RANDOM HOUSE
LARGE PRINT

DISCARD

BOOKS BY ALEXANDER McCALL SMITH
AVAILABLE FROM RANDOM HOUSE
LARGE PRINT

IN THE ISABEL DALHOUSIE SERIES
The Sunday Philosophy Club
Friends, Lovers, Chocolate
The Right Attitude to Rain
The Careful Use of Compliments
The Comforts of a Muddy Saturday

IN THE NO. 1 LADIES' DETECTIVE
AGENCY SERIES
The Full Cupboard of Life
In the Company of Cheerful Ladies

IN THE PORTUGUESE IRREGULAR
VERBS SERIES
Portuguese Irregular Verbs
The Finer Points of Sausage Dogs
At the Villa of Reduced Circumstances

IN THE 44 SCOTLAND STREET SERIES
44 Scotland Street
Espresso Tales

**The Girl Who Married a Lion and
Other Tales from Africa**

Alexander McCall Smith

Two Complete Novels

BLUE SHOES AND HAPPINESS

AND

THE GOOD HUSBAND OF ZEBRA DRIVE

The contents of this book were originally published in two separate volumes under the titles: **Blue Shoes and Happiness**, copyright © 2006 Alexander McCall Smith **The Good Husband of Zebra Drive**, copyright © 2007 Alexander McCall Smith

This 2008 edition is published in the United States of America by Random House Large Print. Distributed by Random House, Inc., New York.

The Library of Congress has established a Cataloging-in-Publication record for this title.

ISBN: 978-0-7393-2830-9

www.randomhouse.com/largeprint

FIRST LARGE PRINT EDITION

10 9 8 7 6 5 4 3 2 1

This Large Print edition published in accord with the standards of the N.A.V.H.

BLUE SHOES AND HAPPINESS

Alexander McCall Smith

RANDOM HOUSE LARGE PRINT

This book is for
Bernard Ditau in Botswana
and
Kenneth and Pravina King in Scotland

BLUE SHOES AND HAPPINESS

CHAPTER ONE

AUNTY EMANG, SOLVER OF PROBLEMS

WHEN YOU ARE JUST the right age, as Mma Ramotswe was, and when you have seen a bit of life, as Mma Ramotswe certainly had, then there are some things that you just know. And one of the things that was well known to Mma Ramotswe, only begetter of the No. 1 Ladies' Detective Agency (Botswana's only ladies' detective agency), was that there were two sorts of problems in this life. Firstly, there were those problems—and they were major ones—about which one could do very little, other than to hope, of course. These were the problems of the land, of fields that were too rocky, of soil that blew away in the wind, or of places where crops would just not thrive for some sickness that lurked in the very earth. But looming greater than anything else there was the problem of drought. It was a familiar feeling in Botswana, this waiting for rain, which often simply did not come, or came too late to save the crops. And then the land, scarred and exhausted, would dry and crack under the relentless sun, and it would seem that nothing short of a miracle would ever bring it to life. But that miracle would eventually arrive, as it always had, and the landscape would turn from brown to green within hours under the kiss of the rain. And there were other colours that would follow the green; yellows, blues, reds would appear in patches across the veld as if great cakes of dye had been crumbled and scattered by an unseen hand. These were the colours of the wild flowers that had been lurking there, throughout the dry season, waiting for the first drops of moisture to awaken them. So at least that sort of problem had its solution, although one often had to wait long, dry months for that solution to arrive.

The other sorts of problems were those which people made for themselves. These were very common, and Mma Ramotswe had seen many of them in the course of her work. Ever since she had set up this agency, armed only with a copy of Clovis Andersen's **The Principles of Private Detection**—and a great deal of common sense—scarcely a day had gone by without her encountering some problem which people had brought upon themselves. Unlike the first sort of problem—drought and the like—these were difficulties that could have been avoided. If people were only more careful, or behaved themselves as they should, then they would not find themselves faced with problems of this sort. But of course people never behaved themselves as they should. "We are all human beings," Mma Ramotswe had once observed to Mma Makutsi, "and human beings can't really help themselves. Have you noticed that, Mma? We can't really help ourselves from doing things that land us in all sorts of trouble."

Mma Makutsi pondered this for a few moments. In general, she thought that Mma Ramotswe was right about matters of this sort, but she felt that this particular proposition needed a little bit more thought. She knew that there were some people who were unable to make of their lives what they wanted them to be, but then there were many others who were quite capable of keeping themselves under control. In her own case, she thought that she was able to resist temptation quite effectively. She did not consider herself to be particularly strong, but at the same time she did not seem to be markedly weak. She did not drink, nor did she over-indulge in food, or chocolate or anything of that sort. No, Mma Ramotswe's observation was just a little bit too sweeping and she would have to disagree. But then the thought struck her: Could she resist a fine new pair of shoes, even if she knew that she had plenty of shoes already (which was not the case)?

"I think you're right, Mma," she said. "Everybody has a weakness, and most of us are not strong enough to resist it."

Mma Ramotswe looked at her assistant. She had an idea what Mma Makutsi's weakness might be, and indeed there might even be more than one.

"Take Mr J.L.B. Matekoni, for example," said Mma Ramotswe.

"All men are weak," said Mma Makutsi. "That is well known." She paused. Now that Mma Ramotswe and Mr J.L.B. Matekoni were married, it was possible that Mma Ramotswe had discovered new weaknesses in him. The mechanic was a quiet man, but it was often the mildest-looking people who did the most colourful things, in secret of course. What could Mr J.L.B. Matekoni get up to? It would be very interesting to hear.

"Cake," said Mma Ramotswe quickly. "That is Mr J.L.B. Matekoni's great weakness. He cannot help himself when it comes to cake. He can be manipulated very easily if he has a plate of cake in his hand."

Mma Makutsi laughed. "Mma Potokwane knows that, doesn't she?" she said. "I have seen her getting Mr J.L.B. Matekoni to do all sorts of things for her just by offering him pieces of that fruit cake of hers."

Mma Ramotswe rolled her eyes up towards the ceiling. Mma Potokwane, the matron of the orphan farm, was her friend, and when all was said and done she was a good woman, but she was quite ruthless when it came to getting things for the children in her care. She it was who had cajoled Mr J.L.B. Matekoni into fostering the two children who now lived in their house; that had been a good thing, of course, and the children were dearly loved, but Mr J.L.B. Matekoni had not thought the thing through and had failed even to consult Mma Ramotswe about the whole matter. And then there were the numerous occasions on which she had prevailed upon him to spend hours of his time fixing that unreliable old water pump at the orphan farm—a pump which dated back to the days of the Protectorate and which should have been retired and put into a museum long ago. And Mma Potokwane achieved all of this because she had a profound understanding of how men worked and what their weaknesses were; that was the secret of so many successful women—they knew about the weaknesses of men.

That conversation with Mma Makutsi had taken place some days before. Now Mma Ramotswe was sitting on the verandah of her house on Zebra Drive, late on a Saturday afternoon, reading the paper. She was the only person in the house at the time, which was unusual for a Saturday. The children were both out: Motholeli had gone to spend the weekend with a friend whose family lived out at Mogiditishane. This friend's mother had picked her up in her small truck and had stored the wheelchair in the back with some large balls of string that had aroused Mma Ramotswe's interest but which she had not felt it her place to ask about.

What could anybody want with such a quantity of string? she wondered. Most people needed very little string, if any, in their lives, but this woman, who was a beautician, seemed to need a great deal. Did beauticians have a special use for string that the rest of us knew nothing about? Mma Ramotswe asked herself. People spoke about face-lifts; did string come into face-lifts?

Puso, the boy, who had caused them such concern over his unpredictable behaviour but who had recently become much more settled, had gone off with Mr J.L.B. Matekoni to see an important football match at the stadium. Mma Ramotswe did not consider it important in the least—she had no interest in football, and she could not see how it could possibly matter in the slightest who succeeded in kicking the ball into the goal the most times—but Mr J.L.B. Matekoni clearly thought differently. He was a close follower and supporter of the Zebras, and tried to get to the stadium whenever they were playing. Fortunately the Zebras were doing well at the moment, and this, thought Mma Ramotswe, was a good thing: it was quite possible, she felt, that Mr J.L.B. Matekoni's depression, from which he had made a good re-covery, could recur if he, or the Zebras, were to suffer any serious set-back.

So now she was alone in the house, and it seemed very quiet to her. She had made a cup of bush tea and had drunk that thoughtfully, gazing out over the rim of her cup onto the gar-den to the front of the house. The sausage fruit tree, the moporoto, to which she had never paid much attention, had taken it upon itself to produce abundant fruit this year, and four heavy sausage-shaped pods had appeared at the end of a branch, bending that limb of the tree under their weight. She would have to do something about that, she thought. People knew that it was dangerous to sit under such trees, as the heavy fruit could crack open a skull if it chose to fall when a person was below. That had happened to a friend of her father's many years ago, and the blow that he had received had cracked his skull and damaged his brain, making it difficult for him to speak. She re-membered him when she was a child, strug-gling to make himself understood, and her father had explained that he had sat under a sausage tree and had gone to sleep, and this was the result.

She made a mental note to warn the children and to get Mr J.L.B. Matekoni to knock the fruit down with a pole before anybody was hurt. And then she turned back to her cup of tea and to her perusal of the copy of **The Daily News,** which she had unfolded on her lap. She had read the first four pages of the paper, and had gone through the small advertisements with her usual care. There was much to be learned from the small advertisements, with their offers of irrigation pipes for farmers, used vans, jobs of various sorts, plots of land with house construction permission, and bargain furniture. Not only could one keep up to date with what things cost, but there was also a great deal of social detail to be garnered from this source. That day, for instance, there was a statement by a Mr Herbert Motimedi that he would not be responsible for any debts incurred by Mrs Boipelo Motimedi, which effectively informed the public that Herbert and Boipelo were no longer on close terms—which did not surprise Mma Ramotswe, as it happened, because she had always felt that that particular marriage was not a good idea, in view of the fact that Boipelo Motimedi had gone through three husbands before she found Herbert, and two of these previous husbands had been declared bankrupt. She smiled at that and skimmed over the remaining advertisements before turning the page and getting to the column that interested her more than anything else in the newspaper.

Some months earlier, the newspaper had announced to its readers that it would be starting a new feature. "If you have any problems," the paper said, "then you should write to our new exclusive columnist, Aunty Emang, who will give you advice on what to do. Not only is Aunty Emang a BA from the University of Botswana, but she also has the wisdom of one who has lived fifty-eight years and knows all about life." This advance notice brought in a flood of letters, and the paper had expanded the amount of space available for Aunty Emang's sound advice. Soon she had become so popular that she was viewed as something of a national institution and was even named in Parliament when an opposition member brought the house down with the suggestion that the policy proposed by some hapless minister would never have been approved of by Aunty Emang.

Mma Ramotswe had chuckled over that, as

she now chuckled over the plight of a young student who had written a passionate love letter to a girl and had delivered it, by mistake, to her sister. "I am not sure what to do," he had written to Aunty Emang. "I think that the sister is very pleased with what I wrote to her as she is smiling at me all the time. Her sister, the girl I really like, does not know that I like her and maybe her own sister has told her about the letter which she has received from me. So she thinks now that I am in love with her sister, and does not know that I am in love with her. How can I get out of this difficult situation?" And Aunty Emang, with her typical robustness, had written: "Dear Anxious in Molepolole: The simple answer to your question is that you cannot get out of this. If you tell one of the girls that she has received a letter intended for her sister, then she will become very sad. Her sister (the one you really wanted to write to in the first place) will then think that you have been unkind to her sister and made her upset. She will not like you for this. The answer is that you must give up seeing both of these girls and you should spend your time working harder on your examinations. When you have a good job and are earning some money, then you can find another girl to fall in love with. But make sure that you address any letter to that girl very carefully."

There were two other letters. One was from a boy of fourteen who had been moved to write to Aunty Emang about being picked upon by his teacher. "I am a hard-working boy," he wrote. "I do all my schoolwork very carefully and neatly. I never shout in the class or push people about (like most other boys). When my teacher talks, I always pay attention and smile at him. I do not trouble the girls (like most other boys). I am a very good boy in every sense. Yet my teacher always blames me for anything that goes wrong and gives me low marks in my work. I am very unhappy. The more I try to please this teacher, the more he dislikes me. What am I doing wrong?"

Everything, thought Mma Ramotswe. That's what you are doing wrong: everything. But how could one explain to a fourteen-year-old boy that one should not **try** too hard; which was what he was doing and which irritated his teacher. It was better, she thought, to be a little bit bad in this life, and not too perfect. If you were too perfect, then you invited exactly this sort of reaction, even if teachers should be above that sort of thing. But what, she wondered, would Aunty Emang say?

"Dear Boy," wrote Aunty Emang. "Teachers do not like boys like you. You should not say you are not like other boys, or people will think that you are like a girl." And that is all that Aunty Emang seemed prepared to say on the subject—which was a bit dismissive, thought Mma Ramotswe, and now that poor, over-anxious boy would think that not only did his teacher not like him, but neither did Aunty Emang. But perhaps there was not enough space in the newspaper to go into the matter in any great depth because there was the final letter to be printed, which was not a short one.

"Dear Aunty Emang," the letter ran. "Four years ago my wife gave birth to our first born. We had been trying for this baby for a long time and we were very happy when he arrived. When it came to choosing a name for this child, my wife suggested that we should call him after my brother, who lives in Mahalapye but who comes to see us every month. She said that this would be a good thing, as my brother does not have a wife himself and it would be good to have a name from a member of the family. I was happy with this and agreed.

"As my son has been growing up, my brother has been very kind to him. He has given him many presents and packets of sweets when he comes to see him. The boy likes his uncle very much and always listens very carefully to the stories that he tells him. My wife thinks that this is a good thing—that a boy should love his kind uncle like this.

"Then somebody said to me: **Your son looks very like his uncle. It is almost as if he is his own son.** And that made me think for the first time: Is my brother the father of my son? I looked at the two of them when they were sitting together and I thought that too. They are very alike.

"I am very fond of my brother. He is my twin, and we have done everything together all our lives. But I do not like the thought that he is the father of my son. I would like to talk to him about this, but I do not want to say anything that may cause trouble in the family. You are a wise lady, Aunty: What do you think I should do?"

Mma Ramotswe finished reading the letter and thought: surely a twin should know how funny this sounds—after all, **they are twins.** If

Aunty Emang had laughed on reading this letter, then it was not apparent in her answer.

"I am very sorry that you are worrying about this," she wrote. "Look at yourself in the mirror. Do you look like your brother?" And once again that was all she had to say on the subject.

Mma Ramotswe reflected on what she had read. It seemed to her that she and Aunty Emang had at least something in common. Both of them dealt with the problems of others and both were expected by those others to provide some solution to their difficulties. But there the similarity ended. Aunty Emang had the easier role: she merely had to give a pithy response to the facts presented to her. In Mma Ramotswe's case, important facts were often unknown and required to be coaxed out of obscurity. And once she had done that, then she had to do rather more than make a clever or dismissive suggestion. She had to see matters through to their conclusion, and these conclusions were not always as simple as somebody like Aunty Emang might imagine.

It would be tempting, she thought, to write to Aunty Emang when next she had a particularly intractable problem to deal with. She would write and ask her what she would do in the circumstances. **Here, Aunty Emang, just you solve this one!** Yes, it would be interesting to do that, she thought, but completely unprofessional. If you were a private detective, as Mma Ramotswe was, you could not reveal your client's problem to the world; indeed, Clovis Andersen had something to say on this subject. "Keep your mouth shut," he had written in **The Principles of Private Detection**. "Keep your mouth shut at all times, but at the same time encourage others to do precisely the opposite."

Mma Ramotswe had remembered this advice, and had to agree that even if it sounded like hypocrisy (if it was indeed hypocrisy to do one thing and encourage others to do the opposite), it was at the heart of good detection to get other people to talk. People loved to talk, especially in Botswana, and if you only gave them the chance they would tell you everything that you needed to know. Mma Ramotswe had found this to be true in so many of her cases. If you want the answer to something, then ask somebody. It always worked.

She put the paper aside and marshalled her thoughts. It was all very well sitting there on her verandah thinking about the problems of others, but it was getting late in the afternoon and there were things to do. In the kitchen at the back of the house there was a packet of green beans that needed to be washed and chopped. There was a pumpkin that was not going to cook itself. There were onions to be put in a pan of boiling water and cooked until soft. That was part of being a woman, she thought; one never reached the end. Even if one could sit down and drink a cup of bush tea, or even two cups, one always knew that at the end of the tea somebody was waiting for something. Children or men were waiting to be fed; a dirty floor cried out to be washed; a crumpled skirt called for the iron. And so it would continue. Tea was just a temporary solution to the cares of the world, although it certainly helped. Perhaps she should write and tell Aunty Emang that. Most problems could be diminished by the drinking of tea and the thinking through of things that could be done while tea was being drunk. And even if that did not solve problems, at least it could put them off for a little while, which we sometimes needed to do, we really did.

CHAPTER TWO

CORRECT AND INCORRECT WAYS OF DEALING WITH A SNAKE

The following Monday morning, the performance of the Zebras in the game against Zambia on Saturday afternoon was the first topic of discussion, at least among the men.

"I knew that we would win," said Charlie, the elder apprentice. "I knew it all the time. And we did. We won."

Mr J.L.B. Matekoni smiled. He was not given to triumphalism, unlike his two apprentices, who always revelled in the defeat of any opposing team. He realised that if you looked at the overall results, the occasional victory tended to be overshadowed by a line of defeats. It was difficult, being a small country—at least in terms of numbers of people—to compete with more populous lands. If the Kenyans wanted to select a football team, then they had many millions of people to choose from, and the same was true, and even more so, of the South Africans. But Botswana, even if it was a land as wide as the sky and even if it was blessed by those great sunburned spaces, had fewer than two million people from whom to select a football team. That made it difficult to stand up to the big countries, no matter how hard they tried. That applied only to sport, of course. When it came to everything else, then he knew, and was made proud by the knowledge, that Botswana could hold its own—and more. It owed no money; it broke no rules. But of course it was not perfect; every country has done some things of which its people might feel shame. But at least people knew what these things were and could talk about them openly, which made a difference.

But football was special.

"Yes," said Mr J.L.B. Matekoni. "The Zebras played very well. I felt very proud."

"Ow!" exclaimed the younger apprentice, reaching for the lever that would expose the engine of a car that had been brought in for service. "Ow! Did you see those people from Lusaka crying outside the stadium?"

"Anybody can lose," cautioned Mr J.L.B. Matekoni. "You need to remember that every time you win." He thought of adding, **and anybody can cry, even a man**, but knew that this would be wasted on the apprentices.

"But we didn't lose, Boss," said Charlie. "We won."

Mr J.L.B. Matekoni sighed. He had been tempted to abandon the task of teaching these apprentices anything about life, but persisted nonetheless. He took the view that an apprentice-master should do more than show his apprentices how to change an oil filter and repair brakes. He should show them, preferably by example, how to behave as honourable mechanics. Anybody can be taught to fix a car—did the Japanese not have machines which could build cars without anybody being there to operate them?—but not everybody could meet the standards of an honourable mechanic. Such a person could give advice to the owner of a car; such a person would tell the truth about what was wrong with a car; such a person would think about the best interests of the owner and act accordingly. That was something which had to be passed on from generation to generation of mechanics, and it was not always easy to do that.

He looked at the apprentices. They were due to go off for another spell of training at the Automotive Trades College, but he wondered if it did them any good. He received reports from the college as to how they performed in the academic parts of their training. These reports did not make good reading; although they passed the examinations—just—their lack of seriousness, and their sloppiness, was always commented upon. What have I done to deserve apprentices like this? Mr J.L.B. Matekoni asked himself. He had friends who also took on apprentices, and they often commented on how lucky they were to get young men who very quickly developed sufficient skill to earn their pay, and more. Indeed, one of these friends, who had taken on a young man from Lobatse, had freely admitted that this young man now knew more than he did about cars and was also very good with the customers. It struck Mr J.L.B. Matekoni as very bad luck that he should get two incompetent apprentices at the same time. To get one would have been understandable bad luck; to get two seemed to be a singular misfortune.

Mr J.L.B. Matekoni looked at his watch. There was no point in wasting time thinking about how things might be if the world were otherwise. There was work to be done that day, and he had an errand which would take him away for much of the morning. Mma Ramotswe and Mma Makutsi had gone off to the post office and the bank and would not be back for a while. It was the end of the month and the banks were always far too busy at such times. It would be better, he thought, if people's pay days were staggered. Some could be paid at the end of the month, as was traditional, but others could get their wages at other times. He had even thought of writing to the Chamber of Commerce about this, but had decided that there was very little point; there were some things that seemed to be so set in stone that nothing would ever change them. Pay day, he thought, was one of those.

He glanced at his watch again. He would have to go off shortly for a meeting with a man who was thinking of selling his inspection ramp. Tlokweng Road Speedy Motors already had one of these, but Mr J.L.B. Matekoni thought that it would be useful to have a second one, particularly if he could get it at a good price. But if he went off on this errand, then the apprentices would be left in sole charge of the garage until Mma Ramotswe and Mma Makutsi arrived. That might be all right, but it might not, and Mr J.L.B. Matekoni was worried about it.

He looked at the car which was being slowly raised on the ramp. It was a large white car which belonged to Trevor Mwamba, who had just been appointed Anglican Bishop of Botswana. Mr J.L.B. Matekoni knew the new bishop well—it was he who had married Mma Ramotswe to him under that tree at the orphan farm, with the choir singing and the sky so high and empty—and would not normally have let the apprentices loose on his car, but it seemed that there was very little choice now. The bishop wanted his car back that afternoon if at all possible, as he had a meeting to attend in Molepolole. There was nothing seriously wrong with the car, which had been brought in for a routine service, but he always liked to check the brakes of any vehicle before he returned it, and there might be some work to

be done there. Brakes were the most important part of a car, in Mr J.L.B. Matekoni's
view. If an engine did not work at all, then
admittedly that was annoying, but it was not
actually dangerous. You could hardly hurt
yourself if you were stationary, but you could
certainly hurt yourself if you were going at
fifty miles an hour and were unable to stop.
And the Molepolole road, as everybody
knew, had a problem with cattle straying
onto it. The cattle were meant to stay on the
other side of the fence—that was the rule—
but cattle were a law unto themselves and always seemed to think that there was better
grass to be had on the other side of the road.

Mr J.L.B. Matekoni decided that he would
have to leave the bishop's car to the mercies of
the apprentices but that he would check up on
their work when he came back just before
lunchtime. He called the older apprentice over
and gave him instructions.

"Be very careful now," he said. "That is
Bishop Mwamba's car. I do not want slapdash
work done on it. I want everything done very
carefully."

Charlie stared down at the ground. "I am always careful, Boss," he muttered resentfully. "When did you ever see me being careless?"

Mr J.L.B. Matekoni opened his mouth to speak, but then thought better of it. It was no use engaging with these boys, he decided. Whatever he said would be no use; they simply would not take it in. He turned away and tore off a piece of paper towel on which to wipe his hands.

"Mma Ramotswe will be here soon," he said. "She and Mma Makutsi are off on some business or other. But until they come in, you are in charge. Is that all right? You look after everything."

Charlie smiled. "A-one, Boss," he said. "Trust me."

Mr J.L.B. Matekoni raised an eyebrow. "Mmm," he began, but said no more. Running a business involved anxieties—that was inevitable. It was bad enough worrying about two feckless young employees; how much more difficult it must be to run a very large company with hundreds of people working for you. Or running a country—that must be a terribly demanding job, and Mr J.L.B. Matekoni wondered how it was possible for people such as prime ministers and presidents to sleep at night with all the problems of the world weighing down upon them. It could not be an easy job being President of Botswana, and if Mr J.L.B. Matekoni had a choice between living in State House or being the proprietor of Tlokweng Road Speedy Motors, he was in no doubt about which one of these options he would choose. That is not to say that it would be uncomfortable occupying State House, with its cool rooms and its shaded gardens. That would be a very pleasant existence, but how difficult it must be for the President when everybody who came to see you, or almost everybody, wanted something: please do this, sir; please do that; please allow this, that, or the next thing. Mind you, his own existence was not all that different; just about everybody he saw wanted him to fix their car, preferably that very day. Mma Potokwane was an example of that, with her constant requests to attend to bits and pieces of malfunctioning machinery out at the orphan farm. Mr J.L.B. Matekoni thought that if he could not resist Mma Potokwane and her demands, then he would not be a very good candidate for the presidency of Botswana. Of course, the President had probably not met Mma Potokwane, and even he might find it a bit difficult to stand up to that most forceful of ladies, with her fruit cake and her way of wheedling things out of people.

The apprentices did not have long to themselves that morning. Shortly after Mr J.L.B. Matekoni had left, they had found themselves comfortable seats on two old up-turned oil drums from which they were able to observe the passers-by on the road outside. Young women who walked past, aware of the eyes upon them, might look away or affect a lack of interest, but would hear the young men's appreciative comments nonetheless. This was fine sport for the apprentices, and they were disappointed by the sudden appearance of Mma Ramotswe's tiny white van only ten minutes or so after the departure of Mr J.L.B. Matekoni.

"What were you doing sitting about like that?" shouted out Mma Makutsi, as she climbed out of the passenger seat. "Don't think we didn't see you."

Charlie looked at her with an expression of injured innocence. "We are as entitled to a tea break as much as anybody else," he replied. "You don't work all the time, do you? You drink tea too. I've seen you."

"It's a little bit early for your tea break," suggested Mma Ramotswe mildly, looking at her wrist-watch. "But no matter. I'm sure that you have lots of work to do now."

"They're so lazy," muttered Mma Makutsi, under her breath. "The moment Mr J.L.B. Matekoni goes anywhere, they down tools."

Mma Ramotswe smiled. "They're still very young," she said. "They still need supervision. All young men are like that."

"Especially useless ones like these," said Mma Makutsi, as they entered the office. "And to think that when they finish their apprenticeships—whenever that will be—they will be let loose on the public. Imagine that, Mma. Imagine Charlie with his own business. Imagine driving into a garage and finding Charlie in control!"

Mma Ramotswe said nothing. She had tried to persuade Mma Makutsi to be a bit more tolerant of the two young men, but it seemed that her assistant had something of a blind spot. As far as she was concerned, the apprentices could do no right, and nothing could be said to convince her otherwise.

The two went into the office. Mma Ramotswe walked over to the window behind her desk and opened it wide. It was a warm day, and already the heat had built up in the small room; the window at least allowed the movement of air, even if the air itself was the hot breath of the Kalahari. While Mma Ramotswe stood before the window, gazing up into the cloudless sky, Mma Makutsi filled the kettle for the first cup of tea of the morning. She then turned round and began to pull her chair out from where she had tucked it under her desk. And that was the point at which she screamed—a scream that cut through the air and sent a small white gecko scuttling for its life across the ceiling boards.

Mma Ramotswe spun round, to see the other woman standing quite still, her face frozen in fear.

"Sn . . . ," she stuttered, and then, "Snake, Mma Ramotswe! Snake!"

For a moment Mma Ramotswe did nothing. All those years ago in Mochudi, she had been taught by her father that with snakes the important thing to do was not to make sudden movements. A sudden movement, only too natural of course, could frighten a snake into striking, which most snakes, he said, were reluctant to do.

"They do not want to waste their venom," he had told her. "And remember that they are as frightened of us as we are of them—possibly even more so."

But no snake could have been as terrified as was Mma Makutsi when she saw the hood of the cobra at her feet sway slowly from side to side. She knew that she should avert her eyes, as such snakes can spit their venom into the eyes of their target with uncanny accuracy; she knew that, but she still found her gaze fixed to the small black eyes of the snake, so tiny and so filled with menace.

"A cobra," she whispered to Mma Ramotswe. "Under my desk. A cobra."

Mma Ramotswe moved slowly away from the window. As she did so, she picked up the telephone directory that had been lying on her desk. It was the closest thing to hand, and she could, if necessary, throw it at the snake to distract it from Mma Makutsi. This was not to prove necessary. Sensing the vibration made by the footfall, the snake suddenly lowered its hood and slid away from Mma Makutsi's desk, heading for a large waste-paper bin which stood at the far side of the room. This was the signal for Mma Makutsi to recover her power of movement, and she threw herself towards the door. Mma Ramotswe followed, and soon the two women were safely outside the office door, which they slammed behind them.

The two apprentices looked up from their work on Bishop Mwamba's car.

"There's a snake in there," screamed Mma Makutsi. "A very big snake."

The two young men ran across from the car to join the shaken women.

"What sort of snake?" asked Charlie, wiping his hands on a piece of waste. "A mamba?"

"No," said Mma Makutsi. "A cobra. With a big hood—this big. Right at my feet. Ready to strike."

"You are very lucky, Mma," said the younger apprentice. "If that snake had struck, then you might be late by now. The late Mma Makutsi."

Mma Makutsi looked at him scornfully. "I know that," she said. "But I did not panic, you see. I stood quite still."

"That was the right thing to do, Mma," said

Charlie. "But now we can go in there and kill this snake. In a couple of minutes your office will be safe again."

He turned to the other apprentice, who had picked up a couple of large spanners and who was now reaching out to hand one to him. Armed with these tools, they slowly approached the door and edged it open.

"Be careful," shouted Mma Makutsi. "It was a very big snake."

"Look near the waste-paper basket," added Mma Ramotswe. "It's over there somewhere."

Charlie peered into the office. He was standing at the half-open door and could not see the whole room, but he could see the basket and the floor about it and, yes, he could make out something curved around its base, something that moved slightly even as his eye fell upon it.

"There," he whispered to the other apprentice. "Over there."

The young man craned his neck forward and saw the shape upon the floor. Letting out a curious half-yell, he hurled the spanner across the room, missing the target, but hitting the wall immediately behind the basket. As the spanner fell to the ground, the snake reared up, its hood again extended, facing the source of the danger. Charlie now threw his spanner, which also struck the wall but in this case fell in such a way that it hit the end of the snake's tail. The tail whipped round as the snake struggled to find its balance. Again the head swayed menacingly, the tongue darting in and out as the reptile sought to make sense of the noise and danger of its surroundings.

Mma Ramotswe clutched Mma Makutsi's arm. "I'm not sure if these boys . . ."

She did not finish the sentence. In their excitement they had not noticed a vehicle draw up and a sunburned young man with fair hair step out.

"Well, Mma Ramotswe," said the man. "What's going on here?"

Mma Ramotswe turned to face their visitor. "Oh, Mr Whitson," she said. "You have come just in time. There is a snake in there. The apprentices are trying to kill it."

Neil Whitson shook his head. "There's no need to kill snakes," he said. "Let me take a look."

He walked up to the door of the office and nodded to the apprentices to stand aside.

"Don't frighten it," he said. "It just makes it worse if you frighten it."

"It is a very large snake," said Charlie resentfully. "We have to kill it, Rra."

Neil looked in through the door and saw the cobra curled at the foot of the waste-paper basket. He turned to Charlie.

"Do you have a stick here?" he said. "Any stick will do. Just a stick."

The younger apprentice went off, while Charlie and Neil continued to watch the snake.

"We will have to kill it," Charlie said. "We cannot have a snake here. What if it bites those ladies over there? What if it bites Mma Ramotswe?"

"It'll only bite Mma Ramotswe if it feels threatened," said Neil. "And snakes only feel threatened if people tread on them or . . . ," he paused, before adding, "or throw things at them."

The younger apprentice now returned with a longish stick from the jacaranda tree which grew at the edge of the garage plot. Neil took this from him and edged his way slowly into the office. The snake watched him, part of its body raised, the hood half up. With a sudden movement, Neil flipped the stick over the snake's back and pressed the neck of the snake down against the floor. Then, leaning forward, he gripped the writhing cobra behind the head and picked it up. The lashing tail, searching for purchase, was soon firmly held in his other hand.

"There," he said. "Now, Charlie, a sack is what we need. You must have a sack some-where."

WHEN MR J.L.B. MATEKONI returned an hour later, he was in a good mood. The inspection ramp which he had viewed was in excellent condition and the owner was not asking very much for it. It was, in fact, a bargain, and Mr J.L.B. Matekoni had already paid a deposit on the purchase. His pleasure in his transaction was evident from his smile, but this was hardly noticed by the apprentices as they greeted him in the workshop.

"We've had big excitement here, Boss," said Charlie. "A snake got into Mma Ramotswe's office. A very large snake, with a head like this. Yes, this big."

Mr J.L.B. Matekoni gave a start. "Mma Ramotswe's office," he stuttered. "Is she all right?"

"Oh, she's all right," said Charlie. "She was

lucky that we were around. If we hadn't been here, then I don't know . . ."

Mr J.L.B. Matekoni looked at the younger apprentice, as if for confirmation.

"Yes, Rra," said the young man. "It is a good thing that we were here. We were able to deal with the snake."

"And where is it?" asked Mr J.L.B. Matekoni. "Where have you thrown it? You must know that if you leave one of these snakes lying around, its mate will come to seek it out. Then we will have trouble."

The younger apprentice glanced at Charlie. "We have had it taken away," said Charlie. "That man from Mokolodi, the one you trade engine parts with. He has taken it away."

"Mr Whitson?" asked Mr J.L.B. Matekoni. "He has taken it?"

Charlie nodded. "You don't need to kill snakes," he said. "It is best just to let them loose. You know that, don't you, Boss?"

Mr J.L.B. Matekoni did not reply. Striding across to the office door, he knocked and entered. Inside, seated at their desks, Mma Ramotswe and Mma Makutsi looked up at him expectantly.

"You have heard about it?" asked Mma Ramotswe. "You heard about the snake?"

Mr J.L.B. Matekoni nodded. "I have heard all about it," he said. "I am only happy that you have not been hurt, Mma Ramotswe. That is all that I am interested in."

"And me?" asked Mma Makutsi from her desk. "What about me, Rra?"

"Oh, I am pleased that you were not bitten, Mma," said Mr J.L.B. Matekoni. "I am very pleased about that. I would not want either of you to be bitten by a snake."

Mma Ramotswe shook her head. "It was a very close thing for Mma Makutsi," she said. "And we were very lucky that your friend happened to come by. He is a man who knows all about snakes. You should have seen him pick it up, Mr J.L.B. Matekoni. He picked it up just as if it were a tshongololo or something like that."

Mr J.L.B. Matekoni looked confused. "But I thought that the boys dealt with it," he said. "Charlie told me that . . ."

Mma Makutsi let out a peal of laughter. "Them? Oh, Rra, you should have seen them. They threw spanners at it and made it all angry. They were no use at all. No use."

Mma Ramotswe smiled at her husband.

"They did their best, of course, but . . ." She broke off. Nobody was perfect, she thought, and she herself had not handled the situation very well. None of us knows how we will cope with snakes until the moment arises, and then most of us find out that we do not do it very well. Snakes were one of the tests which life sent for us, and there was no telling how we might respond until the moment arrived. Snakes and men. These were the things sent to try women, and the outcome was not always what we might want it to be.

CHAPTER THREE

FREE FOOD MAKES
YOU FAT

I T TOOK EVERYBODY some time to settle
down after the incident with the cobra. The apprentices, convinced that they had played a
vital role in dealing with the snake, were full of
themselves for the rest of the day, embroidering
the truth at every opportunity as they told the
story in detail to every caller at the garage. Mr
Polopetsi, the new employee whom Mr J.L.B.
Matekoni had taken on at the garage—on the
understanding that he could also help out,
when required, in the No. 1 Ladies' Detective
Agency—heard all about it when he arrived an
hour or so later. He had been sent by Mr J.L.B.
Matekoni to collect tyres from a depot on the
other side of town, a job which often required a
long wait. Now, returning in the truck which

was used for garage business, he was regaled with an account of the event by Charlie, who this time was careful to mention the presence of the manager of the Mokolodi Game Reserve, even if only in a supporting role.

"Mma Makutsi was very lucky," he said once Charlie had finished the tale. "Those snakes strike like lightning. That quick. You cannot dodge them if they decide to strike."

"Charlie was too quick for it," said the younger apprentice. "He saved Mma Makutsi's life." He paused, and then added, "Not that she thanked him for it."

Mr Polopetsi smiled. "I am sure that she is very grateful," he said. "But you boys should remember that nobody is too quick for a snake. Keep out of their way. I saw some very bad snake-bite cases when I was working at the hospital. Very bad." And he remembered, as he spoke, the woman who had been brought in from Otse; the woman who had been bitten by a puff-adder when she had rolled over in the night and disturbed the fat, languid snake that had slid into her one-room hut for the warmth. He had been on duty in the pharmacy and had been standing outside the entrance to the emergency department when she had been car-

ried out of the government ambulance, and he
had seen her leg, which had swollen so much
that the skin had split. And then he had heard
the next day that she had not lived and that
there were three children and no father or
grandmother to look after them; he had
thought then of all the children there were in
Africa who now had no parents and of what it
must be like for them, not to have somebody
who loved you as your parents loved you. He
looked at the apprentices. They did not think
of things like that, and who could expect them
to? They were young men, and as a young man
one was immortal, no matter what the evidence to the contrary.

At a garage there is no time for thinking
such thoughts; there is work to do. Mr Polopetsi unloaded the new tyres, with their
pristine treads and their chalk markings;
Mr J.L.B. Matekoni attended to the delicate task of adjusting the timing on an old
French station wagon—a car he did not like,
which always went wrong and which in his
view should have been given a decent burial a
long time ago; and the two apprentices finished the servicing of Bishop Mwamba's well-
behaved white car. Inside the adjoining office

of the No. 1 Ladies' Detective Agency, Mma Ramotswe and Mma Makutsi shuffled papers about their desks. They had very little real work to do, as it was a slack period for the agency, and so they took the opportunity to do some filing, a task in which Mma Makutsi took the lead, on account of her training at the Botswana Secretarial College.

"They used to say that good filing was the key to a successful business," she said to Mma Ramotswe as she looked through a pile of old receipts.

"Oh yes," said Mma Ramotswe, not with great interest. She had heard Mma Makutsi on the subject of filing on a number of occasions before and she felt that there was very little more to be said on the subject. The important thing, in her mind, was not the theory behind filing but the simple question of whether it worked or not. A good filing system enabled one to retrieve a piece of paper; a bad filing system did not.

But it seemed that there was more to be said. "You can file things by date," Mma Makutsi went on, as if lecturing to a class. "Or you can file them by the name of the person to whom the document relates. Those are the two main systems. Date or person."

Mma Ramotswe shot a glance across the room. It seemed odd that one could not file according to what the paper was all about. She herself had no office training, let alone a diploma from the Botswana Secretarial College, but surely a subject-based system was possible too. "What about subject matter?" she asked.

"There is that too," Mma Makutsi added quickly. "I had forgotten about that. Subject matter too."

Mma Ramotswe thought for a moment. In her office they filed papers under the name of the client, which she thought was a perfectly reasonable system, but it would be interesting, she thought, to set up a system of cross-referencing according to the subject matter of the case. There would be a large file for adultery, in which she could put all the cases which dealt with that troublesome issue, although it would probably be necessary to subdivide in that case. There could be a section for suspicious husbands and one for suspicious wives, perhaps, and even one for male menopause cases now that she came to think about it. Many of the women who came to see her were worried about their middle-aged husbands, and Mma Ramotswe had read somewhere about the male menopause and all the troubles to which it gave rise. She could certainly add her own views on that, if anybody should ask her.

MMA RAMOTSWE and Mr J.L.B. Matekoni went home for lunch at Zebra Drive, something they enjoyed doing when work at the garage permitted. Mma Ramotswe liked to lie down for twenty minutes or so after the midday meal. On occasion she would drop off to sleep for a short while, but usually she just read the newspaper or a magazine. Mr J.L.B. Matekoni would not lie down, but liked to walk out in the garden under the shade netting, looking at his vegetables. Although he was a mechanic, like most people in Botswana he was, at heart, a farmer, and he took great pleasure in this small patch of vegetables that he coaxed out of the dry soil. One day, when he retired, they would move out to a village, perhaps to Mochudi, and find land to plough and cattle to tend. Then at last there would be time to sit outside on the stoop with Mma Ramotswe and watch the life of the village unfold before them. That would be a good way of spending such days as remained to one; in peace, happy, among the people and cattle of home. It would be good to die among one's cattle, he thought; with their sweet breath on one's face and their dark, gentle eyes watching right up to the end of one's journey, right up to the edge of the river.

MMA RAMOTSWE returned from the lunch break to find Mma Makutsi waiting for her at the office door. The younger woman seemed agitated.

"There's a woman waiting inside."

Mma Ramotswe nodded. "Has she said what she wants, Mma?" she asked.

Mma Makutsi looked rather annoyed. "She is insisting on talking to you, Mma. I offered to listen to her, but she said that she wanted the senior lady. That is what she said. The senior lady. That's you."

Noticing Mma Makutsi's look of disapproval, Mma Ramotswe suppressed a smile. Her assistant was always irritated when this sort of thing happened. People would phone and ask to be put through to the boss, provoking from Mma Makutsi an indignant request for an explanation of what the query was about.

"I do not see why they cannot talk to me first," she said peevishly. "Then I can put them through to you after I have told you who they are and what it's about."

"But that means they might have to repeat themselves," Mma Ramotswe pointed out. "They might think it better to wait until . . ." She broke off. Mma Makutsi was unlikely to be convinced by this argument.

And this woman waiting for her in the office was another of these people who had been unwilling to tell Mma Makutsi what her business was. Well, one had to be understanding; it was often a big step to go and see a private detective about some private trouble, and one had to be gentle with people. She was not sure whether she herself would have the courage to consult a perfect stranger about something intimate. If Mr J.L.B. Matekoni were to begin misbehaving, for example—and it was inconceivable that he should—would she be able to go and talk to somebody about it, or would she suffer in silence? She rather thought that she might suffer in silence; that was her reaction, but others were different, of course. Some people were only too happy to pour out their most private problems into the ear of anybody who would listen. Mma Ramotswe had once sat next to such a woman on a bus; and this woman had told her, in the time that it takes to travel down the road from Gaborone to Lobatse, all about her feelings towards her mother-in-law, her concerns for her son, who was doing very well at school but who had met a girl who had turned his head and taken his mind quite off his schoolwork, and about her prying neighbour whom she had seen on several occasions looking into her bedroom through a pair of binoculars. Perhaps such people felt better if they talked, but it could be trying for those chosen to be their audience.

The woman sitting in the office looked up as Mma Ramotswe came into the room. They exchanged polite greetings—in the prescribed form—while Mma Ramotswe settled herself behind her desk.

"You are Mma Ramotswe?" asked the woman.

Mma Ramotswe inclined her head, taking in the little details that would allow her to place this woman. She was thirty-five, perhaps; of traditional build, like Mma Ramotswe herself (perhaps even more traditional); and, judging from the ring on her finger, married to a man who was able to afford a generously sized gold band. **Clothing**, said Clovis Andersen in **The Principles of Private Detection**, **provides more clues than virtually anything else (other than a pocket book or wallet!). Look at the clothing. It talks.**

Mma Ramotswe looked at the woman's clothing. Her skirt, which was tightly stretched across her traditional thighs, was made of a reasonably good material and was of a neutral grey colour. It said nothing, thought Mma Ramotswe, other than that the woman cared about her clothes and had a bit of money to spend on them. Above the skirt, the blouse was white and . . . She paused. There on one sleeve, just below the elbow, was a red-brown stain. Something had been dribbled down the sleeve, a sauce perhaps.

"Are you a cook, Mma?" asked Mma Ramotswe.

The woman nodded. "Yes," she said, and was about to say something else when she stopped herself and frowned in puzzlement.

"How did you know that, Mma? Have we met one another before?"

Mma Ramotswe waved a hand in the air. "No," she said. "We have not met, but I have this feeling that you are a cook."

"Well, I am," said the woman. "You must be a very clever woman to work that out. I suppose that is why you do the job you do."

"People's jobs tell us a lot about them," said Mma Ramotswe. "You are a cook, perhaps, because . . . Now let me think. Is it because you like eating? No, that cannot be. That would be too simple. You are a cook, then, because . . . You are married to a cook. Am I right?"

The woman let out a whistle of surprise. "I cannot believe that you know all this," she exclaimed. "This is very strange."

For a moment Mma Ramotswe said nothing. It was tempting to take undeserved credit, but she decided that she could not.

"The reason why I know all this, Mma," she said, "is because I read the papers. Three weeks ago—or was it four?—your photograph was in the paper. You were winner of the Pick-and-Pay cooking competition. And the paper said that you were a cook at a college here in Gaborone and that your husband was a cook at the President Hotel." She smiled. "And so that, Mma, is how I know these things."

The disclosure was greeted by a burst of laughter from Mma Makutsi. "So you see, Mma," she said, "we knew these things the moment you walked in here. I did not need to talk to you at all!"

Mma Ramotswe cast a warning glance in Mma Makutsi's direction. She had to watch her with the clients; she could sometimes be rude to them if she thought that they were treating her with inadequate respect. It was a strange tendency, stemming, thought Mma Ramotswe, from this ninety-seven per cent business. She would have to talk to her about it some day and refer her, perhaps, to the relevant section of Clovis Andersen's book in which he described proper relations with clients. One should never seek to score a point at the expense of a client, warned Clovis Andersen. The detective who tries to look smart at the expense of the client is really not smart at all—anything but.

Mma Ramotswe signalled to Mma Makutsi for a cup of tea. Tea helped clients to talk, and this woman looked ill at ease and needed to relax.

"May I ask you your name, Mma?" Mma Ramotswe began.

"It is Poppy," the woman said. "Poppy Maope. I am normally just called Poppy."

"It is a very pretty name, Mma. I should like to be called Poppy."

The compliment drew a smile. "I used to be embarrassed about it," said Poppy. "I used to try to hide my name from people. I thought it was a very silly name."

Mma Ramotswe shook her head. There was nothing embarrassing about the name Poppy, but there was no telling what names people would find embarrassing. Take Mr J.L.B. Matekoni, for instance. Very few people, if any, knew what his initials stood for. He had told her, of course, as he was then her fiancé, but nobody else seemed to know; certainly not Mma Makutsi, who had asked her outright and had been informed that unfortunately she could not be told.

"Some names are private," Mma Ramotswe had said. "This is the case with Mr J.L.B. Matekoni. He has always been known as Mr J.L.B. Matekoni, and that is the way he wishes it to be."

The tea made, Mma Makutsi brought two

cups over and placed them on the desk. As she put them down, Mma Ramotswe saw her looking at the client, as if preparing to say something, and threw her a warning glance.

"I have come to see you on a very private matter," Poppy began. "It is very hard to talk about it."

Mma Ramotswe stretched out a hand across the desk, just far enough to touch Poppy lightly on the forearm. It is a marriage matter, she thought, and these are never easy to talk about; they often bring tears and sorrow, just at the talking of them.

"If it is a marriage question, Mma," said Mma Ramotswe gently, "just remember that we—that is, Mma Makutsi over there and myself—we have heard everything that there is to be said on such matters. There is nothing we have not heard."

"Nothing," confirmed Mma Makutsi, sipping at her tea. And she thought of that client, a man, who had come in the previous week and told them that extraordinary story and how difficult it had been for both of them not to laugh when he had described how . . . Oh, it was important not to think of that, or one would begin to laugh all over again.

Poppy shook her head vehemently. "It is not a marriage matter," she said. "My husband is a good man. We are very happily married."

Mma Ramotswe folded her arms. "I am happy to hear that," she said. "How many people can say that in these troubled times? Ever since women allowed men to think that they did not need to get married, everything has gone wrong. That is what I think, Mma."

Poppy thought for a moment. "I think you may be right," she said. "Look at the mess. Look at what all this unfaithfulness has done. People are dying because of that, aren't they? Many people are dying."

For a moment the three of them were silent. There was no gainsaying what Poppy had said. It was just true. Just true.

"But I have not come to talk about that," said Poppy. "I have come because I am very frightened. I am frightened that I am going to lose my job, and if I do, then how are we going to pay for the house we have bought? All my wages go on the payments for that, Mma. Every thebe. So if I lose my job we shall have to move, and you know how difficult it is to get somewhere nice to live. There are just not enough houses."

Mma Ramotswe took up a pen from her desk and twined her fingers about it. Yes, this woman was right. She, Mma Ramotswe, was fortunate in owning her house in Zebra Drive. If she had to try to buy it today it would be impossible. How did people survive when housing was so expensive? It was a bit of a mystery to her.

Poppy was looking at her.

"Please go on, Mma," said Mma Ramotswe. "I hope you don't mind if I fiddle with this pen. I am still listening to you. It is easier to listen if one has something to do with one's hands."

Poppy made a gesture of assent. "I do not mind, Mma. You can fiddle. I will carry on talking and will tell you why I am frightened. But first I must tell you a little bit about my job, as you must know this if you are to help me.

"I was always interested in cooking, Mma. When I was a girl I was always the one in the kitchen, cooking all the food for the family. My grandmother was the one who taught me. She had always cooked and she could make very simple food taste very good. Maize meal. Sorghum. Those very plain things tasted very good when my grandmother had added her

herbs to them. Herbs or a little bit of meat if
we were lucky, or even chopped-up Mopani
worms. Oh, those were very good. I cannot resist Mopani worms, Mma. Can you?"

"No Motswana can resist them," said Mma
Ramotswe, smiling. "I would love to have
some right now, but I'm sorry, Mma . . ."

Poppy took a sip of her tea. "Yes, Mopani
worms! Anyway, I went off to do a catering
course in South Africa. I was very lucky to
get a place on it, and a scholarship too. It was
one whole year and I learned a very great deal
about cooking while I was on it. I learned
how to cook for one hundred, two hundred
people, as easily as we cook for four or five
people. It is not all that difficult, you know,
Mma Ramotswe, as long as you get the quan-
tities right.

"I came back to Botswana and got my first
job up at one of the diamond mines, the one at
Orapa. They have canteens for the miners
there, and I was assistant to one of the chefs in
charge of that. It was very hard work and those
miners were very hungry! But I learned more
and more, and I also met my husband, who
was a senior cook up there. He cooked in the
guest house that the mining company had for

their visitors. They liked to give these visitors good food and the man I married was the cook who did that.

"My husband decided one day that he had had enough of living up at the diamond mine. 'There is nothing to do here,' he said. 'There is just dust and more dust.'

"I said to him that we should not move until we had made more money, but he was fed up and wanted to come to Gaborone. Fortunately, he got a job very easily through somebody who had stayed in the guest house and who knew that the President Hotel was looking for another chef. So he came down here, and I soon found a job at that college, the big new one which they built over that way—you know the place, Mma. I was very happy with this job and I was happy that we were able to live in Gaborone, where everything is happening and where it is not just dust, dust, dust.

"And everything went very well. I was not the senior cook—there is another woman who has that job. She is called Mma Tsau. She was very good to me and she made sure that I got a pay-rise after I had been there one year. I was very happy, until I discovered something bad that was going on.

"Mma Tsau has a husband, whom I had seen about the place once or twice. One day, one of the cleaning ladies said to me, 'That man is eating all the food, you know. He is eating all the best food.'

"I had no idea what this lady meant, and so I asked her which man she was talking about. She told me that it was Mma Tsau's husband and that there was a storeroom in the college where he came for a meal from time to time and was given all the best meat by his wife. On other days, she said, Mma Tsau would take home packets of the best meat to cook for her husband at their house. This food belonged to the college, she said, but it went straight into the mouth of Mma Tsau's husband, who was getting fatter and fatter as a result of all these good meals he was having.

"I did not believe this at first. I had noticed that he was a very fat man, but I had thought that this must be because he was married to a good cook. The husbands of good cooks are often fatter than other men—and that is natural, I suppose.

"I decided one day to see whether what the cleaning lady had told me was true. I had noticed that at lunchtimes Mma Tsau used to leave the kitchen from time to time, but I was always so busy that I hardly paid any attention to it. There is always something happening in a busy kitchen, and there are many reasons why the head cook may need to leave the stoves for a short time. There are supplies to be checked up on. There are telephones to answer. There are assistants to chase up.

"On that day I kept an eye on Mma Tsau. She went outside at one point to call one of the helpers, who was standing outside in the sun and not doing enough work. I looked out of the window and saw her shaking a finger at this woman and shouting at her, but I did not hear what she said. I had a good idea of it, though.

"Then, a few minutes later, I noticed that she went to the door of one of the warming ovens and took out a covered dish. It was an oven that we never used, as we had too much capacity in that kitchen. She took this dish, which was covered by a metal plate, and went out of the kitchen. I moved over to a window and saw her walking towards a small block near the kitchen. There was an old office there, which was not used any more, and a store-room. She went in, was inside for a few moments, and then came out again, without the dish, but wiping her hands on her apron.

"I waited a few minutes. Mma Tsau was now busy supervising the assistants who were dishing out the stew to the students. She was telling them that they should not give helpings that were too generous, or there would not be enough for the students who came in for their lunch a bit later. I overheard her telling one of them that they should not give more food to those students whom they liked, who smiled at them when they reached the head of the line, or who were related to them. I could not believe that I was hearing that, if what I thought I had just seen was true. I think that you should not say one thing and then do exactly the opposite yourself, should you, Mma Ramotswe? No. That is what I thought too.

"This was now the best time for me to leave the kitchen, while Mma Tsau was lecturing the assistant. I went outside and ran across to the block which I had seen her enter. I had decided that the best thing to do would be to pretend to be looking for something, and so I did not knock on the door, but just pushed it open. There was a man inside, that fat man, the husband of Mma Tsau. He was sitting at a small table with a large plate of steak in front of him. There were vegetables too—some potatoes with gravy on them and a pile of carrots. He had a bottle of tomato sauce on the table in front of him and a copy of **The Daily News**, which he was reading as he ate.

"I pretended to be surprised, although what I saw was exactly what I had expected to see. So I greeted him and said that I was sorry to have disturbed his lunch. He smiled and said that it did not matter, and that I should look for whatever it was that I was searching for. Then he went back to eating his steak, which smelled very good in the small space of that room."

As the story progressed, Mma Ramotswe's mouth opened wider and wider with astonishment. Mma Makutsi also seemed transfixed by the tale which their client was telling, and was sitting quite still at her desk, hanging on every word.

Poppy now paused. "I hope that you do not think that I was being too nosy," she said. "I know that you should not look into things that are not your business."

Mma Ramotswe shook her head. "But it **was** your business, Mma," she said. "It was surely your business. It is always the business of people who work in a place that somebody else in that place is stealing. That is everybody's business."

Poppy looked relieved. "I am glad you said that, Mma. I would not like you to think that I was one of those nosy people. I was worried . . ."

"So," interrupted Mma Ramotswe. "You have to decide what to do. Is that why you have come to see me today?"

This conclusion seemed reasonable to Mma Ramotswe, but Poppy held up her hands in denial. "No, Mma," she said. "I decided what to do straightaway. I went to Mma Tsau the next day and asked her about her husband. I said, 'Why is your husband eating all this college food? Do you not have enough food of your own?'

"She was inspecting a pot at the time, and when I asked her this question she dropped it, she was so surprised. Then she looked closely at me and told me that she did not know what I was talking about and that I should not make up wild stories like that in case anybody believed that what I said was true.

"'But I saw him myself,' I told her. 'I saw

him in the storeroom over there eating steaks from the college kitchen. I saw him, Mma.'"

Mma Makutsi, who had been silent, could no longer contain herself. "Surely she did not try to deny that, Mma," she said. "That wicked woman! Taking the meat from the students and giving it to that fat husband of hers! And our taxes paying for that meat too!"

Poppy and Mma Ramotswe both looked at Mma Makutsi. Her outrage was palpable.

"Well, she didn't," Poppy continued. "Once I had told her that I had seen what was going on, she just became silent for a while. But she was watching me with her eyes narrowed—like this. Then she said that if I told anybody about it, she would make sure that I lost my job. She explained to me that this would be easy for her to do. She said that she would simply tell the college managers that I was not up to the job and that they would have to get somebody else. She said that they would believe her and that there would be nothing I could do."

"I hope that you went straight to the police," said Mma Makutsi indignantly.

Poppy snorted. "How could I do that? I had no proof to give the police, and they would believe her rather than me. She is the senior cook, remember. I am just a junior person."

Mma Ramotswe looked up at the ceiling. She had recently read an article about this sort of problem and she was trying to remember the word which was used to describe it. Whistle-blowing! Yes, that was it. The article had described how difficult it was for whistle-blowers when they saw something illegal being done at work. In some countries, it had said, there were laws to protect the whistle-blower—in some countries, but she was not sure whether this was true of Botswana. There was very little corruption in Botswana, but she was still not sure whether life was made any easier for whistle-blowers.

"Whistle-blowing," she said aloud. "That's what it is—whistle-blowing."

Poppy looked at her blankly. "Who is blowing a whistle?" she asked.

"You are," said Mma Ramotswe. "Or you could blow a whistle."

"I do not see what whistles have to do with it," said Poppy.

"If you went to the police you would be a whistle-blower," explained Mma Ramotswe.

"It's a way of describing a person who lets others know about what is going on behind the scenes."

"Behind what scenes?" asked Poppy.

Mma Ramotswe decided to change tack. There were some people who were rather literal in their understanding of things, and Poppy, it seemed, was one of these.

"Well, let us not think too much about whistles and such things," she said. "The important thing is this: you want us to do something about this woman and her stealing. Is that right?"

The suggestion seemed to alarm Poppy. "No," she said. "I do not want that, Mma. You must wait until I finish telling you my story."

Mma Ramotswe made an apologetic gesture, and Poppy began to speak again.

"I was frightened, Mma. I could not face losing my job and so I did nothing. I did not like the thought of that man eating all that government food, but then I thought of what it would be like not to have a house, and so I just bit my tongue. But then, three days ago, Mma Tsau came to me just as I was about to leave work to go home. My husband has a car and was waiting for me at the end of the road. I could see him sitting in the car, looking up at the sky, as he likes to do. When you are a chef all you see is the kitchen ceiling and clouds of steam. When you are outside, you like to look at the sky.

"Mma Tsau drew me aside. She was shaking with anger and I thought that I had made some very bad mistake in my work. But it was not that. She gripped me by the arm and leaned forward to speak to me. 'You think you're clever,' she said. 'You think that you can get me to give you money not to say anything about my husband. You think that, don't you?'

"I had no idea what she was talking about. I told her that, but she just laughed at me. She said that she had torn up the letter I had written. Then she said that on the very first opportunity that she could find, she would get rid of me. She said that it might take a few months, but she would make very sure that I would lose my job."

Poppy stopped. Towards the end of her tale, her voice had risen, and by the time that she finished, the words were coming in gasps. Mma Ramotswe leaned forward and took her hand. "Do not be upset, Mma," she said gently. "She is just making threats. Often these people don't do what they threaten to do, isn't that right, Mma Makutsi?"

Mma Makutsi glanced at Mma Ramotswe before she answered. She thought that people like that often did exactly what they threatened to do—and worse—but now was not the time to express such doubts. "Hot air," she said. "You would think that in Botswana we had enough hot air, with the Kalahari just over there, but there are still people like this Mma Tsau who add to the hot air. And you do not need to worry about hot air, Mma."

Poppy looked over towards Mma Makutsi and smiled weakly. "I hope that you're right, Mma," she said. "But I am not sure. And anyway, what was this letter? I did not write to her about it."

Mma Ramotswe rose from her seat and walked to the window. Poppy had spoken about how chefs liked to look at the sky when they had the chance; well, so did private detectives, she thought; ladies and private detectives. Indeed, everybody should look at the sky when they could, because the sky had many answers, provided one knew how to see them. And now, as she looked at the sky, over the tops of the acacia trees and up into that echoing emptiness, it seemed to her so very obvious that Poppy was not the only person who knew about the food and that the other person who knew—who, again so obviously, must have been the cleaning woman—was taking the opportunity to blackmail Mma Tsau. Unfortunately for Poppy, she was getting the blame, but that was quite typical of life, was it not? The wrong people often got the blame, the wrong people suffered for what the right people did. And the sky in all this, the sky which had seen so much of it, was neutral, absolutely neutral.

The problem with blackmail, thought Mma Ramotswe, is this: the victim is often a wrongdoer, but, once blackmailed, attracts our sympathy. But why should we feel sorry for somebody who is simply being made to pay for the wrong that he did? It occurred to Mma Ramotswe that this was a problem that deserved serious consideration. Perhaps it was even a question to put to Aunty Emang. Aunty Emang . . .

CHAPTER FOUR

WHAT FEMINISTS HAVE
IN MIND FOR MEN

MMA MAKUTSI made the evening meal that
night for Mr Phuti Radiphuti, her newly acquired fiancé. Phuti Radiphuti was the son of
the elder Mr Radiphuti, successful businessman, farmer, and proprietor of the Double
Comfort Furniture Shop. She had met Phuti
at the dancing classes which they had both attended at the Academy of Dance and Movement. This was not a real academy, in that it
had no buildings and indeed had no staff
other than the woman who took the money
and the instructor, Mr Fano Fanope, an ac-
complished dancer who had danced, success-
fully, in Johannesburg and Nairobi. Word of
the engagement had spread round the dance
class, and Mr Fanope himself had made an of-

ficial announcement at the end of one evening that the academy was proud to have brought the couple together.

"Dancing is about contact between people," he had said in his speech. "When you dance with somebody you are talking to him, even if you do not open your mouth. Your movements can show what is in your heart. That is very important. And that is why so many happy couples meet through dancing. And that is another reason why if you have not already booked your place on our next course, you should do so now. Ladies, you could be like Grace Makutsi and find a good husband here; gentlemen, look at Mr Phuti Radiphuti, who has found this fine lady. May they be very happy together! May they have many happy hours on the dance floor and elsewhere!"

Mma Makutsi had been touched by this speech, in spite of the blatant reference to advance bookings. She liked Mr Fanope, and she knew that he was genuinely pleased about the engagement. She knew, too, that this pleasure was shared by many of the other members of the class, even if not by all. One of the other women, a person by the name of Violet, who had been at the Botswana Secretarial College with her, had smirked during Mr Fanope's speech and had muttered something to the man standing next to her, who had suppressed a laugh. Mma Makutsi had exchanged words with this woman at an earlier session, when Violet had made a disparaging remark about Mma Makutsi's green shoes (of which she was very proud) and had effectively sneered at Phuti Radiphuti. By a supreme effort of will, Mma Makutsi had replied to her courteously and had even gone out of her way to compliment her. This had been difficult indeed, as Violet had achieved a bare pass mark at the Botswana Secretarial College—somewhere around fifty per cent—and was clearly only interested in finding the richest husband available.

As she witnessed the smirk, for a delicious moment Mma Makutsi imagined what she might say to Violet if the opportunity presented itself. And in fact it did, at the end of that evening, when Violet sidled up to her and said, "Well, Mma, that's a kind thing you've done. It's very good of you to look after Mr Radiphuti like that. It must have been very hard for him to find a wife and now you have agreed to marry him. You are a really kind person. But I always knew that, of course."

Mma Makutsi had looked at her enemy. At the back of her mind were the memories of those days at the Botswana Secretarial College when the glamorous girls, of whom Violet was more or less the leader, would sit at the back of the class and discuss their social triumphs and snigger when Mma Makutsi or one of the other hard workers was complimented by the instructor. She had said nothing then, and she really should say nothing now, but the temptation was just too great.

"Thank you, Mma," she had said. "But I am the lucky one, you know. It's not every girl can get a husband like that." She paused before continuing, "But I hope that you have some of my luck in the future. Who knows?" And with that she smiled sweetly.

Violet's eyes widened. "Lucky? Oh, I don't know about that, Grace Makutsi! I'm not so sure that it's lucky to be landed with a man like that. Anyway, I hope that it works out well for you. And it might." And then she herself added, "Who knows?"

Mma Makutsi felt her heart beating fast

within her. It was time for the coup de grâce. "But I am lucky, Mma," she said. "I think that any girl who marries into that family will be very lucky. And rich too."

Violet faltered. "Rich?"

"Ssh," said Grace Makutsi, putting a finger to her lips. "It's not polite to talk about it. So I won't mention the Double Comfort Furniture Shop, which is one of the businesses my fiancé owns, you know. I must not talk about that. But do you know the store, Mma? If you save up, you should come in some day and buy a chair."

Violet opened her mouth to speak, but said nothing. And then Mr Fanope had appeared and had shaken Mma Makutsi's hand and led her away to speak to another member of the class who wanted to congratulate her. Mma Makutsi had glanced back at Violet, who was fiddling with her handbag, but who looked up and caught her eye and could not conceal her envy. There was so much history there; a history of shame, and poverty, and struggle, and she could hear Mma Ramotswe's voice in her head now. "That was not a very kind thing to do, Mma Makutsi," Mma Ramotswe said. "You should not have done that."

"I know," Mma Makutsi answered, mentally. "But I just couldn't help it, Mma."

And the voice of Mma Ramotswe immediately softened. "I know too," she said. "I know." And she did, because although she was kind, Mma Ramotswe was also human, and appreciated that there were times when it was impossible to resist a small triumph, especially one that could make one smile when one remembered it later; smile for hours and hours.

MMA MAKUTSI and Phuti Radiphuti had slipped comfortably into an arrangement. On four days of the week, including Monday, Phuti came for his evening meal at Mma Makutsi's house; on the other three days he ate in turn with his senior aunt, his sister and her husband, and, on Sunday evening, with his aged father. The dinners with his father were sometimes trying for him, as his father's memory was not what it used to be and he frequently repeated himself, especially when talking about cattle. But Phuti was dutiful, and he would sit for hours while his father went over and over the same ground: Did Phuti remember that fine bull that he had sold to that man who lived at Mahalapye? Could Phuti remember how much they had paid for that Brahmin cow that they had bought from that Boer farmer down at Zeerust? That had been a fine cow, but when did she die? Did Phuti remember which year it was? And what about that bull that went to Mahalapye? Did Phuti remember that one? Was he sure?

On occasion, Mma Makutsi would join him for these meals at his father's house, and she would sit through the same conversations, trying hard not to nod off during the narratives or the questions that interspersed them. What were the cattle like up at Bobonong this year? Were they thin? Were they different from the cattle down in the south? She noticed that when he was with his father, Phuti's stammer became more acute. During the dinners that they had at her house, it was barely noticeable now, which spoke to the confidence which she had succeeded in building up in him. In her company, he was now quite capable of uttering long and involved sentences, either in Setswana or in English, without any hesitation or stumbling. This new-found fluency, of which he was so proud, enabled him to say things that he had been unable to say for years, and the words flowed out of him; words about childhood, about being a boy; words about the furniture business and the comfort, or otherwise, of the various sorts of chairs; and words about the pleasure, the sheer pleasure, of having found somebody with whom he would now start to share his life. It was as if a drought had ended—a drought that had made for expanses of silence, as drought will dry up a salt pan and render it white and powdery—and the words were like longed-for rain, turning the land green at last.

She soon found out what Phuti liked to eat, and she made sure that she always cooked these dishes for him. He liked meat, of course, and T-bone steaks in particular, which he would pick up and gnaw at with gusto. He liked marrow and broad green beans doused in melted butter, and he liked chopped-up biltong soaked in gravy and then served over mashed potato. All of these dishes she did for him, and each time he complimented her enthusiastically on her cooking as if it were the first time that he had said anything about it. She loved these compliments, and the nice things he said about her appearance. In her mind she had been no more than a woman with large glasses and a difficult skin; now she found herself described as one of the prettiest women in Botswana, with a nose that reminded him of . . . and here he mumbled and she did not catch what it was that her nose reminded him of, but it was surely a positive association and so she did not mind not knowing what it was.

That evening, after the drama with the snake, Mma Makutsi regaled Phuti with a full account of what had turned into a memorable day. She told him of the apprentices' ridiculous account of their role in the removal of the snake, and he laughed at that. Then she told him about Poppy's visit and her curious tale of the theft of the food and the threat of dismissal.

After Mma Makutsi had finished, Phuti sat in silence for a few minutes. "So?" he said at last. "So what can you do to help this woman? I don't see how you're going to save her job for her. What can you do?"

"We could make sure that the chef—that other woman—is the one to lose her job," said Mma Makutsi. "She's the one who should be fired."

Phuti looked doubtful. "Maybe. But I don't see how you could make that happen. Anyway, where would you start with a case like this? What can you do?"

Mma Makutsi helped him to another portion of mashed potato. "We could find out who is blackmailing Mma Tsau. Then we could tell Mma Tsau that it is not Poppy."

Phuti thought that this was a perfectly sound suggestion, but then a better idea occurred, and he outlined this to Mma Makutsi as he began to eat his mashed potato. "Of course it would be easier, wouldn't it, to tell Mma Tsau that if she fires Poppy, then **we** shall tell the college that she has been stealing. Surely that would be simpler."

Mma Makutsi stared at him. "But that in itself is blackmail," she pointed out. "You can't go round threatening people like that."

"I don't see what's wrong with it," said Phuti, wiping a small speck of mashed potato from his chin. "We're not getting anything from her. It can't be blackmail if you're not getting anything yourself."

Mma Makutsi pondered this. Perhaps Phuti had a point, and yet Mma Ramotswe had always stressed to her that the end did not justify the means, and that one should not commit a wrong to set right another. And yet, Mma

Ramotswe herself had been known to tell the occasional lie while trying to get at the truth. She had obtained information from a government clerk by quoting a non-existent regulation; she had pretended to be somebody she was not when looking into a family dispute for a former minister; the list was really quite long when one came to think of it. In every case, she had done this in her attempts to help somebody who needed help, and it was also true that they were not large lies, but they were lies nonetheless, and so she wondered whether Mma Ramotswe was entirely consistent on this point. She would have to ask her about it, but for the moment it was perhaps better to move on to another topic. So she looked up from her plate and asked Phuti Radiphuti what had happened at the furniture store that day.

He was pleased to leave the philosophical complexities of blackmail, and launched with alacrity into an account of a difficulty they had encountered with the delivery of a table that had only three legs. The factory was adamant that it had left their premises with four, but his warehouse man was equally firm in his view that it had only three on arrival.

"Perhaps that is another one for Mma Ramotswe," said Mma Makutsi. "She is very good at finding out things like that."

Phuti smiled at the suggestion. "There are bigger things for Mma Ramotswe to do," he said. "She has big crimes to solve."

Mma Makutsi had heard of this popular misconception. It flattered her to think that the reputation of the No. 1 Ladies' Detective Agency had been so inflated, but she could not allow Phuti, her own fiancé, to remain in ignorance about what they actually did.

"No," she said. "Mma Ramotswe does not solve crimes. She deals with very small things." To portray the smallness, Mma Makutsi put a thumb and forefinger within a whisker of one another. "But," she went on, "these small things are important for people. Mma Ramotswe has often told me that our lives are made up of small things. And I think she is right."

Phuti thought she was right too. He was slightly disappointed to be disabused of the notion that the No. 1 Ladies' Detective Agency dealt with major crimes. It had been pleasing enough for him to have a fiancée at all, let alone a fiancée who pursued so glamorous a profession, and he had boasted to friends that he was engaged to a well-known detective. And of course that was strictly speaking true—Mma Makutsi was indeed a detective, and it did not matter too much that she concerned herself with mundane matters. In fact, this was probably all for the good. The other sort of detective might be exposed to danger, and that was not what he had in mind for his wife-to-be. There was little danger in the furniture business, and there would always be a place for her there should she decide to abandon detection. He wondered whether he should mention this to her, but decided against it. He did not want her to think that marriage to him would involve her submitting to his plans; he had heard that women were reluctant to accept that sort of thing these days—and a good thing too, he thought. For far too long men had assumed that women would do their bidding, and if women were now questioning that, then he was quite happy to agree with them. Not that he was sympathetic to those people who called themselves feminists: he had heard one of those ladies on the radio and had been shocked by her aggressiveness towards the man who was interviewing her. This woman had more or less accused the reporter of arrogance when he had questioned her statement that men had, in general, fewer abilities than women. She had said that his time was "over" and that men like him would be swept aside by feminism. But if men were to be swept aside, wondered Phuti Radiphuti, then where would men be put? Would there be special homes for them, where they could be given small tasks to perform while women got on with the important business of running things? Would men be allowed out of these homes on selected outings (accompanied, of course)? For some days after he had listened to the interview, Phuti Radiphuti had worried about being swept aside, and had experienced a vivid and uncomfortable dream—a nightmare, really—in which he was indeed swept aside by a large feminist with a broom. It was an unpleasant experience, tumbling head over heels, covered with a cloud of dust, in the face of the frightening woman's aggressive brush-strokes.

He looked at Mma Makutsi as she cut at a piece of meat on her plate. She wielded the knife expertly, pushing the cut meat onto her fork. Then the fork was before her mouth, which opened wide to receive the food before the teeth came together. She smiled at him and nodded to his plate, encouraging him to get on with his meal.

Phuti looked down at his plate. It had just occurred to him that Mma Makutsi might be a feminist. He did not know why he should think this. She had never threatened to sweep him away, but there was no doubt about who had been in charge when they had danced together at the Academy of Dance and Movement. Mr Fano Fanope had explained that it was always the men who led in ballroom dancing, but Phuti had found himself quite unable to lead and had willingly followed the firm promptings of Mma Makutsi's hands planted on his shoulders and in the small of his back. Did this make her a feminist, or merely one who could tell when a man had no idea of how to take the lead in dancing? He raised his eyes from his plate and looked at Mma Makutsi. He saw his reflection in the lenses of her large round glasses, and he saw the smile about her lips. Perhaps it would be best to ask her, he thought.

"Mma Makutsi," he began, "there is something I should like to ask you."

Mma Makutsi put down her knife and fork

and smiled at him. "You may ask me any-thing," she said. "I am your fiancée."

He swallowed. It would be best to be direct. "Are you a feminist?" he blurted out. His nerv-ousness made him stumble slightly on the word "feminist," making the letter "f" sound dou-bled or even tripled. His stammer had been vastly improved since his meeting with Mma Makutsi and her agreeing to marry him, but occasions of stress might still bring it out.

Mma Makutsi looked a bit taken aback by the question. She had not been expecting the topic to arise, but now that she had been asked there was only one answer to give.

"Of course I am," she said simply. Her an-swer given, she stared at him through her large, round glasses; again she smiled. "These days most ladies are feminists. Did you not know that?"

Phuti Radiphuti was unable to answer. He opened his mouth to speak, but words, which had recently been so forthcoming, seemed to have deserted him. It was an old, familiar feel-ing for him; a struggle to articulate the thoughts that were in mind through a voice that would not come, or came in fits and starts.

He had imagined a future of tenderness and mutual cherishing; now it seemed to him that he would face stridency and conflict. He would be swept aside, as he had been swept aside in that dream; but there would be no waking up this time.

He looked at Mma Makutsi. How could he, who was so cautious, have been so wrong about somebody? It was typical of his luck; he had never been noticed by women—it would never be given to him to be admired, to be looked up to; rather, he would be the target of criticism and upbraiding, for that is what he imagined feminists did to men. They put them in their place; they emasculated them; they derided them. All of this now lay ahead of Phuti Radiphuti as he stared glumly at his fiancée and then down again at his plate, where the last scraps of food, a mess of potage in a sense, lay cooling and untouched.

CHAPTER FIVE

MORE CONVERSATIONS
WITH SHOES

"THIS IS A VERY BUSY DAY," said Mr J.L.B.
Matekoni, wiping his hands on a small piece of
lint. "There are so many things that I have to
do and which I will not have the time to do. It
is very hard." He raised his eyes up to the sky,
but not before casting a glance in the direction
of Mma Ramotswe.

She knew that this was a request. Mr J.L.B.
Matekoni was not one to ask for a favour directly. He was always willing to help other
people, as Mma Potokwane, matron of the orphan farm, knew full well, but his diffidence
usually prevented him from asking others to
do things for him. There was sometimes a call
for help, however, disguised as a comment
about the pressures which were always threat-

ening to overcome any owner of a garage; and this was one, to which Mma Ramotswe of course would respond.

She looked at her desk, which was largely clear of papers. There was a bill, still in its envelope but unmistakably a bill, and a half-drafted letter to a client. Both of these were things that she would happily avoid attending to, and so she smiled encouragingly at Mr J.L.B. Matekoni.

"If there is anything I can do?" she asked. "I can't fix cars for you, but maybe there's something else?"

Mr J.L.B. Matekoni tossed the greasy scrap of lint into the waste-paper basket. "Well, there is something, Mma," he said, "now that you ask. And although it has something to do with cars, it doesn't involve actually fixing anything. I know you are a detective, Mma Ramotswe, and not a mechanic."

"I would like to be able to fix cars," said Mma Ramotswe. "Maybe some day I will learn. There are many ladies now who can fix cars. There are many girls who are doing a mechanic's apprenticeship."

"I have seen them," said Mr J.L.B. Matekoni. "I wonder if they are very different from . . ." He did not finish the sentence, but tossed his head in the direction of the workshop behind him, where the two apprentices, Charlie and the younger one—whose name nobody ever used—were changing the oil in a truck.

"They are very different," said Mma Ramotswe. "Those boys spend all their time thinking about girls. You know what they're like."

"And girls don't spend any time thinking about boys?" asked Mr J.L.B. Matekoni.

Mma Ramotswe considered this for a few moments. She was not quite sure what the answer was. When she was a girl she had thought about boys from time to time, but only to reflect on how fortunate she was to be a girl rather than a boy. And when she became a bit older, and was susceptible to male charm, although she occasionally imagined what it would be like to spend time in the company of a particular boy, boys **as a breed** did not occupy her thoughts. Nor did she talk about boys in the way in which the apprentices talked about girls, although it was possible that modern girls were different. She had overheard some teenagers—girls of about seventeen—

talking among themselves one day when she was looking for a book in Mr Kerrison's new book shop, and she had been shocked by what she had heard. Her shock had registered in her expression, and in the dropping of her jaw, and the girls had noticed this. "What's the trouble, Mma?" said one of the girls. "Don't you know about boys?" And she had struggled for words, searching for a reply which would tell these shameless girls that she knew all about boys— and had known about them for many years— while at the same time letting them know that she disapproved. But no words had come, and the girls had gone away giggling.

Mma Ramotswe was not a prude. She knew what went on between people, but she believed that there was a part of life that should be private. She believed that what one felt about another was largely a personal matter, and that one should not talk about the mysteries of the soul. One should just not do it, because that was not how the old Botswana morality worked. There was such a thing as shame, she thought, although there were many people who seemed to forget it. And where would we be in a world without the old Botswana morality? It would not work, in Mma Ramotswe's view, because it would mean that people could do as they wished without regard for what others thought. That would be a recipe for selfishness, a recipe as clear as if it were written out in a cookery book: **Take one country, with all that the country means, with its kind people, and their smiles, and their habit of helping one another; ignore all this; shake about; add modern ideas; bake until ruined.**

Mr J.L.B. Matekoni's question about whether girls thought about boys hung in the air, unanswered. He looked at her expectantly. "Well, Mma?" he asked. "Do girls not think about boys?"

"Sometimes," said Mma Ramotswe nonchalantly. "When there is nothing better to think about, that is." She smiled at her husband. "But that is not what we were discussing," she continued. "What is this thing that you want me to do?"

Mr J.L.B. Matekoni explained to her about the errand he wished her to carry out. It would involve a trip to Mokolodi, which was half an hour away to the south.

"My friend who dealt with the cobra," he said. "Neil. He's the one. He has an old pickup down there, a bakkie, which he kept for years and years. And then . . ." Mr J.L.B. Matekoni paused. The death of a car diminished him, because he was involved with cars. "There was nothing much more I could do for it. It needed a complete engine re-bore, Mma Ramotswe. New pistons. New piston rings." He shook his head sadly, as a doctor might when faced with a hopeless prognosis.

Mma Ramotswe looked up at the ceiling. "Yes," she said. "It must have been very sad."

"But fortunately Neil did not get rid of it," he said. "Some people just throw cars away, Mma Ramotswe. They throw them away."

Mma Ramotswe reached for a piece of paper on her desk and began to fold it. Mr J.L.B. Matekoni often needed some time to get to the point, but she was used to waiting.

"I have a customer with a broken half-shaft," went on Mr J.L.B. Matekoni. "That is part of the rear axle. You know that, don't you? There's a shaft that comes down the middle until it gets to the gear mechanism in the middle of the rear axle. Then, on each side of that there's something called the half-shaft that goes to the wheel on either side."

The piece of paper in Mma Ramotswe's right hand had been folded in two and then

folded again at an angle. As she held it up and
looked past it, it seemed to her that it was now
a bird, a stout bird with a large beak. She narrowed her eyes and squinted at it, so that the
paper became blurred against the background
of the office walls. She thought of the customer
with a broken half-shaft—she understood exactly what Mr J.L.B. Matekoni meant, but she
smiled at his way of expressing it. Mr J.L.B.
Matekoni regarded cars and their owners as in-
terchangeable, or as being virtually one and the
same, with the result that he would talk of people who were losing oil or who were in need
of bodywork. It had always amused Mma
Ramotswe, and in her mind's eye she had seen
people walking with a dribble of oil stretching
out behind them or with dents in their bodies
or limbs. So, too, did she picture this client
with the broken half-shaft; poor man, perhaps
limping, perhaps patched up in some way.

"So," said Mr J.L.B. Matekoni. "So, could
you go and fetch this for me, Mma Ramotswe?
You won't have to lift anything—he'll get one
of his men to do that. All you have to do is to
drive down there and drive back. That's all."

Mma Ramotswe rather liked the idea of a
run down to Mokolodi. Although she lived in

Gaborone, she was not a town person at heart—very few Batswana were—and she was never happier than when she was out in the bush, with the air of the country, dry and scented with the tang of acacia, in her lungs. On the drive to Mokolodi she would travel with the windows down, and the sun and air would flood the cabin of her tiny white van; and she would see, opening up before her, the vista of hills around Otse and beyond, green in the foreground and blue beyond. She would take the turning off to the right, and a few minutes later she would be at the stone gates of the camp and explaining to the attendant the nature of her business. Perhaps she would have a cup of tea on the verandah of the circular main building, with its thatch and its surrounding trees, and its outlook of hills. She tried to remember whether they served bush tea there; she thought they did, but just in case, she would take a sachet of her own tea which she could ask them to boil up for her.

Mr J.L.B. Matekoni looked at her anxiously. "That's all," he said. "That's all I'm asking you to do."

Mma Ramotswe shook her head. "No," she said. "That's fine. I was just thinking."

"What were you thinking?" asked Mr J.L.B. Matekoni.

"About the hills down there," said Mma Ramotswe. "And about tea. That sort of thing."

Mr J.L.B. Matekoni laughed. "You often think about tea, don't you? I don't. I think about cars and engines and things like that. Grease. Oil. Suspension. Those are my thoughts."

Mma Ramotswe put down the piece of paper she had been folding. "Is it not strange, Mr J.L.B. Matekoni?" she said. "Is it not strange that men and women think about such very different things? There you are thinking about mechanical matters, and I am sitting here thinking about tea."

"Yes," said Mr J.L.B. Matekoni. "It is strange." He paused. There was a car needing attention outside and he had to see to it. The owner wanted it back that afternoon or he would be obliged to walk home. "I must get on, Mma Ramotswe," he said. Nodding to Mma Makutsi, he left the office and returned to the garage.

Mma Ramotswe pushed her chair back and rose to her feet. "Would you care to come with me, Mma Makutsi?" she asked. "It's a nice day for a run."

Mma Makutsi looked up from her desk. "But who will look after the business?" she asked. "Who will answer the telephone?"

Mma Ramotswe looked at herself in the mirror on the wall behind the filing cabinet. The mirror was intended for the use of Mma Makutsi and herself, but was used most frequently by the apprentices, who liked to preen themselves in front of it. "Should I braid my hair?" asked Mma Ramotswe. "What do you think, Mma Makutsi?"

"Your hair is very nice as it is, Mma," said her assistant, but added, "Of course, it would be even nicer if you were to braid it."

Mma Ramotswe looked round. "And you?" she asked. "Would you braid your hair too, if I had mine done?"

"I'm not sure," said Mma Makutsi. "Phuti Radiphuti is an old-fashioned man. I'm not sure what his views on braiding would be."

"An old-fashioned man?" asked Mma Ramotswe. "That's interesting. Does he know that you're a modern lady?"

Mma Makutsi considered the question for a moment. "I think he does," she said. "The other night he asked me if I was a feminist."

Mma Ramotswe stiffened. "He asked you that, did he? And what did you reply, Mma?"

"I said that most ladies were feminists these days," said Mma Makutsi. "So I told him, yes, I am."

Mma Ramotswe sighed. "Oh dear," she said. "I'm not sure that that's the best answer to give in such circumstances. Men are very frightened of feminists."

"But I cannot lie," protested Mma Makutsi. "Surely men don't expect us to lie? And anyway, Phuti is a kind man. He is not one of those men who are hostile to feminists because they are insecure underneath."

She's right about that, thought Mma Ramotswe. Men who put women down usually did so because they were afraid of women and wanted to build themselves up. But one had to be circumspect about these things. The term **feminist** could upset men needlessly because some feminists were so unpleasant to men. Neither she nor Mma Makutsi was that sort of person. They liked men, even if they knew that there were some types of men who bullied women. They would never stand for that, of course, but at the same time they would not wish to be seen as hostile to men like Mr J.L.B. Matekoni or Phuti Radiphuti—or Mr Polopetsi, for that matter; Mr Polopetsi, who was so mild and considerate and badly done by.

"I'm not saying that you should lie," said Mma Ramotswe quietly. "All I'm saying is that it's unwise to talk to men about feminism. It makes them run away. I have seen it many times before." She hoped that the engagement would not be threatened by this. Mma Makutsi deserved to find a good husband, especially as she had not had much luck before. Although Mma Makutsi never talked about it, Mma Ramotswe knew that there had been somebody else in Mma Makutsi's life—for a very brief time—and that she had actually married him. But he had died, very suddenly, and she had been left alone again.

Mma Makutsi swallowed hard. Phuti Radiphuti had seemed unnaturally quiet that evening after their conversation. If what Mma Ramotswe said was right, then her ill-considered remarks might prompt him to run away from her, to end their engagement. The thought brought a cold hand to her chest. She would never get another man; she would never find another fiancé like Phuti Radiphuti. She would be destined to spend the rest of her days as an assistant detective, scraping a living while other women found comfortably-off husbands to marry. She had been given a golden chance and she had squandered it through her own stupidity and thoughtlessness.

She looked down at her shoes—her green shoes with the sky-blue linings. And the shoes looked back up at her. **You've done it, Boss**, said the shoes. **Don't expect us to carry you all around town looking for another man. You had one and now you don't. Bad luck, Boss. Bad luck.**

Mma Makutsi stared at the shoes. It was typical of shoes to be so uncaring. They never made any constructive suggestions. They just censured you, crowed at you, rubbed it in; revenge, perhaps, for all the indignities to which they themselves were subjected. Dust. Neglect. Cracking leather. Oblivion.

THEY WERE SILENT as they left Gaborone, with the brooding shape of Kgale Hill to their right, and the road stretching out, undulating, to their front. Mma Ramotswe was silent because she was looking at the shape of the hills and remembering how, all those years ago, she had travelled this road on the way to stay with her cousin, who had been so good to her. And there had been unhappy journeys too, or journeys that had been happy and had become unhappy later on their being remembered. Those were the trips she had made, down this very road, with her former husband, Note Mokoti. Note used to play his trumpet in hotels down in Lobatse, and Mma Ramotswe had accompanied him on these engagements, her heart bursting with pride that she was the wife of this popular and talented man. She had accompanied him until she had realised that he did not want her to come with him. And the reason for that was that he had wanted to pick up women after the concerts, and he could not do that with his young wife there. She remembered this, and thought about it, and tried to put it from her mind; but the unhappy past has a way of asserting itself and sometimes it is best just to let such thoughts run their course. They will pass, she told herself; they will pass.

Beside her, in her own silence, Mma Makutsi was mulling over the brief exchange that she had had with Mma Ramotswe on the subject of feminism. Mma Ramotswe had been right—she was sure of that—and she had inadvertently frightened Phuti Radiphuti. It had been so foolish of her. Of course she believed in those things which the feminists stood up for—the right of women to have a good job and be paid the same amount as men doing the same work; the right of women to be free of bullying by their husbands. But that was all just good common sense, fairness really, and the fact that you supported these goals did not make you one of those feminists who said that men were finished. How could they say such a thing? We were all people— men and women—and you could never say that one group of people was less important than another. She would never say that, and yet Phuti Radiphuti now probably imagined that she would.

They passed a man asking for a ride, waving his hand up and down to stop a well-disposed vehicle. Other cars were driving past regardless, but Mma Ramotswe believed that this was not the old Botswana way and made an elaborate set of hand signals to indicate to him that they were shortly going to turn off. The tiny white van swerved as she did so, and for a moment it must have seemed to the man that they were intending to run him down, but he understood and acknowledged them with a friendly wave.

"People say that these days you should not stop for people like that," said Mma Ramotswe. "But how can they be so heartless? Do you remember when my van broke down and I had to get back to town in the darkness? Somebody stopped for me, didn't they? Otherwise I could still be out here at the side of the road, even now, getting thinner and thinner."

Mma Makutsi was glad to be distracted from her morbid thoughts of engagements broken on the grounds of undisclosed feminism. She laughed at Mma Ramotswe's comment. "That is one way to go on a diet," she said.

Mma Ramotswe threw her a sideways glance. "Do you think that I need to go on a diet, Mma?" she asked.

"No," said Mma Makutsi. "I do not think that you need to go on a diet." She paused, and then added, "Others may, of course."

"Hah!" said Mma Ramotswe. "You must be thinking of those people who hold that it is wrong to be a traditionally built lady. There are such people, you know."

"They should mind their own business," said Mma Makutsi. "I am traditionally built too, you know. Not as traditionally built as you, of course—by a long way. But I am not a very thin lady."

Mma Ramotswe said nothing. She was not enjoying this conversation, and she was glad that the turn-off to Mokolodi had now appeared. Slowing down, she steered the van off the main road and onto the secondary road that ran alongside for a short way until it headed off into the bush. As the van turned, an observer would have noticed that it listed markedly to one side, Mma Ramotswe's side, while Mma Makutsi's side was higher—an appearance that would have confirmed what had just been said by Mma Makutsi. But there was nobody to see this; only the grey lourie on the acacia branch, the go-away bird, which saw so much but confided in none.

CHAPTER SIX

HOW TO DEAL WITH
AN ANGRY OSTRICH

THE ARRIVAL OF Mma Ramotswe and Mma Makutsi at Mokolodi Game Reserve would normally be an occasion for the barking of dogs and for laughter and the shaking of hands. Mma Ramotswe was known here—her father's brother, her senior uncle, was also the uncle (by a second marriage) to the workshop supervisor. And if that were not enough, Mr J.L.B. Matekoni's cousin's daughter worked in the kitchen at the restaurant. So it was in Botswana, almost everywhere; ties of kinship, no matter how attenuated by distance or time, linked one person to another, weaving across the country a human blanket of love and community. And in the fibres of that blanket there were threads of obligation that meant that one could not ignore the claims of others. Nobody should starve; nobody should feel that they were outsiders; nobody should be alone in their sadness.

Now, though, there was nobody on duty at the gate, and they drove in quietly. They parked near an acacia tree. Several people had already had the same idea, as shade was always sought after, and cars competed with one another to find relief from the sun. The tiny white van, by virtue of its size, was able to nose into a space between two large vehicles, leaving just enough room for Mma Ramotswe to get out of her door and, by breathing in, to squeeze through the space between the van and the neighbouring vehicle. It was a tight squeeze, and it brought back to her the subject of her earlier conversation with Mma Makutsi. If she went on a diet, there would be fewer occasions like this where she would find that the passages and doorways of this world were uncomfortably narrow for a person of traditional build. For a moment she was stuck, and Mma Makutsi was poised to render help, but then with a final push she was free.

"People should think a bit more of others when they park their cars," said Mma Ramotswe. "There is enough room in Botswana for everybody's car. There is no need for all this crushing."

Mma Makutsi was about to say something, but did not. Mma Ramotswe had chosen that spot to park, and the owners of the two other cars might well take the view that she, not they, was the cause of the crush. She did not say this, though, but smiled in a way that could have signalled agreement or merely polite tolerance. Mma Ramotswe's views were, in general, very balanced, and Mma Makutsi found no difficulty in agreeing with them. But she had discovered that when it came to any matter connected with the tiny white van, then her otherwise equable employer could become quite touchy. As she stood and watched Mma Ramotswe squeezing herself through the gap between the vehicles, she remembered how a few weeks ago she had asked Mma Ramotswe how two large scratches and a dent had appeared on the side of her van. She had been surprised by the vigour with which Mma Ramotswe denied the evidence.

"There is nothing wrong with my van," she said. "There is nothing wrong."

"But there is a big scratch here," said Mma

Makutsi. "And another one here. And a dent. Look. There it is. I am putting my finger on it. Look."

Mma Ramotswe glanced in a cursory way at the side of the van and shook her head. "That is nothing," she said dismissively. "That is just a bang that happened."

Mma Makutsi had shown her surprise. "A bang?"

"Yes," said Mma Ramotswe. "A bang. It is not a big thing. I was parking the van in town and there was a post. It had no business being there. Somebody had put this post in the wrong place and it hit the side of the van. There was a little bang. That is all."

Mma Makutsi bit her lip. Posts did not move; vans moved. But a warning glance from Mma Ramotswe told her that it would be unwise to pursue the matter further, and she had not. Now at Mokolodi, as then, she thought that it would be best not to say anything on the subject of parking or vans in general, and so they walked together in silence towards the office. A woman came out to greet them, a woman who appeared to recognise Mma Ramotswe.

"He is expecting you, Mma," said the

woman. "Your fiancé telephoned to tell us that you were coming."

"He is my husband now," said Mma Ramotswe, smiling.

"Oh!" exclaimed the woman. "That is very good. You must be very happy, Mma. He is a good man, Mr L.J.B. Matekoni."

"J.L.B.," corrected Mma Ramotswe. "He is Mr J.L.B. Matekoni, and thank you, Mma. He is a very good man."

"I would like to find a man like that," said the woman. "I have a husband down in Lobatse. He never comes to see me. And when I go down there, he is never in."

Mma Ramotswe made a clucking sound of sympathy, and disapproval—sympathy for the woman in her plight, and disapproval of what she thought was only-too-common masculine behaviour. There were many good men in Botswana, but there were some who seemed to think that their women were only there to flatter them and give them a good time when they felt in need. These men did not think of what women themselves needed, which was comfort and support, and a bit of help in the hundred and one tasks which women had to perform if homes were to be kept going. Who did the cooking? Who kept the yard tidy? Who washed and fed the children and put them to bed at night? Who weeded the fields? Women did all these things, and it would be nice, thought Mma Ramotswe, if men could occasionally lend a hand.

It was particularly hard for women now, when there were so many children left without parents because of this cruel sickness. These children had to be looked after by somebody, and this task usually fell to the grandmothers. But in many cases the grandmothers were finding it difficult to cope because there were simply so many children coming to them. Mma Ramotswe had met one woman who had been looking after twelve grandchildren, all orphaned. And there this woman was at seventy-five, at a time when a person should be allowed to sit in the sun and look up at the sky, cooking and washing and scraping around for food for the hungry mouths of all those children. And if that grandmother should become late, she thought, what then?

The woman led them back towards the office, a round building, made of stone, with a thatched roof that came down in low eaves. A man stepped from the door, looked momentarily surprised when he saw Mma Ramotswe and Mma Makutsi, and then gave a broad grin.

"Dumela, Mma Ramotswe," he said, raising a hand in greeting. "And Mma . . ."

"This is Mma Makutsi, Neil," said Mma Ramotswe.

"Of course," said Neil. "This is the lady who keeps cobras under her desk!"

Mma Makutsi laughed. "I do not wish to think about cobras, Rra," she said. "I am only glad that you came when you did. I do not like snakes."

"Those apprentices were not going about it the right way," said Neil, smiling at the recollection. "You don't throw spanners at snakes. It doesn't help."

He gestured for the two women to follow him to the terrace in front of the verandah. Several chairs were set under the shade of a tree, and they sat on these and looked out over the tops of the trees to the hills in the distance. A cicada was screeching somewhere in the grass nearby, a shrill, persistent sound, a call for another cicada, a warning, a protest against some injustice down in the insect world. The sky above was clear, a great echoing bowl of blue, drenched in light. There could be nothing wrong.

"It is very beautiful here," said Mma Ramotswe. "If I worked here I would do no work, I think. I would sit and look at the hills."

"You are welcome to come and look at these hills any time, Mma," said Neil. He paused before continuing. "Are you here on business?"

Mma Ramotswe nodded. "Yes, we are."

Neil signalled to a young woman to bring them tea. "One of our people is in trouble? Is that it?" He frowned as he spoke.

For a moment Mma Ramotswe looked confused. Then she realised. "No, not my business—Mr J.L.B. Matekoni's business. Garage business."

The misunderstanding cleared up, they sat and waited for the tea. Their conversation wandered. Mma Makutsi seemed to be thinking of something else, and Mma Ramotswe found herself expressing a view on something she knew nothing about—a plan to build some houses nearby. Then the subject of ostriches came up. This was more interesting to Mma

Ramotswe, although when she came to think of it, what did she know about ostriches? Very little.

"We've got a number of ostriches over there," said Neil, pointing in the direction of a small hillock in the mid-distance.

Mma Ramotswe followed his gaze. The expanse of bush was wide, the acacia trees like small umbrellas dotted thickly over the land. A patch of high grass on the edge of the clearing in which the camp sat moved slightly in the wind. There was nothing wrong; or was there? Why, thought Mma Ramotswe, do I feel that sensation, not fear, but something like it? Dread, perhaps; the sort of dread that can be felt in broad daylight, like this, with the sun all about and the shadows short and the presence of people—a man whistling as he attended to a task outside the office building, a woman leaning against her broom, chatting with somebody through a window.

"The thing about ostriches," said Neil, "is that they are not very intelligent. In fact, ostriches are very stupid, Mma Ramotswe."

"They are a bit like chickens, then," said Mma Ramotswe. "I have never thought that chickens were very clever."

Neil laughed. "That's a good way of putting it! Yes. Big chickens."

Mma Ramotswe remembered her meeting with Mr Molefelo, who had told her of how he had seen a man kicked by an ostrich and become late, immediately. "Chickens are not so dangerous," she said. "I am not frightened of chickens."

Neil raised an admonitory finger. "Stay away from ostriches, Mma Ramotswe. But, if you find yourself face-to-face with an angry ostrich, do you know what to do? No? I'll tell you. You put your hat on the top of a stick and raise it well above your head. The ostrich will think that you are much taller than he is, and he will back off. It works every time— every time!"

Mma Makutsi's eyes opened wide. What if she had no hat? Could she put something else on a stick and hold it up instead—one of her shoes, one of the green shoes with sky-blue linings perhaps? Or would the ostriches just laugh at that? There was no telling, but it was still an extraordinary piece of information, and she made a mental note to pass it on to Phuti Radiphuti the next time she saw him. She stopped herself; she had forgotten.

She was not sure whether there would be a next time . . .

Neil reached for the tea-pot and poured tea for his guests. "You know, Mma Ramotswe, there's something I want to talk to you about. I wasn't going to mention it to you, but since you're here, you might be just the person to deal with something. I know that you're a . . . what do you call yourself, a detective?"

"Yes, Rra," said Mma Ramotswe. "I call myself a detective. And other people call me that too."

Neil cleared his throat. "Yes, of course," he said. "Well, a detective is maybe what we need around here."

Mma Ramotswe raised her cup to her lips. She had been right—there was something wrong. She had picked it up and, rather than doubting it, she should have trusted her instincts. There were usually ways of telling what was happening; there were signs, if one was ready to see them; there were sounds, if one was ready to hear them.

She looked at Neil across the rim of her cup. He was a very straightforward man, and although he was not a Motswana he was a man who had been born in Africa and lived all his life there. Such people may be white people, but they knew, they understood as well as anybody else. If he was worried about something, then there would be reason to worry.

"I felt that there was something wrong, Rra," she said quietly. "I could tell—I could just tell that there was something wrong." As she spoke, she felt it again—that feeling of dread. She half-turned in her seat and looked behind her, back into the darkened interior of the building behind them, where the kitchen was. A woman was standing in the doorway, just standing, doing nothing. Mma Ramotswe could not quite make out her face, and the woman withdrew, back into the shadows.

Neil had replaced his cup on the table and was rubbing the rim of it gently, as if to coax out a sound. Mma Ramotswe noticed that one of his fingers had been scratched: a small line of dried blood ran across the skin, which was weathered, cracked, the skin of a man who worked with stone and machinery and the branches of thorn trees. She waited for him to speak.

"This is generally a pretty happy place," he began. "You know what it's like, don't you?"

Mma Ramotswe did. She remembered when

Mokolodi had first been set up, the dream of Ian Kirby, who had been a friend of Seretse Khama and his family. He had created the game park and had given it over to a trust for the nation so that people could come out from Gaborone, which was so close, and see animals in the wild. It was an idealistic place, and it attracted people who loved the bush and wanted to preserve it. These were not people to argue or fight with one another. Nor was it the sort of place where a dishonest or difficult person would wish to work. And yet there was something wrong. What was it? What was it? She closed her eyes, but opened them again quickly. It was fear; it was unmistakable.

"I know what this place is like normally," she said. "It is happy. I have a cousin here, you know. She has always liked working here."

"Well, it's not like that now," said Neil. "There's something very odd going on, and I don't seem able to find out what the trouble is. I've asked people and they just clam up. They look away. You know how people do that when they don't want to talk. They look away."

Mma Ramotswe understood that. People did not always talk about the things that were worrying them. Sometimes this was because they thought it rude to burden others with their troubles; sometimes it was because they did not know how to say what had to be said; there were many reasons. But fear was always a possible explanation: you did not talk about things that you were worried might happen. If you did, then the very things you worried about could come to pass.

"Tell me, Rra," she asked, "how do you know that there is something? How can you tell?"

Neil picked up a dried leaf which had blown onto the table and crushed it slowly between his fingers. "How do I know? Well, I'll give you an example. Last Saturday I wanted to drive round the reserve at night. I do that from time to time—we've had a bit of trouble with poachers, and I like to go out at odd times, without lights, so that if there's anybody thinking of getting up to anything they will know that we're in the habit of coming round the corner at any time, night or day. I usually take two or three of the men when I do this.

"Normally there's no difficulty in getting some men to come with me. They take it in turns, and pitch up of their own accord. Well, last Saturday it seemed to be a very different situation. Nobody was willing to volunteer, and when I went down to the houses to see what was going on, everybody's door was firmly shut."

Mma Ramotswe raised an eyebrow. "They were scared?"

"That's the only explanation," said Neil.

"Scared of poachers?"

Neil shrugged his shoulders. "It's difficult to say. I would have thought that was unlikely. The sort of poachers we get round here will usually run a mile rather than come up against any of us. They're not a very impressive breed of poacher, I'm afraid."

"So?" pressed Mma Ramotswe. "Was there anything else?"

Neil thought for a moment. "There have been other odd things. One of the women who works in the kitchen ran out screaming her head off the other day. She was hysterical. She said that she had seen something in the storeroom."

"And?" encouraged Mma Ramotswe.

"I called one of the other women to calm her down," said Neil. "Then I went and had a look in the storeroom. Of course, there was nothing. But when I tried to get the women to come in with me so that I could show them that there was nothing there, they both refused. Both of them. The woman who was trying to calm her friend down was just as bad."

Mma Ramotswe listened carefully. This was beginning to sound familiar to her. Although it happened relatively infrequently, it still happened. Witchcraft. Somebody was practising witchcraft, and the moment that happened, then all reason, all sound ideas and rationality, could be abandoned. Just below the surface, there were deep wells of fear and superstition that could suddenly be revealed by something like this. It was less common than it used to be, but it was there.

She looked at her watch. Mr J.L.B. Matekoni needed that axle, and she and Mma Makutsi did not have the time to sit and talk much longer, pleasant though it was to sit under that tree.

"I will come back sometime soon," said Mma Ramotswe. "And when I come back, I shall look into these things for you. In the meantime, we must get that axle for Mr J.L.B. Matekoni. That is what we need to do first. The other thing can wait."

Mma Ramotswe went back to her van and

drove it down to the workshop area, while Neil and Mma Makutsi walked together down the track to meet her there. It took no more than a few minutes for the half-axle to be found among a pile of greasy spare parts. Then it was loaded into the back of the tiny white van, where it rested on some spread-out newspapers. Mma Ramotswe noticed that the two men who picked up the axle and manoeuvred it into the van said nothing beyond a mumbled greeting, completing their task in silence and then turning away, melting back into the workshop.

"You won't forget to come out soon?" Neil said as Mma Ramotswe prepared to leave.

"I won't," said Mma Ramotswe. "Don't worry. I'll come out and have a word with a few people."

"If they'll talk," said Neil gloomily. "It's as if somebody has stuck their lips together with tape."

"Somebody probably has," said Mma Ramotswe quietly. "It's just that we can't see the tape."

She drove back up the Mokolodi road to join the main road back to Gaborone. Mma Makutsi was still silent, sitting next to her, morosely looking out of her window. Mma Ramotswe glanced at her companion and was on the point of saying something, but did not. It seemed to her as if she was surrounded by silence—those silent men at the workshop, the silent woman beside her, the silent sky.

She looked again at Mma Makutsi. She had been about to say: "You know, Mma, I might just as well have come out here by myself, for all the fun you're being." But she did not. If I said anything like that, she told herself, I rather think Mma Makutsi would burst into tears. She wanted to reach across and lay a hand on Mma Makutsi's arm, to comfort her, but could not. They were coming to a bend in the road, and they would end up in a ditch if she took her hands off the wheel. That would not help, thought Mma Ramotswe.

CHAPTER SEVEN

MR POLOPETSI, AND THE COMPLICATIONS IN HIS LIFE

Mr J.L.B. MATEKONI was very pleased with the half-axle that he had obtained from Mokolodi. Fitting it, though, was a major job, requiring the assistance of the two apprentices—who needed to be instructed on this matter anyway. So the next morning, while the three of them conferred under the raised vehicle, Mr Polopetsi, who was the most recent addition to the staff of Tlokweng Road Speedy Motors, was left in charge of the routine work of the garage. He had been recruited after Mma Ramotswe's van had knocked him off his bicycle and she had arranged for it to be fixed by Mr J.L.B. Matekoni. It was after this that he had revealed what had happened to him, how he had been sent to prison for negligence after the wrong drug had been dispensed from the hospital pharmacy in which he worked. It had not been his fault, but lies had been told by another, and the magistrate had felt that a conviction and prison sentence were necessary to satisfy the outrage of the patient's family. Mma Ramotswe had been moved by the story and by his plight, and had arranged work for him in the garage. It had been a good choice: Mr Polopetsi was a methodical worker who had rapidly learned how to service a car and carry out the more mundane repairs. He was an intelligent man, and discreet too, and Mma Ramotswe foresaw the day when he would be useful in the No. 1 Ladies' Detective Agency. He could never be a partner in the agency, as a ladies' detective agency could not allow that, but he could certainly perform some of the tasks for which a man would be useful. It would be handy, for instance, to have a man who could go and observe what was going on in a particular bar, if that should be necessary in a case. A lady detective could not very well do that, as she would spend half her time fending off the men who pestered ladies in bars.

One of the pleasures of having Mr Polopetsi in the garage was that he would often come

through to the office to have his tea break with
Mma Ramotswe and Mma Makutsi. Mr J.L.B.
Matekoni was frequently too busy to take a tea
break, and the apprentices liked to have their
tea sitting on upturned oil drums and watching
girls walk past along the road outside. But Mr
Polopetsi would come through with his mug
and ask Mma Makutsi if there might be
enough tea for him. He would always receive
the answer that there certainly would be and
that he should take a seat on the client's chair
and they would fill his mug for him. And Mr
Polopetsi would always say the same thing in
reply, as if it were a mantra: "You are very kind,
Mma Makutsi. There are not many ladies as
kind as you and Mma Ramotswe. That's the
truth." He did not seem to notice that he said
the same thing every time, and the ladies never
pointed out to him that they had heard the remark before. "We say the same things all the
time, you know," Mma Ramotswe had once
observed to Mma Makutsi, and Mma Makutsi
had replied, "You're right about that, Mma
Ramotswe"—which is something that she always said.

Mr Polopetsi came into the office that

morning wiping his brow from the heat. "I think that it's tea-time," he said, placing his mug on the top of the metal filing cabinet. "It's very hot through there. Do you know why drinking a hot liquid like tea can cool you down, Mma Ramotswe?"

Mma Ramotswe had, in fact, thought about this but had reached no conclusion. All she knew was that a cup of bush tea always refreshed her in a way in which a glass of cold water would not. "You tell me, Rra," she said. "And Mma Makutsi will turn on the kettle at the same time."

"It's because hot liquids make you sweat," explained Mr Polopetsi. "Then as the sweat dries off the skin it gives a feeling of coolness. That is how it works."

Mma Makutsi flicked the switch of the kettle. "Very unlikely," she said curtly.

Mr Polopetsi turned to her indignantly. "But it's true," he said. "I learned that on my pharmacy course at the hospital. Dr Moffat gave us lectures on how the body works."

This did not impress Mma Makutsi. "I don't sweat when I drink tea," she said. "But it still cools me off."

"Well, you don't have to believe me if you don't want to," he said. "I just thought that I would tell you—that's all."

"I believe you, Rra," said Mma Ramotswe soothingly. "I'm sure that you're right." She glanced at Mma Makutsi. There was definitely something worrying her assistant; it was unlike her to snap at Mr Polopetsi, whom she liked. She had decided that it was something to do with that conversation which she had had with Phuti Radiphuti—the conversation in which she had confessed to feminism. Had he taken that to heart? She very much hoped he had not; Mma Ramotswe was appalled at the thought of something going wrong with Mma Makutsi's engagement. After all those years of waiting and hoping, Mma Makutsi had eventually found a man, only to ruin everything by frightening him off. Oh, careless, careless Mma Makutsi! thought Mma Ramotswe. And foolish, foolish man to take a casual remark so seriously!

Mma Ramotswe smiled at Mr Polopetsi. "I know Dr Moffat's wife," she said. "I can go and ask her myself. She can speak to the doctor. We can settle this matter quite easily."

"It is already settled," said Mr Polopetsi. "There is no doubt in my mind, at least."

"Well, then," said Mma Ramotswe. "You need not worry about it any more."

"I wasn't worried," said Mr Polopetsi, as he sat down in the client's chair. "I have bigger things to worry about. Unlike some people." The last few words were said softly, but Mma Ramotswe heard them. Mma Makutsi, for whom they were half-intended, did not. She was standing by the kettle, waiting for it to boil, looking up at the tiny white gecko suspended by its minute suction pads on the ceiling.

Mma Ramotswe saw this as an opportunity to change the subject. When Mma Makutsi was in that sort of mood, then she had found that the best tactic was to steer away from controversy. "Oh?" she said. "Bigger worries? What are they, Rra?"

Mr Polopetsi glanced over his shoulder at Mma Makutsi. Mma Ramotswe noticed this, and made a discreet signal with her hand. It was a "don't you worry about her" signal, and he understood immediately.

"I am very tired, Mma," he said. "That is

my problem. It is all this bicycle-riding in this heat. It is not easy."

Mma Ramotswe looked out of the window. The sun that day was relentless; you felt it on the top of your head, pressing down. Even in the early mornings, shortly after breakfast, a time when one might choose to walk about the yard and inspect the trees—even then, it was hot and uncomfortable. And it would stay like this, she knew—or get even worse until the rains came, cooling and refreshing, like a cup of tea for the land itself, she found herself thinking.

She looked back at Mr Polopetsi. Yes, he looked exhausted, poor man, sitting there in the client's chair, crumpled, hot.

"Couldn't you come in by minibus?" she said. "Most other people do."

Mr Polopetsi seemed to crumple even more. "You have been to my house, Mma Ramotswe. You know where it is. It is no good for minibuses. There is a long walk to the nearest place that a minibus stops. Then they are often late."

Mma Ramotswe nodded sympathetically. It was not easy for people who lived out of town. The cost of housing in Gaborone itself was going up and up, and for most people a house in town would be an impossible dream. That left places like Tlokweng, or even further afield, and a long journey into work. It was all right, she supposed, if one were young and robust, but Mr Polopetsi, although he was only somewhere in his forties, did not look strong: he was a slight man, and with that crumpled look of his . . . If a powerful gust of wind should come sweeping in from the Kalahari, he could easily be lifted up and blown away. In her mind's eye, she saw Mr Polopetsi in his khaki trousers and khaki shirt, arms flailing, being picked up by the wind and cartwheeled through the sky, off towards Namibia somewhere, and dropped down suddenly on the ground, confused, in another land. And then she saw Herero horsemen galloping towards him and shouting and Mr Polopetsi, dusting himself off, trying hard to explain, pointing to the sky and gesturing.

"Why are you smiling, Mma Ramotswe?" asked Mr Polopetsi.

She corrected herself quickly. "I'm sorry," she said. "I was thinking of something else."

Mr Polopetsi shifted in his chair. "It must have been funny," he muttered.

Mma Ramotswe looked away. "Funny

things come to mind," she said. "You can be thinking of something serious, and then something very funny comes to mind. But look, Rra, what about a car? Would it not be possible now to buy a car—now that you're earning here; and your wife has a job, doesn't she? Could you not afford a cheap car, an old one, which is still going? Mr J.L.B. Matekoni would be able to find something for you."

Mr Polopetsi shook his head vehemently. "I cannot afford a car," he said. "I would love one, and it would solve all my troubles. I could give people a ride in with me and pay for the petrol that way. My neighbour works not far away— he could come in with me, and he has a friend too. They would love to come by car. My brother has a car. He is lucky."

The tea was now ready, and Mma Makutsi brought over Mr Polopetsi's mug and placed it on the edge of Mma Ramotswe's desk in front of him.

"You are very kind, Mma Makutsi," said Mr Polopetsi. "There are not many ladies as kind as you and Mma Ramotswe. That's the truth."

Mma Ramotswe lowered her head briefly to acknowledge the compliment. "This brother of yours, Mr Polopetsi," she said. "Is he a wealthy man?"

Mr Polopetsi took a sip of his tea. "No," he answered. "He is not a rich man. He has a good job, though. He works in a bank. But that is not how he managed to get the car. He was given a loan by my uncle. It was one of those loans that you can pay off in such small installments that you never notice the cost. My uncle is a generous man. He has a lot of money in the bank."

"A rich uncle?" said Mma Ramotswe. "Could this rich uncle not lend you money too? Why should he prefer your brother? Surely an uncle . . ." She tailed off. It occurred to her that there was a very obvious reason why this uncle would prefer one brother to another, and she saw, from the embarrassment in his demeanour, that she was right.

"He has not forgiven me," said Mr Polopetsi simply. "He has not forgiven me for . . . for being sent to prison. He said that it brought shame on the whole family when I was sent to that place."

Mma Makutsi, who had poured her own tea now and had taken it to her desk, looked up indignantly. "He should not think that," she expostulated. "What happened was not your fault. It was an accident."

"I tried to tell him that," said Mr Polopetsi, turning to address Mma Makutsi, "but he would not listen to me. He refused. He just shouted." He hesitated. "He is an old man, you know. Old men sometimes do not want to listen."

There was silence as Mma Ramotswe and Mma Makutsi digested this information. Mma Ramotswe understood. There were some older people in Botswana—men in particular—who had very strong ideas of what was what and who were notoriously stubborn in their attitudes. Her father, the late Obed Ramotswe, had not been like that at all—he had always had an open mind—but she remembered some of his friends being very difficult to persuade. He had even spoken of one of them who had been hostile to independence, who had wanted the Protectorate to continue. This man had said that it would be better to have somebody to protect the country against the Boers, and had continued to say this even when Obed had asked him: "Where are these troops you say will protect us? Where are they?" And, of course, there were none. He could understand, though, loyalty to Queen Elizabeth. She was a friend of Africa, Obed said; she had always been, for she understood all about loyalty and duty, and about how, during the war, there had been many men from the Protectorate who had gone to fight. They had been brave men, who had seen terrible things in Italy and North Africa, and now most people had forgotten about them. We should not forget these things, he had said; we should not forget.

"I understand," she said to Mr Polopetsi. "Sometimes when somebody makes up his mind, it is difficult to shift him. The elders are sometimes like that." She paused. "What is the name of this uncle of yours, Mr Polopetsi? Where does he live?"

Mr Polopetsi told her. He drained the rest of the tea from his mug and rose to his feet; he did not see Mma Ramotswe reaching for a pencil and writing a note on a scrap of paper. And then this scrap of paper she tucked in her bodice, the safest place to keep anything. She never forgot to do anything filed in that particular place, and so she would not forget the details on that piece of paper: Mr Kagiso Polopetsi, Plot 2487, Limpopo Drive. After which she had scrawled—**mean old uncle**.

MMA MAKUTSI went back to the house early that afternoon. She had told Mma Ramotswe that she would be cooking a meal for Phuti Radiphuti that evening and wanted to make it a special one. Mma Ramotswe had told her that this was a very good idea and that it would also be a good idea to talk to him about feminism.

"Set his mind at rest," she said. "Tell him that you are not going to be one of those women who will give him no peace. Tell him that you are really quite traditional at heart."

"I will do that," agreed Mma Makutsi. "I will show him that he need not fear that I will always be criticising him." She stopped and looked at Mma Ramotswe. There was misery in her expression, and Mma Ramotswe felt an immediate rush of sympathy for her. It was different for her. She was married to Mr J.L.B. Matekoni and felt quite secure; if Mma Makutsi lost Phuti Radiphuti she would have nothing—just the prospect of hard work for the rest of her life, making do with the small salary she earned and the little extra she made from the Kalahari Typing School for Men. The typing school was a valuable source of extra funds, but she had to work so hard keeping that going that she had very little time to herself.

Back at her house, Mma Makutsi made the evening meal with care. She boiled a large pot of potatoes and simmered a thick beef stew into which she had put carrots and onions. The stew smelled rich and delicious, and she dipped a finger into the pot to taste it. It needed a little bit more salt, but after that it was perfect. She sat down to wait for Phuti Radiphuti, who normally arrived at seven o'clock. It was now six thirty, and she flicked through a magazine, only half-concentrating, for the remaining half hour.

At seven thirty she looked out of the window, and at eight o'clock she went out to stand at her gate and peer down the road to see if he was coming. It was a warm evening and the air was heavy with the smell of cooking and dust. From her neighbour's house she heard the sound of a radio, and laughter. Somebody coughed; she felt the brush of insect wings against her leg.

She walked back up the path to her front door and into her house. She sat down on her sofa and stared up at the ceiling. I am a girl from Bobonong, she said to herself. I am a girl from Bobonong, with glasses. There was a man who was going to marry me, a kind man, but I frightened him away through my foolish talk. Now I am alone again. That is the story of my life; that is the story of Grace Makutsi.

CHAPTER EIGHT

A MEETING IN THE TINY WHITE VAN

THE FOLLOWING DAY, Mma Ramotswe went to see Mma Tsau, the cook for whom Poppy worked, the wife of the man who had grown prosperous-looking on government food. It was an auspicious day—a Friday at the end of the month. For most people, that was pay day, and for many it was the end of the period of want that always seemed to occur over the last few days of the month, no matter how careful one was with money for the other twenty-five days or so. The apprentices were a good example of this. When they had first started to work at Tlokweng Road Speedy Motors, Mr J.L.B. Matekoni had warned them that they should husband their resources carefully. It was tempting, he pointed out, to view money as something to be spent the moment it came into one's hands. "That is very dangerous," he said. "There are many people whose bellies are full for the first fifteen days of the month who then have hungry stomachs for the last two weeks."

Charlie, the older apprentice, exchanged a knowing glance with his younger colleague. "That makes twenty-nine days," he said. "What about the other two days, Boss?"

Mr J.L.B. Matekoni sighed. "That is not the point," he said, his tone level. It would be easy to lose his temper with these boys, he realised, but that was not what he intended to do. He was their apprentice-master, and that meant that he should be patient. One got nowhere if one shouted at young people. Shouting at a young person was like shouting at a wild animal—both would run away in their confusion.

"What you should do," said Mr J.L.B. Matekoni, "is work out how much money you need for each week. Then put all your money in the post office or somewhere safe like that and draw it out weekly."

Charlie smiled. "There is always credit," he said. "You can buy things on credit. It is cheaper that way."

Mr J.L.B. Matekoni looked at the young man. Where does one start? he thought. How does one make up for all the things that young people do not know? There was so much ignorance in the world—great swathes of ignorance like areas of darkness on a map. That was the job of teachers, to put this ignorance to flight, and that was why teachers were respected in Botswana—or used to be. He had noticed how people these days, even young people, treated teachers as if they were the same as anybody else. But how would people learn if they did not respect a teacher? Respect meant that they would be prepared to listen, and to learn. Young men like Charlie, thought Mr J.L.B. Matekoni, imagined that they knew everything already. Well, he would simply have to try to teach them in spite of their arrogance.

Grace Makutsi and Mma Ramotswe knew all about the end of the month. Mma Ramotswe's financial position had always been considerably easier than most people's, thanks to the late Obed Ramotswe's talent for the spotting of good cattle, but she was well aware of the enforced penny-pinching that was the daily lot of those about her. Rose, the woman who cleaned her house in Zebra Drive, was an example. She had a number of children—Mma Ramotswe had never been sure just how many—and these children had all known what it was to go to bed hungry, in spite of their mother's best efforts. And one of the children, a small boy, had difficulties with his breathing and needed inhalers, which were expensive to buy, even with the help of the government clinic. And then there was Mma Makutsi herself, who had supported herself at the Botswana Secretarial College by doing cleaning work in a hotel in the early mornings before she went to her classes at the college. That could not have been easy, getting up at four in the morning, even in the winter, when the skies were sharp-empty (as Mma Makutsi put it) with cold and the ground hard below the feet. But she had been careful, husbanding every spare thebe, and now, at long last, had achieved some measure of comfort with her new house (or half house, to be precise), her new green shoes with sky-blue linings, and, of course, her new fiancé . . .

The end of the month, pay day; and now Mma Ramotswe parked her tiny white van near the kitchen building of the college and waited. She looked at her watch. It was three o'clock, and she imagined that Mma Tsau would have finished supervising the clean-up after lunch. She was not sure where the cook had her office, but it was likely to be in the same building as the kitchens, and there was no doubt which building that was; one only had to wind down the window and sniff the air to know where the kitchens were. What a lovely smell it was, the smell of food. That was one of the great pleasures of life, in Mma Ramotswe's view—the smell of cooking drifting on the wind; the smell of maize cobs roasting on the open fire, of beef sizzling in its fat, of large chunks of pumpkin boiling in the pot. All these smells were good smells, part of the smells of Botswana, of home, that warmed the heart and made the mouth water in anticipation.

She looked towards the kitchen building. There was an open door at one end and a large window, through which she could just make out the shape of a cupboard and an overhead fan turning slowly. There were people in it too; a head moved, a hand appeared at the window, briefly, and was withdrawn. That was the office, she thought, and she could always just go up to it, knock on the door, and ask for Mma Tsau. Mma Ramotswe had always believed in the direct approach, no matter what advice Clovis Andersen gave in **The Principles of Private Detection**. Clovis Andersen seemed to endorse circumspection and the finding out of information by indirect means. But in Mma Ramotswe's view, the best way of getting an answer to any question was to ask somebody face-to-face. Experience had shown her that if one suspected that there was a secret, the best thing to do was to find out who knew the secret and then ask that person to tell it to you. It nearly always worked. The whole point about secrets was that they demanded to be told, they were insistent, they burned a hole in your tongue if you kept them for too long. That was the way it worked for most people.

For her part, Mma Ramotswe knew how to keep a secret, if the secret was one which needed to be kept. She did not divulge her clients' affairs, even if she felt that she was bursting to tell somebody, and even Mr J.L.B. Matekoni would not be told of something if it really had to be kept confidential. Only very occasionally, when she felt that the burden of some bit of knowledge was too great for one person to shoulder, would she share with Mr J.L.B. Matekoni some hidden fact which she had uncovered or which had been imparted to her. This had happened when she had heard from one client that he was planning to defraud the Botswana Eagle Insurance Company by making a false claim. He had told her this in a matter-of-fact way, as if she should not be surprised; after all, was this not the way in which practically everybody treated insurance companies? She had gone to Mr J.L.B. Matekoni to discuss this with him, and he had advised her to bring her professional relationship with that client to an end, which she did, and was crudely threatened for her pains. That had resulted in a trip to the Botswana Eagle Insurance Company, which had been most grateful for the information Mma Ramotswe had provided, and had taken steps to protect its interests.

But the direct approach would not work now. If she went to the office, there was every chance that she would see Poppy, and that would lead to difficulties. She had not warned Poppy that she was coming to speak to Mma Tsau, and she would not want the cook to suspect that Poppy had consulted her. No, she would have to make sure that she spoke to Mma Tsau by herself.

A small group of students emerged from a building beside the kitchen. It was the end of a class, and they stood in groups of two or three outside the classroom, talking among themselves, laughing at shared jokes. It was the end of the month for them too, Mma Ramotswe assumed, and they would have their allowances in their pockets and thoughts of the weekend's socialising ahead of them. What was it like, she wondered, to be one of them? Mma Ramotswe herself had gone from girlhood to the world of work without anything in between and had never known the student life. Did they know, she wondered, just how fortunate they were?

One of the students detached herself from a group and started to walk across the patch of ground that separated the van from the kitchen building. When she drew level with the van, she glanced in Mma Ramotswe's direction.

"Excuse me, Mma," shouted Mma Ramotswe through the open window of her van. "Excuse me, Mma!"

The young woman stopped and looked across at Mma Ramotswe, who was now getting out of the van.

"Yes, Mma," said the student. "Are you calling me?"

Mma Ramotswe made her way over to stand before the young woman. "Yes, Mma," she said. "Do you know the lady who works in the kitchen? Mma Tsau? Do you know that lady?"

The student smiled. "She is the cook," she said. "Yes, I know her."

"I need to speak to her," said Mma Ramotswe. "I need to speak to her out here, in my van. I do not want to speak to her when there are other people about."

The student looked blank. "So?" she said.

"So I wonder if you would go and tell her, Mma," said Mma Ramotswe. "Could you go and tell her that there is somebody out here who needs to speak to her?"

The young woman frowned. "Could you not go yourself, Mma? Why do you need me to do this for you?"

Mma Ramotswe looked searchingly into the face of the young woman before her. What bond was there between them? Were they strangers, people who would have no reason to do anything for one another? Or was this still a place where one might go and speak to another, even a complete stranger, and make a request for help, as had been possible in the past?

"I am asking you," said Mma Ramotswe

quietly. "I am asking you . . ." And then she hesitated, but only for a moment, before she continued, "I am asking you, my sister."

For a moment the young woman said nothing, but then she moved her head slightly; she nodded. "I will do that," she said. "I will go."

MMA TSAU, a squat, rather round woman, appeared from the door of the kitchen office, paused, and looked out over the grounds of the college. Her gaze fell upon the tiny white van and she hesitated for a moment. Within the van, Mma Ramotswe raised a hand, which Mma Tsau did not see, but she saw the van, and the young woman had said, "There is a woman who needs to see you urgently, Mma. She is outside in a small white van. She is too big for that van, if you ask me, but she wants to see you there."

The cook made her way across the ground to the van. She had a curious gait, Mma Ramotswe observed; a slight limp perhaps, or feet that pointed out to the side rather than forwards. Mma Makutsi was slightly inclined to do that, Mma Ramotswe had noticed, and although she had never said anything about it, one day she would pluck up the courage to suggest that she should think about the way she walked. One had to be careful, though: Mma Makutsi was sensitive about her appearance and might be demoralised by such a remark, even if it was meant helpfully.

Mma Tsau peered into the van. "You are looking for me, Mma?" The voice was a loud one, surprisingly loud for one of such small stature; it was the voice of one who was used to shouting at people. Professional cooks had a reputation for shouting, Mma Ramotswe recalled. They shouted at the people who worked for them in their kitchen, and some of them—the really famous ones—threw things too. There was no excuse for that, of course. Mma Ramotswe had been shocked when she had read in a magazine about a famous chef somewhere overseas who threw cold soup over the heads of his junior staff if they did not measure up to his expectations. He swore at them too, which was almost as bad. To use strong language, she thought, was a sign of bad temper and lack of concern for others. Such people were not clever or bold simply because they used such language; each time they opened their mouths they proclaimed **I am a person**

who is poor in words. Was Mma Tsau one of those chefs, she wondered; this round little person with the blue spotted scarf tied round her head like a doek? It seemed unlikely that she would throw cold soup over somebody's head.

"Yes, Mma," said Mma Ramotswe, trying to put to the back of her mind the sudden mental picture which had come to her of Mma Tsau tipping a pot of soup over . . . Charlie. What a picture! And it was replaced immediately by an image of Mr J.L.B. Matekoni, frustrated by some piece of sloppy work, doing a similar thing to the apprentice; and Mma Makutsi pouring soup over . . . She stopped herself. "I would like to talk to you, please."

Mma Tsau wiped her brow. "I am listening," she said. "I can hear you."

"This is private," said Mma Ramotswe. "We could talk in my van, if you don't mind."

Mma Tsau frowned. "What is this private business?" she asked. "Are you trying to sell something, Mma?"

Mma Ramotswe looked about her, as one might do if about to impart a confidence. "It is about your husband," she said.

The words had their desired effect. When her husband was mentioned, Mma Tsau gave a start, as if somebody had poured ... She moved her head back and squinted at Mma Ramotswe through narrowed eyes.

"My husband?"

"Yes, Mma, your husband." Mma Ramotswe nodded in the direction of the passenger door. "Why don't you get into the van, Mma? We can talk in here."

For a moment it seemed as if Mma Tsau was going to turn around and go back to her office. There was a moment of hesitation; the eyes moved; she continued to stare at Mma Ramotswe. Then she started to walk round the front of the van, slowly, her eyes still on Mma Ramotswe.

"You can wind down that window, Mma," said Mma Ramotswe as the other woman lowered herself into the seat beside her. "It will be cooler that way. It is very hot today, isn't it?"

Mma Tsau had folded her hands on her lap and was staring down at them. She did not respond to Mma Ramotswe's remark. In the confines of the van, her breathing was audibly laboured. Mma Ramotswe said nothing for a moment, allowing her to get her breath back. But there was no change in Mma Tsau's breathing, which sounded as if the air was working its way through a small thicket of leaves, a rustling sound, the sound of a tree in the wind. She turned and looked at her visitor. She had been prepared to dislike this woman who had been stealing food from the college; this woman who had so unfairly threatened the inoffensive Poppy with dismissal. But now, in the flesh, with her laboured breathing and her odd walk, it was difficult not to feel sympathy. And of course it was always difficult for Mma Ramotswe not to feel sympathy for another, however objectionable his conduct might be, however flawed his character, simply because she understood, at the most intuitive, profound level what it was to be a human being, which is not easy. Everybody, she felt, could do evil, so easily; could be weak, so easily; could be selfish, so easily. This meant that she could understand—and did—which was not the same thing as condoning—which she did not—or taking the view—which she did not—that one should not judge others. Of course one could judge others, and Mma Ramotswe used the standards of the old Botswana morality to make these judgements. But there was nothing in the old Botswana morality which said that one could not forgive those who were weak; indeed, there was much in the old Botswana morality that was very specifically about forgiveness. One should not hold a grudge against another, it said, because to harbour grudges was to disturb the social peace, the bond between people.

She felt sorry, then, for Mma Tsau, and instinctively, without giving it any thought, she reached out and touched the other woman gently on the forearm, and left her hand there. Mma Tsau tensed, and the breath caught in her throat, but then she turned her head and looked at Mma Ramotswe, and her eyes were moist with tears.

"You are the mother of one of those girls," Mma Tsau said quietly. It was not a question; it was a statement. Her earlier confidence was drained from her, and she seemed even smaller now, hunched in her seat.

Mma Ramotswe did not understand, and was about to say so. But then she thought, and it came to her what this other woman meant. It was a familiar story, after all, and nobody should be surprised. The husband, the father, the respectable citizen; such a man might still carry on with other women in spite of everything, in spite of his wife's pain, and many did.

And some of these men went further, and picked up girls who were far younger than themselves, some still at high school. They felt proud of themselves, these men, with their youthful girlfriends, whose heads they turned because they had money to throw around, or a fast car, or power perhaps.

"I hear what you say, Mma," Mma Ramotswe began. "Your husband. I did not mean . . ."

"It has been going on for many years," Mma Tsau interrupted her. "Just after we were married—even then, he started this thing. I told him how stupid he looked, running after these young girls, but he ignored me. I told him that I would leave him, but he just laughed and said that I should do that. But I could not, Mma. I could not . . ."

This was a familiar story to Mma Ramotswe. She had come across so many women who could not leave unworthy men because they loved them. This was quite different from those cases where women could not leave because they were frightened of the man, or because they had no place to go; some women could not leave simply because, in spite of everything that had been done to them, in spite

of all the heartbreak, they stubbornly loved the
man. This, she suspected, was what was happening here. Mma Tsau loved Rra Tsau, and
would do so to the end.

"You love him, Mma?" she probed gently.
"Is that it?"

Mma Tsau looked down at her hands. Mma
Ramotswe noticed that one of them had a light
dusting of flour on it; the hand of a cook.

"Eee," said Mma Tsau, under her breath,
using the familiar, long-drawn-out Setswana
word of assent. "Eee, Mma. I love that man.
That is true. I am a weak woman, I know. But I
love him."

Mma Ramotswe sighed. There was no cure
for such love. That was the most basic thing
one found out about human affairs, and one
did not have to be a private detective to know
that simple fact. Such love, the tenacious love
of a parent or a devoted spouse, could fade—
and did—but it took a long time to do so and
often persisted in the face of all the evidence
that it was squandered on an unworthy choice.

"I was going to say that I hadn't come about
that," said Mma Ramotswe. "I do not know
your husband."

It took Mma Tsau a few moments to take

in what Mma Ramotswe had told her. When she did, she turned to look at her. She was still defeated.

"What have you come about?" she asked. There was no real curiosity in her voice now. It was as if Mma Ramotswe had come about the supply of eggs, or potatoes perhaps.

"I have come because I have heard that you have threatened to dismiss one of your staff," she said. She did not want to suggest that Poppy had complained, and so she said, quite truthfully—in the strictest sense—that nobody had asked her to come. That was not a lie. It was more what Clovis Andersen called **an indirect statement;** and there was a distinction.

Mma Tsau shrugged. "I am the head cook," she said. "I am called the catering manager. That is who I am. I take on some staff—and push some staff out. Some people are not good workers." She dusted her hands lightly, and for a moment Mma Ramotswe saw the tiny grains of flour, like specks of dust, caught in a slant of sunlight.

The sympathy that Mma Ramotswe had felt for her earlier was now being replaced by irritation. She did not really like this woman, she decided, although she admired her, perhaps, for her loyalty to her philandering husband. "People get dismissed for other reasons," she said. "Somebody who was stealing food, for example—that person would be dismissed if it were found out that government food was being given to her husband."

Mma Tsau was quite still. She reached her hand out and touched the hem of her skirt, tugging at it gently, as if testing the strength of the seam. She took a breath, and there was the rattling sound of phlegm.

"Maybe it was you who wrote that letter," she said. "Maybe . . ."

"I did not," said Mma Ramotswe. "And nor did that girl."

Mma Tsau shook her head. "Then who did?"

"I have no idea," said Mma Ramotswe. "But it had nothing to do with that girl. There is somebody else who is blackmailing you. That is what this is, you know. This is blackmail. It is normally a matter for the police."

Mma Tsau laughed. "You think I should go to the police? You think that I should say to them: **I have been giving government food to my husband. Now somebody is threatening me**? I'm not stupid, Mma."

Mma Ramotswe's voice was even. "I know

that you're not stupid, Mma Tsau. I know that." She paused. She doubted that Mma Tsau intended now to do anything more about Poppy, and that meant that she could regard the matter as closed. But it left the issue of the blackmail unresolved. It was a despicable act, she thought, and she was offended that somebody might do such a thing and get away with it. She might look into it, perhaps, if she had the time, and there were always slack periods when she and Mma Makutsi had nothing to do. Perhaps she could even put Mma Makutsi on the case and see what she made of it. No blackmailer would be a match for Mma Makutsi, assistant detective at the No. 1 Ladies' Detective Agency and graduate of distinction of the Botswana Secretarial College—Mma Ninety-Seven Per Cent, as Mma Ramotswe sometimes irreverently thought of her. She could imagine a confrontation between the blackmailer and Mma Makutsi, with the latter's large round glasses flashing with the fire of indignation and the blackmailer, a wretched, furtive man cowering in the face of female wrath.

"What are you smiling at?" asked Mma Tsau. "I do not think this is funny."

"No," said Mma Ramotswe, bringing herself back to reality. "It is not funny. But tell me, Mma—do you still have that letter? Could you show it to me? Perhaps I can find out who this person is who is trying to blackmail you."

Mma Tsau thought for a moment. "And you won't do anything about . . . about my husband?"

"No," said Mma Ramotswe. "I am not interested in your husband." And that was true, of course. She could just imagine Mma Tsau's husband, a lazy womaniser, being fed by his devoted wife and getting fatter and fatter until he could no longer see the lower part of his body, so large had his stomach become. That would serve him right, thought Mma Ramotswe. Being a traditionally built lady was one thing; being a traditionally built man was quite another. And it was certainly not so good.

The thought made her smile again, but Mma Tsau did not see the smile, as she was struggling with the door handle, preparing to go off and retrieve the letter which she had in her office, in one of the secret places she had there.

CHAPTER NINE

FILING CABINETS,
LOCKS, CHAINS

MMA RAMOTSWE looked into her tea cup.
The red bush tea, freshly poured, was still very
hot, too hot to drink, but good to look at in its
amber darkness, and very good to smell. It was
a pity, she thought, that she had become accustomed to the use of tea-bags, as this meant that
there were no leaves to be seen swirling around
the surface or clinging to the side of the cup.
She had given in on the issue of tea-bags, out of
weakness, she admitted; tea-bags were so over-
whelmingly more convenient than leaf tea,
with its tendency to clog drains and the spouts
of tea-pots too if one was not careful. She had
never worried about getting the occasional tea
leaf in her mouth, indeed she had rather enjoyed this, but that never happened now, with

these neatly packed tea-bags and their very precise, enmeshed doses of chopped leaves.

It was the first cup of the morning, as Mma Ramotswe did not count the two cups that she took at home before she came to work. One of these was consumed as she took her early stroll around the yard, with the sun just up, pausing to stand under the large acacia tree and peer up into the thorny branches above her, drawing the morning air into her lungs and savouring its freshness. That morning she had seen a chameleon on a branch of the tree and had watched the strange creature fix its riveting eye upon her, its tiny prehensile feet poised in mid-movement. It was a great advantage, she thought, to have a chameleon's eyes, which could look backwards and forwards independently. That would be a fine gift for a detective.

Now at her desk, she raised the cup to her lips and took a sip of the bush tea. She looked at her watch. Mma Makutsi was usually very punctual, but today she was late for some reason. This would be the fault of the minibuses, thought Mma Ramotswe. There would be enough of them coming into town from Tlokweng at that hour of the morning, but not enough going in the opposite direction. Mma

Makutsi could walk, of course—her new house was not all that far away—but people did not like to walk in the heat, understandably enough.

She had a report to write, and she busied herself with this. It was not an easy one, as she had to detail the weaknesses she had found in the hiring department of a company which provided security guards. They imagined that they screened out applicants with a criminal record when they sought jobs with the company; Mma Ramotswe had discovered that it was simplicity itself to lie about one's past on the application form and that the forms were usually not even scrutinised by the official in charge of the personnel department. This man, who had got the job through lying about his qualifications and experience, rubber-stamped the applications of virtually anybody, but particularly of applications submitted by any of his relatives. Mma Ramotswe's report would not make comfortable reading for the company, and she knew to expect some anger over the results. This was inevitable—people did not like to be told uncomfortable truths, even if they had asked for them. Uncomfortable truths meant that one had to go back and in-

vent a whole new set of procedures, and that
was not always welcome when there were so
many other things to do.

As she listed the defects in the firm's arrange-
ments, Mma Ramotswe thought of how difficult it was to have a completely secure system
for anything. The No. 1 Ladies' Detective
Agency was a case in point. They kept all their
records in two old filing cabinets, and neither
of these, she realised, had a lock, or at least a
lock that worked. There was a lock on the office door, naturally enough, but during the day
they rarely bothered to use that if both of them
went out on some errand. There were always
people around the garage, of course—either
Mr J.L.B. Matekoni or the apprentices, and
surely intruders would be deterred by their
presence . . . No, she thought, perhaps not. Mr
J.L.B. Matekoni was often so absorbed in tinkering with an engine that he would not notice
it if the President himself drew up in his large
official car. And as for the apprentices, they
were completely unobservant and missed the
most glaring features of what went on round
about them. Indeed, she had given up on asking them for descriptions of clients who might
have called while she was out and spoken to

one of them. "There was a man," they would say. "He came to see you. Now he is gone." And in response to questioning for some clue as to the caller's identity, they would say, "He was not a very tall man, I think. Or maybe he was a bit tall. I could not tell."

Her pen stopped in mid-sentence. Who was she to criticise when it would be possible for virtually anybody to walk into the office of the No. 1 Ladies' Detective Agency at an unguarded moment and rifle through the secrets of their clients? Are you interested in who is suspected by his wife of adultery? Please, help yourself: there are plenty of reports about that in an old filing cabinet on the Tlokweng Road—just help yourself! And why was that man dismissed from that hotel last month, with no reason given? Well, the report on that—freely available from the No. 1 Ladies' Detective Agency, and signed by Mma Grace Makutsi, Dip. Sec. (Botswana Secretarial College) (97%)—may be obtained by the simple expedient of looking in the top drawer of the second desk of an unlocked office beside Tlokweng Road Speedy Motors.

Mma Ramotswe rose to her feet and made her way over to the filing cabinet nearest her.

Bending forward, she peered at the lock which was built into the top of the cabinet. It was a small, oval silver-coloured plate with an incised key-hole. At the top of the plate the maker's sign, a small rampant lion, was stamped into the metal. The lion looked back at Mma Ramotswe, and she shook her head. There was rust in the key-hole, and the edges of the hole were dented. Even if they could locate the key, it would be impossible to insert it. She looked at the lion, a symbol of the pride which some-body must once have felt, somewhere, in the construction of the cabinet. And perhaps this pride was not entirely misplaced—the cabinet must have been made decades ago, perhaps even forty or fifty years previously, and it still worked. How many modern cabinets, with their plastic trimmings and their bright colours, would still be holding files in fifty years' time? And it was the same with people, she thought. Bright, modern people were all very well, but did they last the course? Tradi-tionally minded (and traditionally built) peo-ple might not seem so fashionable, but they would always be there, doing what they always did. A traditional mechanic, for example— somebody like Mr J.L.B. Matekoni—would be able to keep your car going when a modern mechanic—somebody like Charlie—would shrug his shoulders and say that everything needed to be renewed.

She reached out and gave the filing cabinet an affectionate pat. Then, on impulse, she bent down and kissed its scratched and dented metal surface. The metal felt cool to her lips and smelled acrid, as metal can—a smell of rust and sharpness.

"Dumela, Mma," said Mma Makutsi from the doorway.

Mma Ramotswe straightened up.

"Don't worry about me," said Mma Makutsi. "Just carry on doing whatever it was that you were doing . . ." She glanced at the filing cabinet and then at her employer.

Mma Ramotswe returned to her desk. "I was thinking about that filing cabinet," she said. "And suddenly I felt very grateful to it. I know that it must have looked very strange to you, Mma."

"Not at all," said Mma Makutsi. "I am grateful to it too. It keeps all our records safe."

Mma Ramotswe frowned. "Well, I'm not sure if they're completely safe," she said. "In fact, I was just wondering whether we should do something about locking them. Confidentiality is very important. You know that, Mma."

Mma Makutsi looked thoughtfully at the filing cabinets. "That is true," she said. "But I do not think we would ever find a key for those old locks." She paused. "Maybe we could put a chain around them, with a padlock?"

Mma Ramotswe did not think that this would be a good idea. It would look absurd to have chained filing cabinets, and would give quite the wrong impression to clients. It was bad enough having an office inside a garage, but it would be worse to have something quite so odd-looking as a chain around a cabinet. It would be better to buy a couple of new filing cabinets, even if they would not be as sturdy and substantial as these old ones. There was probably enough money in the office account to do this, and they had not spent very much on equipment recently. In fact, they had spent nothing, apart from three pula for a new teaspoon, which had been required after one of the apprentices had used their existing teaspoon to fix a gearbox and had broken it. The thought of furniture reminded her. Mma Makutsi was about to marry, was she not?

And was she not about to marry into the furniture trade?

"Phuti Radiphuti!" Mma Ramotswe exclaimed.

Mma Makutsi looked up sharply. "Phuti?"

"Your fiancé, Mma," went on Mma Ramotswe. "Does he do office furniture as well as house furniture?"

Mma Makutsi looked down at her shoes. **Fiancé?** she imagined hearing the shoes say. **We used to be engaged to a pair of men's shoes but we haven't seen them for some time! Is it still on, Boss?**

Mma Ramotswe smiled across her desk. "I wouldn't expect a new filing cabinet for nothing," she said. "But he could give us a trade price, could he not? Or he would know where we could get it cheaply." She noticed Mma Makutsi's expression, and tailed off. "If he could . . ."

Mma Makutsi seemed reluctant to speak. She looked up at the ceiling for a moment, and then out of the door. "He did not come to my place last night," she said. "I had cooked for him. But he did not come."

Mma Ramotswe caught her breath. She had feared that something like this would happen.

Ever since Mma Makutsi had become engaged, she had been concerned that something would go wrong. That had nothing to do with Phuti Radiphuti himself, who seemed a good candidate for marriage, but it had everything to do with the bad luck that seemed to dog Mma Makutsi. There were some people who were badly treated by life, no matter how hard they worked and no matter what efforts they made to better their circumstances. Mma Makutsi had done her very best, but perhaps she would never get any further than she had already got, and would remain an assistant detective, a woman from Bobonong, with large round glasses, and a house that, although comfortable, had no hot water supply. Phuti Radiphuti could have changed everything, but now would not. He would be just another missed opportunity, another reminder of what might have been had everything been different.

"I think that he must have been working late," said Mma Ramotswe. "You should call him on the telephone and find out. Yes, just use the office phone. That is fine. Call Phuti."

Mma Makutsi shook her head. "No, I cannot do that. I cannot chase him."

"You're not chasing him," said Mma Ramotswe. "It is not chasing a man just to speak to him on the telephone and ask him why he did not come to your house. Men cannot let women cook for them and not eat the food. Everybody understands that."

This remark did not seem to help, and in the face of Mma Makutsi's sudden and taciturn gloominess, Mma Ramotswe herself became silent.

"That is why I'm late this morning," Mma Makutsi said suddenly. "I could not sleep at all last night."

"There are many mosquitoes," said Mma Ramotswe. "They do not make it easy."

"It had nothing to do with mosquitoes," Mma Makutsi mumbled. "They were sleeping last night. It was because I was thinking. I think it is all over, Mma."

"Nonsense," said Mma Ramotswe. "It is not over. Men are very strange—that is all. Sometimes they forget to come to see ladies. Sometimes they forget to get married. Look at Mr J.L.B. Matekoni. Look at how long it took him to get round to marrying me."

"I cannot wait that long," said Mma Makutsi. "I was thinking of being engaged for six months at the most." She reached for a piece of paper on her desk and stared at it. "Now I shall be doing this filing for the rest of my life."

Mma Ramotswe realised that she could not allow this self-pity to continue. That would only make it worse, in her view. So she explained to Mma Makutsi that she would have to seek out Phuti Radiphuti and reassure him. If she did not wish to do that, then she herself, Mma Ramotswe, could do it for her. Her offer was not taken up, but she repeated it, and it was reflected upon. Then the working day began. It was the day on which bills were due to be sent out, and that was always an enjoyable experience. If only there were a day on which bills were all returned, fully paid, that would be even more enjoyable. But the working world was not like that, and there were always more that went out than came in, or so it seemed. And in this sense, Mma Ramotswe mused, the working world reflected life; which was an adage worthy of Aunty Emang herself, even if she was not quite sure whether it was true or not.

THE BILLS ALL TYPED UP and sealed in their neat white envelopes, Mma Ramotswe remembered that she had something that she wanted to show to Mma Makutsi. Reaching into the old leather bag that she used for carrying papers and lists and the one hundred and one other accoutrements of her daily life, she extracted the letter which Mma Tsau had handed over to her the previous day. She crossed the room and handed it to Mma Makutsi.

"What do you make of this?" she said.

Mma Makutsi unfolded the letter and laid it on the desk before her. The paper, she noted, was crumpled, which meant that somebody could have crunched it up and tossed it away. This was not a cherished letter. This was a letter which had brought only anger and fear.

"So, Mma Tsau," Mma Makutsi read out. "So there you are in that good job of yours. It is a good job, isn't it? You have lots of people working for you. You get your cheque at the end of the month. Everything is fine for you, isn't it? And for that husband of yours too. He is very happy that you have this good job, as he can go and eat for nothing, can't he? It must be very nice to eat for nothing in this life. There are very few people who can do that, but he is one.

"But, you see, I know that you are stealing food for him. I saw him getting fatter and fatter, and I thought: that's a man who is eating for nothing! I could tell that. Of course you wouldn't want other people to know that, and so, you listen to me, listen carefully please: I will be getting in touch with you about how you can keep me from telling anybody about this. Don't worry—you'll hear from me."

When she had finished reading out the letter, Mma Makutsi looked up. Her earlier expression of defeat, brought on by Phuti Radiphuti's non-appearance and by her contemplation of her future, had been replaced by one of anger. "That's blackmail," she said. "That's . . . that's . . ." Her outrage had got the better of her; there were no words strong enough to describe what she felt.

"That's simple wickedness," supplied Mma Ramotswe. "Even if Mma Tsau is a thief, the writer of that letter is much worse."

Mma Makutsi was in strong agreement with this. "Yes. Wickedness. But how are we going to find out who wrote it? It's anonymous."

"Such letters always are," said Mma Ramotswe.

"Have you got any ideas?"

Mma Ramotswe had to confess that she had none. "But that doesn't mean that we shall not find out," she said. "I have a feeling that we are very close to that person. I don't know why I feel that, but I am sure that we know that lady."

"A lady?" asked Mma Makutsi. "How do we know it's a lady?"

"I just feel it," said Mma Ramotswe. "That's a woman's voice."

"Are you sure that that's not just because I was reading it?" said Mma Makutsi.

Mma Ramotswe replied with care. No, it was not just that. The voice—the voice inside the letter—was the voice of a woman. And, as she explained to Mma Makutsi, she had the feeling, vague and elusive though it might be, that she **knew** this woman.

CHAPTER TEN

YOU ARE FRIGHTENED OF SOMETHING

THAT AFTERNOON Mma Ramotswe made one of her lists. She liked to do this when life seemed to be becoming complicated, which it was now, as the mere fact of listing helped to get everything into perspective. And there was more to it than that; often the listing of a problem produced a solution, as if the act of writing down the issues gave the unconscious mind a nudge. She had heard that sleep could have the same effect. "Go to sleep on a problem," Mr J.L.B. Matekoni had once advised her, "and in the morning you will have your answer. It always works." He had then proceeded to describe how he had gone to sleep wondering why a rather complicated diesel engine would not fire and had dreamed that night of loose connections in the solenoid. "And when I got to the garage that morning," he said, "there it was—a very bad connection, which I replaced. The engine fired straightaway."

So that was what he dreamed about, thought Mma Ramotswe. Diesel engines. Solenoids. Fuel pipes. Her dreams were quite different. She often dreamed of her father, the late Obed Ramotswe, who had been such a kind man, and a loving one; a man whom everybody respected because he was such a fine judge of cattle, but also because he showed in all his actions the dignity which had been the hallmark of the Motswana of the old school. Such men knew their worth, but did not flaunt it. Such men could look anybody in the eye without flinching; even a poor man, a man with nothing, could stand upright in the presence of those who had wealth or power. People did not know, Mma Ramotswe felt, just how much we had in those days—those days when we seemed to have so little, we had so much.

She thought of her father, the Daddy as she called him, every day. And when she had those dreams at night, he was there, as if he had never died, although she knew, even in the dream, that he had. One day she would join him, she knew, whatever people said about how we came to an end when we took our last breath. Some people mocked you if you said that you joined others when your time came. Well, they could laugh, those clever people, but we surely had to hope, and a life without hope of any sort was no life: it was a sky without stars, a landscape of sorrow and emptiness. If she thought that she would never again see Obed Ramotswe, then it would make her shiver with loneliness. As it was, the thought that he was watching gave a texture and continuity to her life. And there was somebody else she would see one day, she hoped—her baby who had died, that small child with its fingers that had grasped so tightly around hers, whose breathing was so quiet, like the sound of the breeze in the acacia trees on an almost-still day, a tiny sound. She knew that her baby was with the late children in whatever place it was that the late children went, somewhere over there, beyond the Kalahari, where the gentle white cattle allowed the children to ride upon their backs. And when the late mothers came, the children would flock to them and they would call to them and take them in their arms. That was what she hoped, and it was a hope worth having, she felt.

But this was a time for making lists, not for dreaming, and she sat at her desk and wrote down on a piece of paper, in order of their priority, the various matters which concerned her. At the top of the list she simply wrote **blackmail**, and under that she left a blank space. This was where ideas might be noted, and a few words were immediately scribbled in: **Who could know?** Then below that there was **Mr Polopetsi**. Mr Polopetsi himself was not a problem, but Mma Ramotswe had been moved by his description of his wealthy uncle and his cutting out of his nephew. That was an injustice, in her view, and Mma Ramotswe found it hard to ignore injustice. Under Mr Polopetsi's name she wrote: **Mean uncle—speak to him?** Then there was **Mokolodi**, under which was written: **something very odd going on.** And then, finally, almost as an afterthought, she wrote: **Phuti Radiphuti: Could I say something to him about Mma Makutsi?** Her pencil poised at the end of the last question, she then added: **Mind own business?** And finally, she wrote: **Find new shoes.** That was simple, or at least it sounded simple; in reality the question of shoes could be a complicated one. She had been meaning for some time to buy herself a pair of shoes to replace the ones which she always wore to the office and which were becoming a bit down-at-heel. Traditionally built people could be hard on shoes, and Mma Ramotswe sometimes found it difficult to get shoes which were sufficiently well constructed. She had never gone in for fashionable shoes—unlike Mma Makutsi, with her green shoes with the sky-blue linings—but she wondered now whether she should not follow her assistant's lead and choose shoes which were perhaps just slightly more elegant. It was a difficult decision to make, and it would require some thought, but Mma Makutsi might help her, and this would at least take her mind off her problems with Phuti Radiphuti.

She looked at her list, sighed, and let the slip of paper fall from her hand. These were difficult issues, indeed, and not one of them, as far as she could see, involved a fee. The trickiest one was undoubtedly the blackmail problem, and now that she had established that Poppy was unlikely to lose her job—for which she could hardly charge very much, if anything—there was no financial reason to become further involved. There was a moral reason, of course, and that would inevitably prevail, but the setting of wrong to right often brought no financial reward. She had sighed, but it was not a sigh of desperation; she knew that there would be other cases, lucrative ones in which bills could be sent to firms that could well afford to pay. And had they not just posted a whole raft of such bills, each of which would bring in a comfortable cheque? And was there not an awful lot of banging and clattering going on in the garage next door, all of which meant money in the till and food on several tables? So she could afford to spend the time, if she wanted to, on these unremunerative matters, and she need not feel bad about it.

She picked up the list again and looked at it. Blackmail was too difficult. She would come back to it, she knew, but for now she felt like dealing with something which was more manageable. The word **Mokolodi** stood out on the page. She looked at her watch. It was three o'-clock. She had nothing to do (ignoring, for the moment, everything else on the list), and it would be pleasant to drive down to Mokolodi and talk to her cousin perhaps and see whether she could find out what was happening down

there. She could take Mma Makutsi with her
for company; but no, that would not be much
fun, with Mma Makutsi in her current
mood. She could go by herself or, and here another possibility came to mind, she could take
Mr Polopetsi. She was keen to train him to do
the occasional piece of work for the agency, as
well as the work that he did for the garage. He
was always interesting company and would
keep her entertained on the short drive south.

"I HAVE NEVER BEEN to this place," said
Mr Polopetsi. "I have heard of it, but I have
never been here."

They were no more than a few minutes
away from the main gate of Mokolodi, with
Mma Ramotswe at the wheel of the van and
Mr Polopetsi in the passenger seat, his arm resting on the sill of the open window as he looked
with interest at the passing landscape.

"I do not like wild animals very much," he
continued. "I am happy for them to be there,
out in the bush, but I do not like them to be
too close."

Mma Ramotswe laughed. "Most people
would agree with you," she said. "There are

some wild animals that I would prefer not to come across."

"Lions," said Mr Polopetsi. "I don't like to think that there are things which would like to have me for breakfast." He shuddered. "Lions. Of course, they would probably go for you first, Mma Ramotswe, rather than me." He made the remark without thinking, almost as a joke, and then he realised that it was not in very good taste. He glanced quickly at Mma Ramotswe, wondering whether she had missed what he had said. She had not.

"Oh?" she said. "And why would a lion prefer to eat me rather than you, Rra? Why would that be?"

Mr Polopetsi looked up at the sky. "I'm sure that I'm wrong," he said. "I thought that they might eat you first because . . ." He was about to say that it was because he would be able to run faster than Mma Ramotswe, but he realised that the reason that he would be able to run faster was because she was too large to run fast, and that she would think that he was commenting on her size, which was the real reason for his original remark. Of course any lion would prefer Mma Ramotswe, in the same way as any customer in a butcher's shop would prefer a tasty rump steak to a scrap of lean meat. But he could not say that either, and so he was silent.

"Because I'm traditionally built?" prompted Mma Ramotswe.

Mr Polopetsi raised his hands in a defensive gesture. "I did not say that, Mma," he protested. "I did not."

Mma Ramotswe smiled at him reassuringly. "I know you didn't, Rra," she said. "Don't worry. I don't mind. I've been thinking, you know, and I've decided that I might go on a diet."

They had now arrived at the Mokolodi gate, where stone-built rondavels guarded the entrance to the camp. This gave Mr Polopetsi the respite he needed: there need be no further talk of lions or diets now that they had people to talk to. But he would not put to the back of his mind the extraordinary news which Mma Ramotswe had so casually imparted to him and which he would breathlessly pass on to Mma Makutsi the moment he saw her. It was news of the very greatest import: if Mma Ramotswe, stern and articulate defender of the rights of the fuller-figured as she was, could contemplate going on a diet, then what would happen to the ranks of the traditionally built? They would be thinned, he decided.

MMA RAMOTSWE HAD TOLD Mr Polopetsi that there was something brewing at Mokolodi. She could not be more specific than that, as that was all she knew, and she wondered whether, as a man, he would understand. It seemed to her that men were often unaware of an atmosphere and could assume that all was well when it very clearly was not. This was not the case with all men; there were some who were extremely intuitive in their approach, but many men, alas, were not. Men were interested in hard facts, and sometimes hard facts were simply not available and one had to make do with feelings.

Mr Polopetsi looked puzzled. "So what do you want me to do?" he asked. "Why are we here?"

Mma Ramotswe was patient. "Private detection is all about soaking things up," she said. "You speak to people. You walk around with your eyes wide open. You get a feel for what's happening. And then you draw your conclusions."

"But I don't know what I'm meant to be reaching conclusions about," protested Mr Polopetsi.

"Just see what you feel," said Mma Ramotswe. "I'm going to talk to a relative of mine. You just . . . just walk about the place as if you're a visitor. Have a cup of tea. Look at the animals. See if you **feel** anything."

Mr Polopetsi still looked doubtful, but he was beginning to be intrigued by the assignment. It was rather like being a spy, he thought, and that was something of a challenge. When he was a boy he had played at being a spy and had positioned himself beneath a neighbour's window and listened to the conversation within. He had noted down what was said (the conversation had mostly been about a wedding which was going to take place the following week), and he was in the middle of writing when a woman came out of the house and shouted at him. Then she had hit him with a broom, and he had run away and hidden in a small cluster of paw-paw trees. How strange it was, he thought, that here he was now doing what he had done as a boy, although he could not see himself crouching beneath a window. If Mma Ramotswe expected him to do that, then she would have to think again; she could crouch under windows herself, but he would certainly not do that, even for her.

Mma ramotswe's relative, the nephew (by a second marriage) of her senior uncle, was the supervisor of the workshop. Leaving Mr Polopetsi in the parking place, where he stood, rather awkwardly, wondering what to do, she made her way down the track that led to the workshops. This track took her past a small number of staff houses, shady buildings finished in warm earth, with comfortable windows of the traditional type—eyes for the building, thought Mma Ramotswe; eyes that made the buildings look human, which is how buildings should look. And then, at the bottom of the track, close to the stables, was the workshop, a rambling set of buildings around a courtyard. With its grease and its working litter—an old tractor, engine parts, the metal bars of an animal cage awaiting welding—it had some of the feel of Tlokweng Road Speedy Motors, the sort of place in which one might expect the wife of a mechanic to feel at home. And Mma Ramotswe did. Had Mr J.L.B.

Matekoni himself strolled out of a doorway, wiping his hands on a piece of lint, she would not have been surprised; instead of him, though, it was her relative, looking at her in surprise, and breaking into a broad grin.

They exchanged family news, standing there in the courtyard. Was his father well? No, but he was still cheerful, and spent a lot of his time talking about the old days. He had talked about Obed Ramotswe recently, and still missed his advice on cattle. Mma Ramotswe lowered her eyes; there was nobody who knew more about cattle than her late father, and it touched her that this knowledge should still be talked about; wise men are remembered, they always are.

And what was she doing? Was it true that she had a detective agency, of all things? And that husband of hers? He was a good man, as everybody knew. There was a local man whose car had broken down in Gaborone and who had been helped by Mr J.L.B. Matekoni, who had seen this man standing in despair beside that car and who had stopped and towed him back to the garage, where he had fixed the car—for nothing. That had been talked about.

So the conversation continued, until Mma

Ramotswe, hot under the slanting afternoon sun, had mopped her brow and had been invited inside for a mug of tea. It was the wrong sort of tea, of course, but it was still welcome, even if it did cause a slight fluttering of the heart, which ordinary tea or coffee always did to her.

"Why have you come out here?" the relative asked. "I heard that you were here the other day. I was in town. I did not see you."

"I was collecting a part for Mr J.L.B. Matekoni," she explained. "Neil had found it for him. But I didn't manage to speak to anybody. So I thought I would come back and say hallo."

The relative nodded. "You are always welcome," he said. "We like to see people out here."

There was a silence. Mma Ramotswe picked up the mug of tea he had prepared and took a sip. "Is everything going well here?" she asked. It was an innocent-seeming question, but one which was asked with an ulterior motive, and it did not sound innocent to her.

The relative looked at her. "Going well? I suppose so."

Mma Ramotswe waited for him to say something else, but he did not. She saw, though, that he was frowning. People did not normally frown when they said that something was going well.

"You look unhappy," she said.

This remark seemed to take the relative by surprise. "You noticed?" he said.

Mma Ramotswe tapped the table with a finger. "That is what I am paid to do," she said. "I am paid to notice things. Even when I am off duty, I notice things. And I can tell that there's something uncomfortable going on here. I can tell."

"What can you tell, Mma Ramotswe?" said the relative.

Mma Ramotswe patiently explained to him about atmospheres, and about how one could always tell when people were frightened. It showed in their eyes, she said. Fear always showed in the eyes.

The relative listened. He looked away as she spoke, as people will do when they did not wish their eyes to be seen. This confirmed her impression.

"You yourself are frightened of something," she coaxed, her voice low. "I can tell."

The relative glanced back at her. His look was a pleading one. He rose to his feet and closed the door. There was only one small window in the room, a small rectangle of sky, and they were immediately enveloped in gloom. It was slightly cold too, as the floor of the room was of uncovered concrete and the warming sunlight which had slanted in through the door was now excluded. In the background, against one of the walls, a tap that ran into a dirty basin dripped water.

Mma Ramotswe had suspected it, but had put the thought to the back of her mind. Now, to her dismay, the possibility returned, and it chilled her. She could cope with anything. She understood very well what people were capable of, how cruel they could be, how perverse in their selfishness, how ruthless; she could cope with all that, and with all the general misfortunes of life. She was not afraid of human wickedness, which was usually tawdry and banal, something to be pitied, but there was one thing, one dark thing, which frightened her no matter how much she saw it for what it was. That thing, she now felt, might be present here, and it might explain why people were frightened.

She reached out and took her relative's

hand. And at that moment she knew that she had been right. His hand was shaking.

"You must tell me, Rra," she whispered. "You must tell me what it is that is frightening you. Who has done it? Who has put a curse on this place?"

His eyes were wide. "There is no curse," he said, his voice low. "There is no curse . . . yet."

"Yet?"

"No. Not yet."

Mma Ramotswe digested this information in silence. She was convinced that behind this there would be some scruffy witch doctor somewhere, a traditional healer, perhaps, who had found the profits of healing too small and had taken to the selling of charms and potions. It was a bit like a lion turning man-eater: an old lion, or an injured one, would discover that he could no longer run down his usual prey and turned to those slower two-legged creatures for easier pickings. It was easy for a healer to be tempted. **Here's something to make you strong; here's something to deal with your enemies.**

Of course, there was much less of that sort of thing than there used to be, but it still existed, and its effects could be potent. If you heard that somebody had put a curse on you, then however much you might claim not to believe in all that mumbo-jumbo, you would still feel uneasy. This was because there was always a part of the human mind that was prepared to entertain such notions, particularly at night, in the world of shadows, when there were sounds that one could not understand and when each one of us was in some sense alone. Some people found this intolerable, and succumbed, as if life itself simply gave out in the face of such evil; and when this happened, it served only to strengthen the belief of some that such things worked.

She looked at the relative, and saw his terror. She put her arms around him and whispered something. He looked at her, hesitated, and then whispered something in return.

Mma Ramotswe listened. On the roof, a small creature, a lizard perhaps, scuttled across the tin, making a tiny tapping sound. Rats did that, thought Mma Ramotswe; made such a sound at night in the rafters, which could wake up a light sleeper and leave her tossing and turning in the small hours of the morning.

The relative finished, and Mma Ramotswe

moved her arms. She nodded, and placed a finger against his lips in a gesture of conspiracy.

"We don't want him to know," he said. "Some of us are ashamed of this."

Mma Ramotswe shook her head. No, she thought, one need not be ashamed about such a thing. Superstitions persist. Anybody—even the most rational people—can be a little worried about things like that. She had read that there are people who throw salt over their shoulder if they spilled some, or who would not walk under ladders, or sit in any seat numbered thirteen. No culture was immune to that sort of thing, and there was no reason for African people to be ashamed of such beliefs, just because they did not sound modern.

"You need not feel ashamed," she said. "And I shall think of some way of dealing with this. I shall think of some tactful way."

"You are very kind, Mma Ramotswe," he said. "Your late father would have been proud of you. He was a kind man too."

It was the most generous remark that anybody could possibly have made, and for a moment Mma Ramotswe was unable to respond. So she closed her eyes and there came to her, unbidden, the image of Obed Ramotswe, standing before her, holding his hat in his hands, and smiling. He was there for a moment, and then the image faded and was gone, leaving her alone, but not alone.

THAT WAS NOT the only encounter Mma Ramotswe had at Mokolodi that day. From the workshop she walked up the path to the restaurant next to the office. A few visitors, clad in khaki with field guides stuffed into pockets, sat at tables set out on the platform in front of the restaurant. At one table, a woman smiled at Mma Ramotswe and waved, and she returned the greeting warmly. It pleased her to see these visitors, who came to her country and seemed to fall head over heels in love with it. And why should they not do this? The world was a sad enough place and it needed a few points of light, a few places in which people could find comfort, and if Botswana was one of these, then she was proud of that. **If only more people knew**, thought Mma Ramotswe. **If only more people knew that there was more to Africa than all the problems they saw. They could love us too, as we love them.**

The woman stood up. "Excuse me, Mma," she said. "Would you mind?"

She pointed to her friend, a thin woman with a camera around her neck. Such thin arms, thought Mma Ramotswe, with pity; like the arms of a praying mantis, like sticks.

Mma Ramotswe did not mind, and gestured to the woman to stand beside her while the other woman took her camera from its case.

"You can stand here with me, Mma," she said to the woman.

The woman joined her, standing close to her. Mma Ramotswe felt her arm against hers, flesh against flesh, warm and dry as the touch of human flesh so often and so surprisingly is. She had sometimes thought that this is what snakes said about people: **And, do you know, when you actually touch these creatures they aren't slimy and slippery, but warm and dry?**

She moved, so that they were now standing arm in arm: two ladies, she thought, a brown lady from Botswana and a white lady from somewhere far away, America perhaps, somewhere like that, some place of neatly cut lawns and air conditioning and shining buildings, some place where people wanted to love others if only given the chance.

The photograph was taken, and the thin woman with the camera asked if she might hand over the camera and in turn stand beside Mma Ramotswe, to which Mma Ramotswe readily agreed. And so they stood together, and Mma Ramotswe took her arm too, but was afraid that she might break it, so fragile it seemed. This woman was wearing a heavy scent, which Mma Ramotswe found pleasant, and she wondered whether she might one day be able to wear such a perfume and leave a trail of exotic flowers behind her, as this thin woman must.

They said goodbye to one another. Mma Ramotswe noticed that the first woman was fumbling with the camera as she gave it back to her friend. But she managed to get it back into its case, and as Mma Ramotswe walked away, this woman followed her and took her aside.

"That was very kind of you, Mma," she said. "We are from America, you see. We have come to your country to see it, to see animals. It is a very beautiful country."

"Thank you," said Mma Ramotswe. "I am glad that . . ."

The foreign woman reached out and took her hand. Again there was this feeling of dryness. "My friend is very ill," she said, her voice lowered. "You may not have noticed it, but she is not well."

Mma Ramotswe cast a glance in the direction of the thin woman, who was busying herself with the pouring of orange juice from a jug on their table. She noticed that even the lifting of the jug seemed an effort.

"You see," went on the other woman, "this trip is a sort of farewell. We used to go everywhere together. We went to many places. This will be our last trip. So thank you for being so kind and having your photograph taken with us. Thank you, Mma."

For a moment Mma Ramotswe stood quite still. Then she turned and walked back to the table, to stand beside the woman, who looked up at her in surprise. Mma Ramotswe went down on her haunches, squatting beside the thin woman, and slipped an arm around her shoulder. It was bony beneath the thin blouse, and she was gentle, but she hugged her, carefully, as one might hug a child. The woman reached for her hand, and clasped it briefly in her own and pressed it, and Mma Ramotswe whispered very quietly, but loudly enough for the woman to hear, **The Lord will look after**

you, my sister, and then she stood up and said goodbye, in Setswana, because that is the language that her heart spoke, and walked off, her face turned away now, so that they should not see her tears.

CHAPTER ELEVEN

YOU WILL BE VERY HAPPY
IN THAT CHAIR

MMA MAKUTSI LOOKED at her watch. Mma Ramotswe and Mr Polopetsi were away on their trip to Mokolodi—she had felt slightly irritated that Mma Ramotswe should have chosen him to accompany her rather than herself; but she should not begrudge him the experience, she reminded herself, particularly if he was in due course to become her own assistant, an assistant–assistant detective. With the two of them gone for the rest of the afternoon and everything in the office, filing and typing, up-to-date, there was no real reason for her to stay at her desk now that it was four o'clock. In the garage itself, Mr J.L.B. Matekoni had finished the work he had been doing on a customer's persnickety French car and had sent the apprentices home. He would probably stay for an hour or so and clear up; if the telephone went, then he could answer it and take a message. It was unlikely to ring, though, as clients very rarely got in touch in the late afternoon. The morning was the time of important telephone calls, as it was at the start of the day that people plucked up the courage to contact a private detective; for an act of courage was what it often was, an admission of a troubling possibility, something suppressed and not thought about, something fretted over and dreaded. The morning brought the strength to tackle such matters; the dying hours of the day were hours of defeat and resignation.

Yet here was Mma Makutsi, in the late afternoon, reaching a decision which required considerable courage. She had been putting off doing anything about Phuti Radiphuti, but now she felt that she should seek him out and see what he had to say about his failure to appear for dinner the previous night. It had suddenly occurred to her that there might be a perfectly reasonable explanation for his absence. People got days mixed up; she herself had spent an entire Tuesday last week under the impression that it was a Wednesday, and if she could do that—she who was so organised in her personal life, thanks to that early, invaluable training at the Botswana Secretarial College—then how easy it would be for a man who had a whole business to run to get the days mixed up. If that had happened, then Phuti might have gone to eat at his father's house, and his father would not have found anything amiss, even if it was the wrong day for his meal with him, as most of the time these days the old man seemed to be unaware of what day of the week it was. His memory of the distant past, of old friends, of much-loved cattle; all those memories which such people carried of the early days, of the days of the Protectorate, of Seretse Khama's father, of times even earlier than that; that was all still there. But now the recent past, the crowded, hurried present, seemed to pass him by. She had seen this before, in others; he would not have pointed out to Phuti that this was not his day for coming to eat.

The thought that Phuti might merely have mistaken the day cheered her, but only briefly. Phuti went to eat at his father's house on a Sunday, and it was unlikely that he would have mistaken a Sunday for any other day, as he did not go to work on a Sunday. If, then, he had mixed the days up and gone to eat elsewhere, it could only have been because he had gone to either his sister's or his aunt's house, as those were the only other houses where he went to eat. Neither the aunt nor the sister would have failed to point out to him that he had come to them on the wrong day. Both were very well aware of what day of the week it was, especially the aunt. That aunt, who had played an important role in the building up of the family furniture business, was noted for the acuity of her mind. Phuti himself had told Mma Makutsi how his aunt had an uncanny ability for remembering the details of what everything cost, and this applied not only to present-day prices, but to prices going back to the days before independence. She knew, for example, what the traders in the local store used to ask for paraffin in those silver-coloured jerry cans, and how much a large tin of Lyons golden syrup or a can of Fray Bentos bully beef cost in the late nineteen-fifties; or Lion matches, for that matter, or a Supersonic Radio imported from the radio factory in Bulawayo. Such an aunt would have informed Phuti that he was in the wrong house on the wrong day, had he come to her door unexpectedly.

No, she realised that this was clutching at straws; Phuti Radiphuti had not come to dinner because he had gone cool on her after her feminist disclosure. He had been frightened off, he had been discouraged by the thought that he would have to live with a feminist who would nag and bully him. Whatever the rights and wrongs of it were, some men, and he must be one of them, wanted women who did not make them feel guilty for wanting the things that they wanted. And she should have sensed that, she told herself. Phuti Radiphuti so obviously had a confidence problem, with his speech impediment and his hesitant ways, and of course such a man would not want to marry a woman who would be too forceful. He would want a woman who looked up to him, just a little, and who made him feel manly. She should have understood that, she realised, and she should have built him up rather than made him feel threatened.

She looked at her watch again, and then she looked down at her shoes. **Don't look at us**, they seemed to be saying. **Don't look at us**,

Miss Feminist! There was clearly no help from that quarter; there never was. She would have to sort her troubles out by herself, and that meant that she would have to go right now, without any further delay, to the Double Comfort Furniture Shop and speak to Phuti before he left work. She would ask Mr J.L.B. Matekoni to drive her there; he was a kind man, and never turned down a request for a favour. And then an idea occurred. Mma Ramotswe had spoken about the need to get Mr J.L.B. Matekoni a new chair. She could go with him to the store on the pretext of helping him to choose this chair. And in that way she could speak to Phuti without giving him the impression that she had come specially to see him.

She left her desk and made her way into the garage, where she found Mr J.L.B. Matekoni standing at the entrance, staring out on to the Tlokweng Road. He was wiping his hands on an old cloth, almost absent-mindedly, as if he was thinking about something much more important than the problem of oil on the skin.

"I am glad to see that you have nothing to do, Rra," she said, as she came up behind him. "I have had an idea."

Mr J.L.B. Matekoni turned round and looked at her vacantly. "I was very far away," he said. "I was thinking."

"I have been thinking too," said Mma Makutsi. "I was thinking about that new chair which Mma Ramotswe said that she wanted to buy you."

Mr J.L.B. Matekoni tucked the piece of cloth into his pocket. "It would be good to be able to sit comfortably again," he said. "I cannot find a comfortable position in any of the chairs in Zebra Drive. I don't know what has happened to them. They are full of lumps and springs."

Mma Makutsi knew very well what had happened to the furniture in Zebra Drive, but did not want to say as much. She had always suspected that Mma Ramotswe was hard on anything with springs—look at the way in which the tiny white van listed to one side (the driver's side)—and then there was her office chair, which, although it had no springs, also had a marked inclination to the right, where one of the legs had buckled slightly under Mma Ramotswe's traditional form.

"You will be very comfortable in a new chair," she said. "And I think we should go off to the store right now to take a look. Not to buy anything, of course—that can wait until Mma Ramotswe has the time to get out there. But at least we could go and take a look and put your name on something comfortable."

Mr J.L.B. Matekoni glanced at his watch. "It would mean closing the garage early."

"Why not?" said Mma Makutsi. "The apprentices have gone home. Mma Ramotswe and Mr Polopetsi are out at Mokolodi. There is nothing for us to do here."

Mr J.L.B. Matekoni hesitated, but only briefly. "Very well," he said. "We can go out there and then I can drop you at your place afterwards. That will save you a walk."

Mma Makutsi thanked him and went to fetch her things from the office. It would be easy to find a suitable chair for Mr J.L.B. Matekoni, she thought, but how easy would it be to talk to Phuti Radiphuti now that she had frightened him off? And what would he say to her? Would he simply say that he was sorry, but it was now time to end their engagement? Would he find the words to do that, or would he simply stare at her, as he used to do, while his tongue tried desperately to find the words that simply would not come?

AT THE DOUBLE COMFORT Furniture
Shop Phuti Radiphuti was standing at the window of his office, looking out over the
barn-like showroom. The lay-out had been de-
signed with just that in mind: from where he
stood the manager could look down and signal
to the staff below. If customers brought children who bounced on the chairs, or if people
came to try out the beds and showed signs of
lying too long on the comfortable mattresses—
which they sometimes did, even those who had
no intention at all of buying a bed but who
merely wanted a few minutes of comfort before
continuing with their shopping tasks elsewhere—he could draw the attention of his assistants to the problem and tell them what to
do with a quick hand signal. A finger pointed
in the direction of the door meant **out;** the
clenching of a fist meant **tell them to keep
their children under control;** and the shaking
of a finger directed at a member of staff meant
**there are customers waiting to be served and
you are sitting there talking to your friends.**

He saw Mma Makutsi come in with Mr
J.L.B. Matekoni and for a moment he did

nothing. He swallowed hard. He had meant to telephone Mma Makutsi and apologise for his failure to turn up last night, but it had been a frantic day, with the visit to the hospital to see his aunt and the list of things that she had given him to do. She had been admitted to the Princess Marina Hospital the previous morning, her face drawn with pain, and they had removed the bloated appendix barely an hour later. It had been close to bursting, they explained, and that would have been perilous. As it was, she had been sitting up in bed that morning, ready to give him instructions, and he had spent much of the rest of the day performing the chores that she had set him. There had been no time to telephone Mma Makutsi, and now here she was in search of an explanation, with Mr J.L.B. Matekoni in support, and he would have to explain everything to her. As he watched her enter the showroom, he felt that familiar knot of anxiety in his stomach— the knot that he had always felt in the past when he had been faced with the need to talk and which always seemed so effectively to paralyse his tongue and vocal cords.

He turned away from the window and went down into the showroom. Mma Makutsi had not spotted him yet, although he had seen her glancing around as if to look for him. Now she was standing before a large armchair covered in black leather and was pointing it out to Mr J.L.B. Matekoni, who was bending down to examine the label attached to the chair. Oddly, Phuti found himself trying to remember the price. It was not expensive, that chair, covered as it was in soft leather, but it was certainly not a bargain. He wondered whether Mr J.L.B. Matekoni was the sort of man to spend a lot of money on a chair. He remembered, of course, that Mma Makutsi had said that Mma Ramotswe had a comfortable house in Zebra Drive and so there was some money there. And perhaps that garage of his on the Tlokweng Road did well, although on the few occasions that he had been there he had not seen signs of great activity.

He made his way past a display of dining-room tables, noting with irritation that somebody had placed a sticky hand print on one of them, the finest in the room, with its highly polished black surface. It would be somebody's child, he thought; a child had reached out and touched the furniture with a hand that had been used to push sweets into his mouth. And the same hand would have been placed on the light red velvet of the sofas on the other side of the table, and they would have to get some of that cleaning fluid . . . He sighed. There was no point getting exercised over this; the country was full of dust and children with sticky hands, and termites that liked nothing better than to eat people's furniture; that was just how it was, and if one worried about it, then it simply made one stammer all the more and feel hot at the back of the neck. Mma Makutsi had told him that he should stop worrying, and he had made a real effort to do so, with the result that he stammered less and felt less hot. He was a fortunate man, he thought, to be engaged to a woman like that. Many women made life worse for their husbands with their nagging and hectoring; one saw such men in the store, defeated men, men with all the cares of the world on their shoulders, looking at the furniture as if it was just one more thing to worry about in lives already full of anxieties.

"That is a very g . . . goo . . . ," said Phuti Radiphuti as he approached Mma Makutsi and Mr J.L.B. Matekoni.

He closed his eyes. There was that sensation

of heat at the back of his neck and the familiar, cramping feeling in the muscles of the tongue. He saw the word **good** written down on an imaginary piece of paper; he had only to read it out, as she had told him to do, but he could not. She had read a book about this problem and she had helped him, but now he could not say that this chair was good.

"A ve . . ." He tried again, but it would not come. He should have telephoned her, and told her, and now she would be angry with him and might be having second thoughts about their marriage.

"It looks very comfortable," said Mr J.L.B. Matekoni, reaching out to touch the leather on one of the armrests. "This leather . . ."

"So soft," said Mma Makutsi quietly. "Some of these leather chairs you see are very hard. They are from old, old cows."

"Chairs like that are called cowches," said Mr J.L.B. Matekoni, and laughed.

Mma Makutsi looked at him. Mr J.L.B. Matekoni was a good man, and much admired, but he was not noted for his witty remarks. Now it was possible that he had said something very amusing, and she found herself so taken by surprise that she did not laugh.

Phuti Radiphuti fiddled nervously with a shirt button. Making a conscious effort to relax, he opened his mouth again and made a statement. This time the words came more easily.

"A couch usually has two or three seats," he said. "It is also called a sofa. That chair over there—the big one—is a couch. This one is just a chair."

Mma Makutsi nodded. She had been taken aback by his sudden appearance and now she was uncertain what to do. She had imagined that she would start their conversation by asking after his health, as was polite, but now he had launched into a technical discussion of couches, and so she explained that Mr J.L.B. Matekoni was looking for a new chair and they wondered whether something like this would be suitable.

Phuti Radiphuti listened attentively. Then he turned to Mr J.L.B. Matekoni. "Do you like this chair, Rra?" he asked. "Why don't you sit down in it and see how you feel? It is always best to sit in a chair before you make up your mind."

"I was just looking around," said Mr J.L.B. Matekoni hurriedly. "I saw this chair, but there are many other chairs . . ." He had seen the price on the ticket and had realised that the chair was not cheap. One could get an engine re-bore for the price of that chair.

"Just sit in it, Rra," said Phuti Radiphuti, smiling at Mma Makutsi. "Then you will know for sure if it is a good chair."

He sat down, and Phuti Radiphuti looked at him enquiringly.

"Well, Rra?" said Phuti. "It is very comfortable, isn't it? That chair is made in Johannesburg, in a big chair factory there. There are many chairs like that in Johannesburg."

"It is very comfortable," said Mr J.L.B. Matekoni. "Yes, it is very comfortable. But I must look at some other chairs. I think that there will be many other good chairs in your store."

"Oh, there are," said Phuti. "But when you find a chair that is right, then it is a good idea to choose that one."

Mr J.L.B. Matekoni glanced at Mma Makutsi. He wanted her help now, but she seemed to be having thoughts of her own. She was watching Phuti Radiphuti, staring at him in a way which Mr J.L.B. Matekoni found rather disconcerting. It was as if she was expecting him to say something which he was not saying; some private business between them, he thought, which they should go away and discuss rather than exchanging glances like this. Women always had private business to raise with men, he reflected. There was always something going on in the background—some plotting or mulling over some slight or lack of attention, quite unintended, of course, but noted and filed away for subsequent scrutiny. And much of the time men would be unaware of it, until it all came out in a torrent of recrimination and tears. Fortunately, Mma Ramotswe was not like that, he thought. She was cheerful and direct; but this Mma Makutsi, with her big round glasses, might be different when it came to men, and this poor man, this Phuti Radiphuti, could be in for a difficult time. He would not like to be engaged to Mma Makutsi. Certainly not. He would be terrified of her, with her ninety-seven per cent, or whatever it was, and her determined ways. Poor Phuti Radiphuti.

Mma Makutsi had not said anything since the arrival of Phuti Radiphuti, but now she spoke. "It is very important for a man to have a good chair," she announced. "Men have so many important decisions to make, they need to have good chairs in which to sit and think about these things. I have always thought that."

When she had finished making this observation, she stole a glance at Phuti Radiphuti and then looked down at her shoes. It was almost as if she expected the shoes to contradict her, to reproach her for this sudden departure from the view that she had always held that women made the really important decisions for men, subtly and without letting the men know that they were doing it, but doing it nonetheless. She had enjoyed countless conversations with Mma Ramotswe along those lines, and the two women had always agreed on that point. And now here she was cravenly suggesting that it was men, seated in their comfortable chairs, who did all the deciding. She stared at her shoes for a moment, but they were silent, stunned into speechlessness, perhaps, by the suddenness of the volte-face.

Phuti Radiphuti looked at Mma Makutsi. He was smiling, as a man might when he makes a new and pleasant discovery. "That is true," he said. "But everyone deserves a good chair. Women too. They have important things to think about."

Mma Makutsi was quick to nod her assent. "Yes, they do, but, and you can call me old-fashioned maybe, but I have always thought that men are particularly important. That is just the way I have been brought up, you see."

This remark seemed to make Phuti Radiphuti smile even more. "I hope that you are not too traditional in your views," he said. "Modern men do not like that. They like wives who have their own views."

"Oh, I have those all right," said Mma Makutsi quickly. "I do not let anybody else do my thinking for me."

"That is g . . . g . . . good," said Phuti Radiphuti. He had realised that he had been speaking smoothly and without a stutter, and the realisation made him stumble slightly, but he felt relieved that his omitting to tell Mma Makutsi why he had not arrived for dinner seemed not to have upset her. And now the words came tumbling out, as he explained about his aunt's illness and about his trip to the hospital. She reassured him that although she had noticed his absence, she had realised that he must have a good reason and that she had not been worried.

You're such a liar, Boss, her shoes suddenly said to her. But Mma Makutsi, listening to the man who, once again, was to be her husband, had no time for the grumbling of shoes and did not hear them.

"Now, then," said Phuti Radiphuti. "Shall we look at other chairs, or is that the one you like?"

Mr J.L.B. Matekoni stroked the leather stretched across the arms of the chair. It had a soft feel, and he could imagine himself in the sitting room at Zebra Drive, ensconced in the chair, stroking the leather on the arms and staring up at the ceiling in contemplation. In the background, in the kitchen, Mma Ramotswe would be preparing the evening meal and the tantalising smell of one of her rich stews would come wafting down the corridor. It was a vision of perfection, a glimpse of what heaven might be like, if one ever got there. Was there anything wrong with men sitting in such chairs and thinking such thoughts? he asked himself. Not really, although there did seem to be rather a lot of people about these days who wanted to make men feel guilty about that. He had heard one on the radio recently, and she had said that men were fundamentally lazy and just wanted to be waited on hand and foot by women. What a thing to say! He, for one, was not in the slightest bit lazy. He worked hard all day at Tlokweng Road Speedy Motors, he never let his customers down, and he handed over all the money he earned to Mma Ramotswe for their joint expenses. And if he wanted to sit in a chair from time to time and rest his weary bones, then was there anything wrong with that? Mma Ramotswe liked cooking, and if he went into the kitchen to try to help her, she would chase him out with very little ceremony. No, such people were very unfair about men, and very wrong too. But then he thought of the apprentices, and suddenly he realised that perhaps there was some truth in what had been said. They were the ones who gave men a bad name, with their slipshod ways and their arrogant attitudes towards women. They were the ones.

"So that's the chair you like?" Phuti Radiphuti's question brought Mr J.L.B. Matekoni back to the Double Comfort Furniture Shop and to the realisation that he was sitting in a chair that he would be unlikely to be able to afford.

"I like it," he said. "But I think that perhaps we should look at something that is not quite so costly. I do not think that Mma Ramotswe . . ."

Phuti Radiphuti raised his hands to stop him. "But that chair has just gone on sale," he said. "It is fifty per cent off. Right now. Specially for you."

"Fifty per cent!" exclaimed Mma Makutsi. "That is very good. You must buy that chair, Mr J.L.B. Matekoni. It is a very big bargain."

"But what will Mma Ramotswe . . ."

"She will thank you for it," said Mma Makutsi firmly. "Mma Ramotswe likes a bargain as much as any other woman. She will be very pleased."

Mr J.L.B. Matekoni hesitated. He longed for a comfortable chair. His life had been full of axles and engine parts and grease. It had been a battle, all of it; a battle to keep engines going in spite of the dust and the bumps in the road that were such enemies of machinery; a battle to keep the apprentices from ruining any engine they touched. It had all been a struggle. At the end of the day a chair like this could make up for a lot. It was irresistible.

He looked at Phuti Radiphuti. "Can you deliver it to Zebra Drive?"

"Of course," said Phuti Radiphuti. He reached out and patted the back of the chair. "You will be very happy in that chair, Rra. Very happy."

CHAPTER TWELVE

BLOOD PRESSURE

IF ONE PRESSED Mma Ramotswe on the point, really pressed, she would admit that very little happened in the No. 1 Ladies' Detective Agency. Very little in general, that was; certainly there were spikes of activity, in which suddenly there would be several problems to be looked into at once. These, though, were the exception; normally the issues with which the agency was required to deal were very small ones, which were readily solved by Mma Ramotswe's simple expedient of asking somebody a direct question and getting a direct answer. It was all very well for Clovis Andersen to go on about the complexity of many investigations, and indeed the danger in at least some of them, but that was

not really what life in the No. 1 Ladies' Detective Agency was like.

But there were times, thought Mma Ramotswe, when even Clovis Andersen would be
impressed by the number of major issues with
which she and Mma Makutsi had to deal, and
over the days that followed the trip out to
Mokolodi, it seemed to her that this was rapidly
becoming one such period.

On the morning after she and Mr Polopetsi
had paid their visit, one of those glorious mornings in which the sun is not too fierce, when the
air is clear, and when even the doves in their
leafy kingdoms seem to be more alert and alive
than usual; on that morning Mma Makutsi announced that she could see a woman standing
outside the door of the agency, hesitant about
knocking.

"There is a lady wanting to come in," she
said to Mma Ramotswe. "I think that she is
one of the ones who are embarrassed to come
to us."

Mma Ramotswe craned her neck to see. "Go
and invite her in," she said. "Poor woman."

Mma Makutsi rose from her desk. Adjusting
her glasses, those big, round glasses that she

wore, she made her way to where she had seen the woman standing.

She greeted their caller politely. Then she asked, "Are you wanting to come in, Mma? Or are you just standing?"

"I'm looking for Mma Ramotswe," said the young woman. "Are you that lady?"

Mma Makutsi shook her head. "I am a different lady," she said. "I am Mma Makutsi. I am the assistant detective."

The young woman glanced at her, and then looked away. Mma Makutsi noticed that she was fiddling with a handkerchief that she was holding in her hands, twisting it in her anxiety. I used to do the same thing, she thought. I used to do exactly the same thing with my handkerchief when I was anxious. I twisted it at interviews; I twisted it in examinations. And the thought made her feel a rush of sympathy for this woman, whoever she was, and for the problem that had brought her to their doorstep. It would be a man problem, of course; it so often was. She would have been treated badly by some man, perhaps by a man to whom she had lent money. Perhaps she had taken the money from her employer and then lent it to some worthless man. That happened so often that it was hardly a matter of remark. And now here was another case.

Mma Makutsi reached out and touched the young woman lightly on the arm. "If you come with me, my sister," she said, "I will take you to Mma Ramotswe. She is sitting inside."

"I do not want to trouble her," said the woman. "She is very busy."

"She is not busy right now," said Mma Makutsi. "She will be happy to see you."

"How much does . . ."

Mma Makutsi put a finger to her lips. "We do not need to talk about that just yet," she said. "It is not as expensive as you think. And we charge according to how much people can afford to pay. We do not charge very much."

The reassuring words had their effect, and as she entered the office with Mma Makutsi, the young woman was visibly more relaxed. And seeing Mma Ramotswe sitting behind her desk, beaming at her encouragingly, seemed to allay her fears even more.

"Mma Makutsi will make us some tea," said Mma Ramotswe. "And I believe we have some doughnuts too! Are there doughnuts this morning, Mma Makutsi?"

"There are doughnuts," said Mma Makutsi. "I bought three, just in case." She had bought the third one for herself, to eat on the way home, but she would happily give it to this young woman who was now settling into the chair in front of Mma Ramotswe's desk.

"Well," said Mma Ramotswe. "What is it, Mma? What can the No. 1 Ladies' Detective Agency do for you?"

"I am a nurse," began the young woman.

Mma Ramotswe nodded. This did not surprise her. There was something about nurses that she could always pick up—a neatness, a clinical carefulness. She could always tell.

"It is a good job," said Mma Ramotswe. "But you have not told me your name yet."

The young woman stared down at her hands, which she had folded across her lap. "Do I have to tell you who I am? Do I have to?"

Mma Ramotswe and Mma Makutsi exchanged glances across the room.

"It would be better if you did," said Mma Ramotswe gently. "We do not speak to other people about what we hear in this room, do we, Mma Makutsi?"

Mma Makutsi confirmed that they did not.

But there was still some hesitation from the young woman.

"Look, Mma," said Mma Ramotswe. "We have heard everything that there is to be heard. There is no need to be ashamed."

The young woman gave a start. "But I am not ashamed, Mma," she protested. "I have done nothing wrong. I am not ashamed."

"Good," said Mma Ramotswe.

"You see, I am frightened," said the young woman. "I am not ashamed; I am frightened."

For a few moments, the young woman's words hung in the air. Mma Ramotswe sat at her desk, her elbows resting comfortably on its surface, her shoes slipped off, allowing the cool of the polished concrete floor to chill the soles of her feet. She thought: **This is the second time in two days in which I have heard these words**. First there was her cousin at Mokolodi, and now there was this woman. Fear might be talked about in the clear light of day, when people were going about their business, and when the sun was strong in the sky, and yet it was nonetheless chilling for that. She looked at the woman before her, this nurse who worked in a world of white walls and disinfectant, and who was, in spite of that, preyed upon by something dark and dangerous. Fear was like that; it worked from the inside and was indifferent to what was going on outside.

Mma Ramotswe signalled to Mma Makutsi. The kettle needed to be switched on and tea made. Whatever was troubling this young woman, the making and drinking of tea would help to take her mind off her fears. Tea was like that. It just worked.

"You need not be frightened here," said Mma Ramotswe gently. "We are your friends here. You need not be frightened."

The young woman looked at her for a moment and then she spoke. "My name is Boitelo," she said. "I am Boitelo Mampodi."

Mma Ramotswe nodded encouragingly. "I am glad that you have told me," she said. "Now, Mma, we can have some tea together and you can tell me what is frightening you. You can take your time. Nobody is in a hurry in this place. You can take as long as you like to tell me what this trouble is. Do you understand?"

Boitelo nodded. "I'm sorry, Mma," she said. "I hope that you did not think that I distrusted you."

"I did not think that," said Mma Ramotswe.

"It's just that you are the first person I have talked to about . . . about this thing."

"It is not easy," said Mma Ramotswe. "It is not easy to talk about things that are worrying you. Sometimes we cannot even talk to our friends about these things."

From the back of the room there came the hissing sound of the kettle as it began to bring the water to the boil. Outside, in the branches of the acacia tree that shaded the back wall of the building, a grey dove cooed to its mate. **They mate for life**, thought Mma Ramotswe inconsequentially. **Those doves. For life.**

"Do you mind if I start from the beginning?" asked Boitelo.

This was more than most people did, thought Mma Ramotswe. Most people started at the end, or somewhere around the middle. Very few people put events in order and explained clearly to others what happened. But Boitelo, of course, was a nurse, and nurses knew how to take a history from people, separating unrelated facts from each other and getting to the bottom of a matter that way. She gestured to Boitelo to begin, while Mma Makutsi spooned red bush tea into one tea-pot and black tea into another (for herself). It is

important to give the client a choice, thought
Mma Makutsi. Mma Ramotswe, by contrast,
imagined that everybody would like bush tea,
and not everybody did. She, for one, preferred
ordinary tea, and so did Phuti Radiphuti.
Phuti Radiphuti! Just the thought of him
made her feel warm and contented. My man,
she thought; I have a man. I have a fiancé. And
soon I shall have a husband. Which is more, I
suspect, than this poor Boitelo has.

"I AM FROM A SMALL VILLAGE," began
Boitelo. "Over that way. Near Molepolole. You
will not have heard of it, I think, because it is
very small. I trained at the hospital in Molepolole—you know the one? The one they used
to call the Scottish Livingstone Hospital. The
one where Dr Merriweather worked."

"He was a very good man," said Mma
Ramotswe.

Boitelo's reply came quickly. "Some doctors
are good men," she said.

There was a note in her voice which
alerted Mma Ramotswe. And then she
thought: **Yes, that is it!** That is the oldest
problem that nurses have. Doctors who make

advances to them. This young woman has had
a doctor pestering her. That is why she is frightened. It's simple. There is very little new in the
affairs of people. The same things happen again
and again.

But then Boitelo continued. "Do you think
that a doctor can be a criminal, Mma?" she
asked.

Mma Ramotswe remembered the doctors
she had met all those years ago—those two
doctors, twins, involved in a profitable fraud in
which they shared only one medical quali-
fication between them. Yes, doctors could be
criminals. Those had been criminal doctors;
they had shown no concern for the safety of
their patients, just like those doctors one read
about who deliberately killed their patients as
if out of sheer bravado. Those stories were
shocking because they represented the most extreme breach of trust imaginable, but it appeared that they were true. And for a moment
Mma Ramotswe considered the terrible possibility that Boitelo had found herself working
for one of those homicidal doctors, right here
in Gaborone. That would be a powerful cause
for fear; indeed, just to think of it made her
flesh come up in goose bumps.

"Yes," she answered. "I do think that. There have been some very wicked doctors who have even killed their patients." She paused, hardly daring to ask the question. "You haven't stumbled across something like that, Mma?"

She had hoped that Boitelo's answer would be a swift denial, but it was not. For a moment the young woman seemed to dwell on the question, and then at last she answered. "Not quite," she said.

Behind her, Mma Makutsi let out a little gasp. Mma Ramotswe had been to the doctor only a few days earlier and had been given a bottle of small white pills which she had been taking religiously. It would be so easy for a doctor to substitute something fatal, should he wish to do so, in the knowledge that his trusting patient would pop the poison into her mouth. But why would any doctor want to do that? What drove a doctor to kill the very person he was meant to save? Was it a madness of some sort; an urge that people have from time to time to do something utterly bizarre and out of character? She herself had felt that once or twice when she had been suddenly tempted to throw a tea-pot at Mr J.L.B. Matekoni. She had been astonished that such an outrageous thought had even entered her mind, but it had, and she had sat there wondering what would happen if she picked up the tea-pot from the table and threw it across the room at poor Mr J.L.B. Matekoni as he sat drinking his afternoon tea, his head full of thoughts of gearboxes and brakes, or whatever it was that Mr J.L.B. Matekoni's head was full of. Of course she had not done it, and never would, but the thought had been there, an unwelcome visitor to her otherwise quite rational mind. Perhaps it was the same with those strange cases of the doctors who deliberately killed their patients. Perhaps . . .

"Not quite?" asked Mma Ramotswe. "Do you mean . . ."

Boitelo shook her head. "I mean I don't think that the doctor I'm talking about would go up to a patient and inject too much morphine. No, I don't mean that. But I still think that what he is doing is wicked." She paused. "But I was going to start at the beginning, Mma. Would you like me to do that?"

"Yes," said Mma Ramotswe. "And I won't interrupt you again. You just start. But first, Mma Makutsi will give you a cup of tea. It's red bush tea, Mma. Do you mind?"

"This tea is very good for you," said Boitelo,

taking the cup which Mma Makutsi was handing her. "My aunt, who is late, used to drink it."

Mma Ramotswe could not help smiling. It seemed strange to say that something was good for one and in the same breath say that one who used it is now late. There need be no connection, of course, but it seemed strange nonetheless. She imagined an advertisement: **Red Bush Tea: much appreciated by people who are late.** That would not be a good recommendation, she felt, whatever the intention behind it.

Boitelo took a sip of the bush tea and put her cup down on the table in front of her.

"After I qualified, Mma," Boitelo went on, "I came to work in the Princess Marina. I became a theatre nurse there, and I think that I was good at the job. But then, after a while, I became tired of standing behind the doctors all the time and passing them things. I also didn't like the bright lights, which I think gave me headaches. And I don't think that they are good for your eyes, those lights. When I came out of the theatre and closed my eyes I could still see bright circles, as if the lights were still there. So I decided to do something different, and I saw an advertisement for a nurse to work in a general practitioner's clinic. I was interested in this. The surgery was not too far from where I lived, and I would even be able to walk there in the cooler weather. So I went for an interview.

"My interview was on a Monday afternoon, after the doctor had finished seeing his patients. I was due to work that day, but I was able to change my duties around so that I was free to go. I went along and there was Dr . . ." She had been on the point of giving the name, but she checked herself.

"You don't have to tell me," said Mma Ramotswe, remembering that Boitelo had confessed to feeling frightened.

Boitelo looked relieved. "The doctor was there. He was very kind to me and said that he was very pleased to see that I had been a theatre nurse, as he thought that such people were hard workers, and that I would be a good person to have in his clinic. Then he spoke about what the job would involve. He asked me if I understood about confidentiality and about not talking to people about things that I might see or hear while I was working in the clinic. I said I did.

"Then he said to me, 'I have a friend who

has just had an operation in the Princess Marina. Maybe you can tell me how he is doing.'

"He gave me the name of his friend, who is a well-known person because he plays football very well and is very handsome. I had been on duty for that operation and I was about to say that I thought that it had gone very well. But then I realised that this was a trick and that I should say nothing. So I said, 'I cannot speak about these things. I'm sorry.'

"He looked at me, and for a little while I thought that he was very cross and would shout at me for not answering his question. But then he smiled and he said, 'You are very good at keeping confidences. Most people are not. I think that you will be a very good nurse for this clinic.' "

Boitelo took a further sip of her tea. "I had to work out a month's notice at the Princess Marina, but that was simple enough. Then I started and I found that the work was very enjoyable. I did not have to stand about as I had to do in the theatre, and I was also permitted to do things that nurses sometimes are not allowed to do. He let me do little surgical procedures on people—dealing with an in-growing toe-nail, for example, or freezing off a wart. I liked freezing off warts, as the dry ice made my fingers tingle with the cold.

"I was happy in my work, and I thought that I must have been one of the luckiest nurses in the country, to work for this doctor and to be allowed to do all these things. But then something happened which made me wonder. I was puzzled by something, and I decided to check up on it. And that was when I learned something which made me very worried. I have been worrying about this thing so much that I decided to come and speak to you, Mma Ramotswe, because people say that you are a good woman and that you are very kind to those who come to you with their troubles. That is why I am here."

Mma Ramotswe, listening intently, had allowed her bush tea to become cooler than she liked it. She preferred to drink bush tea when it was fresh from the pot, piping hot, and this cup, now, was lukewarm. Boitelo's story was a familiar one, at least in that it followed a pattern which she had come across so often. Things started well for somebody and then, and then . . . well, then a path was crossed with a person who would change everything. That had happened to her, with her former husband,

Note Mokoti, the jazz player and ladies' man who had, for a brief period, transformed her world from one of happiness and optimism to one of suffering and fear. Such people—men like Note—went through life spreading unhappiness about them like weedkiller, killing the flowers, the things that grew in the lives of others, wilting them with their scorn and spite.

As a young woman she had been too naïve to see evil in others. The young, Mma Ramotswe thought, believe the best of people, or don't imagine that people they know, people of their own age, can be cruel or worthless. And then they find out, and they see what people can do, how selfish they can be, how ruthless in their dealings. The discovery can be a painful one, as it was for her, but it is one that has to be made. Of course it did not mean that one had to retreat into cynicism; of course it did not mean that. Mma Ramotswe had learned to be realistic about people, but this did not mean that one could not see some good in most people, however much that might be obscured by the bad. If one persisted, if one gave people a chance to show their better nature, and—and this was important—if one was prepared to forgive, then people could show a remarkable ability to change their ways. Except for Note Mokoti, of course. He would never change, even though she had forgiven him, that final time, when he had come to see her and asked her for money and had shown that his heart, in spite of everything, was as hard as ever.

Boitelo was looking at her. Mma Ramotswe thought that the nurse must be wondering what she was thinking. She would have no idea that the woman before her, the traditionally built detective with her cup of rapidly cooling bush tea before her, was dreaming about human nature and forgiveness and matters of that sort.

"I'm sorry, Mma," said Mma Ramotswe. "Sometimes my mind wanders. Something you said made my mind wander. Now it is back. Now it is listening to you again."

"One of the things that I didn't do," continued Boitelo, "was to take the blood pressure of patients. All nurses can do that. There is an instrument which you wind round the patient's arm and then you pump a bulb. You will have had your blood pressure taken, Mma? You will know what I am talking about."

Mma Ramotswe did. Her blood pressure had been taken and had caused her doctor to say something to her about trying to keep her weight down. She had tried for a short time, and somehow had failed. It was difficult. Sometimes doctors did not know how difficult it was. Traditionally built doctors did, of course, but not those young thin doctors, who had no feeling for tradition.

"My blood pressure was a bit high," said Mma Ramotswe.

"Then you should lose weight," said Boitelo. "You should go on a diet, Mma Ramotswe. That is what I have to say to many of the ladies who come to the clinic. Many of them are . . . are the same shape as you. Go on a diet and reduce your salt intake. No biltong or other things with lots of salt in them."

Mma Ramotswe thought that she heard Mma Makutsi snigger at this, but she did not look in her assistant's direction. She had never been told before by a client to go on a diet, and she wondered what Clovis Andersen would make of such a situation. He was always stressing the need to be courteous to the client—indeed, there was a whole chapter on the subject in **The Principles of Private Detection**—but it said nothing, she thought, on the subject of clients who told one to go on a diet.

"I will think about that, Mma," she said politely. "Thank you for the advice. But let us get back to this thing that you found out. What has it got to do with blood pressure?"

"Well," said Boitelo, "I was rather surprised that I was never asked to take the patients' blood pressure. The doctor always did that, and he kept the sphygmomanometer in his room, in a desk drawer. I saw him using it if I came into the room to give him something, but he never let me use it. I thought that maybe it was because he liked pumping up the instrument— you know how men are sometimes a bit like boys in that way—and I did not think too much about it after that. But then one day I used the instrument myself, and that was when I had a big surprise.

"It was a Friday, I think, not that that matters, Mma. But it was because it was a Friday that the doctor was not in the clinic at the time. On Fridays he likes to meet some of his friends for lunch at the President Hotel, and sometimes he is not back until after three o'clock. There are some other Ugandan doctors who work here, and he likes to meet with them. Their lunch sometimes goes on a bit long.

"I never make an appointment for a patient

between two and three on a Friday afternoon,
to give him time to get back from the hotel.
Well, on that Friday the patient for the three
o'clock appointment arrived early. It was a man
from the Ministry of Water Affairs, a nice man
who goes to the church round the corner from
my place. I have seen him on Sundays, walking
with his wife and their young son to church.
Their dog follows them and sits outside the
church until the service is over. It is a very faithful dog, that one.

"This man had half an hour to wait, and he
started talking to me. He told me that he was
worried about his blood pressure and that he
had been trying hard to get it down, but the
doctor said that it was still too high. The doctor's door was open while this man was saying
this, and I saw the sphyg on his desk. So I
thought that there would be no harm in my
taking his blood pressure, just out of interest,
and just to keep up my skills. So I said to the
patient that I would do this, and he rolled up
the sleeve on his right arm.

"I inflated the band around the arm and
looked at the mercury. The pressure was normal in every respect. So I did it again, and I was
about to say to the patient that everything was

fine. But I stopped and thought, and I realised that if I did this, then he would say to the doctor that I had taken the reading and that it was now normal. I was worried that this would make the doctor cross with me for doing something to a patient without his permission. So I muttered something about not being able to understand these figures and I replaced the instrument before the doctor came back.

"Now, Mma, that was not a busy afternoon and I was able to catch up on the filing of the patient records. Every so often I go through the files just to check up that all the records are in the right order. The doctor gets very cross if he cannot have the records on his desk when a patient comes in to see him. Well, I was sorting out the records and I came across the record of the man who had come for the three o'clock appointment. And I noticed that the latest entry was about the consultation that this man had just had."

Boitelo paused. Mma Ramotswe was sitting quite still, as was Mma Makutsi. The nurse had a simple, direct way of talking, and the two women had been caught up in her narrative.

"I see," said Mma Ramotswe. "The record.

Yes. Please go on, Mma. This is a very interesting story."

Boitelo looked down at her hands. "The doctor had taken his blood pressure and had entered the reading. It was very high."

Mma Ramotswe frowned. "Does blood pressure go up and down?"

The nurse shrugged. "It can do. If you are very excited your blood pressure can go right up, but it doesn't seem very likely, does it?"

Mma Makutsi now intervened. "Perhaps there was something wrong with the instrument. Things go wrong, you know, with these complicated machines."

Boitelo half-turned to stare at Mma Makutsi. "These instruments are very simple," she said quietly. "They are not complicated machines."

"Then it must have been a mistake," said Mma Ramotswe. "Does the doctor drink over lunch?"

"He never drinks," said Boitelo. "He says that he does not like the taste of alcohol, and he also says that it is far too expensive. Water is cheaper, he says."

There was a brief silence as Mma Ramotswe

and Mma Makutsi contemplated the possibilities. Neither was sure about the significance of the misreading—if that was what it was. It sounded important, but what did it mean? Doctors made mistakes all the time—as everybody did—and why should this make the nurse so anxious? It seemed that an important part of the story was yet to come, and this was what Boitelo now provided.

"I was puzzled by this," she said. "As you said, it could have been a mistake, but now there was something that was making me wonder if something strange was going on. It seemed odd that the doctor should be so determined that I should not take blood pressure and then that he himself should go and make such a mistake. So I decided to carry out a little investigation myself. I have a friend who is a nurse too. She works in another clinic, and she had once told me that there was some old equipment lying about in a cupboard there. I asked her if there was a sphyg, and she said that she would look and see. When she reported back that there was one, I asked her if I could borrow it for a few weeks. She was a bit surprised, but she agreed.

"I hid the sphyg in my drawer at work. And then I waited for my chance, which eventually arrived. I had been paying attention to the medical records now, and each time I got them out for the doctor I looked to see whether it was a high blood pressure case. There were many of them, I noticed, and I began to wonder about them. All of them were on the same drug, which is quite an expensive one. We give them supplies of it from the clinic."

Mma Ramotswe sat up, almost upsetting her cup of cold tea as she did so. "Now, Mma," she exclaimed, "I think that I can already see what is happening here. The doctor is giving false blood pressure readings. He tells patients that they have high blood pressure when they really do not. Then he makes them take the expensive drug, which he provides for them. It must be a very good business for him."

Boitelo stared at her. "No, Mma," she said flatly. "That is not what is happening."

"Then why did he enter the false reading? Why did he do that?"

"It must have been a genuine mistake," said Boitelo.

Mma Ramotswe sighed. "But you said that

you yourself were suspicious of it. You didn't think it was a mistake."

Boitelo nodded. "I didn't," she said. "You are right, Mma. I did not. But now I do. You see, I did two further tests. In each case it was while the doctor was busy with somebody else and there was one of these blood pressure patients in the waiting room. I took their blood pressure and then I compared the results I got with the results that the doctor later noted on their records."

"And?"

"And they were the same."

Mma Ramotswe thought for a moment. She was no statistician, but she had read Clovis Andersen on the subject of unusual occurrences. **The fact that something happens once**, the author of **The Principles of Private Detection** had written, **does not mean that it will happen again. And remember that some events are pure one-offs. They are freaks. They are coincidences. Don't base a whole theory on them.** Clovis Andersen was probably right in general, and if he was also right in this particular case, then there was nothing untoward occurring. But if that were so, then why had Boitelo come to see her?

"You are probably wondering what happened," said Boitelo.

"I am, Mma," said Mma Ramotswe. "I am not very sure where this is going. I thought I did, but now . . ."

"Well, I will tell you. I shall tell you what happened. One of our patients had a stroke. It was not a serious stroke, and he recovered very well. But he had a stroke. And he was one of the ones with high blood pressure."

Mma Ramotswe nodded. "I have heard that this is a danger from high blood pressure." She shifted in her chair. That was why that doctor had told her to lose some weight. He had talked about heart problems and strokes, and it had all made her feel most uncomfortable. What use, she wondered, was a doctor who made people feel uncomfortable? Doctors were meant to provide reassurance, which of course made people feel better. Everybody knew that.

"Yes," Boitelo went on. "High blood pressure can lead to strokes. And this patient ended up in hospital for a few days. I don't think that there was any real danger, but the doctor became quite agitated about it. He asked me to get out the patient's records and he kept them with him for a while. Then he gave them back to me for filing."

"And you looked?" asked Mma Makutsi.

Boitelo smiled. "Yes, Mma. I was nosy. I looked."

"And did you see anything unusual?" prompted Mma Ramotswe.

Boitelo spoke slowly, seemingly aware of the dramatic effect that her words were having. "I found that the figures for a blood pressure reading had been changed."

A large fly landed on the table in front of Mma Ramotswe and she watched it as it took a few steps towards the edge. It hesitated and then launched itself into the air again, its tiny buzz just audible. Boitelo had been watching it too, and she swatted ineffectively at it.

"Rubbed out?" asked Mma Ramotswe. "Were there marks on the page?"

"No," answered Boitelo. "There was no sign of that. It must have been done very skilfully."

"Then how could you tell?" challenged Mma Makutsi. "How did you know?"

Boitelo smiled. "Because the patient was the first one whose blood pressure I had taken in the waiting room while the doctor was busy. It was the same person. And I had written down my reading on a scrap of paper which I had put away in my drawer. I remember comparing those figures with the ones which the doctor put on the card that day. They were the same. But now, that very same figure had been changed. A high reading had been changed to a low one."

Boitelo sat back in her chair and looked at Mma Ramotswe. "I think, Mma," she said, "I think that this doctor is doing something very wrong. I went to see somebody in the Ministry of Health and I told him about it. But he said that I had no proof. And I don't think that he believed me anyway. He said that from time to time they had complaints from nurses who did not like the doctor they worked for. He said that they had to be very careful, and until I could come up with something more concrete I should be careful what I said."

She looked at Mma Ramotswe defensively, as if she, too, would pour scorn on her story. But Mma Ramotswe did not do this. She was noting something down on a piece of paper, and she did not react in any way when Boitelo went on to explain that she had brought this matter to the attention of the No. 1 Ladies' Detective Agency out of a sense of public duty and she hoped that in the circumstances there would be no fee, which she would be unable to pay anyway.

CHAPTER THIRTEEN

BLUE SHOES

MMA RAMOTSWE KNEW that she should
not have left the office that afternoon. She now
had rather more to do than she wanted, and
none of the problems which had landed on her
desk appeared to have any answer. There was a
series of issues, each of them demanding to be
resolved but each curiously resistant to solution. There was Mokolodi, which she should
do something about sooner or later; there was
Mma Tsau and the blackmailing letter; and
then there was the question of Mr Polopetsi's
mean uncle and his favouritism towards Mr
Polopetsi's brother, for whom he had bought a
car. She thought about that. No, there was
nothing that she could do—just now—about
that. The world was imperfect, and there were

just too many claims. One day, perhaps, but not now. So that came off the list, which left one remaining item, the most difficult of course: the doctor. She admired Boitelo for coming to see her; many people would just have given up in the face of a wrong which they could not right, but she had brought the issue to her. And Boitelo had been correct, Mma Ramotswe thought, about civic duty. It was her duty not to stand by in the face of evidence of medical wrongdoing; and it was Mma Ramotswe's civic duty to do something now that the issue had been brought to her attention. But it was difficult to think what to do, and, as she often did in such circumstances, Mma Ramotswe decided that the best thing to do would be to go shopping. She often found that ideas came to her when shopping, halfway down the vegetable aisle in the supermarket, or when trying on a skirt—which would inevitably be just a little bit too tight—she would have an idea and what had previously been a log-jam would gradually begin to shift.

"We shall go shopping, Mma Makutsi," she announced after Boitelo had taken her leave. "We shall go downtown."

Mma Makutsi looked up from her desk. She

Nor for Mr J.L.B. Matekoni, thought Mma
Makutsi ruefully. But what was this about a
Mercedes-Benz? Why did Mma Ramotswe
nk that she might buy a Mercedes-Benz? It
an impossible thought . . . and yet, it was
that Phuti was quite a rich man; perhaps
hould get used to being the wife of a man
ven if not very wealthy was nonetheless
rtably off by any standards. It was a
thought. Phuti Radiphuti was so mod-
unassuming, and yet he undoubtedly
resources to live a showier life if he
lo so.

Phuti and I get married," said Mma
we will not act like rich people. We
the same as we always have been.
vay we are."

it is very good," said Mma
was not the Botswana way to be
it was quietness and discretion
ired. A great person was a quiet
B. Matekoni, for instance; he
nd a great man too, like many
en who worked well with
here were many such men in
se lives had been ones of

was working on a rather complex matter at the
moment, the pursuit of a debtor on behalf of
a firm of lawyers. The debtor, a Mr Cedric
Disani, had established a hotel which had gone
spectacularly bankrupt. It was thought that
he had extensive holdings in land, and they
now had a list of properties from the land regis-
ter and were trying to work out which were
owned by companies in which he had an interest. It was one of the most testing cases Mma
Makutsi had ever been allocated, but at least it
had a fee attached to it—a generous one—and
this would make up for all the public-spirited
work which Mma Ramotswe seemed to be taking on.

"Yes, yes," urged Mma Ramotswe. "You can
leave those lists for a while. It will do us both
good to get downtown and do some shopping.
And maybe we'll have some ideas while we're
about it. I always find that shopping clears the
head, don't you agree, Mma?"

"And it clears the bank account," joked
Mma Makutsi as she closed the file in front of
her. "This Mr Cedric Disani must have done
a bit of shopping—you should see how much
he owes."

"I knew a lady of that name once," said

Mma Ramotswe. "She was a very fashionable lady. You used to see her in very expensive clothes. She was a very fancy lady."

"That will be his wife," said Mma Makutsi. "The lawyers told me about her. They said that Mr Disani put a lot of things in her name so that his creditors cannot touch them. They said that she still drives around in a Mercedes-Benz and wears very grand clothing."

Mma Ramotswe made a clucking sound of disapproval. "Those Mercedes-Benzes, Mma— have you noticed how whenever we come across them in our line of work they are driven by the same sort of people? Have you noticed that, Mma?"

Mma Makutsi replied that she had. "I would never get a Mercedes-Benz," she said. "Even if I had the money. They are very fine cars, but people would talk."

Mma Ramotswe, halfway to the door, paused and looked at Mma Makutsi. "You said **Even if I had the money**, Mma. Do you realise that?"

Mma Makutsi looked blank. "Yes," she said. "That is what I said."

"But, Mma," said Mma Ramotswe. "Don't you realise that now you could have a Mercedes-

Benz if you wanted one? Remember who y going to marry. Phuti Radiphuti is very w with that Double Comfort Furniture Sh his. Yes, he is well off—not that I really l furniture that he sells in that shop, Mm to say that, but it's not really to my tast

Mma Makutsi looked at Mma R for a moment, and swallowed hard. I occurred to her that Mr J.L.B. Matel fail to inform her of his purchase chair, but now it struck her that cisely what had happened. And ht a tually came to explain that he had chair, he would reveal, no dou to taken him there and had e to make the purchase. She w her whether she should tell M self; whether she should t it, or whether she shoul natural course.

"So you would nev sa asked innocently. " Say, fifty per cent o

Mma Ramotsw re tl seven per cent it's the furniture is for me."

hardship and suffering, but who were great men nonetheless.

MMA RAMOTSWE locked the door of the office behind them and said goodbye to Mr J.L.B. Matekoni. He was bent over the engine of a car, explaining something to the apprentices, who stood up and stared at the two women.

"We are going shopping," said Mma Makutsi, taunting the young men. "That is what women like to do, you know. They much prefer shopping to going out with men. That is very well known."

The younger apprentice let out a howl of protest. "That is a lie!" he shouted. "Boss, listen to how that woman lies! You cannot have a detective who lies, Mma Ramotswe. You need to fire that woman. Big glasses and all. Fire her."

"Hush!" said Mr J.L.B. Matekoni. "We have plenty of work to do. Let the ladies go shopping if it makes them feel better."

"Yes," said Mma Ramotswe, as she let herself into the tiny white van. "It certainly makes us feel better."

They drove down the Tlokweng Road to the busy roundabout. There were hawkers at the side of the road selling rough-hewn stools and chairs, and a woman with a smoking brazier on which maize cobs were being grilled. The smell of the maize, the sharp-sweet smell that she knew so well and which spoke so much of the African roadside, wafted through the window of the tiny white van, and for a moment she was back in Mochudi, a child again, at the fireside, waiting for a cob to be passed over to her. And she saw herself all those years ago, standing away from the fire, but with the woodsmoke in her nostrils; and she was biting into the succulent maize, and thinking that this was the most perfect food that the earth had to offer. And she still thought that, all these years later, and her heart could still fill with love for that Africa that she once knew, our mother, she thought, our mother who is always with us, to provide for us, to nourish us, and then to take us, at the end, into her bosom.

They passed the roundabout and drove on to the busy set of shops that had sprung up near Kgale Hill. She did not like these shops, which were ugly and noisy, but the fact of the matter was that there were many different stores there and their selection of merchandise was better than any other collection of shops in the country. So they would put up with the crowds and the noise and see what the shops had to offer. And it would not be all window-shopping. Mma Ramotswe had long promised herself a pressure cooker, and Mr J.L.B. Matekoni had urged her to buy one. They could look for a pressure cooker, and even if they did not buy it today it would be interesting to see what was on offer.

The two women spent an enjoyable half hour browsing in a shop that sold kitchen equipment. There was a bewildering array of cooking utensils—knives and chopping boards and instruments with which to slice onions into all sorts of shapes.

"I have never needed anything like that to cut up onions," Mma Ramotswe observed. "I have found that a knife is usually enough."

Mma Makutsi agreed with her on this, but made a secret mental note of the name of the implement. When Phuti Radiphuti gave her the money to restock her kitchen—as he had promised to do—then she would undoubtedly buy one of those onion-slicers, even if Mma Ramotswe said that they were unnecessary.

Mma Ramotswe was certainly a good cook, but she was not an expert on onions, and if somebody had invented an onion-slicer, then it must have been because there was a need for one.

They left the shop having identified and priced a pressure cooker. "We shall find another shop that sells those cookers," said Mma Ramotswe, "and then we shall compare their prices. It is not good to waste money. Seretse Khama himself said that, you know. He said that we should not waste money."

Mma Makutsi was non-committal. Mma Ramotswe had a habit of quoting Seretse Khama on a wide range of subjects, and she was not at all sure whether her employer was always strictly accurate in this. She had once asked Mma Ramotswe to supply chapter and verse for a particular quotation and had been fobbed off with a challenge. "Do you think I invent his words?" Mma Ramotswe had asked indignantly. "Just because people are beginning to forget what he said, that doesn't mean that I've forgotten."

Mma Makutsi had left it at that, and now said very little when the late President was quoted. It was a harmless enough habit, she thought, and if it helped to keep alive the memory of that great man, then it was, all in all, a good thing. But she wished that Mma Ramotswe would be a little bit more **historically** accurate; just a bit. The problem was that she had not been to the Botswana Secretarial College, where the motto, proudly displayed above the front entrance to the college, was **Be Accurate.** Unfortunately, there was a spelling mistake, and the motto read **Be Acurate**. Mma Makutsi had spotted this and had pointed it out to the college, but nothing had been done about it so far.

They walked together in the direction of another shop that Mma Ramotswe had identified as a possible stockist of pressure cookers. All about them there were well-dressed crowds, people with money in their pockets, people buying for homes that were slowly beginning to reflect Botswana's prosperity. It had all been earned, every single pula of it, in a world in which it is hard enough to make something of one's country, in a world of selfish and distant people who took one's crops at rock-bottom prices and wrote the rules to suit themselves. There were plenty of fine words, of course—and lots of these came from Africa itself—but at the end of the day the poor, the people who lived in Africa, so often had nothing to show for their labours, nothing. And that was not because they did not work hard—they did, they did—but because of something that was wrong which made it so hard for them to get anywhere, no matter how hard they tried. Botswana was fortunate, because it had diamonds and good government, and Mma Ramotswe was well aware of that, but her pride did not allow her to forget the suffering of others, which was there, not far away, a suffering which made mothers see their children fade away before their eyes, their little bodies thin and rickety. One could not forget that in the middle of all this plenty. One could not forget.

But now Mma Makutsi stopped, and took Mma Ramotswe by the arm, pointing to a shop window. A woman was peering into the window, a woman in a striped blue dress, and for a moment Mma Ramotswe thought that it was this woman who had attracted Mma Makutsi's attention. Was she a client, perhaps, or somebody else who had come to the attention of the No. 1 Ladies' Detective Agency, one of those adulterous wives that men sometimes asked them to follow and report upon? But Mma Makutsi was not pointing at the woman, who now moved away from the window, but to the contents of the window display itself.

"Look, Mma Ramotswe," she said. "Look over there!"

Mma Ramotswe looked into the window. There was a sale of some sort on, with large reductions, the window claimed. Indeed, shouted a sign within, the sale amounted to madness on the part of the shoe shop.

"Bargains," said Mma Ramotswe. "There always seem to be so many bargains."

But it was not the bargain shoes that had made Mma Makutsi stop and look—it was the full-price offerings, all neatly arrayed along a shelf and labelled **Exclusive models, as worn in London and New York**.

"You see that pair over there?" said Mma Makutsi, pointing into the window. "You see that pair? The blue pair?"

Mma Ramotswe's gaze followed the direction in which Mma Makutsi was pointing. There, set aside from the other exclusive models, but still in the category of the exclusive, was a pair of fashionable blue shoes, with delicate high heels and toes which came to a point, like the nose of a supersonic aircraft. It was difficult to see the linings from where they were, but by standing on her tip-toes and craning her neck Mma Makutsi was able to report on their colour.

"Red linings," she said with emotion. "Red linings, Mma Ramotswe!"

Mma Ramotswe stared at the shoes. They were certainly very smart, as objects, that is, but she doubted whether they were much use as shoes. She had not been to London or New York, and it was possible that people wore very fashionable shoes in those places, but she could not believe that many people there would be able to fit into such shoes, let alone walk any distance in them.

She glanced at Mma Makutsi, who was staring at the shoes in what seemed to be a state of near-rapture. She was aware of the fact that Mma Makutsi had an interest in shoes, and she had witnessed the pleasure that she had derived from her new pair of green shoes with sky-blue linings. She had entertained her doubts about the suitability of those particular shoes, but now, beside this pair that she was staring at in the window, those green shoes seemed practicality itself. She drew a breath. Mma Makutsi was a grown woman and could look after herself, but she felt, as her employer and as the person who had inducted her into the profession of private detection, that she had at least some degree of responsibility to ensure that Mma Makutsi did not make too many demonstrably bad decisions. And any decision to buy these shoes would be unambiguously bad—the sort of decision that one would not want a friend to make.

"They are very pretty shoes," Mma Ramotswe said cautiously. "They are a very fine colour, that is certainly true, and . . ."

"And the toes!" interrupted Mma Makutsi. "Look at how pointed those toes are. Look at them." And, as she herself looked, she let out a whistle of admiration.

"But nobody is that shape," said Mma Ramotswe. "I have never met anybody with pointed feet. If your feet were pointed like that, then you would have only one toe." She paused, uncertain as to how her comments were being received; it was difficult to tell. "Perhaps those are shoes for one-toed people. Perhaps they are specialist shoes."

She laughed at her own comment, but Mma Makutsi did not.

"They are not for one-toed people, Mma," she said disapprovingly. "They are very fine shoes."

Mma Ramotswe was apologetic. "I'm sorry, Mma. I know that you do not like to joke about shoes." She looked at her watch. "I think that we should move on now. There is much to do."

Mma Makutsi was still gazing intently at the shoes. "I did not think we had all that much to do," she said. "There is plenty of time to look at pots and pans."

It seemed to Mma Ramotswe that looking at pots and pans, as Mma Makutsi put it, was a rather more useful activity than looking at blue shoes in shop windows, but she did not say this. If Mma Makutsi wished to admire shoes in a window, then she would not spoil her fun. It was an innocent enough activity, after all; like looking at the sky, perhaps, when the sun was going down and had made the clouds copper-red, or looking at a herd of fine cattle moving slowly over the land when rains had brought on the sweet green grass. These were pleasures which the soul needed from time to time, and she would wait for Mma Makutsi until she had examined the shoes from all angles. But a word of caution, perhaps, would not go amiss, and so Mma Ramotswe cleared her throat and said, "Of course, Mma, we must remember that if we have traditionally shaped feet, then we should stick to traditionally shaped shoes."

For a moment, in spite of all the hustle and bustle about the shops, there was a cold silence. Mma Makutsi glanced down at Mma Ramotswe's feet. She saw the wide-fitting flat shoes, with their sensible buckles, rather like the shoes which Mma Potokwane wore to walk around the orphan farm (though perhaps not quite so bad). Then she glanced at her own feet. No, there was no comparison, and at that moment she decided that she must have those blue shoes. She simply had to have them.

They went inside, with Mma Makutsi in the lead and Mma Ramotswe following passively. Mma Ramotswe remained silent during the resulting transaction. She watched as Mma Makutsi pointed to the window. She watched as the assistant reached for a box from a shelf and took out a pair of the blue shoes. She said nothing as Mma Makutsi, seated on a stool, squeezed her foot into one of the shoes, to the encouragement of the assistant who pushed and poked at her foot with vigour. And she remained silent as Mma Makutsi, reaching into her purse, paid the deposit that would have the shoes set aside for her; the precious, hard-earned Bank of Botswana notes being placed down on the counter; those notes with the pictures of cattle, which in their heart of hearts the people of Botswana thought were the real foundation of the country's wealth.

As they left the shop, Mma Ramotswe made amends and told Mma Makutsi that she really thought the blue shoes very beautiful. There was no point in disapproving of a purchase once the deed had been done. She remembered learning this lesson from her father, the late Obed Ramotswe, about whom she thought every day, yes, every day, and who had been, she believed, one of the finest men in Botswana. He had been asked for his view of a bull which a man in Mochudi had bought, and although he had already confided in Precious that the bull would not be good for the herd—too lazy, he had said; a bull who would often say to the cows that he was too tired—although that was his view, he had not said that to the new owner.

"That is a bull who will give you no trouble," he had said.

And that, she thought, had been just the right thing to say about that particular bull. But could she say the same thing about Mma Makutsi's new shoes? She thought not. For those shoes would most certainly give Mma Makutsi trouble—the moment she tried to walk anywhere in them. That, thought Mma Ramotswe, was glaringly obvious.

CHAPTER FOURTEEN

AT DINNER

THAT EVENING, Mr Polopetsi had his dinner early, almost immediately after he had returned from Tlokweng Road Speedy Motors. It had been a hard afternoon for him, as he had been replacing tyres on a large cattle truck owned by a loyal friend of Mr J.L.B. Matekoni. This client, who had a fleet of such trucks, could have taken his vehicles to one of the large garages which specialised in looking after such concerns, but chose instead to stick with his old friend. With the growth of the cattle transport firm, their business had become increasingly valuable, and now accounted for almost one eighth of the income of Tlokweng Road Speedy Motors.

Changing the tyres on such large trucks was

very physical work, and Mr Polopetsi, who was a relatively slight man, found that it sorely taxed his strength. But it was not physical tiredness that caused him to ask for an early dinner; there was quite another reason. "I have work to do tonight," he announced to his wife, slightly mysteriously. "Work for the agency."

Mma Polopetsi raised an eyebrow. "Does Mma Ramotswe ask you to do overtime? Will she pay you?"

"No," he said. "She does not know that I am doing this work. I am doing it quietly."

Mma Polopetsi stirred the pot of maize meal. "I see," she said. "It's nothing illegal, is it?" She remembered her husband's imprisonment—how could one forget that spell of loneliness and shame?—and she had not been very enthusiastic about the thought that he would engage in detective work, which could so easily go wrong. And yet everything she had heard about Mma Ramotswe had inspired confidence, and she shared her husband's gratitude to one whom she regarded as the family's saviour.

Mr Polopetsi hesitated for a moment, but then shook his head. "It is not illegal," he said. "And the only reason I have not told Mma

Ramotswe is that it is a problem which is worrying her. I have found out what is happening and I can fix it. I want it to be a nice surprise for her."

The surprise, as he called it, had required some planning, and the co-operation of his friend and neighbour David, who had a battered old taxi which he used to ferry office-workers home from a parking place under a tree near the central mall. David owed Mr Polopetsi a favour, going back to an argument which had flared up with other neighbours over the ownership of a goat. Mr Polopetsi had sided with him and helped his side of the case to prevail, and this had cemented the friendship between the two men. So when Mr Polopetsi had asked him to drive him down to Mokolodi and to help him with something that needed doing down there, he readily agreed.

They set off shortly after seven. In town, this was still a busy time, with the traffic quite heavy, but by the time they reached the last lights of Gaborone and the dark shape of Kgale Hill could be made out to their side, it was difficult to imagine that there were people about, not far behind them. There was the occasional car on the Lobatse Road, but nothing very much, and on either side of the road there were just the dark shapes of the acacia trees, caught briefly in their headlights and then lost to the night. Mr Polopetsi had not told David about the precise nature of the errand, but now he did so.

"You don't have to come with me," he said. "You just park the car nearby. I'll do the rest."

David stared at the road ahead. "I'm not happy about this," he said. "You didn't tell me."

"It is quite safe," said Mr Polopetsi. "You aren't superstitious, are you?"

It was a challenge that had to be met. "I am not scared of these things," said David.

They reached the turn-off to Mokolodi, and David nosed the taxi down the road which led in the direction of the game park. There were several houses in the bush to one side, and lights shone out from one or two of these, but for the rest they were in darkness. After a while, Mr Polopetsi tapped his friend on the shoulder and told him to extinguish the headlights.

"We can go very slowly from here," he said. "Then you can park under a tree and wait until I come back. Nobody will see you."

They stopped, and the car's engine was turned off. Now Mr Polopetsi got out of the car and closed the door quietly behind him. It was utterly still, apart from the sound of insects, the persistent chirruping sound that seems to come from nowhere and from everywhere. It was a curious sound, which some people said was the sound of the stars calling their hunting dogs. He looked up. There was no moon that night, and the sky was filled with stars, so high, so white, that they were like an undulating blanket above him. He turned round to find south, and there it was, low down in the sky, as if suspended by something that he could not see, the Southern Cross. He had seen that constellation at night from the window of the prison, from the board and blankets that was his bed, and it had, in a strange way, sustained him. He was unjustly imprisoned; what had happened had not been his fault, and the sight of the stars had reminded him of the smallness of the world of men and their injustices.

Now he made his way to a point in the fence below the main gate. He pulled the strands of wire apart and slipped through. To his right there were the lights of the staff houses, squares of yellow in the black. He paused, waiting to see if there was anybody about; people might sit outside their houses on a warm night like this, but tonight there was nobody. Mr Polopetsi moved on. He knew exactly what he had to do, and he hoped that there would be no noise. If there was, then he would have to run off into the bush and crouch down until it had subsided. But with the bag that he had in his hand, there was no reason why it should not be quiet, and quick. And in the morning they would find out what had happened and there would be talk, but the fear, the dread that he had sensed, would be over. They would be pleased—all of them—although they would never be able to thank him because he would have acted in complete secrecy. Mma Ramotswe would thank him for it; he was sure of that.

As it happened, at the precise moment that Mr Polopetsi was creeping through the darkness, imagining the gratitude of his employer, Mma Ramotswe was sitting with Mr J.L.B. Matekoni at their dining table, having just completed a short conversation on the subject of Mr Polopetsi and his good work in the garage. The two foster children, Motholeli and Puso, were sitting at their places, eyes fixed on the pot of stew which she was about to serve. At a signal from Mr J.L.B. Matekoni, the children folded their hands together and closed their eyes.

"We are grateful for this food which has been cooked for us," he said. "Amen."

The grace completed, the children opened their eyes again and watched as Mma Ramotswe ladled their helpings onto their plates.

"I have not seen this uncle," said Motholeli. "Who is he?"

"He is working at the garage," said Mma Ramotswe. "He is a very good mechanic, just like you, Motholeli."

"He is not a mechanic," Mr J.L.B. Matekoni corrected her. "A mechanic is somebody who has had the proper training. You are not a mechanic until you have completed an apprenticeship." The mention of apprenticeships seemed to make him sombre, and he stared grimly at his plate for a few moments. He had reminded himself of his two apprentices, and as a general rule he did not like to think too much about them. He was not sure when they would finish their apprenticeships, as both of them had failed to complete one of the courses they had been sent off on, and would have to repeat it. They had said that they had failed only because of a mix-up in the papers and an ambiguity in one of the questions about diesel systems. He had looked at them with pity; did they really expect him to swallow such a story? No, it was best not to think too much about those two when he was away from the garage.

"What I mean is that he is good with cars," said Mma Ramotswe. "And he is a good detective too."

"But is he really a detective?" Mr J.L.B. Matekoni asked, loading his fork with a piece of meat. "You cannot call just anybody a detective. There must be some training . . ." He tailed off. Mma Ramotswe had had no training, of course, although she had at least read **The Principles of Private Detection** by Clovis Andersen. He doubted whether Mr Polopetsi had read even that.

"Being a private detective is different from being a mechanic," said Mma Ramotswe. "You can be a detective without formal qualifications. There is no detective school, as far as I know. I do not think that Mr Sherlock Holmes went to a detective school."

"Who is this Rra Holmes?" asked Motholeli.

"He was a very famous detective," said Mma Ramotswe. "He smoked a pipe and was very clever."

Mr J.L.B. Matekoni stroked his chin. "I do not know if he really existed," he said. "I think that he was just in a book."

Motholeli looked to Mma Ramotswe for clarification. "Maybe," said Mma Ramotswe. "Perhaps."

"He is from a book," said Puso suddenly. "My teacher told us about him. She said that he went to a waterfall and fell over the edge. She said that is what sometimes happens to detectives."

Mma Ramotswe looked thoughtful. "I have never been to the Victoria Falls," she said.

"If you fell over the Victoria Falls," said Mr J.L.B. Matekoni cheerfully, "I do not think that you would drown. You are too traditionally built for that. You would float over and bounce up at the bottom like a big rubber ball. You would not be hurt."

The children laughed, and Mma Ramotswe

smiled, at least for a moment. Then her smile faded. She normally paid no attention to any references to her traditional build—indeed, she was proud of it and would mention it herself. But now, it seemed to her, rather too many people were drawing attention to it. There had been that remark from Mr Polopetsi, an ill-considered, casual remark it is true, but still a suggestion that lions would like to eat her because she was large and juicy. And then the nurse had said that she should watch her blood pressure and that one way to do this was to go on a diet. And now here was Mr J.L.B. Matekoni himself suggesting that she looked like a round rubber ball and the children laughing at the idea (and presumably agreeing).

Mma Ramotswe looked down at her plate. She did not think that she ate too much—if one excluded cake and doughnuts and pumpkin, and perhaps a few other things—and the fact that she was traditionally built was just the way she was. And yet there was no doubt but that she could afford to shed a few pounds, even if only to avoid the embarrassment which had arisen the other day when she had stooped to sit down on her office chair and the seams of her skirt had given way. Mma Makutsi had been tactful about this, and had pretended not to hear anything, but she had noticed and her eyes had widened slightly. There were many arguments in favour of being traditionally built, but it had to be said that it would be pleasant if these digs from other people could be headed off. Perhaps there was an argument for going on a diet after all and showing everybody that she could lose weight if she wanted to. And of course what they said about diets was that you had to start straightaway—the moment the idea crossed your mind. If you put it off, and said that your diet would start the following day, or the following week, then you would never do it. There would always be some reason why it was impossible or inconvenient. So she should start right now, right at this very moment, while the tempting plate of stew lay before her.

"Motholeli and Puso," she said, sitting up straight in her chair. "Would you like the stew on my plate? I do not think I am going to eat it."

Puso nodded quickly and pushed out his plate for the extra portion, and his sister soon followed his lead. Mr J.L.B. Matekoni, though, looked at Mma Ramotswe in astonishment. He lowered his fork to his plate and let it lie there.

"Are you not feeling well, Mma Ramotswe?" he asked. "I have heard that there is something going round the town. People are having trouble with their stomachs."

"I am quite well," said Mma Ramotswe. "I have just decided that from now on I shall eat just a little bit less."

"But you will die," said Puso anxiously. "If you do not eat, then you die. Our teacher told us that."

"I am not going to stop eating altogether," said Mma Ramotswe, laughing at the suggestion. "Don't worry about that. No, it's just that I have decided that I should go on a diet. That is all. I shall eat something, but not as much as before."

"No cake," said Motholeli. "And no doughnuts."

"That is right," said Mma Ramotswe. "Next time Mma Potokwane offers me any of that fruit cake of hers, I shall say, 'No thank you, Mma.' That is what I shall say."

"I shall eat your share of fruit cake," said Mr J.L.B. Matekoni. "I do not need to go on a diet."

Mma Ramotswe said nothing. She was already beginning to feel hungry, and the diet had only been going for a few minutes. Perhaps she should have just a little bit of the stew—there was still some left in the pot in the kitchen. She rose to her feet.

Mr J.L.B. Matekoni smiled. "Is that you going into the kitchen to help yourself to stew in secret?" he asked.

Mma Ramotswe sat down. "I was not going into the kitchen," she said hotly. "I was just adjusting my dress. It's feeling rather loose, you see."

She looked up at the ceiling. She had heard that dieting was not easy. Some time ago, before any question of a diet had arisen, she had seen an article in the paper about how diets encouraged people to become dishonest with others—and with themselves. There had been a survey conducted at one of the places where people went to diet, and it was revealed that just about everybody who went on the course took with them a secret supply of snacks. She had found that funny; the idea of adults behaving like children and smuggling in sweets and chocolate had struck her as being an amusing one. And yet now that she herself was on a diet, it did not seem so funny after all. In fact, it seemed rather sad. Those poor people wanting to eat and not being allowed to. Dieting was cruel; it was an abuse of human rights. Yes, that's what it was, and she should not allow herself to be manipulated in this way.

She stopped herself. Thinking like that was nothing more than coming up with excuses for breaking the diet. Mma Ramotswe was made of sterner stuff than that, and so she persisted. As the others ate the pudding she had prepared for them—banana custard with spoonfuls of red jam in the middle, she sat as if fixed to her seat, watching them enjoying themselves.

"Are you sure you won't have some of this custard, Mma Ramotswe?" asked Mr J.L.B. Matekoni.

"No," she said. And then said, "Yes. Yes, I am sure that I won't. Which means no."

Mr J.L.B. Matekoni smiled. "It is very good," he said.

This is how we are tempted, thought Mma Ramotswe. But at least some of us are strong.

She closed her eyes. It was easier to be strong, she thought, if one had one's eyes closed; although that would only work to a limited extent. One could not go around indefinitely with one's eyes closed, especially if one was a detective. Quite apart from anything else, that was in direct contradiction of the advice which Clovis Andersen gave in **The Principles of Private Detection**, one chapter of which was entitled "The Importance of Keeping Your Eyes Open." Had Clovis Andersen ever been on a diet? she wondered. There was a picture of him on the back cover, and although Mma Ramotswe had never paid much attention to it, now that she brought it to mind, one salient feature of it leapt out. Clovis Andersen was traditionally built.

CHAPTER FIFTEEN

MR POLOPETSI TRIES
TO BE HELPFUL

MMA MAKUTSI was already in the office of the No. 1 Ladies' Detective Agency when Mma Ramotswe arrived there the following morning.

"So, Mma," said Mma Ramotswe, after formal greetings had been exchanged. "So, there you are chasing after our friend, Mr Cedric Disani. What have you managed to uncover today?"

Mma Makutsi picked up a piece of paper and brandished it. "There is a small farm down near Lobatse. I have the details here. It is meant to be the property of his brother, but I have already spoken on the telephone to the people down there who sell cattle dip. They say that it is always Mr Cedric Disani who comes to buy the dip and it is always his name on the cheques. The lawyers will be interested to hear this. I think they want to show that he is really the owner."

"They will be very pleased with your work," said Mma Ramotswe, adding, "And Mr Disani will be very displeased."

Mma Makutsi laughed. "We cannot please everybody."

They chatted for a few minutes more before Mma Makutsi offered to make Mma Ramotswe a cup of tea.

"I have brought in some doughnuts," she said. "Phuti gave me some last night. He has sent one for you and one for Mr J.L.B. Matekoni."

Mma Ramotswe's face lit up. "That is very kind of him," she said. "A doughnut . . ." She trailed off. She had remembered about her diet. She had eaten one slice of toast that morning, and a banana, and her stomach felt light and empty. A doughnut was exactly what she wanted; a doughnut with a dusting of coarse sugar on the outside, enough to give a bit of a crunch and to line one's lips with white, and a layer of sweetened oil soaked into the dough itself. Such bliss. Such bliss.

"I don't think that I shall have a doughnut, Mma," she said. "You may eat mine today."

Mma Makutsi shrugged. "I will be happy to have two," she said. "Or should I give it to the apprentices to share? No, I don't think I'll do that. I will eat it myself."

Mma Makutsi rose from her chair and began to walk across the room towards the kettle. Mma Ramotswe noticed immediately that she was walking in an unusual way. Her steps were small and she appeared to totter as she put one leg before the other. The new shoes, of course; she had collected her new shoes that morning.

Mma Ramotswe leaned forward at her desk and looked. "Your new shoes, Mma!" she exclaimed. "Those beautiful new shoes!"

Mma Makutsi stopped where she was. She turned round to face Mma Ramotswe. "So you like them, Mma Ramotswe?"

Mma Ramotswe did not hesitate. "Of course I do," she said. "They look very good on you."

Mma Makutsi smiled modestly. "Thank you, Mma. I am just breaking them in at the moment. You know how that takes a bit of time."

Mma Ramotswe did know. And she knew too, but did not say anything, that there were some pairs of shoes that would never be broken in. Shoes that were too small were usually too small for a reason: they were intended for people with small feet. "You'll get used to them," she said. But her voice lacked conviction.

Mma Makutsi continued her journey to the kettle—painfully, thought Mma Ramotswe. Then she went back to her desk and sat down, with relief. Watching this, Mma Ramotswe had to suppress a smile. It was her assistant's one weak point—this interest in unsuitable shoes—but, as failings went, this was not a great one; how much more dangerous was an interest in unsuitable men. And Mma Makutsi did not show any sign of that. In fact, she showed herself to be very sensible when it came to men, even if her last friend had been misleading her. He had not been unsuitable in any way, apart from the fact that he was already married, of course.

Once the kettle had boiled, Mma Makutsi made the tea—Tanganda tea for her and red bush tea for Mma Ramotswe—and she took Mma Ramotswe's cup over to her. Mma Ramotswe suppressed the urge to offer to help her by getting the tea herself, in view of the obvious pain which walking now caused Mma Makutsi. It would not be helpful, she thought, for Mma Makutsi to know that she realised how uncomfortable she was. It would be difficult enough for her to acknowledge her mistake to herself, let alone to others.

The doughnuts were then produced from a grease-stained paper bag, and Mma Makutsi began to eat hers.

"This is very delicious," she said as she chewed on a mouthful. "Phuti says that he knows the baker at that bakery up in Broadhurst, and he always gives him the best doughnuts. They are very good, Mma. Very good." She paused to lick the sugar off her fingers. "You must have had a big breakfast today, Mma Ramotswe. Either that or you're getting sick."

"We don't have to eat doughnuts all day," said Mma Ramotswe. "There are other things to do."

Mma Makutsi raised an eyebrow. It was a bit extreme of Mma Ramotswe to suggest that doughnuts were being consumed all day. Two doughnuts in one morning was not excessive, surely, and Mma Ramotswe would not normally turn up her nose at the possibility of a couple of doughnuts. Unless . . . Well, that would be an extraordinary development. Mma Ramotswe on a diet!

Mma Makutsi looked across at Mma Ramotswe. "You'd never go on a diet, would you, Mma Ramotswe?" The question was asked casually, but Mma Makutsi knew immediately that she had guessed correctly. Mma Ramotswe looked up sharply, with exactly that look of irritation mixed with self-pity that people in the early stages of a diet manifest.

"As a matter of fact, Mma, I am on a diet," said Mma Ramotswe. "And it doesn't make it any easier for me if you eat doughnuts like that in front of me."

It was an uncharacteristically sharp retort from Mma Ramotswe, who was normally so kind and polite, and for that reason Mma Makutsi did not take it to heart. Short temper was a known hazard of dieting—and who could blame people for being a bit irritable when they were constantly hungry? But at the same time, normal life had to go on around dieters, and doughnuts were just a part of normal life.

"You can't expect everybody else to stop

eating, Mma Ramotswe," Mma Makutsi pointed out.

Nothing more was said on the subject, but it occurred to Mma Ramotswe that this was exactly the sort of question one should put to Aunty Emang. She imagined the letter: "Dear Aunty Emang, I am on a diet and yet the lady in the office with me insists on eating doughnuts in front of me. I find this very difficult. I do not want to be rude, but is there anything I can do about this?"

Aunty Emang would come up with one of her rather witty responses to that, thought Mma Ramotswe. She reflected on Aunty Emang. It must be strange having people write to one about all sorts of problems. One would end up being party to so many secrets . . . She stopped. An idea had come to her, and she noted it down quickly on a scrap of paper so that it might not be lost, as was the fate of so many ideas, brilliant and otherwise.

SHORTLY BEFORE LUNCH, Mr Polopetsi knocked on the office door. They had not seen him that morning, but this was not unusual. Mr J.L.B. Matekoni had discovered that Mr Polopetsi was a safe driver—unlike the apprentices, who broke the speed limit at every opportunity—and he had decided to use him to collect spares and deliver the cars of customers who could not manage to get in to the garage to collect them. Mr Polopetsi did not mind walking back from the customers' houses, or taking a minibus, whereas the apprentices insisted on being collected by Mr J.L.B. Matekoni in his truck. But all this was time-consuming for him, and sometimes Mr Polopetsi would be out of the garage for hours on end.

"Mr Polopetsi!" said Mma Ramotswe. "Have you been off on one of your long errands, Rra? All over the place? Here and there?"

"He is known all over the town," said Mma Makutsi, laughing. "He is the best-known messenger. Like Superman."

"Superman was not a messenger," said Mma Ramotswe. "He was . . ." She did not complete her sentence. What exactly did Superman do? She was not sure if that was ever made clear.

Mr Polopetsi ignored this talk of Superman. He had noticed that sometimes these ladies got into a silly mood and talked all sorts of non-sense, which was meant to be funny. He did not find it particularly amusing. "I have been collecting some spare parts for Mr J.L.B. Matekoni," he explained patiently. "I had to get some fuses and we had run out of fan belts and . . ."

"And blah blah blah," said Mma Makutsi. "All this garage business. It is of no interest to us, Mr Polopetsi. We are interested in more se-rious matters on this side of the building."

"You would find fan belts serious enough if yours broke halfway to Francistown," retorted Mr Polopetsi. He was about to continue with an explanation of the importance of mechani-cal matters, but he stopped. Mma Makutsi had risen from her desk to take a file back to the fil-ing cabinet, and he now saw her new blue shoes. And he noticed, too, the odd way in which she was walking.

"Have you hurt yourself, Mma?" he asked solicitously. "Have you sprained an ankle?"

Mma Makutsi continued on her tottering journey. "No," she said. "I have not hurt my-self. I am fine, thank you, Rra."

Mr Polopetsi did not intercept the warning

glance from Mma Ramotswe, and continued, "Those look like new shoes. My! They are very fashionable, aren't they? I can hardly see them, they're so small. Are you sure they fit you?"

"Of course I am," mumbled Mma Makutsi. "I am just breaking them in, that's all."

"I would have thought that your feet were far too wide for shoes like that, Mma," Mr Polopetsi went on. "I do not think that you would be able to run in those, do you? Or even walk."

Mma Ramotswe could not help but smile, and she peered down at her desk with intense interest, trying to hide her expression from Mma Makutsi.

"What do you think, Mma Ramotswe?" asked Mr Polopetsi. "Do you think that Mma Makutsi should wear shoes like that?"

"It is none of my business, Rra," said Mma Ramotswe. "Mma Makutsi is old enough to choose her own shoes."

"Yes," said Mma Makutsi defiantly. "I don't comment on your shoes, and you should not comment on mine. It is very rude for a man to comment on a woman's shoes. That is well known, isn't it, Mma Ramotswe?"

"Yes, it is," said Mma Ramotswe loyally.

"And anyway, Mr Polopetsi, did you want to see us about something?"

Mr Polopetsi walked across the room and sat in the client's chair, uninvited. "I have something to show you," he said. "It is out at the back. But first I will tell you something. You remember when we went out to Mokolodi? There was something wrong there, wasn't there?"

Mma Ramotswe nodded, but was non-committal. "I do not think that everything was right."

"People were frightened, weren't they?" pressed Mr Polopetsi. "Did you notice that?"

"Maybe," said Mma Ramotswe.

"Well, I certainly noticed it," said Mr Polopetsi. "And while you were talking to people, I did a bit of investigating. I dug a bit deeper."

Mma Ramotswe frowned. It was not for Mr Polopetsi to dig deeper. That was not why she had taken him down to Mokolodi. He was a perceptive man, and an intelligent one, but he should not think that he could initiate enquiries. Not even Mma Makutsi, with her considerable experience in the field, initiated investigations without first talking to Mma

Ramotswe about it. This was a simple question of accountability. If anything went wrong, then it would be Mma Ramotswe who would have to bear responsibility as principal. For this reason she had to know what was going on.

She composed herself to talk firmly to Mr Polopetsi. She did not relish doing this, but she was the boss, after all, and she could not shirk her duty.

"Mr Polopetsi," she began. "I do not think . . ."

He cut her off, brightly raising a finger in the air, as if to point to the source of his inspiration.

"It was all to do with a bird," he said. "Would you believe it, Mma Ramotswe? A bird was responsible for all that fear and worry."

Mma Ramotswe was silenced. Of course it was to do with a bird—she had found that out eventually, had winkled the information out of that girl in the restaurant. But she had not expected that Mr Polopetsi, who had no contacts there, would have found out the same thing.

"I did know about the bird," she said gravely. "And I was going to do something about it for them."

Mr Polopetsi raised another finger in the air.

"I've done it already," he said brightly. "I've solved the problem."

Mma Makutsi, who had been listening with increasing interest, now broke into the conversation. "What is all this about a bird?" she asked. "How can a bird cause all this trouble?"

Mr Polopetsi turned in his chair to face Mma Makutsi. "It's not just any ordinary bird," he explained. "It's a hornbill—a ground hornbill."

Mma Makutsi gave an involuntary shudder. There were ground hornbills up in the north, where she came from. She knew that they were bad luck. People avoided the ground hornbill if they could. And they were wise to do so, in her view. One only had to look at those birds, which were as big as turkeys and had those great beaks and those old-looking eyes.

"Yes," went on Mr Polopetsi. "This bird had been brought to the Mokolodi animal sanctuary. Somebody had found it lying on the road up north and brought it down. It had a broken wing and a broken leg, and they bound these up and kept it there to recover. And everybody was very frightened because they knew that this bird would bring death. It would just bring death."

"So why did they not say something?" asked Mma Makutsi.

"Because they were embarrassed," said Mr Polopetsi. "Nobody wanted to be the one to go and tell Neil that the people did not want that bird about the place. Nobody wanted to be thought to be superstitious and not modern. That was it, wasn't it, Mma Ramotswe?"

Mma Ramotswe nodded, somewhat reluctantly. Mr Polopetsi had reached exactly the same conclusion as she had. But what had he done about it? She had considered the issue to be of such delicacy that she would have to think very carefully about what to do. Mr Polopetsi, it would seem, had blundered right in.

"You said that you had solved the problem," she said. "And how did you do that, Rra? Did you tell the bird to fly away?"

Mr Polopetsi shook his head. "No, not that, Mma. I took the bird. I took it away at nighttime."

Mma Ramotswe gasped. "But you can't do that . . ."

"Why not, Mma?" asked Mr Polopetsi. "It's a wild creature. Nobody owns wild birds. They had no right to keep it there."

"They would release it once it was healed," said Mma Ramotswe, a note of anger showing in her voice.

"Yes, but before that, what would happen?" Mr Polopetsi challenged. "Somebody could kill the bird. Or some awful thing might happen out there and everybody would then blame Neil for allowing the bird to come. It could have been a terrible mess."

Mma Ramotswe thought for a moment. What Mr Polopetsi said was probably right, but it still did not justify his taking matters into his own hands. "Where did you let it go, Rra?" she asked. "Those birds don't live down here. They live up there." She pointed northwards, in the direction of the empty bush of the Tuli Block, of the Swapong Hills, of the great plains of Matabeleland.

"I know that," said Mr Polopetsi. "And that is why I have not let it go yet. I have asked one of the truck drivers to take it up there when he drives up to Francistown tomorrow. He will let it go for us. I have given him a few pula to do this. And some cigarettes."

"So where is this bird now?" interjected Mma Makutsi. "Where are you hiding it?"

"I am not hiding it anywhere," said Mr

Polopetsi. "It is in a cardboard box outside. I will show it to you."

He rose to his feet. Mma Ramotswe exchanged a glance with Mma Makutsi—a glance which was difficult to interpret, but which was a mixture of surprise and foreboding. Then the two of them followed him out of the office and round to the back of the building. Against the wall, unprotected from the sun, was a large cardboard box, air holes punched into the top.

Mr Polopetsi approached the box cautiously. "I will open the lid just a little bit," he said. "I do not want the bird to escape."

Mma Ramotswe and Mma Makutsi stood immediately behind him as he gently tugged at one of the flaps of the box. "Look inside," he whispered. "There he is. He is resting."

Mma Ramotswe peered into the box. There at the bottom lay the great shape of the ground hornbill, its unwieldy bill lying across its chest, half open. She stared for a moment, and then she stood up.

"The bird is dead, Rra," she said. "It is not resting. It is late."

She was gentle with Mr Polopetsi, who was too upset to help them bury the bird in the bush behind Tlokweng Road Speedy Motors. She did not point out to him the foolishness of leaving the bird for several hours out in the hot sun, in a box in which the temperature must have climbed too high for the bird to survive. She did not say that, and a warning glance to Mma Makutsi prevented her from pointing it out either. Instead she said that anybody could make a mistake and that she knew that he was trying to be helpful. And then, as politely as she could, she told him that he should in future get her agreement to any proposed solutions he might have to problems. "It's better that way," she said quietly, touching him gently on the shoulder in an act of reassurance and forgiveness.

She and Mma Makutsi carried the lifeless form of the bird out into the bush. They found a place, a good place, under a small acacia tree, where the earth looked soft enough to dig a hole. And Mma Ramotswe dug a hole, a grave for a bird, using an adze borrowed from a man who had a plot of land next to the garage. She swung the adze high and brought it down into the ground in much the same way as women before her, many generations of women of her family and her tribe, had done in years gone past as they readied the soil of Botswana, the good soil of their country, for the crops. And Mma Makutsi scraped the soil away and prepared the bird for its grave, lowering it in gently, as one may lay a friend to rest.

Mma Ramotswe looked at Mma Makutsi. She wanted to say something, but somehow she could not bring herself to say it. **This bird is one of our brothers and sisters. We are returning it to the ground from which it came, the ground from which we came too. And now we put the soil upon it** . . . And they did that, breaking the soil gently upon the bird, on the great beak, on the large, defeated body, so unfortunate in its short life and its ending, until it was covered entirely.

Mma Ramotswe nodded to Mma Makutsi, and together they walked back to the garage, barefoot, in simplicity, as their mothers and grandmothers had walked before them across the land that meant so much to them, and which was the resting place of us all—of people, of animals, of birds.

CHAPTER SIXTEEN

DR MOFFAT MAKES A DIAGNOSIS

MR POLOPETSI, mortified by what he had done, was now anxious to do anything to make up for the awful outcome of his venture. The next morning he put his head round the door of the No. 1 Ladies' Detective Agency several times, asking if there was anything Mma Ramotswe wanted him to do. She replied politely that there was nothing very much that needed doing, but that she would call on him if something arose.

"Poor man," said Mma Makutsi. "He is feeling very bad, don't you think, Mma?"

"Yes, he is," said Mma Ramotswe. "It cannot be easy for him."

"You were very kind to him, Mma," said

Mma Makutsi. "You didn't shout. You didn't show that you were angry."

"What's the point of being angry?" asked Mma Ramotswe. "When we are cross with somebody, what good does that do? Especially if they did not mean to cause harm. Mr Polopetsi was sorry about it—that's the important thing."

She thought for a moment. It was clear that Mr Polopetsi wanted some sign from her, some sign that she still trusted him in the performance of occasional tasks. He dearly wanted to do more detective work—he had made that much very plain—and he was no doubt concerned that this debacle would put an end to that. She would find something. She would give him a sign that she still respected his abilities.

Mma Ramotswe thought about her list of tasks. The Mokolodi matter had been resolved—in a very unfortunate way, of course, but still resolved. That left the matter of the doctor and the matter of Mma Tsau's being blackmailed. She already had an idea of what to do about the doctor, and she would attend to that soon, but the blackmail affair still had to be dealt with. Could she use Mr Polopetsi for that? She decided that she could.

Mma Makutsi summoned Mr Polopetsi into the office, and he sat down in the client's chair, wringing his hands anxiously.

"You know, Mr Polopetsi," began Mma Ramotswe. "You know that I have always respected your ability as a detective. And I still do. I want you to know that."

Mr Polopetsi beamed with pleasure. "Thank you, Mma. You are very kind. You are my mother, Mma Ramotswe."

Mma Ramotswe waved the compliment aside. **I am nobody's mother,** she thought, **except for my little child in heaven. I am the mother of that child.**

"You were asking earlier on for something to do, Rra. Well, I have something for you to look into. There is a young woman called Poppy who came to see us. She works for a lady who had been stealing government food to feed to her husband. This lady, Mma Tsau, has received a blackmail threat. She thought it came from Poppy, because Poppy was the only one who knew."

"And was she?" asked Mr Polopetsi.

"I don't think so," said Mma Ramotswe. "I think that she must have told at least one other person."

"And if we can find out who that person is, then that will be the blackmailer?"

Mma Ramotswe smiled. "There you are!" she said. "I knew that you were a good detective. That is exactly the conclusion one should draw." She paused. "Go and speak to this Poppy and ask her this question. Ask her this: Did you write to anybody, anybody about your troubles? That is all you have to ask her. Use those exact words, and see what she says."

She explained to Mr Polopetsi where Poppy worked. He could go there immediately, she said, and ask to see her. He could tell them that he had a message for her. People were always sending messages to one another, and she would come to receive it.

After Mr Polopetsi had left, Mma Ramotswe smiled at Mma Makutsi. "He is a good detective, that man," she said. "He would be a very good assistant for you, Mma Makutsi."

Mma Makutsi welcomed this. She relished the thought of having an assistant, or indeed anybody who was junior to her. She had done a course in personnel management at the Botswana Secretarial College and had secured a very good mark in it. She still had her notes somewhere and would be able to dig them out and read them through before she started to exercise actual authority over Mr Polopetsi.

"But now," said Mma Ramotswe, glancing at her watch, "I have a medical appointment. I mustn't miss it."

"You aren't ill, are you, Mma Ramotswe?" enquired Mma Makutsi. "This diet of yours . . ."

Mma Ramotswe cut her off. "My diet is going very well," she said. "No, it is nothing to do with the diet. It's just that I thought I should go and have my blood pressure checked."

IT HAD BEEN EASY to find out which doctor Boitelo had been talking about. She had let slip, without thinking, that he was Ugandan, and that his clinic was close enough to where she lived for her to walk to work. She had Boitelo's address and that meant a simple trawl of the list of medical practitioners in the telephone book. The Ugandan names were easily enough spotted—there were a number of them—and after that it was a simple matter to see that Dr Eustace Lubega ran a clinic just round the corner from the street in which Boitelo lived. After that, all that was required was a telephone call to the clinic to make an appointment.

It had been Boitelo who answered the telephone. Mma Ramotswe announced who she was, and there was a silence at the other end of the line.

"Why are you phoning this place?" said Boitelo, her voice lowered.

"I want to make an appointment—as a patient—with your good Dr Lubega," said Mma Ramotswe. "And don't worry. I shall pretend not to recognise you. I shall say nothing about you."

This reassurance was followed by a brief silence. "Do you promise?" asked Boitelo.

"Of course I promise, Mma," said Mma Ramotswe. "I will protect you. You don't need to worry."

"What do you want to see him about?" asked Boitelo.

"I want my blood pressure checked," said Mma Ramotswe.

Now, parking the tiny white van in front of the sign that announced the clinic of Dr Eustace Lubega, MB, ChB (Makerere), she made her way through the front door and into the waiting room. The clinic had been a private house before—one of those old Botswana Housing Corporation houses with a small verandah, not unlike her own house in Zebra Drive—and the living room was now used as the reception area. The fireplace, in which many wood fires would have burned in the cold nights of winter, was still there, but filled now with an arrangement of dried flowers and seed pods. And on one wall a large noticeboard had been mounted, on which were pinned notices about immunisation and several large warnings about the care that people should take now in their personal lives. And then there was a picture of a mosquito and a warning to remain vigilant about stagnant water.

There was another patient waiting to see the doctor, a pregnant woman, who nodded politely to Mma Ramotswe as she came in. Boitelo gave no sign of recognising Mma Ramotswe and invited her to take a seat. The pregnant woman did not seem to need long with the doctor, and so now it was Mma Ramotswe's turn to go in.

Dr Lubega looked up from his desk. Gesturing for Mma Ramotswe to sit down beside his desk, he held out a card in front of him.

"I don't have any records for you," he said.

Mma Ramotswe laughed. "I have not seen a doctor for a long time, Dr Lubega. My records would be very old."

The doctor shrugged. "Well, Mma Ramotswe, what can I do for you today?"

Mma Ramotswe frowned. "My friends have been talking to me about my health," she said. "You know how people are. They said that I should have my blood pressure taken. They say that because I am a bit traditionally built . . ."

Dr Lubega looked puzzled. "Traditionally built, Mma?"

"Yes," said Mma Ramotswe. "I am the shape that African ladies are traditionally meant to be."

Dr Lubega started to smile, but his professional manner took over and he became grave. "They are right about blood pressure. Overweight people need to be a little careful of that. I will check that for you, Mma, and give you a general physical examination."

Mma Ramotswe sat on the examination couch while Dr Lubega conducted a cursory examination. She glanced at him quickly as he listened to her heart; she saw the spotless white shirt with its starched collar, the tie with a university crest, the small line of hair beneath the side of his chin that his razor had missed.

"Your heart sounds strong enough," he said. "You must be a big-hearted lady, Mma."

She smiled weakly, and he raised an eyebrow. "Now, then," he said. "Your blood pressure."

He started to wrap the cuff of the sphygmomanometer around her upper arm, but stopped.

"This cuff is too small," he muttered, unwrapping it. "I must get a traditionally built cuff."

He turned away and opened a cabinet drawer from which he extracted a larger cuff. Connecting this to the instrument, he wound it round Mma Ramotswe's arm and took the reading. She saw that he noted figures down on a card, but she did not see what he wrote.

Back at the side of the doctor's desk, Mma Ramotswe listened to what he had to say.

"You seem in reasonable shape," he said, "for a . . . for a traditionally built lady. But your blood pressure is a bit on the high side, I'm afraid. It's one hundred and sixty over ninety. That's marginally high, and I think that you will need to take some drugs to get it down a bit. I can recommend a very good drug. It is two drugs in one—what we call a beta-blocker and a diuretic. You should take these pills."

"I will do that," said Mma Ramotswe. "I will do as you say, Doctor."

"Good," said Dr Lubega. "But there is one thing I should tell you, Mma. This very good drug is not cheap. It will cost you two hundred pula a month. I can sell it to you here, but that is what it will cost."

Mma Ramotswe whistled. "Ow! That is a lot of money just for some little pills." She paused. "But I really need it, do I?"

"You do," said Dr Lubega.

"In that case I will take it. I do not have two hundred pula with me, but I do have fifty pula."

Dr Lubega made a liberal gesture with his hands. "That will get you started. You can come back for some more, once you have the money."

ARMED WITH HER SMALL BOTTLE of light blue pills, Mma Ramotswe went that evening to the house of her friend Howard Moffat. He and his wife were sitting in their living room when she called at their door. Dr Moffat's bad-tempered brown dog, of whom Mma Ramotswe had a particular distrust, barked loudly but was silenced by his master and sent to the back of the house.

"I'm sorry about that dog," said Dr Moffat. "He is not a very friendly dog. I don't know where we went wrong."

"Some dogs are just bad," said Mma Ramotswe. "It is not the fault of the owners. Just like some children are bad when it is not the fault of the parents."

"Well, maybe my dog will change," said Dr Moffat. "Maybe he will become kinder as he grows older."

Mma Ramotswe smiled. "I hope so, Doctor," she said. "But I have not come here to be unkind about that dog of yours. I have come to ask you a quick favour."

"I am always happy to do anything for you, Mma Ramotswe," said Dr Moffat. "You know that."

"Will you take my blood pressure, then?"

If Dr Moffat was surprised by the request, he did not show it. Ushering Mma Ramotswe into his study at the back of the house, he took a sphygmomanometer out of his desk drawer and began to wrap the cuff round Mma Ramotswe's proffered arm.

"Have you been feeling unwell?" he asked quietly as he inflated the instrument.

"No," said Mma Ramotswe. "It's just that I needed to know."

Dr Moffat looked at the mercury. "It's a tiny bit higher than would be wise," he said. "It's one hundred and sixty over ninety. In a case like that we should probably do some other tests."

Mma Ramotswe stared at him. "Are you sure about that reading?" she asked.

Dr Moffat told her that he was. "It's not too bad," he said.

"It's exactly what I thought it would be."

He gave her a curious look. "Oh? Why would you think that?"

She did not answer the question, but

reached into her pocket and took out the bottle of pills which Dr Lubega had sold her. "Do you know these pills?" she asked.

Dr Moffat looked at the label. "That is a well-known pill for high blood pressure," he said. "It's very good. Rather costly. But very good. It's a beta-blocker combined with a diuretic."

He opened the bottle and spilled a couple of pills out onto his hand. He seemed interested in them, and he held one up closer to examine it.

"That's a bit odd," he said, after a moment. "I don't remember this drug looking like that. I seem to recall it was white. I could be wrong, of course. These are . . . blue, aren't they? Yes, definitely blue."

He replaced the pills in the bottle and crossed the floor of his study to reach for a volume from the bookshelf. "This is a copy of the **British National Formulary**," he said. "It lists all the proprietary drugs and describes their appearance. Let me take a look."

It took him a few minutes to find the drug, but when he did he nodded his agreement with what he read. "There it is," he said, reading from the formulary. "White tablets. Each tablet contains fifty milligrams of beta-blocker and twelve point five milligrams of diuretic." He closed the book and looked at Mma Ramotswe over the top of his spectacles.

"I think you're going to have to tell me where these came from, Mma Ramotswe," he said. "But would it be easier to do so over a cup of tea? I'm sure that Fiona would be happy to make us all a cup of tea while you tell me all about it."

"Tea would be very good," said Mma Ramotswe.

At the end of the story, Dr Moffat shook his head sadly. "I'm afraid that the only conclusion we can reach is that this Dr Lubega is substituting a cheap generic for a costly drug but charging his patients the full cost."

"And that would harm them?" she asked.

"It could," said Dr Moffat. "Some of the generics are all right, but others do not necessarily do what they're meant to. There's an issue of purity, you see. Of course, this doctor may have thought that everything would be all right and that no harm would come to anybody, but that's not good enough. You don't take that sort of risk. And you definitely don't commit fraud on your patients." He shook his head. "We'll have to report this, of course. You know that?"

Mma Ramotswe sighed. That was the trouble with getting involved in these things; one got drawn in. There were reports. Dr Moffat sensed her weariness. "I'll have a word with the ministry," he said. "It's easier that way."

Mma Ramotswe smiled her appreciation and took a sip of her tea. She wondered why a doctor would need to defraud his patients when he could already make a perfectly comfortable living in legitimate practice. Of course, he could have hire-purchase payments or school fees or debts to pay off; one never knew. Or he could need the money because somebody was extorting money out of him. Blackmail drove people to extremes of desperation. And a doctor would be a tempting target for blackmail if he had a dark secret to conceal . . . But it seemed a little bit unlikely to her. It was probably just greed, simple greed. The desire to own a Mercedes-Benz, for example. That could drive people to all sorts of mischief.

CHAPTER SEVENTEEN

WAITING FOR A VISIT

THE NEXT MORNING when Mma Ramotswe arrived at the shared premises of Tlokweng Road Speedy Motors and the No. 1 Ladies' Detective Agency, she found Mr Polopetsi with his head under a car. She was always wary of calling out to a mechanic when he was under a car, as they inevitably bumped their heads in surprise. And so she bent down and whispered to him, "Dumela, Rra. Have you anything to tell me?"

Mr Polopetsi heaved himself out from under the car and wiped his hands on a piece of cloth. "Yes, I do," he said keenly. "I have some very interesting news for you."

"You found Poppy?"

"Yes, I found her."

"And you had a word with her?"

"Yes, I did."

Mma Ramotswe looked at him expectantly. "Well?"

"I asked her whether she had written a letter to anybody about what had happened. That is exactly what I asked her."

Mma Ramotswe felt herself becoming impatient. "Come on, Mr Polopetsi. Tell me what she said."

Mr Polopetsi raised a finger in one of his characteristic gestures of emphasis. "You'll never believe who she wrote to, Mma Ramotswe. You'll never guess."

Mma Ramotswe savoured her moment. "Aunty Emang?" she said quietly.

Mr Polopetsi looked deflated. "Yes. How did you know that?"

"I had a hunch, Mr Polopetsi. I had a hunch." She affected a careless tone. "I find that sometimes I have a hunch, and sometimes they are correct. Anyway, that's very useful information you came up with there. It confirms my view of what is happening."

"I do not know what is happening," said Mr Polopetsi.

"Then I will tell you, Rra," said Mma Ramotswe, pointing to her office. "Come inside and sit down, and I will tell you exactly what is going on and what we need to do."

BOTH MMA MAKUTSI and Mr Polopetsi listened attentively as Mma Ramotswe gave an account of where she had got to in the blackmail investigation.

"Now what do we do?" asked Mma Makutsi. "We know who it is. Do we go to the police?"

"No," said Mma Ramotswe. "At least, not yet."

"Well?" pressed Mr Polopetsi. "Do we go and talk to Aunty Emang, whoever she is?"

"No," said Mma Ramotswe. "I have a better idea than that. We get Aunty Emang to come and talk to us. Here in our office. We get her to sit in that chair and tell us all about her nasty ways."

Mr Polopetsi laughed. "She will never come, Mma! Why should she come?"

"Oh, she will come all right," said Mma Ramotswe. "Mma Makutsi, I should like to dictate a letter. Mr Polopetsi, you stay and listen to what I have to say."

Mma Makutsi liked to use her shorthand, which had been described by the examiners at the Botswana Secretarial College as "quite the best shorthand we have ever seen, in the whole history of the college."

"Are you ready, Mma?" asked Mma Ramotswe, composing herself at her desk. She was aware of being watched closely by Mr Polopetsi, who appeared to be hanging on her every word. This was a very important moment.

"The letter goes to," she said, ". . . to Aunty Emang, at the newspaper. Begin. Dear Aunty Emang, I am a lady who needs your help and I am writing to you because I know that you give very good advice. I am a private detective, and my name is Mma Ramotswe of the No. 1 Ladies' Detective Agency (but please do not print that bit in the paper, dear Aunty, as I would not like people to know that I am the person who has written this letter)."

She paused, as Mma Makutsi's pencil darted across the page of her notebook.

"Ready," said Mma Makutsi.

"A few weeks ago," dictated Mma Ramotswe, "I met a lady who told me that she was being blackmailed about stealing food and giving it to her husband. I wondered if this lady was telling the truth, but I found out that she was when she showed me the letter and I saw that it was true. Then I found out something really shocking. I spoke to somebody who told me that the blackmailer was a lady who worked at your newspaper! Now I do not know what to do with this information. One part of me tells me that I should just forget about it and mind my own business. The other tells me that I should pass on this name they gave me to the police. I really do not know what to do, and I thought that you would be the best person to advise me. So please, Aunty Emang, will you come and see me at my office and tell me in person what I should do? You are the only one I have spoken to about this, and you are the one I trust. You can come any day before five o'-clock, which is when we go home. Our office is part of Tlokweng Road Speedy Motors, which you cannot miss if you drive along the Tlok-weng Road in the direction of Tlokweng. I am waiting for you. Your sincere friend, Precious Ramotswe."

Mma Ramotswe finished with a flourish. "There," she said. "What do you think of that?"

"It is brilliant, Mma," said Mr Polopetsi.

"Shall I deliver it right now? To the newspaper office?"

"Yes, please," said Mma Ramotswe. "And write 'urgent' on the envelope. I think that we shall have a visit from Aunty Emang before we go home from work today."

"I think so too," said Mma Makutsi. "Now I will type it and you can sign it. This is a very clever letter, Mma. Perhaps the cleverest letter you have ever written."

"Thank you, Mma," said Mma Ramotswe.

How slowly the hours can pass, thought Mma Ramotswe. After the writing of the letter to Aunty Emang, the letter that she was confident would draw the blackmailer from her lair, she found it difficult to settle down to anything. Not that she had a great deal of work to do; there were one or two routine matters that required to be worked upon, but both of these involved going out and speaking to people and she did not wish to leave the office that day in case Aunty Emang should arrive. So she sat at her desk, idly paging through a magazine. Mma Ramotswe loved magazines, and could not resist the stand of tempting titles that were on constant display at the Pick-and-Pay super-market. She liked magazines that combined practical advice (hints for the kitchen and the garden) with articles on the doings of famous people. She knew that these articles should not be taken seriously, but they were fun nonethe-less, a sort of gossip, not at all dissimilar to the gossip exchanged in the small stores of Mochudi or with friends on the verandah of the President Hotel, or even with Mma Makutsi when they both had nothing to do. Such gossip was fascinating because it dealt with day-to-day life; the second marriage of the man who ran the new insurance agency in the shopping centre; the unsuitable boyfriend of a well-known politician's daughter; the unex-pected promotion of a senior army officer and the airs and graces of his wife, and so on.

She turned the pages of the magazine. There was Prince Charles inspecting his organic bis-cuit factory. That was very interesting, thought Mma Ramotswe. She had her strong likes and dislikes. She liked Bishop Tutu and that man with the untidy hair who sang to help the hun-gry. She liked Prince Charles, and here was a picture of a box of his special biscuits, which he sold for his charity. Mma Ramotswe looked at them and wondered what they would taste like. She thought that they would go rather well with bush tea, and she imagined having a packet of them on her desk so that she and Mma Makutsi could help themselves at will. But then she remembered her diet, and her stomach gave a lurch of disappointment and longing.

She continued to page through the magazine. There was a picture of the Pope getting into a helicopter, holding on to the round white cap that he was wearing so that it should not blow away. There were a couple of cardinals in red standing behind him, and she noted that they were both very traditionally built, which was reassuring for her. If I ever see God, she thought, I am sure that he will not be thin.

At midday, Charlie, the older apprentice, came in and asked Mma Makutsi for a loan. "Now that you have a rich husband," he said, "you can afford to lend me some money."

Mma Makutsi gave him a disapproving look. "Mr Phuti Radiphuti is not yet my husband," she said. "And he is not a very rich man. He has enough money, that is all."

"Well, he must give you some, Mma," Charlie persisted. "And if he does, then surely you can lend me eight hundred pula."

Mma Makutsi looked to Mma Ramotswe for support. "Eight hundred pula," she said. "What do you want with eight hundred pula? That is a lot of money, isn't it, Mma Ramotswe?"

"It is," said Mma Ramotswe. "What do you need it for?"

Charlie looked embarrassed. "It is for a present for my girlfriend," he said. "I want to buy her something."

"Your girlfriend!" shrieked Mma Makutsi. "That's interesting news. I thought you boys didn't stay around long enough to call anybody your girlfriend. And now here you are talking about buying her a present. This is very important news!"

Charlie glanced resentfully at Mma Makutsi and then looked away.

"And what are you thinking of buying her?" asked Mma Makutsi. "A diamond ring?"

Charlie looked down at the ground. He had his hands clasped behind his back, like a man appearing on a charge, and Mma Ramotswe felt a sudden surge of sympathy for him. Mma Makutsi could be a bit hard on the apprentices on occasion; even if they were feckless boys for much of the time, they still had their feelings and she did not like to see them humiliated.

"Tell me about this girl, Charlie," said Mma Ramotswe. "I am sure that she is a very pretty girl. What does she do?"

"She works in a dress shop," said Charlie. "She has a very good job."

"And have you known her long?" asked Mma Ramotswe.

"Three weeks," said Charlie.

"Well," said Mma Makutsi. "What about this present? Is it a ring?"

Her question had not been intended seriously, and she was not prepared for the answer. "Yes," said Charlie. "It is for a ring."

Silence descended on the room. Outside, in the heat of the day, cicadas screeched their endless mating call. The world seemed still at such a time of day, in the heat, and movement seemed pointless, an unwanted disturbance. This was a time for sitting still, doing nothing, until the shadows lengthened and the afternoon became cooler.

Mma Makutsi spoke softly. "Isn't three weeks a bit early to get somebody a ring? Three weeks . . ."

Charlie looked up and fixed her with an intense gaze. "You don't know anything about it, Mma. You don't know what it is like to be in love. I am in love now, and I know what I'm talking about."

Mma Makutsi reeled in the face of the outburst. "I'm sorry . . . ," she began.

"You don't think I have feelings," said Charlie. "All the time you have just laughed at me. You think I don't know that? You think I can't tell?"

Mma Makutsi held up a hand in a placatory gesture. "Listen, Charlie, you cannot say . . ."

"Yes, I can," said Charlie. "Boys have feelings too. I don't want eight hundred pula from you. I do not even want two pula. If you offered to give it to me, I would not take it. Warthog."

Mma Ramotswe rose to her feet. "Charlie! You are not to call Mma Makutsi a warthog. You have done that before. I will not allow it. I shall have to speak to Mr J.L.B. Matekoni."

He moved towards the door. "I am right. She is a warthog. I do not understand why that Radiphuti wants to marry a warthog. Maybe he is a warthog too."

By three o'clock in the afternoon, Mma Ramotswe had taken to looking at her watch anxiously. She wondered now whether the premise upon which she had based her letter to Aunty Emang was entirely wrong. She had no proof that Aunty Emang was the black-mailer—it was no more than surmise. The facts fitted, of course, but facts could fit many situations and still not be the full explanation. If Aunty Emang was not the blackmailer, then she would treat her letter simply as any other one which she received from her readers, and would be unlikely to put herself out by com-ing to the office. She looked at her watch again. The excitement of Charlie's outburst earlier on had dissipated, and now there was nothing more to look forward to but a couple of hours of fruitless waiting.

Shortly before five, when Mma Ramotswe had reluctantly decided that she had been mistaken, Mma Makutsi, who had a better view from her desk of what was happening outside, hissed across to her, "A car, Mma Ramotswe, a car!"

Mma Ramotswe immediately tidied the magazines off her desk and carefully placed her half-finished cup of bush tea into her top drawer. "You go outside and meet her," she said to Mma Makutsi. "But first tell Mr Polopetsi to come in."

Mma Makutsi did as she was asked and walked out to where the car was parked under the acacia tree. It was an expensive car, she noticed, not a Mercedes-Benz, but close enough. As she approached, a remarkably small woman, tiny indeed, stepped out of the vehicle and approached her. Mma Ramotswe, craning her neck, saw this from within the office, and watched intently as Mma Makutsi bent to talk to the woman.

"She's very small," Mma Ramotswe whispered to Mr Polopetsi. "Look at her!"

Mr Polopetsi's jaw had opened with surprise. "Look at her," he echoed. "Look at her."

Aunty Emang was ushered into the office by Mma Makutsi. Mma Ramotswe stood up to greet her, and did so politely, with the traditional Setswana courtesies. After all, she was her guest, even if she was a black-mailer.

Aunty Emang glanced about the office casually, almost scornfully.

"So this is the No. 1 Ladies' Detective

Agency," she said. "I have heard of this place. I did not think it would be so small."

Mma Ramotswe said nothing, but indicated the client's chair. "Please sit down," she said. "I think you are Aunty Emang. Is that correct?"

"Yes," said the woman. "I am Aunty Emang. That is me. And you are this lady, Precious Ramotswe?" Her voice was high-pitched and nasal, like the voice of a child. It was not a voice that was comforting to listen to, and the fact that it emanated from such a tiny person made it all the more disconcerting.

"I am, Mma," said Mma Ramotswe. "And this is Mma Makutsi and Mr Polopetsi. They both work here."

Aunty Emang looked briefly in the direction of Mma Makutsi and Mr Polopetsi, who was standing beside her. She nodded abruptly. Mma Ramotswe watched her, fascinated by the fact that she was so small. She was like a doll, she thought; a small, malignant doll.

"Now this letter you wrote to me," said Aunty Emang. "I came to see you because I do not like the thought of anybody being worried. It is my job to help people in their difficulties."

Mma Ramotswe looked at her. Her visitor's small face, with its darting, slightly hooded eyes, was impassive, but there was something in the eyes which disturbed her. Evil, she thought. That is what I see. Evil. She had seen it only once or twice in her life, and on each occasion she had known it. Most human failings were no more than that—failings—but evil went beyond that.

"This person who says that she knows somebody who is a blackmailer is just talking nonsense," went on Aunty Emang. "I do not think that you should take the allegation seriously. People are always inventing stories, you know. I see it every day."

"Are they?" said Mma Ramotswe. "Well, I hear lots of stories in my work too, and some of them are true."

Aunty Emang sat quite still. She had not expected quite so confident a response. This woman, this fat woman, would have to be handled differently.

"Of course," Aunty Emang said. "Of course you're right. Some stories are true. But why would you think this one is?"

"Because I trust the person who told me," said Mma Ramotswe. "I think that this person is telling the truth. She is not a person to make anything up."

"If you thought that," said Aunty Emang, "then why did you write to me for my advice?"

Mma Ramotswe reached for a pencil in front of her and twisted it gently through her fingers. Mma Makutsi saw this and recognised the mannerism. It was what Mma Ramotswe always did before she was about to make a revelation. She nudged Mr Polopetsi discreetly.

"I wrote to you," said Mma Ramotswe, "because you are the blackmailer. That is why."

Mr Polopetsi, watching intently, swayed slightly and thought for a moment that he was going to faint. This was the sort of moment that he had imagined would arise in detective work: the moment of denouement when the guilty person faced exposure, when the elaborate reasoning of detection was revealed. **Oh, Mma Ramotswe**, he thought, **what a splendid woman you are!**

Aunty Emang did not move, but sat staring impassively at her accuser. When she spoke, her voice sounded higher than before, and there was a strange clicking when she started talking, like the clicking of a valve. "You are speaking lies, fat woman," she said.

"Oh, am I?" retorted Mma Ramotswe. "Well, here are some details. Mma Tsau. She was the one who was stealing food. You black-mailed her because she would lose her job if she was found out. Then there is Dr Lubega. You found out about him, about what happened in Uganda. And a man who was having an affair and was worried that his wife would find out." She paused. "I have the details of many cases here in this file."

Aunty Emang snorted. "Dr Lubega? Who is this Dr Lubega? I do not know anybody of that name."

Mma Ramotswe glanced at Mma Makutsi and smiled. "You have just shown me that I was right," she said. "You have confirmed it."

Aunty Emang rose from her chair. "You can-not prove anything, Mma. The police will laugh at you."

Mma Ramotswe sat back in her chair. She put the pencil down. And she thought, How might I think if I were in this woman's shoes? How do you think if you are so heartless as to blackmail those who are frightened and guilty? And the answer that came back to her was this: hate. Somewhere some wrong had been done, a wrong connected with who she was perhaps, a wrong which turned her to despair and to hate.

And hate had made it possible for her to do all this.

"No, I cannot prove it. Not yet. But I want to tell you one thing, Mma, and I want you to think very carefully about what I tell you. No more Aunty Emang for you. You will have to earn your living some other way. If Aunty Emang continues, then I will make it my business—all of us here in this room, Mma Makutsi over there, who is a very hard-working detective, and Mr Polopetsi there, who is a very intelligent man—we shall all make it our business to find the proof that we don't have at the moment. Do you understand me?"

Aunty Emang turned slightly, and it seemed for a moment that she was going to storm out of the room without saying anything further. Yet she did not leave immediately, but glanced at Mma Makutsi and Mr Polopetsi and then back at Mma Ramotswe.

"Yes," she said.

"YOU LET HER GO," said Mma Makutsi afterwards, as they sat in the office, discussing what had happened. They had been joined by

Mr J.L.B. Matekoni, who had finished work in the garage and who had witnessed the angry departure of Aunty Emang, or the former Aunty Emang, in her expensive car.

"I had no alternative," said Mma Ramotswe. "She was right when she said that we had no proof. I don't think we could have done much more."

"But you had other cases of blackmail," said Mr Polopetsi. "You had that doctor and that man who was having an affair."

"I made up the one about the man having an affair," said Mma Ramotswe. "But I thought it likely that she would be blackmailing such a person. It's very common. And I think I was right. She didn't contradict me, which confirmed that she was the one. But I don't think that she was blackmailing Dr Lubega. I think that he is a man who needed money because he liked it."

"I am very confused about all this," said Mr J.L.B. Matekoni. "I do not know who this doctor is."

Mma Ramotswe looked at her watch. It was time to go home, as she had to cook the evening meal, and that would take time. So they left the office, and after saying goodbye to

Mr Polopetsi, she and Mr J.L.B. Matekoni gave Mma Makutsi a ride home in Mr J.L.B. Matekoni's truck. The tiny white van could stay at the garage overnight, said Mma Ramotswe. Nobody would steal such a vehicle, she thought. She was the only one who could love it.

On the way she remarked to Mma Makutsi that she was not wearing her new blue shoes that day. Was she giving them a rest? "One should rotate one's shoes," said Mma Ramotswe. "That is well known."

Mma Makutsi smiled. She was embarrassed, but in the warm intimacy of the truck, at such a moment, after the emotionally cathartic showdown they had all just witnessed, she felt that she could speak freely of shoes.

"They are a bit small for me, Mma," she confessed. "I think you were right. But I felt great happiness when I wore them, and I shall always remember that. They are such beautiful shoes."

Mma Ramotswe laughed. "Well, that's the important thing, isn't it, Mma? To feel happiness, and then to remember it."

"I think that you're right," said Mma Makutsi. Happiness was an elusive thing. It had something to do with having beautiful shoes, sometimes; but it was about so much else. About a country. About a people. About having friends like this.

THE FOLLOWING DAY was a Saturday, which was Mma Ramotswe's favourite day, a day on which she could sit and reflect on the week's events. There was much to think about, and there was good reason, too, to be pleased that the week was over. Mma Ramotswe did not enjoy confrontation—that was not the Botswana way—and yet there were times when finding oneself head-to-head with somebody was inevitable. That had been so when her first husband, the selfish and violent Note Mokoti, had returned unannounced and tried to extort money from her. That moment had tested her badly, but she had stood up to him, and he had gone away, back into his private world of bitterness and distrust. But the encounter had left her feeling weak and raw, as arguments with another so often do. How much better to avoid occasions of conflict altogether, provided that one did not end up running away from things; and that, of course, was the rub. Had she not faced up to Aunty Emang, then the blackmail would have continued because nobody else would have stood up to her. And so it was left to Mma Ramotswe to do so, and Aunty Emang had folded up in the same way that an old hut made of elephant grass and eaten by the ants would collapse the moment one touched its fragile walls.

Now she sat on her verandah and looked out over her garden. She was the only one in the house. Mr J.L.B. Matekoni had taken Puso and Motholeli to visit one of his aunts, and they would not be back until late afternoon, or, more likely, the evening. That particular aunt was known for her loquaciousness and had long stories to tell. It did not matter if the stories had been heard before—as they all had—they would be repeated that day, in great detail, until the sun was slanting down over the Kalahari and the evening sky was red. But it was important, she thought, that the children should get to know that aunt, as there was much she could teach them. In particular, she knew how to renew the pressed mud floor of a good traditional home, a skill that was dying out. The children sometimes helped her with this, although they would never themselves live in a house with a mud-floored yard, for those houses were going and were not being replaced. And all that was linked to them, the stories, the love and concern for others, the sense of doing what one's people had done for so many years, could go too, thought Mma Ramotswe.

She looked up at the sky, which was empty, as it usually was. In a few days, though, perhaps even earlier, there would be rain. Heavy clouds would build up and make the sky purple, and then there would be lightning and that brief, wonderful smell would fill the air, the smell of the longed-for rain, a smell that lifted the heart. She dropped her gaze to her garden, to the withered plants that she had worked so hard to see through the dry season and which had lived only because she had given them each a small tinful of water each morning and each evening, around the roots; so little water, and so quickly absorbed, that it seemed unlikely that it would make a difference under that relentless sun. But it had, and the plants had kept in their leaves some green against the brown. When the rains came, of course, then everything would be different, and the brown which covered the land, the trees, the stunted grass, would be replaced by green, by growth, by tendrils stretching out, by leaves unfolding. It would happen so quickly that one might go to bed in a drought and wake up in a landscape of shimmering patches of water and cattle with skin washed sleek by the rain.

Mma Ramotswe leaned back in her chair and closed her eyes. She knew that there were places where the world was always green and lush, where water meant nothing because it was always there, where the cattle were never thin and listless; she knew that. But she did not want to live in such a place because it would not be Botswana, or at least not her part of Botswana. Up north they had that, near Maun, in the Delta, where the river ran the wrong way, back into the heart of the country. She had been there several times, and the clear streams and the wide sweeps of Mopani forest and high grass had filled her with wonder. She had been happy for those people, because they had water all about them, but she had not felt that it was her place, which was in the south, in the dry south.

No, she would never exchange what she had for something else. She would never want to be anything but Mma Ramotswe, of Gaborone, wife of Mr J.L.B. Matekoni of Tlokweng Road Speedy Motors, and daughter of the late Obed Ramotswe, retired miner and fine judge of cattle, the man of whom she thought every day, but every day, and whose voice she heard so often when she had cause to remember how things had been in those times. God had given her gifts, she thought. He had made her a Motswana, a citizen of this fine country which had lived up so well to the memory of Sir Seretse Khama, that great statesman, who had stood with such dignity on that night when the new flag had been unfurled and Botswana had come into existence. When as a young girl she had been told of that event and had been shown pictures of it, she had imagined that the world had been watching Botswana on that night and had shared the feelings of her people. Now she knew that this was never true, that nobody had been at all interested, except a few perhaps, and that the world had never paid much attention to places like Botswana, where everything went so well and where people did not squabble and fight. But slowly they had seen, slowly they had come to hear of the secret, and had come to understand.

She opened her eyes. The old van driven by Mma Potokwane had arrived at the gate, and the matron had manoeuvred herself out of the driver's seat and was fiddling with the latch. Mma Potokwane had been known to come to see Mma Ramotswe on a Saturday morning, usually to ask her to get Mr J.L.B. Matekoni to do something for the orphan farm, but such visits were rare. Now, the gate unlatched and pushed back, Mma Potokwane got back into the van and drove up the short driveway to the house. Mma Ramotswe smiled to herself as her visitor nosed her van into the shady place used by Mr J.L.B. Matekoni to park his truck. Mma Potokwane would always find the best place to park, just as she could always be counted upon to find the best deal for the children whom she looked after.

"So, Mma," said Mma Ramotswe to her visitor after they had greeted one another. "So, you have come to see me. This is very good, because I was sitting here with nobody to talk to. Now that has changed."

Mma Potokwane laughed. "But you are a great lady for thinking," she said. "It does not matter to you if there is nobody around, you can just think."

"And so can you," replied Mma Ramotswe. "You have a head too."

Mma Potokwane rolled her eyes upwards. "My poor head is not as good as yours, Mma Ramotswe," she said. "Everybody knows that. You are a very clever lady."

Mma Ramotswe made a gesture of disagreement. She knew that Mma Potokwane was astute, but, like all astute people, the matron was discreet about her talents. "Come and sit with me on the verandah," she said. "I shall make some tea for us."

Once her guest was seated, Mma Ramotswe made her way into the kitchen. She was still smiling to herself as she put on the kettle. Some people never surprised one, thought Mma Ramotswe. They always behave in exactly the way one expects them to behave. Mma Potokwane would talk about general matters for ten minutes or so, and then would come the request. Something would need fixing at the orphan farm. Was Mr J.L.B. Matekoni by any chance free—she was not expecting him to do anything immediately—just to take a look? She thought about this as the kettle boiled, and then she thought: And I'm just as predictable as

Mma Potokwane. Mma Makutsi can no doubt anticipate exactly what I'm going to do or say even before I open my mouth. It was a sobering thought. Had she not said something about how I liked to quote Seretse Khama on everything? Do I really do that? Well, Seretse Khama, Mma Ramotswe told herself, said a lot of things in his time, and it's only right that I should quote a great man like that.

Mma Makutsi, in fact, cropped up in the conversation after Mma Ramotswe had returned to the verandah with a freshly brewed pot of red bush tea.

"That secretary of yours," said Mma Potokwane. "The one with the big glasses . . ."

"That is Mma Makutsi," said Mma Ramotswe firmly. There had been a number of minor clashes between Mma Potokwane and Mma Makutsi—she knows her name, thought Mma Ramotswe; she knows it.

"Yes, of course, Mma Makutsi," said Mma Potokwane. "That is the lady." There was a pause before she continued, "And I hear that she is now engaged. That must be sad for you, Mma, as she will probably not want to work after she is married. So I thought that perhaps you would like to take on a girl who comes from the orphan farm but who has now finished her training at the Botswana Secretarial College. I can send her to you next week . . ."

Mma Ramotswe interrupted her. "But Mma Makutsi has no intention of giving up her job, Mma," she said. "And she is an assistant detective, you know. She is not just any secretary."

Mma Potokwane digested this information in silence. Then she nodded. "I see. So there is no job?"

"There is no job, Mma," said Mma Ramotswe. "I'm sorry."

Mma Potokwane took a sip of her tea. "Oh well, Mma," she said. "I shall ask some other people. I am sure that this girl will find a job somewhere. She is very good. She is not one of those girls who think about boys all the time."

Mma Ramotswe laughed. "That is good, Mma." She looked at her visitor. One of the attractive things about Mma Potokwane was her cheerfulness. The fact that she had failed in her request did not seem to upset her unduly; there would be plenty of other such chances.

The conversation moved on to other things. Mma Potokwane had a niece who was doing very well with her music—she played the piano—and she was hoping to get her a place in David Slater's music camp. Mma Ramotswe heard all about this and then she heard about the troubles that Mma Potokwane's brother was having with his cattle, which had not done well in the dry season. Two of them had also been stolen, and had appeared in somebody's herd with a new brand on them. That was a terrible thing, did Mma Ramotswe not agree, and you would have thought that the local police would have found it easy to deal with such a matter. But they had not, said Mma Potokwane, and they had believed the story offered up by the man in whose herd they had been found. The police were easy to fool, Mma Potokwane suggested; she herself would not have been taken in by a story like that.

Their conversation might have continued for some time along these lines had it not been for the sudden arrival of another van, this time a large green one, which drove smartly through the open gate and drew to a halt in front of the verandah. Mma Ramotswe, puzzled by this further set of visitors, rose to her feet to investigate as a man got out of the front of the van and saluted her cheerfully.

"I am delivering a chair," he announced. "Where do you want me to put it?"

Mma Ramotswe frowned. "I have not bought a chair," she said. "I think that this must be the wrong house."

"Oh?" said the man, consulting a piece of paper which he had extracted from his pocket. "Is this not Mr J.L.B. Matekoni's house?"

"It is his house," said Mma Ramotswe. "But . . ."

"Then this is the right place after all," said the man. "Mr J.L.B. Matekoni bought a chair the other day. Now it is ready. Mr Radiphuti told me to bring it."

So, thought Mma Ramotswe, Mr J.L.B. Matekoni has been shopping, and she could hardly send the chair back. She nodded to the man and gestured to the door behind her. "Please put it through there, Rra," she said. "That is where it will go."

As the chair was carried past them, Mma Potokwane let out a whistle. "That is a very fine chair, Mma," she said. "Mr J.L.B. Matekoni has made a very good choice."

Mma Ramotswe did not reply. She could only imagine the price of such a chair, and she

wondered what had possessed Mr J.L.B.
Matekoni to buy it. Well, they could talk about
it later, when he came back. He could explain
himself then.

She turned to Mma Potokwane and noticed
that her friend was studying her, watching her
reaction. "I'm sorry," said Mma Ramotswe.
"It's just that he did not consult me. He does
that sort of thing from time to time. It is a very
expensive chair."

"Don't be hard on him," said Mma Potokwane. "He is a very good man. And doesn't he
deserve a comfortable chair? Doesn't he deserve
a comfortable chair after all that hard work?"

Mma Ramotswe sat down. It was true. If Mr
J.L.B. Matekoni wanted a comfortable chair,
then surely he was entitled to one. She looked
at her friend. Perhaps she had been too hard in
her judgement of Mma Potokwane; here she
was selflessly supporting Mr J.L.B. Matekoni,
praising his hard work. She was a considerate
woman.

"Yes," said Mma Ramotswe. "You are right,
Mma Potokwane. Mr J.L.B. Matekoni has
been using an old chair for a long time. He deserves a new chair. You are quite right."

There was a brief silence. Then Mma Potokwane spoke. "In that case," she said, "do you
think that you could give his old chair to the orphan farm? We would be able to use a chair like
that. It would be very kind of you to do that,
Mma, now that you no longer need it."

There was very little that Mma Ramotswe
could do but agree, although she reflected, ruefully, that once again the matron had managed
to get something out of her. Well, it was for the
orphans' sake, and that, she felt, was the best
cause of all. So she sighed, just very slightly, but
enough for Mma Potokwane to hear, and
agreed. Then she offered to pour Mma Potokwane a further cup of tea, and the offer was
quickly accepted.

"I have some cake here," said Mma Potokwane, reaching for the bag she had placed at
her feet. "I thought that you might like a
piece."

She opened the bag and took out a large par-
cel of cake, carefully wrapped in greaseproof
paper. Mma Ramotswe watched intently as her
visitor sliced the slab into two generous por-
tions and laid them on the table, two pieces of
paper acting as plates.

"That's very kind of you, Mma," said Mma Ramotswe. "But I think that I'm going to have to say no thank you. You see, I am on a diet now."

It was said without conviction, and her words faded away at the end of the sentence. But Mma Potokwane had heard, and looked up sharply. "Mma Ramotswe!" she exclaimed. "If you go on a diet, then what are the rest of us to do? What will all the other traditionally built ladies think if they hear about this? How can you be so unkind?"

"Unkind?" asked Mma Ramotswe. "I do not see how this is unkind."

"But it is," protested Mma Potokwane. "Traditionally built people are always being told by other people to eat less. Their lives are often a misery. You are a well-known traditionally built person. If you go on a diet, then everybody else will feel guilty. They will feel that they have to go on a diet too, and that will spoil their lives."

Mma Potokwane pushed one of the pieces of cake over to Mma Ramotswe. "You must take this, Mma," she said. "I shall be eating my piece. I am traditionally built too, and we traditionally built people must stick together. We really must."

Mma Potokwane picked up her piece of cake and took a large bite out of it. "It is very good, Mma," she mumbled through a mouth full of fruit cake. "It is very good cake."

For a moment Mma Ramotswe was undecided. **Do I really want to change the way I am?** she asked herself. **Or should I just be myself, which is a traditionally built lady who likes bush tea and who likes to sit on her verandah and think?**

She sighed. There were many good intentions which would never be seen to their implementation. This, she decided, was one of them.

"I think my diet is over now," she said to Mma Potokwane.

They sat there for some time, talking in the way of old friends, licking the crumbs of cake off their fingers. Mma Ramotswe told Mma Potokwane about her stressful week, and Mma Potokwane sympathised with her. "You must take more care of yourself," she said. "We are not born to work, work, work all the time."

"You're right," said Mma Ramotswe. "It is important just to be able to sit and think."

Mma Potokwane agreed with that. "I often tell the orphans not to spend all their time working," she said. "It is quite unnatural to work like that. There should be some time for work and some for play."

"And some for sitting and watching the sun go up and down," said Mma Ramotswe. "And some time for listening to the cattle bells in the bush."

Mma Potokwane thought that this was a fine sentiment. She too, she said, would like to retire one day and go and live out in her village, where people knew one another and cared for one another.

"Will you go back to your village one day?" she asked Mma Ramotswe. And Mma Ramotswe replied, "I shall go back. Yes, one of these days I shall go back."

And in her mind's eye she saw the winding paths of Mochudi, and the cattle pens, and the small walled-off plot of ground where a modest stone bore the inscription **Obed Ramotswe.** And beside the stone there were wild flowers growing, small flowers of such beauty and perfection that they broke the heart. They broke the heart.

africa
africa africa
africa africa africa
africa africa
africa

THE GOOD HUSBAND
OF ZEBRA DRIVE

Alexander McCall Smith

RANDOM HOUSE
LARGE PRINT

This book is for
Tom and Sheila Tlou

THE GOOD HUSBAND OF ZEBRA DRIVE

CHAPTER ONE

A VERY RUDE PERSON

It is useful, people generally agree, for a wife to wake up before her husband. Mma Ramotswe always rose from her bed an hour or so before Mr J.L.B. Matekoni—a good thing for a wife to do because it affords time to accomplish at least some of the day's tasks. But it is also a good thing for those wives whose husbands are inclined to be irritable first thing in the morning—and by all accounts there are many of them, rather too many, in fact. If the wives of such men are up and about first, the husbands can be left to be ill-tempered by themselves—not that Mr J.L.B. Matekoni was ever like that; on the contrary, he was the most good-natured and gracious of men, rarely raising his voice, except occasionally when dealing

with his two incorrigible apprentices at Tlokweng Road Speedy Motors. And anybody, no
matter how even-tempered he might be, would
have been inclined to raise his voice with such
feckless young men. This had been demonstrated by Mma Makutsi, who tended to shout
at the apprentices for very little reason, even
when one of them made a simple request, such
as asking the time of day.

"You don't have to shout at me like that,"
complained Charlie, the older of the two. "All I
asked was what time it was. That was all. And
you shout **four o'clock** like that. Do you think
I'm deaf?"

Mma Makutsi stood her ground. "It's because I know you so well," she retorted. "When
you ask the time, it's because you can't wait to
stop working. You want me to say five o'clock,
don't you? And then you would drop everything and rush off to see some girl or other,
wouldn't you? Don't look so injured. I know
what you do."

Mma Ramotswe thought of this encounter as she hauled herself out of bed and
stretched. Glancing behind her, she saw the
inert form of her husband under the blankets, his head half covered by the pillow,

which was how he liked to sleep, as if to block out the world and its noise. She smiled. Mr J.L.B. Matekoni had a tendency to talk in his sleep—not complete sentences, as one of Mma Ramotswe's cousins had done when she was young, but odd words and expressions, clues each of them to the dream he was having at the time. Just after she had woken up and while she was still lying there watching the light grow behind the curtains, he had muttered something about brake drums. So that was what he dreamed about, she thought—such were the dreams of a mechanic; dreams of brakes and clutches and spark plugs. Most wives fondly hoped that their husbands dreamed about them, but they did not. Men dreamed about cars, it would seem.

Mma Ramotswe shivered. There were those who imagined that Botswana was always warm, but they had never experienced the winter months there—those months when the sun seemed to have business elsewhere and shone only weakly on southern Africa. They were just coming to the end of winter now, and there were signs of the return of warmth, but the mornings and the evenings could still be bitterly cold, as this particular morning was. Cold air, great invisible clouds of it, would sweep up from the south-east, from the distant Drakensberg Mountains and from the southern oceans beyond; air that seemed to love rolling over the wide spaces of Botswana, cold air under a high sun.

Once in the kitchen, with a blanket wrapped about her waist, Mma Ramotswe switched on Radio Botswana in time for the opening chorus of the national anthem and the recording of cattle bells with which the radio started the day. This was a constant in her life, something that she remembered from her childhood, listening to the radio from her sleeping mat while the woman who looked after her started the fire that would cook breakfast for Precious and her father, Obed Ramotswe. It was one of the cherished things of her childhood, that memory, as was the mental picture that she had of Mochudi as it then was, of the view from the National School up on the hill; of the paths that wound through the bush this way and that but which had a destination known only to the small, scurrying animals that used them. These were things that would stay with her forever, she thought, and which

would always be there, no matter how bustling
and thriving Gaborone might become. This
was the soul of her country; somewhere there,
in that land of red earth, of green acacia, of cattle bells, was the soul of her country.

She put a kettle on the stove and looked out
of the window. In mid-winter it would barely
be light at seven; now, at the tail end of the cold
season, even if the weather could still conjure
up chilly mornings like this one, at least there
was a little more light. The sky in the east had
brightened and the first rays of the sun were beginning to touch the tops of the trees in her
yard. A small sun bird—Mma Ramotswe was
convinced it was the same one who was always
there—darted from a branch of the mopipi tree
near the front gate and descended on the stem
of a flowering aloe. A lizard, torpid from the
cold, struggled wearily up the side of a small
rock, searching for the warmth that would en-
able him to start his day. Just like us, thought
Mma Ramotswe.

Once the kettle boiled, she brewed herself a
pot of red bush tea and mug in hand went out
into the garden. She drew the cold air into her
lungs and when she breathed out again her
breath hung in the air for a moment in a thin

white cloud, quickly gone. The air had a touch of wood smoke in it from somebody's fire, perhaps that of the elderly watchman at the nearby Government offices. He kept a brazier fire going, not much more than a few embers, but enough for him to warm his hands on in the cold watches of the night. Mma Ramotswe sometimes spoke to him when he came off duty and began to walk home past her gate. He had a place of sorts over at Old Naledi, she knew, and she imagined him sleeping through the day under a hot tin roof. It was not much of a job, and he would have been paid very little for it, so she had occasionally slipped him a twenty-pula note as a gift. But at least it was a job, and he had a place to lay his head, which was more than some people had.

She walked round the side of the house to inspect the strip of ground where Mr J.L.B. Matekoni would be planting his beans later in the year. She had noticed him working in the garden over the last few days, scraping the soil into ridges where he would plant, constructing the ramshackle structure of poles and string up which the bean stalks would be trained. Everything was dry now, in spite of one or two unexpected winter showers that had laid the dust, but it would be very different if the rains were good. If the rains were good . . .

She sipped at her tea and made her way to the back of the house. There was nothing to see there, just a couple of empty barrels that Mr J.L.B. Matekoni had brought back from the garage for some yet-to-be-explained purpose. He was given to clutter, and the barrels would be tolerated only for a few weeks before Mma Ramotswe would quietly arrange for their departure. The elderly watchman, Mr Nthata, was useful for that; he was only too willing to take away things that Mr J.L.B. Matekoni left lying about in the yard; Mr J.L.B. Matekoni forgot about these things fairly quickly and rarely noticed that they had gone.

It was the same with his trousers. Mma Ramotswe kept a general watch on the generously cut khaki trousers that her husband wore underneath his work overalls, and eventually, when the trouser legs became scuffed at the bottom, she would discreetly remove them from the washing machine after a final wash and pass them on to the woman at the Anglican Cathedral who would find a good home for them. Mr J.L.B. Matekoni often did not notice that he was putting on a new pair of trousers, particularly if Mma Ramotswe distracted him with some item of news or gossip while he was in the process of getting dressed. This was necessary, she felt, as he had always been unwilling to get rid of his old clothes, to which, like many men, he became excessively attached. If men were left to their own devices, Mma Ramotswe believed, they would go about in rags. Her own father had refused to abandon his hat, even when it became so old that the brim was barely attached to the crown. She remembered itching to replace it with one of those smart new hats that she had seen on the top shelf of the Small Upright General Dealer in Mochudi, but had realised that her father would never give up the old one, which had become a talisman, a totem. And they had buried that hat with him, placing it lovingly in the rough board coffin in which he had been lowered into the ground of the land that he had loved so much and of which he had always been so proud. That was long ago, and now she was standing here, a married woman, the owner of a business; a woman of some status in the community; standing here at the back of her house with a mug that was now drained of tea and a day of responsibilities ahead of her.

She went inside. The two foster children, Puso and Motholeli, were good at getting themselves up and did so without any prompting by Mma Ramotswe. Motholeli was already in the kitchen, sitting at the table in her wheelchair, her breakfast of a thick slice of bread and jam on a plate before her. In the background, she could hear the sound of Puso slamming the door of the bathroom.

"He cannot shut doors quietly," said Motholeli, putting her hands to her ears.

"He is a boy," said Mma Ramotswe. "That is how boys behave."

"Then I am glad that I am not a boy," said Motholeli.

Mma Ramotswe smiled. "Men and boys think that we would like to be them," she said. "I don't think they know how pleased we are to be women."

Motholeli thought about this. "Would you like to be somebody else, Mma? Is there anybody else you would like to be?"

Mma Ramotswe considered this for a moment. It was the sort of question that she always found rather difficult to answer—just as she found it impossible to reply when people asked when one would like to have lived if one did not live in the present. That question was particularly perplexing. Some said that they would have liked to live before the colonial era, before Europe came and carved Africa up; that, they said, would have been a good time, when Africa ran its own affairs, without humiliation. Yes, it was true that Europe had devoured Africa like a hungry man at a feast—and an un-invited one too—but not everything had been perfect before that. What if one had lived next door to the Zulus, with their fierce militarism? What if one were a weak person in the house of the strong? The Batswana had always been a peaceful people, but one could not say that about everybody. And what about medicines and hospitals? Would one have wanted to live in a time when a little scratch could turn septic and end one's life? Or in the days before dental anaesthetic? Mma Ramotswe thought not, and yet the pace of life was so much more human then and people made do with so much less. Perhaps it would have been good to live then, when one did not have to worry about money, because money did not exist; or when one did not have to fret about being on time for any-thing, because clocks were as yet unknown. There was something to be said for that; there was something to be said for a time when all one had to worry about was the cattle and the crops.

And as for the question of who else she would rather be, that was perhaps as unanswerable. Her assistant, Mma Makutsi? What would it be like to be a woman from Bobonong, the wearer of a pair of large round glasses, a graduate—with ninety-seven per cent—of the Botswana Secretarial College, an assistant detective? Would Mma Ramotswe exchange her early forties for Mma Makutsi's early thirties? Would she exchange her marriage to Mr J.L.B. Matekoni for Mma Makutsi's engagement to Phuti Radiphuti, proprietor of the Double Comfort Furniture Store—and of a considerable herd of cattle? No, she thought she would not. Manifold as Phuti Radiphuti's merits might be, they could not possibly match those of Mr J.L.B. Matekoni, and even if it was good to be in one's early thirties, there were compensations to being in one's early forties. These were . . . She stopped. What precisely were they?

Motholeli, the cause of this train of thought, now interrupted it; there was to be no enumeration of the consolations of being forty-ish. "Well, Mma," she said. "Who would you be? The Minister of Health?"

The Minister, the wife of that great man, Professor Thomas Tlou, had recently visited Motholeli's school to present prizes and had delivered a stirring address to the pupils. Motholeli had been particularly impressed and had talked about it at home.

"She is a very fine person," said Mma Ramotswe. "And she wears very beautiful head-dresses. I would not mind being Sheila Tlou . . . if I had to be somebody else. But I am quite happy, really, being Mma Ramotswe, you know. There is nothing wrong with that, is there?" She paused. "And you're happy being yourself, aren't you?"

She asked the question without thinking, and immediately regretted it. There were reasons why Motholeli would prefer to be somebody else; it was so obvious, and Mma Ramotswe, flustered, searched for something to say that would change the subject. She looked at her watch. "Oh, the time. It's getting late, Motholeli. We cannot stand here talking about all sorts of things, much as I'd like to . . ."

Motholeli licked the remnants of jam off her

fingers. She looked up at Mma Ramotswe. "Yes, I'm happy. I'm very happy. And I don't think that I would like to be anybody else. Not really."

Mma Ramotswe sighed with relief. "Good. Then I think . . ."

"Except maybe you," Motholeli continued. "I would like to be you, Mma Ramotswe."

Mma Ramotswe laughed. "I'm not sure if you would always enjoy that. There are times when I would like to be somebody else myself."

"Or Mr J.L.B. Matekoni," Motholeli said. "I would like to know as much about cars as he does. That would be good."

And dream about brake drums and gears? wondered Mma Ramotswe. And have to deal with those apprentices, and be covered in grease and oil half the time?

ONCE THE CHILDREN had set off for school, Mma Ramotswe and Mr J.L.B. Matekoni found themselves alone in the kitchen. The children always made a noise; now there was an almost unnatural quiet, as at the end of a thunderstorm or a night of high winds. It was a time for the two adults to finish their tea in companionable silence, or perhaps to exchange a few words about what the day ahead held. Then, once the breakfast plates had been cleared up and the porridge pot scrubbed and put away, they would make their separate ways to work, Mr J.L.B. Matekoni in his green truck and Mma Ramotswe in her tiny white van. Their destination was the same—the No. 1 Ladies' Detective Agency shared premises with Tlokweng Road Speedy Motors—but they invariably arrived at different times. Mr J.L.B. Matekoni liked to drive directly to the top of the Tlokweng Road along the route that went past the flats at the end of the university, while Mma Ramotswe, who had a soft spot for the area of town known as the Village, would meander along Oodi Drive or Hippopotamus Road and approach the Tlokweng Road from that direction.

As they sat at the kitchen table that morning, Mr J.L.B. Matekoni suddenly looked up from his teacup and started to stare at a point on the ceiling. Mma Ramotswe knew that this preceded a disclosure; Mr J.L.B. Matekoni looked at the ceiling when something needed to be said. She said nothing, waiting for him to speak.

"There's something I meant to mention to you," he said casually. "I forgot to tell you about it yesterday. You were in Molepolole, you see."

She nodded. "Yes, I went to Molepolole."

His eyes were still fixed on the ceiling. "And Molepolole? How was Molepolole?"

She smiled. "You know what Molepolole is like. It gets a bit bigger, but not much else has changed. Not really."

"I'm not sure that I would want Molepolole to change too much," he said.

She waited for him to continue. Something important was definitely about to emerge, but with Mr J.L.B. Matekoni these things could take time.

"Somebody came to see you at the office yesterday," he said. "When Mma Makutsi was out."

This surprised Mma Ramotswe and, in spite of her equable temperament, irritated her. Mma Makutsi had been meant to be in the office throughout the previous day, in case a client should call. Where had she been?

"So Mma Makutsi was out?" she said. "Did she say where?" It was possible that some urgent matter of business had arisen and this had required Mma Makutsi's presence elsewhere, but she doubted that. A more likely explanation, thought Mma Ramotswe, was urgent shopping, probably for shoes.

Mr J.L.B. Matekoni lowered his gaze from the ceiling and fixed it on Mma Ramotswe. He knew that his wife was a generous employer, but he did not want to get Mma Makutsi into trouble if she had deliberately disobeyed instructions. And she had been shopping; when she had returned, just before five in the afternoon—a strictly token return, he thought at the time—she had been laden with parcels and had unpacked one of these to show him the shoes it contained. They were very fashionable shoes, she had assured him, but in Mr J.L.B. Matekoni's view they had been barely recognisable as footwear, so slender and insubstantial had seemed the criss-crossings of red leather which made up the upper part of the shoes.

"So she went shopping," said Mma Ramotswe, tight-lipped.

"Perhaps," said Mr J.L.B. Matekoni. He tended to be defensive about Mma Makutsi, whom he admired greatly. He knew what it was like to come from nowhere, with nothing, or next to nothing, and make a success of one's life. She had done that with her ninety-seven per cent and her part-time typing school, and now, of course, with her well-heeled fiancé. He would defend her. "But there was nothing going on. I'm sure she had done all her work."

"But something did turn up," pointed out Mma Ramotswe. "A client came to see me. You've just said that."

Mr J.L.B. Matekoni fiddled with a button on the front of his shirt. He was clearly embarrassed about something. "Well, I suppose so. But I was there to deal with things. I spoke to this person."

"And?" asked Mma Ramotswe.

Mr J.L.B. Matekoni hesitated. "I was able to deal with the situation," he said. "And I have written it all down to show you." He reached into a pocket and took out a folded sheet of paper, which he handed to Mma Ramotswe.

She unfolded the paper and read the pencil-written note. Mr J.L.B. Matekoni's handwriting was angular, and careful—the script of one who had been taught penmanship, as he had been, at school all those years ago, a skill he had never forgotten. Mma Ramotswe's own handwriting was less legible and was becoming worse. It was something to do with her wrists, she thought, which had become chubbier over the years and which affected the angle of the hand on the paper. Mma Makutsi had suggested that her employer's handwriting was becoming increasingly like shorthand and that it might eventually become indistinguishable from the system of pencilled dashes and wiggles that covered the pages of her own notebook.

"It will be a first," she remarked, as she squinted at a note which Mma Ramotswe had left her. "It will be the first time that anybody has started to write shorthand without learning it. It may even be in the papers."

Mma Ramotswe had wondered whether she should feel offended by this, but had decided to laugh instead. "Would I get ninety-seven per cent for it?" she asked.

Mma Makutsi became serious. She did not like her result at the Botswana Secretarial College to be taken lightly. "No," she said. "I was only joking about shorthand. You would have to work very hard at the Botswana Secretarial College to get a result like that. Very hard." She gave Mma Ramotswe a look which implied that such a result would be well beyond her.

Now, on the paper before her, were Mr J.L.B. Matekoni's notes. "Time," he had written, "3:20 p.m. Client: woman. Name: Faith Botumile. Complaint: husband having an affair. Request: find out who the husband's girlfriend is. Action proposed: get rid of girlfriend. Get husband back."

Mma Ramotswe read the note and looked at her husband. She was trying to imagine the encounter between Faith Botumile and Mr J.L.B. Matekoni. Had the interview taken place in the garage, while his head was buried in some car's engine compartment? Or had he taken her into the office and interviewed her from the desk, wiping his hands free of grease as she told her story? And what was Mma Botumile like? What age? Dress? There were so many things that a woman would notice which would provide vital background to the handling of the case which a man simply would not see.

"This woman," she asked, holding up the note. "Tell me about her?"

Mr J.L.B. Matekoni shrugged. "Just an ordinary woman," he said. "Nothing special about her."

Mma Ramotswe smiled. It was as she had

imagined, and Mma Botumile would have to be interviewed again from scratch.

"Just a woman?" she mused.

"That's right," he said.

"And you can't tell me anything more about her?" asked Mma Ramotswe. "Nothing about her age? Nothing about her appearance?"

Mr J.L.B. Matekoni seemed surprised. "Do you want me to?"

"It could be useful."

"Thirty-eight," said Mr J.L.B. Matekoni.

Mma Ramotswe raised an eyebrow. "She told you that?"

"Not directly. No. But I was able to work that out. She said that she was the sister of the man who runs that shoe shop near the supermarket. She said that she was the joint owner, with him. She said that he was her older brother—by two years. I know that man. I know that he had a fortieth birthday recently because one of the people who brings in his car for servicing said that he was going to his party. So I knew . . ."

Mma Ramotswe's eyes widened. "And what else do you know about her?"

Mr J.L.B. Matekoni looked up at the ceiling

again. "Nothing, really," he said. "Except maybe that she is a diabetic."

Mma Ramotswe was silent.

"I offered her a biscuit," said Mr J.L.B. Matekoni. "You know those iced ones you have on your desk. In that tin marked **Pencils.** I offered her one of those and she looked at her watch and then shook her head. I have seen diabetics do that. They sometimes look at their watch because they have to know how long it is before their next meal." He paused. "I am not sure, of course. I just thought that."

Mma Ramotswe nodded, and glanced at her own watch. It was almost time to go to the office. It was, she felt, going to be an unusual day. Any day on which one's suppositions are so rudely shattered before eight o'clock is bound to be an unusual day, a day for discovering things about the world which are quite different from what you thought they were.

She drove into work slowly, not even trying to keep up with Mr J.L.B. Matekoni's green truck ahead of her. At the top of Zebra Drive she nosed her van out across the road that led north, narrowly avoiding a large car which swerved and sounded its horn; such rudeness, she thought, and so unnecessary. She drove on, past the entrance to the Sun Hotel and beyond it, against the hotel fence, the place where the women sat with their crocheted bedspreads and table-cloths hung out for passers-by to see and, they hoped, to buy. The work was intricate and skilfully done; stitch after stitch, loop after loop, worked slowly and painstakingly out from the core in wide circles of white thread, like spider-webs; the work of women who sat there so patiently under the sun, women of the sort whose work was often forgotten or ignored in its anonymity, but artists really, and providers. Mma Ramotswe needed a new bedspread and would stop to buy one before too long; but not today, when she had things on her mind. Mma Botumile. Mma Botumile. The name had been tantalising her, because she thought that she had encountered it before and could not recall where. Now she remembered. Somebody had once said to her: **Mma Botumile: rudest woman in the whole of Botswana. True!**

CHAPTER TWO

THE RULE OF THREE

So, MMA," said Mma Makutsi from behind her desk. "Another day."

It was not an observation that called for an immediate reply; certainly one could hardly contradict it. So Mma Ramotswe merely nodded, glancing at Mma Makutsi and taking in the bright red dress—a dress which she had not seen before. It was very fetching, she thought, even if a bit too formal for their modest office; after all, new clothes, grand clothes, can show just how shabby one's filing cabinets are. When she had first come to work for Mma Ramotswe, Mma Makutsi had possessed only a few dresses, two of which were blue and the others of a faded colour between green and yellow. With the success of her part-time typing school for men, she had been able to afford rather more, and now, following her engagement to Phuti Radiphuti, her wardrobe had expanded even further.

"Your dress, Mma," said Mma Ramotswe. "It's very smart. That colour suits you well. You are a person who can wear red. I have always thought that."

Mma Makutsi beamed with pleasure. She was not used to compliments on her appearance; that difficult skin, those too-large glasses—these made such remarks only too rare. "Thank you, Mma," she said. "I am very pleased with it." She paused. "You could wear red too, you know."

Mma Ramotswe thought: **Of course I can wear red.** But she did not say this, and simply said instead, "Thank you, Mma."

There was a silence. Mma Ramotswe was wondering where the money for the dress came from, and whether it had been bought during that unauthorised absence from work. She thought that she might know the answer to the first question: Phuti Radiphuti was obviously giving Mma Makutsi money, which was quite proper, as he was her fiancé, and that was part of the point of having a fiancé. And as for the second question, well, she would be able to find that out readily enough. Mma Ramotswe strongly believed that the simplest way to obtain information was to ask directly. This technique had stood her in good stead in the course of countless enquiries. People were usually willing to tell you things if asked, and many people moreover were prepared to do so even if unasked.

"I always find it so hard to make up my mind when I'm choosing clothes," said Mma Ramotswe. "That's why Saturday is such a good time for clothes-shopping. You have the time then, don't you? Unlike a working day. There's never time for much shopping on a work day, don't you find, Mma Makutsi?"

If Mma Makutsi hesitated, it was only for a moment. Then she said, "No, there isn't. That's why I sometimes think that it would be nice not to have to work. Then you could go to the shops whenever you wanted."

Silence again descended on the office. For Mma Ramotswe, the meaning of Mma Makutsi's comment was quite clear. It had occurred to her before now that her assistant's engagement to a wealthy man might mean her departure from the agency, but she had quickly put the idea out of her mind; it was a possibility so painful, so unwelcome, that it simply did not bear thinking about. Mma Makutsi might have her little ways, but her value as a friend and colleague was inestimable. Mma Ramotswe could not imagine what it would be like to sit alone in her office, drinking solitary cups of bush tea, unable to discuss the foibles of clients with a trusted confidante, unable to share ideas about difficult cases, unable to exchange a smile over the doings of the apprentices. Now she felt ashamed of herself for having begrudged Mma Makutsi her shopping trip during working hours. What did it matter if a conscientious employee slipped out of the office from time to time? Mma Ramotswe herself had done that on numerous occasions, and had never felt guilty about it. Of course, she was the owner of the business and had nobody to account to apart from herself, but that fact alone did not justify having one rule for herself and one for Mma Makutsi.

Mma Ramotswe cleared her throat. "Of course, one might always take a few hours off in the afternoon. There's nothing wrong with that. Nothing at all. One cannot work all the time, you know."

Mma Makutsi was listening. If she had intended her remark to be a warning, then it had been well heeded. "Actually, I did just that the other day, Mma," she said casually. "I knew that you wouldn't mind."

Mma Ramotswe was quick to agree. "Of course not. Of course not, Mma."

Mma Makutsi smiled. This was the response she had hoped for, but Mma Ramotswe could not be let off that easily. "Thank you." She looked out of the window for a moment before continuing. "Mind you, it must be a very nice, free feeling not to work at all."

"Do you really think so, Mma?" asked Mma Ramotswe. "Don't you think you'd become bored rather quickly? Particularly if you left a job like this, which is such an interesting one. I would miss it very badly, I'm afraid."

Mma Makutsi appeared to give the matter some thought. "Maybe," she said, non-committedly. And then added, as if to emphasise the doubtfulness of Mma Ramotswe's proposition, "Perhaps."

The matter was left at that. Mma Makutsi had made her point—that she was now a woman who did not actually need the job she occupied, and who would go shopping if she wished; and for her part, Mma Ramotswe had been made to understand that there had been a subtle shift in power, like a change in the wind, barely noticeable, but nonetheless there. She had always been a considerate employer, but her seniority in age, and in the business, had lent her a certain authority that Mma Makutsi had always recognised. Now that things appeared to be changing, she wondered if it would be Mma Makutsi, rather than herself, who decided when tea break was to be. And would it stop at that? There was always Mr Polopetsi to be considered. He was the exceedingly mild man to whom Mma Ramotswe had given a job—of sorts—after she had knocked him off his bicycle and had heard of his misfortunes. He had proved to be a keen worker, capable of helping Mr J.L.B. Matekoni in the garage as well as taking on small tasks for the agency. He was both unobtrusive and eager to please, but she had already heard Mma Makutsi referring to him as "my assistant" in a tone of voice that was distinctly proprietorial, even though there had never been any question but that she was herself an assistant detective. Mma Ramotswe wondered whether Mma Makutsi might now claim to be something more than that, a **co-detective,** perhaps, or better still an **associate detective;** there were many ways in which people could inflate the importance of their jobs by small changes to their titles. Mma Ramotswe had met an associate professor from the university, a man who brought his car to Mr J.L.B. Matekoni for repair. She had reflected on his title, imagining that this would be appropriate for one who was allowed to associate with professors, without actually being allowed to be one himself. And when they had tea, these professors, did the associate professors drink their tea while sitting at the edge of the circle, or a few yards away perhaps—of the group but not quite of it? She had smiled at the thought; how silly people were with their little distinctions, but here she was herself thinking of some way of bringing Mma Makutsi forward, but not too far forward. That, of course, would be a way of keeping her assistant. It would be easy enough to give her a nominal promotion, particularly if no salary increase was required. This would be an exercise in window-dressing, in tokenism; but no, she would do this because Mma Makutsi actually deserved it. If she was to become an associate detective, with all that that implied—

whatever that was—it would be because she had earned the title.

"Mma Makutsi," she began. "I think that it is time to have a review. All this talk of jobs and not working and such matters has made me realise that we need to review things . . ."

She got no further. Mma Makutsi, who had been looking out of the window again, had seen a car draw up to park under the acacia tree.

"A client," she said.

"Then please make tea," said Mma Ramotswe.

As Mma Makutsi rose to her feet to comply, Mma Ramotswe breathed a discreet sigh of relief. Her authority, it seemed, was intact.

"So, we're cousins!" said Mma Ramotswe, her voice halfway between enthusiasm and caution. One had to be careful about cousins, who had a habit of turning up in times of difficulty—for them—and reminding you of cousinship. And the old Botswana morality, of which Mma Ramotswe was a stout defender, required that one should help a relative in need, even if the connection was a distant one. There was nothing wrong with that, thought Mma Ramotswe, but at times it could be abused. It all depended, it seemed, on the cousin.

She glanced discreetly at the man sitting in the chair in front of her desk, the man whom Mma Makutsi had spotted arriving and whom she had ushered into the office. He was well dressed, in a suit and tie, and his shoe laces, she noticed, were carefully tied. That was a sign of self-respect, and such evidence, together with his open demeanour and confident articulation, made it clear that this was not a distant cousin on the scrounge. Mma Ramotswe relaxed. Even if a favour was about to be asked for, it would not be one which would require money. That was something of a relief, given that the income of the agency over the past month had been so low. For a moment she allowed herself to think that this might even be a paying case, that the fact that the client was a cousin would make no difference when it came to the bill. But that, she realised, was unlikely. One could not charge cousins.

The man smiled at her. "Yes, Mma. We are cousins. Distant ones, of course, but still cousins."

Mma Ramotswe made a welcoming gesture with her hands. "It is very good to meet a new cousin. But I was wondering . . ."

"How we are related?" the man interrupted. "I can tell you that quite simply, Mma. Your father was the late Obed Ramotswe, was he not?"

Mma Ramotswe nodded in confirmation: Obed Ramotswe—her beloved Daddy—the man who had raised her after the death of the mother she could not remember; Obed Ramotswe, the man who had scrimped and saved during all those hard, dark years down the mines and who had built up a herd of cattle that any man might be proud of. Not a day went past, not a day, but that she thought of him.

"He was a very fine man, I have been told," said the visitor. "I met him once when I was much younger, but we had left Mochudi, you see, and we were living down in Lobatse. That is why we did not meet, you and I, even though we are cousins."

Mma Ramotswe encouraged him to continue. She had decided that she liked this man, and she felt slightly guilty about her initial suspicions. You had to be careful, some people said; you had to be, because that was how the

world had become, or so such people argued.
They said that you could no longer trust people, because you did not know where other
people came from, who their people were; and
if you did not know that, then how could you
trust them? Mma Ramotswe saw what was
meant by such pronouncements, but did not
agree with this cynical view. Everybody came
from somewhere; everybody had their people.
It was just a bit harder to find out about them
these days; that was all. And that was no reason
for abandoning trust.

Their visitor took a deep breath. "Your late
father was the son of Boamogetswe Ramotswe, was he not? That was your grandfather,
also late?"

"That was." She had never known him, and
there were no pictures of him, as was usually
the case with people of that generation. Nobody knew any more how they looked, how
they dressed. All that was lost now.

"And he had a sister whose name I cannot
remember," the man went on. "She married a
man called Gotweng Dintwa, who worked on
the railways back in the Protectorate days. He
was in charge of a water tower for the steam
trains."

"I remember those towers," said Mma Ramotswe. "They had those long canvas pipes hanging down from them, like an elephant's trunk."

The man laughed. "That is what they were like." He leaned forward. "He had a daughter who married a man called Monyena. He was your father's generation and they knew one another, not very well, but they knew one another. And then this Monyena went to Johannesburg and was thrown in jail for not having the right papers. He came back home to his wife and settled near Mochudi. That is where I come in. I am that man's son. I am called Tati Monyena."

He uttered the last sentence with an air of pride, as a storyteller might do at the end of a saga when the true identity of the hero is at last revealed. Mma Ramotswe, digesting the information, allowed her gaze to move off her guest and out of the window. There was nothing happening outside the window, but you never knew. The acacia tree might be still, its thorny branches unmoved by any breeze, with just the pale blue sky behind them, but birds landed there and watched, and moved, and led their lives. She thought of what had been told her—

this potted story of a family that had shared roots with her own. A few words could sum up a lifetime; a few more could deal with a sweep of generations, whole dynasties, with here and there a little detail—a water tower, for instance—that made everything so human, so immediate. It was a distant link indeed, and she was as closely connected to him as she was to hundreds, possibly thousands of other people. Ultimately, in a country like Botswana, with its sparse population, everybody was connected in one way or another with virtually everybody else. Somewhere in the tangled genealogical webs there would be a place for everybody; nobody was without people.

Mma Makutsi, who had been listening from her desk, now decided to speak. "There are many cousins," she said.

Tati Monyena turned round and looked at her in surprise. "Yes," he said. "There are many cousins."

"I have so many cousins," Mma Makutsi continued. "I cannot count the number of cousins I have. Up in Bobonong. Cousins, cousins, cousins."

"That is good, Mma," said Tati Monyena.

Mma Makutsi snorted. "Sometimes, Rra.

Sometimes it is good. But I see many of these cousins only when they want something. You know how it is."

At this, Tati Monyena stiffened in his chair. "Not everybody sees their cousin for that reason," he muttered. "I am not one of those who . . ."

Mma Ramotswe threw a glance at her assistant. She might be engaged to Phuti Radiphuti now, but she had no right to speak to a client like that. She would have to talk to her about it, gently, of course, but she would have to remonstrate with her.

"You are very welcome, Rra," Mma Ramotswe said hurriedly. "I am glad you came to see me."

Tati Monyena looked at Mma Ramotswe. There was gratitude in his eyes. "I haven't come to ask a favour, Mma," he said. "I mean to pay for your services."

Mma Ramotswe tried to hide her surprise, but failed, as Tati Monyena felt constrained to reassure her once more. "I shall pay, Mma. It is not for me, you see, it's for the hospital."

"Don't worry, Rra," she said. "But what hospital is this?"

"Mochudi, Mma."

That triggered so many memories: the old Dutch Reformed Mission Hospital in Mochudi, now a Government hospital, near the meeting place, the kgotla; the hospital where so many people she knew had been born, and had died; the broad eaves of which had witnessed so much human suffering, and kindness in the face of suffering. She thought of it with fondness, and now turned to Tati Monyena and said, "The hospital, Rra? Why the hospital?"

His look of pride returned. "That is where I work, Mma. I am not quite the hospital administrator, but I am almost."

The words came quickly to Mma Ramotswe. "Associate administrator?"

"Exactly," said Tati Monyena. The description clearly pleased him, and he savoured it for a few moments before continuing, "You know the hospital, Mma, don't you? Of course you do."

Mma Ramotswe thought of the last time she had been there, but put that memory out of her mind. So many had died of that terrible disease before the drugs came and stopped the misery in its tracks, or did so for many; too late, though, for her friend of childhood, whom she had visited in the hospital on that hot day. She had felt so powerless then, faced with the shadowy figure on the bed, but a nurse had told her that holding a hand, just holding it, could help. Which was true, she thought later; leaving this world clasping the hand of another was far better than going alone.

"How is the hospital?" she asked. "I have heard that you have a lot of new things there. New beds. New X-ray machines."

"We have all of that," said Tati Monyena. "The Government has been very generous."

"It is your money," chipped in Mma Makutsi from behind his chair. "When people say that the Government has given them this thing or that thing, they are forgetting that the thing which the Government gave them belonged to the people in the first place!" She paused, and then added, "Everybody knows that."

In the silence that followed, a small white gecko, one of those albino-like creatures that cling to walls and ceilings, defying gravity with their tiny sucker-like toes, ran across a section of ceiling board. Two flies, which had landed on the same section, moved, but languidly, to escape the approaching danger. Mma Ramotswe's gaze followed the gecko, but then dropped to Mma Makutsi, sitting defiantly below. What she said might be true—in fact, it was self-evidently true—but she should not have used that disparaging tone, as if Tati Monyena were a schoolboy who needed the facts of public finance spelled out for him.

"Rra Monyena knows all that, Mma," said Mma Ramotswe quietly.

Tati Monyena gave a nervous glance over his shoulder in the direction of Mma Makutsi. "What she says is right," he said. "It is our money."

"You wouldn't think that some politicians knew that," said Mma Makutsi.

Mma Ramotswe decided that it was time to get the conversation off politics. "So the hospital wants me to do something," she said. "I am happy to help. But you must tell me what the problem is."

"That's what doctors say," offered Mma Makutsi from the other side of the office. "They say, **What seems to be the problem?** when you go to see them. And then they say . . ."

"Thank you very much, Mma," said Mma Ramotswe firmly. "No, Rra, what is this problem that the hospital has?"

Tati Monyena sighed. "I wish we had only one problem," he began. "In fact, we have many problems. All hospitals have problems. Not enough funds. Not enough nurses. Infection control. It would be a very big list if I were to tell you about all our problems. But there is one problem in particular that we decided I needed to ask you about. One very big problem."

"Which is?"

"People have died in the hospital," he said.

Mma Ramotswe caught Mma Makutsi's eye. She did not want any further remarks from that quarter, and she gave her assistant a severe look. She could imagine what Mma Makutsi might have said to that: that people were always dying in hospitals, and that it was surely no cause for complaint if this happened from time to time. Hospitals were full of sick people, and sick people died if the treatment did not work.

"I am sorry," said Mma Ramotswe. "I can imagine that the hospital does not like its patients to become late. But, after all, hospitals . . ."

"Oh, we know that we're going to lose a certain number of patients," said Tati Monyena quickly. "You can't avoid that."

"So, why would you need my services?" asked Mma Ramotswe.

Tati Monyena hesitated before he replied. "This will go no further?" he asked. His voice was barely above a whisper.

"This is a confidential consultation," Mma Ramotswe reassured him. "It is just between you and me. Nobody else."

Tati Monyena looked over his shoulder again. Mma Makutsi was staring at him through her large round glasses and he quickly looked back again.

"My assistant is bound to secrecy too," said Mma Ramotswe. "We do not talk about our clients' affairs."

"Except when . . . ," began Mma Makutsi, but she was cut off by Mma Ramotswe, who raised her voice.

"Except never," she said. "Except never."

Tati Monyena looked uncomfortable at this display of disagreement and hesitated a moment. But then he continued, "People become late in a hospital for all sorts of reasons. You would be surprised, Mma Ramotswe, at how many patients decide that now that they've arrived in hospital it's time to go . . ." He pointed up at the ceiling. "To go up there. And then there are those who fall out of bed and those who have a bad reaction to some drug and so on. There are many unfortunate things that happen in a hospital.

"But then there are those cases where we just don't know why somebody became late—we just don't know. There are not many of these cases, but they do happen. Sometimes I think that is because of a broken heart. That is something that you cannot see, you know. The pathologist does a post-mortem and the heart looks fine from outside. But it is broken inside, from some sadness. From being far from home, maybe, and thinking that you will never again see your family, or your cattle. That can break the heart."

Mma Ramotswe nodded her agreement at that. She knew about broken hearts, and she understood how they can occur. Her father had told her about that many years ago; about how some men who went off to the mines in South Africa died for no reason at all, or so it seemed. A few weeks after they had arrived in Johannesburg, they simply died, because they were so far from Botswana, and their hearts were broken. She remembered that now.

"A broken heart," mused Tati Monyena. "But to have a broken heart you have to be awake, Mma, would you not agree?"

Mma Ramotswe looked puzzled. "Awake?"

"Yes. Let me tell you what happened, Mma, and then you will see what I mean. I'm not sure if you know much about hospitals, but you know about a ward they have which is called intensive care. That is for people who are very ill and have to be looked after by nurses all the time, or just about all the time. Sometimes these people are in comas, on ventilators, which help them to breathe. You know about those machines, Mma?"

Mma Ramotswe did.

"Well," continued Tati Monyena, "we have a ward like that in the hospital. And of course when people become late in that ward, nobody is too surprised. They are very sick when they go in and not all of them will come out. But . . ." He raised a finger in the air to emphasise the point. "But, when you have three deaths in six months and each of those takes place in the same bed, then you begin to wonder."

"Coincidence," muttered Mma Makutsi. "There are many coincidences."

This time, Tati Monyena did not turn to answer her, but addressed his reply to Mma Ramotswe. "Oh, I know about coincidences," he said. "That could easily be a coincidence. I know that. But what if those three deaths take place at more or less exactly the same time on a Friday? All of them?" He raised three fingers in the air. "Friday." One finger went down. "Friday." The second finger. "Friday." The third.

CHAPTER THREE

I HAVE FOUND YOU

MMA MAKUTSI went home that day thinking about what Tati Monyena had said. She preferred not to dwell upon her work once she left the office—something that they had strongly recommended at the Botswana Secretarial College. "Don't go home and write letters all over again in your head," said the lecturer. "It is best to leave the problems of the office where they belong—in the office."

She had done that, for the most part, but it was not easy when there was something as unusual—as shocking, perhaps—as this. Even though she tried to put out of her mind the account of the three unusual hospital deaths, the image returned of Tati Monyena holding up three fingers and bringing them down one by one. So might the passing of one's life be marked—by the raising and lowering of a finger. She thought of this again as she unlocked the door of her house and flicked the light switch. On, off; like our lives.

It had not been a good day for Mma Makutsi. She had not sought out that altercation with Mma Ramotswe—if one could call it that—and it had left her feeling uncomfortable. It was Mma Ramotswe's fault, she decided; she should not have made those remarks about shopping during working hours. One might reasonably require a junior clerk to keep strict hours, but when it came to those at a higher level, such as herself, then a certain leeway was surely normal. If one went to the shops in the afternoon they were full of people who were senior enough to take the time off to do their shopping. One could not expect such people—and she included herself in that category—to struggle to get everything done on a Saturday morning, when the whole town was trying to do the same thing. If Mma Ramotswe did not appreciate that, she said to herself, then she would have to employ somebody else.

She stopped. She was standing in the middle

of the room when this thought crossed her mind, and she realised that it was the first time she had seriously contemplated leaving her job. And now that she had articulated the possibility, even if only to herself, she found that she felt ashamed. Mma Ramotswe had given her her first job when she had been beaten to so many others by those feckless, glamorous girls from the Botswana Secretarial College, with their measly fifty per cent results in the final examinations. It had been Mma Ramotswe who had seen beyond that and had taken her on, even when the agency could hardly afford to pay her wages. That had been one of Mma Ramotswe's many acts of kindness, and there had been others. There had been her promotion; there had been her support after the death of her brother, Richard, when Mma Ramotswe had given her three weeks off and had paid half the cost of the funeral. She had expected and wanted no thanks, had done it out of the goodness of her heart, and here was she, Mma Makutsi, thinking of leaving simply because her circumstances had improved and she was in a position to do so. She felt a flush of shame. She would apologise to Mma Ramotswe the next day and offer to work some overtime for nothing—well, perhaps not quite that, but she would make a gesture.

Mma Makutsi put the bag she was carrying on the table and started to unpack it. She had called in at the shops on the way home and had bought the supplies that she needed for Phuti Radiphuti's dinner. He came to eat at her house on several evenings a week—on the others he still ate with his father or his aunt—and she liked to prepare him something special. Of course she knew what he liked, which was meat, good beef fed on the sweet, dry grass of Botswana; beef served with rice and thick gravy and broad beans. Mma Ramotswe always liked to cook boiled pumpkin with beef, but Mma Makutsi preferred beans, and so did Phuti Radiphuti. It was a good thing, she thought, that they liked the same things, on the table and elsewhere, and that boded well for the marriage, when it eventually happened. That was something she wanted to talk to Phuti about, without appearing to be either too anxious or too keen about it. She was acutely aware of the fact that Mma Ramotswe's engagement to Mr J.L.B. Matekoni had been a long-drawn-out affair, concluded only when he was more or less manoeuvred into position for the wedding by no less a person than Mma Potokwane. She did not want her engagement to last that long, and she would have to get Phuti Radiphuti to agree to a date for the wedding. He had already spoken of that, and had shown no signs of the reluctance, dithering really, which had held back Mr J.L.B. Matekoni from naming a day.

The winter day died with the quickness of those latitudes. It seemed to be only for a few moments that the sun made the sky to the west red, and then it was gone. The night would be a cold one, clear and cold, with the stars suspended above like crystals. She looked out of her window at the lights of the neighbouring houses. Through the windows she saw her neighbours on the other side of the road seated round the fire that she knew they liked to keep going in their hearth throughout the winter months, triggering the memory, long overlaid but still there, of sitting round the fire at the cattle posts. Mma Makutsi had no fireplace in her house, but she would have, she thought, when she moved to Phuti's house, which had more than one; mantelpieces too, on which she could put the ornaments which she currently kept in a box behind her settee. There would be so much room in her new life; room for all the things that she had been unable to do because of poverty, and if she did not have to work—that thought returned unbidden—then she would be able to do so much. And she could stay in bed too, if she wished, until eight in the morning; such a prospect—no dashing for the minibus, no crowding with two other people into a seat made for two; and so often, it seemed, those others were ladies of traditional build who could have done with an entire bench seat to themselves.

She prepared a stew for Phuti Radiphuti and carefully measured out the beans that would accompany it. Then she laid the table with the plates that she knew he liked, the ones with the blue and red circles, with his teacup, a large one with a blue design that she had bought at the bring-and-buy sale at the Anglican Cathedral. "That teacup," Mma Ramotswe had said, "belonged to the last Dean. He was such a kind man. I saw him drinking from it."

"It belongs to me now," said Mma Makutsi.

Like Mma Ramotswe, Phuti Radiphuti drank red bush tea, which he thought was much better for you, but he had never asked Mma Makutsi for it and had simply taken what was served to him. He was planning, though, to make the request, but the moment had not yet arisen and with each pot of ordinary tea served it became more difficult for him to ask for something different. That had been Mma Makutsi's own quandary, resolved when she had eventually plucked up all her courage and blurted out to Mma Ramotswe that she would like to have India tea and would have preferred that all along.

There were one or two other matters which Phuti Radiphuti would have liked to raise with his fiancée but which he had found himself unable to bring up. They were small things, of course, but important in a shared life. He did not take to her curtains; yellow was not a colour that appealed to him in the slightest. In his view, the best colour for curtains was undoubtedly light blue—the blue of the national flag. It was not a question of patriotism; although there were those who painted their front doors that blue for reasons of pride. And why should they not do so, when there was a lot to be proud of? It was more a question of restfulness. Blue was a peaceful colour, Phuti Radiphuti thought. Yellow, by contrast, was an energetic, unsettled colour; a colour of warning, every bit as much as red was; a colour which made one feel vaguely uncomfortable.

But when he arrived at her house that evening, he did not want to discuss curtain colour. Quite suddenly, Phuti Radiphuti felt grateful; simply relieved that of all the men she must have come across, Mma Makutsi had chosen him. She had chosen him in spite of his stammer and his inability to dance; had seen past all that and had worked with such success on both of these defects. For that he felt thankful, so thankful, in fact, that it hurt; for it so easily might have been quite different. She might have laughed at him, or simply looked away with embarrassment as she heard his uncooperative tongue mangle the liquid syllables of Setswana; but she did not do that because she was a kind woman, and now she was about to become his wife.

"We must decide on a day for the wedding," he said as he sat down at the table. "We cannot leave that matter up in the . . ." The importance of what he was about to say made the words stick; they would not come.

"Up in the air," said Mma Makutsi quickly.

"Yes," he said. "Yes. We must share . . . must share . . . our . . . our . . ."

For a moment Mma Makutsi thought that the next word was **blanket,** and almost supplied that, for this was a common metaphor in Setswana—to share a blanket. But then she realised that Phuti Radiphuti would never be so forward as to say such a thing, and she stopped herself just in time.

"Our ideas on that," went on Phuti Radiphuti.

"Of course. We must share our ideas on that."

Phuti Radiphuti was relieved that he had made a start and went on to deal with the details. Now he spoke easily again, with none of the stumbling that had at one time dogged him when he had something important to say.

"I think that we should get married in January," said Phuti. "January is a month when people are looking for things to do. A wedding will keep them busy. You know, all the aunties and people like that."

Mma Makutsi laughed. There was so much to think of—so many exciting things—but this reference to aunts gave her a reason to chuckle. And beyond the amusement there was the heady, intoxicating fact: he had said it! He may not have named a day, but at least he had named a month! Her marriage was now not just some sort of vague possibility in the future; it was a singled-out time, as definite, as cast in stone, as the dates on her calendar in the office from the Good Impression Printing Company: 30 September—Botswana Independence Day; 1 July—Birthday of Sir Seretse Khama. Those dates she remembered, as everyone did, because they were holidays, and Mma Ramotswe remembered a few more: 21 April—Queen Elizabeth II's birthday; 4 July—Independence Day of the United States of America. There were others in the calendar that the Good Impression Printing Company thought important enough to note, but which escaped the attention of the No. 1 Ladies' Detective Agency. Some of these were other national days; 1 October, for example, was Nigeria's national day, and was marked in the calendar, but not observed in any way by Mma Ramotswe. When Mma Makutsi had drawn Mma Ramotswe's attention to the significance of that day, there had been a brief silence and then, "That may be so, Mma, and I am happy for them. But we cannot observe everybody's national day, can we, or life would be one constant celebration."

The apprentices had been hovering nearby when this remark was passed and Charlie, the older one, had opened his mouth to say, "And what would be wrong with that?" but had stopped himself and instead nodded his head in exaggerated agreement.

She sat quite still at the table, her eyes lowered to the plate before her. "Yes. January would be a good time. That gives people six months to get ready. That should be enough."

Phuti agreed. It had always struck him as strange that people took such trouble over weddings, with two parties—one for each family—and a great deal of coming and going by anybody who was related, even distantly, to the couple. Six months would be reasonable, and would not encourage unnecessary activity; if one allowed a year, then people would think of a year's worth of things to do.

"You have an uncle . . . ," he began. This, he knew, was the delicate part of the matter. Mma Makutsi would have to be paid for, and an uncle would probably wish to negotiate the bride price. Her uncle would speak to his father and his uncles, and together they would agree the figure, notionally in head of cattle.

He stole a glance at his fiancée. A woman of

her education and talents could expect a fairly good dowry—perhaps nine cattle—even if her background would not normally justify more than seven or eight. But would this uncle, if he existed, try to raise the price once he found out about the Double Comfort Furniture Store and all those Radiphuti cattle out at the cattle post? In Phuti Radiphuti's experience, uncles did their homework in these situations.

"Yes," said Mma Makutsi. "I have an uncle. He is my senior uncle, and I think that he will want to talk about these things."

It was delicately put, and it made it possible for Phuti Radiphuti to move on from this potentially awkward topic to the safer ground of food. "I know somebody who is a very good caterer," he said. "She has a truck with a fridge in it. She is very good at this sort of thing."

"She sounds just right," said Mma Makutsi.

"And I can get hold of chairs for the guests to sit on," went on Phuti Radiphuti.

Of course, thought Mma Makutsi; the Double Comfort Furniture Store would come in useful for that. There was nothing worse than a wedding where there were not enough chairs for people to sit on and they ended up eating with their plates balanced on all sorts of things, ant heaps even, and getting food on their smart clothes. She vowed to herself, That will not happen at my wedding, and the thought filled her with pride. **My wedding. My wedding guests. Chairs.** It was a long way from those days of penury as a student at the Botswana Secretarial College, of rationing herself in what she ate; of making do with just one of anything, if that. Well, those days were over now.

And Phuti Radiphuti, for his part, thought, **My days of loneliness are finished. My days of being laughed at because of the way I speak and because no woman would look at me—those are over now. Those are over.**

He reached out and took Mma Makutsi's hand. She smiled at him. "I am very lucky to have found you," he said.

"No, I am the lucky one. I am the one."

He thought that unlikely, but he was moved very deeply that somebody should consider herself lucky to have him, of all people. The previously unloved may find it hard to believe that they are now loved; that is such a miracle, they feel; such a miracle.

ᒧᒧᒧ

ᴌE MMA MAKUTSI and Phuti Radiphuti
reflecting on their good fortune, Mma
ᴴᴼᵗswe and Mr J.L.B. Matekoni, who
ᵗhemselves had on many occasions pondered
their own good luck, were engaged in a conversation of an entirely different nature. They had
finished their dinner and the children had been
dispatched to bed. Both were tired—he because he had removed an entire engine that afternoon, a task which involved considerable
physical exertion, and she because she had
awoken the night before and lost an hour or
two of sleep. The kitchen clock, which always
ran ten minutes fast, revealed that it was eight
thirty, eight twenty after adjustment. One
could not decently go to bed before eight
thirty, Mma Ramotswe felt; and so she sat back
and chatted with her husband about the day's
events. She was not particularly interested in
the removal of the engine, and listened to his
comments on that with only half an ear. But
then he said something which engaged her full
attention.

"That woman I spoke to," he said. "Mma
What's-her-name. The one with the husband."

tiality. That would be a good recommendation, she thought; how a person divided a shared doughnut was a real test of integrity. A good person would cut the doughnut into two equal pieces. A shifty, selfish person would divide it into two pieces, but one would be bigger than the other and he would take that one himself. She had seen that happen.

No, every job had its repetitive side and most people, surely, recognised that. She glanced again at Mr J.L.B. Matekoni. She knew that many men of his age started to feel trapped and began to wonder if this was all that life offered. It was understandable; anyone might feel that, not just men, although they might feel it particularly acutely, as they felt themselves weaken and began to realise that they were no longer young. Women were better at coming to terms with that, thought Mma Ramotswe, as long as they were not the worrying sort. If one was of traditional build and not given to fretting . . . If one drank plenty of bush tea . . .

"You know," she said to Mr J.L.B. Matekoni, "all of us have things that are the same in our jobs. Even in the sort of work I do, the same sort of thing happens quite a lot. I don't think there is anything much that you can do."

It was not like Mr J.L.B. Matekoni to argue, but now, if there was a stubborn streak in his character, it showed. "No," he said. "I think there is something that you can do. You can try something different."

Mma Ramotswe was silent. She reached for her teacup. It was cold. She looked at him. It was inconceivable that Mr J.L.B. Matekoni could be anything but a mechanic; he was a truly great mechanic, a man who understood engines, who knew their every mood. She tried to picture him in the garb of some other profession—in a banker's suit, for example, or in the white coat of a doctor, but neither of these seemed right, and she saw him again in his mechanic's overalls, in his old suede boots so covered in grease, and that somehow rang true, that was just what he should wear.

Mr J.L.B. Matekoni broke the silence. "I'm not thinking of stopping being a mechanic, of course. Certainly not. I know that I must do that to put bread on our table."

Mma Ramotswe's relief showed, and this

caused him to smile reassuringly. "It's just that I would like to do a little bit of detective work. Not much. Just a little."

That, she thought, was reasonable enough. She had no desire to fix engines, but there was no harm in his wanting to see her side of the business. "Just to find out what it's like? Just to get it out of your system?" she asked, smiling. Most men, she thought, fantasised about doing something exciting, about being a soldier, or a secret agent, or even a great lover; that was how men were. That was normal.

Mr J.L.B. Matekoni frowned. "Please don't laugh at me, Mma Ramotswe."

She leaned forward and rested her hand on his forearm. "I would never laugh at you, Mr J.L.B. Matekoni. I would never do that. And of course you can look after a case. How about this Mma Botumile matter? Would that do?"

"That is the one that I want to investigate," he said. "That is the one."

"Then you shall investigate," she said.

Even as she spoke, she had her misgivings, unexpressed. The thought of Mma Botumile's reputation disturbed her, and she was not sure whether she should put Mr J.L.B. Matekoni in the path of a woman like that. But it was too late to do anything about it, and so she looked at her watch and rose to her feet. She would not think about it any more, or she would have difficulty in getting to sleep.

CHAPTER FOUR

MMA RAMOTSWE GOES TO MOCHUDI WITH MR POLOPETSI, IN THE TINY WHITE VAN

MMA RAMOTSWE TRAVELLED to Mochudi the next day. She decided to take Mr Polopetsi with her; there was nothing for him to do in the garage that morning and he had asked Mma Makutsi three times if there was anything that he could help her with in the office. She had tried to think of some task, and failed, and so Mma Ramotswe had invited him to accompany her on the Mochudi trip. She enjoyed his company, and it would be good to have somebody to talk to. Whether he would contribute anything to her enquiries there was another matter; Mr Polopetsi, she feared, would never distinguish himself in the role of detective, as he tended to jump to conclusions and to act impetuously. But there was something appealing about him that made all that forgivable—an earnestness combined with a slight air of vulnerability that made people, particularly women, want to protect him. Even Mma Makutsi, who was famously short with the two apprentices and who tended to talk to men as if they were children, had been won over by Mr Polopetsi. "There are many men for whom there does not appear to be any reason," she once said to Mma Ramotswe. "But I don't feel that about Mr Polopetsi. Even when he is standing there, doing nothing, I don't think that."

It had been a curious thing to say, but then Mma Makutsi often said things that surprised Mma Ramotswe and she had become used to her pronouncements. But what made this re-mark particularly unusual was the fact that it was made while Mr Polopetsi was in the office, busying himself with the making of a pot of tea. Mma Makutsi must have been aware of his coming into the room, but must simply have forgotten his presence after a few moments and addressed Mma Ramotswe without thinking. And there was no doubt in Mma Ramotswe's mind that Mr Polopetsi had heard what was said about him, for he stopped stirring the tea for a moment, as if frozen, and then, after a few seconds, began to rattle the spoon about the pot more vigorously than before. Mma Ramotswe had felt acutely embarrassed, but had decided that the remark was hardly unflattering to Mr Polopetsi, even if he had scurried out of the room, his mug of tea in his hand, studiously avoiding looking at the author of the remark. For Mma Makutsi's part, she had simply raised an eyebrow when she realised that he had heard her, and shrugged, as if this was merely one of those things that happened in offices.

They drove out to Mochudi on the old road, because that was the way that Mma Ramotswe had always travelled and because it was quieter. It was a bright morning, and there was warmth in the air; not the heat that would come in a month or so and build up over the final months of the year, but a pleasant feeling of a benign sun upon the skin. As they left Gaborone behind them, the houses and their surrounding plots gave way to the bush, to the expanses of dry grass dotted with acacia and smaller thorn bushes that were halfway between trees and shrubs. Here and there was a dry river bed, a scar of sand that would remain parched until the rainy season, when it would be covered with swift-moving dun-coloured water, a proper river for a few days until it all drained off and the bed would cake and crack in the sun.

For a while they did not talk. Mma Ramotswe looked out of the window of her tiny white van, savouring the feeling of heading somewhere she was always happy to be going; for Mochudi was home, the place from which she had come and to which she knew that she would one day return for good. Mr Polopetsi looked straight ahead, at the road unfolding ahead of them, lost in thoughts of his own. He was waiting for Mma Ramotswe to tell him about the reason for their trip to Mochudi; she had simply said at the office that she needed to go there and would tell him all about it on the way up.

He glanced at her sideways. "This business . . ."

Mma Ramotswe was thinking of something quite different, of this road and of how she had once travelled down it by bus, unhappy to the very core of her being; but that was years ago, years. She moved her hands on the wheel. "We don't usually get involved in cases where people have died, Rra," she said. "We may be detectives, but not that sort."

Mr Polopetsi drew in his breath. Ever since he had joined the staff of the No. 1 Ladies' Detective Agency—even in his ill-defined adjunct role—he had been waiting for something like this. Murder was what detectives were meant to investigate, was it not, and now at last they were embarked on such an enquiry.

"Murder," he whispered. "There have been murders?"

Mma Ramotswe was about to laugh at the suggestion. "Oh no," she began. But then she stopped herself, and the thought occurred to her that perhaps this was exactly what they were letting themselves in for. Tati Monyena had described the deaths as **mishaps** and had hinted, at the most, that there was some form of unexplained negligence behind them; he had said nothing about deliberate killing. And yet it was possible, was it not? She remembered reading somewhere about cases where hospital patients had been deliberately killed by doctors or nurses. She thought hard, probing the recesses of her memory, and it came to her. Yes, there had been such a doctor in Zimbabwe, in Bulawayo, and she had read about him. He had started to poison people while he was still at medical school in America and had continued to do so for years. These people existed. Was it possible that a person like that could have slipped into Botswana? Or could it be a nurse? They did it too sometimes, she believed. It gave them power, somebody had said. They felt powerful.

She half-turned to Mr Polopetsi. "I hope not," she said. "But we must keep an open mind, Rra. It is possible, I suppose."

They were ten miles from Mochudi now, and Mma Ramotswe spent the rest of the journey describing to Mr Polopetsi what Tati Monyena had told her: three Fridays, three unexplained deaths, and all in the same bed.

"That cannot be a coincidence," he said, shaking his head. "That sort of thing just does not happen." He paused. "You know that I worked in this hospital once, Mma Ramotswe? Did I tell you that?"

Mma Ramotswe knew that Mr Polopetsi had worked as an assistant in the pharmacy at the Princess Marina Hospital in Gaborone, and she knew of the injustice that occurred there which led to his spell in prison. But she did not know that he had been at Mochudi.

"Yes," Mr Polopetsi explained. "I was there for eight months, while they were short-staffed. That was about four years ago. I was in the pharmacy." He lowered his voice as he mentioned the pharmacy, in shame, she thought. All that had turned sour for him, and all because of a lying witness and the transfer of blame. It was so unfair, but she had gone over all that with him before, several times, and she knew—they both knew—that they could do nothing to remedy it. "You are innocent in your heart," she had said to him. "That is the most important thing." And he had thought about that for a few moments before shaking his head and saying, "I would like that to be true, Mma, but it is not. It is what other people think. **That** is the most important thing."

Now, as they made their way through the outskirts of Mochudi, past the rash of small hairdressing establishments with their hand-painted grandiose signs, past the turn-offs that led to the larger houses of those who had made good in Gaborone and returned to the village, past the tax office and the general dealers, he said to her casually, almost as if he were thinking aloud, "I wouldn't like to be one of his patients."

"Of whose patients?"

"There was a doctor who worked at the hospital when I was there," he said. "I didn't like him. Nobody did. And I remember thinking: I would be frightened to be in that doctor's care. I really would."

She changed gear. A donkey had wandered onto the road and was standing directly in the path of the tiny white van. It was a defeated, cowed creature, and seemed to be looking directly up at the sun.

"That donkey is blind," said Mr Polopetsi. "Look at him."

She guided the van round the static animal. "Why?" she said.

"Why does he stand there? That is what they do. That is just the way they are."

"No," she said. "That is not what I meant. I wondered what frightened you about him."

He thought for a few moments before answering. "You get a feeling sometimes. You just do." He paused. "Maybe we'll see him."

"Is he still there, Rra?"

Mr Polopetsi shrugged. "He was last year. I heard from a friend. I don't know if he has moved since then. Maybe not. He was married to a woman from Mochudi, so maybe he will still be there. He is a South African himself. Xhosa mother, Boer father."

Mma Ramotswe was thoughtful. "Do you know many others from the hospital staff? From that time?"

"Many," said Mr Polopetsi.

Mma Ramotswe nodded. It had been a good idea, she decided, to bring Mr Polopetsi with her. Clovis Andersen, author of **The Principles of Private Detection,** said in one of his chapters that there was no substitute for local knowledge. **It cuts hours and days off an investigation,** he wrote. **Local knowledge is like gold.**

Mma Ramotswe glanced at her modest assistant. It was difficult to think of Mr Polopetsi in these golden terms; he was so mild and diffident. But Clovis Andersen was usually right about these things, and she muttered **gold** under her breath.

"What?" asked Mr Polopetsi.

"We have arrived," said Mma Ramotswe.

TATI MONYENA was clearly proud of his office, which was scrupulously clean and which exuded the smell of polish. In the centre of the room stood a large desk on which rested a telephone, three stacked letter trays, and a small wooden sign, facing out, on which was inscribed **Mr T. Monyena.** Against one wall stood two grey metal filing cabinets, considerably more modern than those in Mma Ramotswe's office, and on another wall, directly behind Tati Monyena's chair, was a large framed picture of His Excellency, the President of the Republic of Botswana.

Mma Ramotswe and Mr Polopetsi sat in the straight-backed chairs in front of the desk. It was a tight fit for Mma Ramotswe, and the chair-arm on each side pushed uncomfortably into her traditional waistline. Mr Polopetsi, though, barely filled his seat, and perched nervously on the edge of it, his hands clasped together on his lap.

"It is very good of you to come so quickly," said Tati Monyena. "We are at your disposal." He paused. He had made a magnanimous beginning, but he was not at all sure what he could do to help Mma Ramotswe. She would want to speak to people, he imagined, even though he had spoken to the ward nurses again and again, and had had several conversations with the doctors in question, in this very office;

conversations in which the doctors sat where Mma Ramotswe was sitting and defensively insisted that they had no idea how these patients had died.

"I should like to speak to the nurses," said Mma Ramotswe. "And I should like to see the ward too, if possible."

Tati Monyena's hand reached for the telephone. "I can arrange for both of those things, Mma. I shall show you the ward, and then we will bring the nurses back here so you can talk to them in this office. There are three of them who were there at the time."

Mma Ramotswe frowned. She did not wish to be rude, but it would not be a good idea to interview the nurses in front of Tati Monyena. "It might be better for me to see them by themselves," she said. "Just Mr Polopetsi here and myself. That's not to suggest . . ."

Tati Monyena raised a hand to stop her. "Of course, Mma! Of course. How tactless of me! You can speak to them in private. But I don't think they will say anything. When things go wrong, people become very careful. They forget what they have seen. They saw nothing. Nothing happened. It is always the same thing."

"That is human nature," interjected Mr Polopetsi. He had been silent until then, and they both looked at him intently.

"Of course it is," said Tati Monyena. "It is human nature to protect ourselves. We are no different from animals in that respect."

"Except that they can't tell lies," said Mr Polopetsi.

Tati Monyena laughed. "Of course. But that's only because they cannot speak. I think that if they could, then they would probably lie too. Would a dog own up if some meat had been stolen? Would it say, **I am the one who has eaten the meat?** I do not think so."

Mma Ramotswe wondered whether to join in this speculative conversation, but decided against it, and sat back until the two of them should finish. But Tati Monyena rose to his feet instead and gestured towards the door. "I shall take you to the ward," he said. "You will see the bed where these things happened."

They left his office and walked down a green-painted corridor. There was a hospital smell in the air, that mixture of humanity and disinfectant, and, in the background, the sound that seemed to go so well with that smell—voices somewhere, the sound of a child crying, the noise of wheels being pushed over uneven floors, the faint hum of machinery. There were posters on the wall: warnings about disease and the need to be careful; a picture of a blood spill. This, ultimately, was what our life was about, she thought, and hospitals were there to remind us: biology, human need, human suffering.

They passed a nurse in the corridor. She was carrying a pan of some sort, covered with a stained cloth, and she smiled and half-turned to let them pass. Mma Ramotswe kept her gaze studiously away from the pan and on the nurse's face. It was a kind face, the sort that one trusted, unlike, she imagined, the face of the doctor whom Mr Polopetsi had described.

"It's changed since your father was here," said Tati Monyena. "In those days we had to make do with so little. Now we have much more."

"But there is never enough, is there?" said Mr Polopetsi. "We get drugs for one illness and then a new illness comes along. Or a new type of the same thing. Same devil, different clothes. Look at TB."

Tati Monyena sighed. "That is true. I was talking to one of the doctors the other day and he said, **We thought that we had it cracked. We really did. And now . . .**"

But at least we can try, thought Mma Ramotswe. That is all we can do. We can try. And that, surely, is what doctors did. They did not throw up their hands and give up; they tried.

They turned a corner. A small boy, three or four years old, wearing only a vest, his tiny stomach protruding in a small mound, his eyes wide, stood in their way. The hospital was full of such children, the offspring of patients or patients themselves, and Tati Monyena barely saw him. But the child looked at Mma Ramotswe and came up to her and reached for her hand, as children will, especially in Africa, where they will still come to you. She bent down and lifted him up. He looked at her and snuggled his head against her chest.

"The mother of that one is late," said Tati Monyena in a matter-of-fact voice. "Our people are deciding what to do. The nurses are looking after him."

The child looked up at Mma Ramotswe. She saw that his eyes were shallow; there was no light in them. His skin, she felt, was dry.

Tati Monyena waited for her to put the

child down. Then he indicated towards a further corridor to the right. "It is this way," he said.

The ward doors were open. It was a long room, with six beds on either side. At the far end of the room, at a desk with several cabinets about it, a nurse was sitting, looking at a piece of paper with another nurse who was leaning over her shoulder. Halfway down the ward, another couple of nurses were adjusting the sheets on one of the beds, propping up the patient against a high bank of pillows. A drugs trolley stood unattended at the foot of another bed, an array of small containers on its top shelf.

When she saw them at the door, the nurse at the desk rose to her feet and walked down the ward to meet them. She nodded to Mma Ramotswe and Mr Polopetsi and then looked enquiringly at Tati Monyena.

"This lady is dealing with that . . . that matter," said Tati Monyena, nodding at the bed on his left. "I spoke to you about her." He turned to Mma Ramotswe. "This is Sister Batshegi."

Mma Ramotswe was watching the nurse's expression. She knew that the first moments were the significant ones, and that people gave away so much before they had time to think and to compose themselves. Sister Batshegi had looked down, not meeting Mma Ramotswe's gaze, and then had looked up again. Did that mean anything? Mma Ramotswe thought that it meant that she was not particularly pleased to see her. But that in itself did not tell her very much. People who are busy with some task—as Sister Batshegi clearly had been—were not always pleased to be disturbed.

"I am happy to see you, Mma," said Sister Batshegi.

Mma Ramotswe replied to the greeting and then turned to Tati Monyena. "That is the bed, Rra?"

"It is." He looked at Sister Batshegi. "Have you had anybody in it over the last few days?"

The nurse shook her head. "There has been nobody. The last patient was that man last week—the one who had the motorcycle accident near Pilane. He got better quickly." She turned to Mma Ramotswe. "Every time I see a motorcyle, Mma, I think of the young men we get in here . . ." She shrugged. "But they never think of that. They don't."

"Young men often don't think," said Mma

Ramotswe. "They cannot help it. That is how they are." She thought of the apprentices, and reflected on what a good illustration they were of the proposition she had just made. But they would start to think sooner or later, she told herself; even Charlie would start to think. She looked at the bed, covered in its neat white sheet. Although the sheet was clean, there were brown stains on it, the stains of blood that the hospital laundry could not remove. At the top of the bed, to the side, she saw a machine with tubes and dials on a stand.

"That is a ventilator," said Tati Monyena. "It helps people to breathe. All three patients . . ." He paused, and looked at Sister Batshegi, as if for confirmation. "All three patients were on it at the time. But the machine was thoroughly checked and there was nothing wrong with it."

Sister Batshegi nodded. "The machine was working. And we checked the alarm. It has a battery, which was working fine. If the machine had been faulty we would have known."

"So you can rule out a defective ventilator," said Tati Monyena. "That is not what caused it."

Sister Batshegi was vigorously of the same

mind. "No. It is not that. That is not what happened."

Mma Ramotswe looked about her. One of the patients at the end of the ward was calling out, a cracked, unhappy voice. A nurse went over to the bed quickly.

"I have to get on with my work," said Sister Batshegi. "You may look round, Mma, but you will find nothing. There is nothing to see in this place. It is just a ward. That is all."

MMA RAMOTSWE and Mr Polopetsi spoke to Sister Batshegi again, along with two other nurses, in Tati Monyena's office. He had left them alone, as he had promised, but through the window they saw him hovering around anxiously in the courtyard outside, looking at his watch and fiddling with a line of pens that he had clipped in his shirt pocket. Sister Batshegi said little more than she had said in the ward, and the other two nurses, both of whom had been on duty at the time of the incidents, seemed very unwilling to say much at all. The deaths had been a surprise, they said, but they often lost very ill patients. Neither had been nearby at the time, they said, although they were quick to point out that they were both keeping a close watch on the patients involved. "If anything had happened, we would have known it," said one of the nurses. "It is not our fault, you see, Mma. It is just not our fault."

It did not take long to interview them, and then Mma Ramotswe and Mr Polopetsi were alone in the office before Tati Monyena came back.

"Those nurses were scared about something," said Mr Polopetsi. "Did you see the way they looked? Did you hear it in their voices?"

Mma Ramotswe had to agree. "But what are they scared of?" she asked.

Mr Polopetsi thought for a moment. "They are scared of some person," he said. "Some unknown person is frightening them."

"Sister Batshegi?"

"No. Not her."

"Then who else is there? Tati Monyena?"

Mr Polopetsi did not think this likely. "I think that he is somebody who would protect his staff rather than punish them," he said. "Tati Monyena is a kind man."

"Well, I don't know what to think," said

Mma Ramotswe. "But it's time for us to leave anyway. I don't think that there is anything more we can do here."

They drove back to Gaborone. They spoke to each other on the journey, but not about the visit to the hospital, as neither had much to say about that. Mr Polopetsi told Mma Ramotswe about one of his sons, who was turning out to be very good at mental arithmetic. "He is like a calculator," he said. "He is already doing calculations that I cannot do, and he is only eight."

"You must be very proud of him," said Mma Ramotswe.

Mr Polopetsi beamed with pleasure. "I am, Mma," he said. "He is the most precious thing I have in this world." He seemed about to say something else, but stopped. He looked at Mma Ramotswe hesitantly, and she knew that he was about to make a request. It will be for money, she thought. There will be school fees to be paid, or shoes to be bought for this boy, or even a blanket; children needed all these things, all the time.

"He needs a godmother," said Mr Polopetsi. "He had a godmother, and now she is late. He needs a new one."

There was only one answer Mma Ramotswe could give. "Yes," she said. "I will do that, Rra."

There would be birthdays from now on, as well as shoes and school fees and so forth. But we cannot always choose whose lives will become entangled with our own; these things happen to us, come to us uninvited, and Mma Ramotswe understood that well. And just as she had not chosen Mr Polopetsi's son, she reflected, so too had the boy not chosen her.

CHAPTER FIVE

RESIGNATION SHOES

MMA MAKUTSI was eager for a report the next day. She would have preferred to have gone to Mochudi in the place of Mr Polopetsi, who she thought would not have been likely to add very much to the investigation. But she was cautious about giving offence to Mma Ramotswe after the misunderstandings of the previous day, and she kept those feelings to herself. In fact, she went further than that and told Mma Ramotswe what a good idea it had been to take Mr Polopetsi. "If you're a woman, sometimes people don't take you seriously enough," she said. "That is when it is useful to have a man around."

Mma Ramotswe was non-committal about that. Men were learning, she thought, and a great deal had changed. Mma Makutsi, perhaps, was fighting battles which had already been largely won, at least in the towns. It was different in the villages, of course, where men still thought that they could do what they liked. But she was thinking of other things: she had been pondering Mr J.L.B. Matekoni's planned investigation and was wondering whether she could discreetly suggest that Mma Makutsi assist him. She could try that, certainly, but she was not sure whether he would welcome it; in fact, she was sure that he would not. Mr J.L.B. Matekoni might not be the most assertive of men, but there were sensitivities there that surfaced from time to time.

"Be that as it may," she said to Mma Makutsi, as they began to attend to the morning mail. "There was not very much that we could find out at the hospital. I saw the ward where it happened. I spoke to the nurses, who said almost nothing. And that was it."

Mma Makutsi thought for a moment. "And what can you do now?" she asked.

It was difficult for Mma Ramotswe to answer that. She very rarely gave up on a case, as solutions had a habit of cropping up as long as one was patient. But it was difficult at any particular point to say what would happen next. "I shall wait," she said. "There is no special hurry, Mma. I shall wait and see what happens."

"Well, I don't see what can possibly happen," said Mma Makutsi. "These things don't solve themselves, you know."

Mma Ramotswe bit her lip and turned to the letter she had just opened. It was a letter of thanks from the parents of a young man whom she had eventually located in Francistown. There had been a family row and he had gone missing, leaving no address. There had been a girlfriend, about whom the parents knew nothing, and the young woman had eventually confided to Mma Ramotswe that he was in Francistown, although she was not sure exactly where. So Mma Ramotswe had quizzed her about his interests, which, she revealed, included jazz. From that it was a simple step to enquire of the only place in Francistown where jazz was played. Yes, they knew of him, and yes he would be playing the following evening. Would she like to come? She would not, but the young man's parents did, and they were reunited with their son. He had wanted to contact them, but was too proud; the fact that his parents had come all the way from Gaborone meant that honour was satisfied. Everybody forgave one another and started again, which, Mma Ramotswe reflected, is how many of the world's problems might be solved. We should forgive one another and start all over again. But what if those who needed to be forgiven hung on to the things that they had wrongly acquired: What then? That, she decided, was a matter that would require further thought.

"It is so easy to thank people," said Mma Ramotswe, passing the letter over to Mma Makutsi. "And most people don't bother to do it. They don't thank the person who does something for them. They just take it for granted."

Mma Makutsi looked out of the window. Mma Ramotswe had done her plenty of favours in the past, and she had never written to thank her. Could the remark be aimed at her? Could Mma Ramotswe have been harbouring a grudge, as people did, sometimes for years and years? She looked at her employer and decided that this was unlikely. Mma Ramotswe could not harbour a grudge **convincingly;** she would start to laugh, or offer the object of her grudge a cup of tea, or do something which indicated that the grudge was not real.

Mma Makutsi read the letter. "Where shall I file this, Mma?" she asked. "We do not have a file for letters of thanks. We have a file for letters of complaint, of course. Should it go there?"

Mma Ramotswe did not think this a good idea. They could open a new file, but their filing cabinets were already overcrowded and she did not think it would be worthwhile opening a file which might never contain another letter. "We can throw it away now," she said.

Mma Makutsi frowned. "At the Botswana Secretarial College we were taught never to throw anything away for at least a week," she said. "There might always be some follow-up."

"There will be no follow-up to a letter of thanks," said Mma Ramotswe. "That is it. There will be no more. That case is closed."

With a slow show of reluctance, Mma Makutsi held the letter over the bin and dropped it in. As she did so, the door of the office opened and Charlie, the older of the two apprentices, walked in. He had removed his work overalls to reveal a pair of jeans and a tee-shirt underneath. The tee-shirt, Mma Ramotswe noticed, had a picture of a jet aircraft on it

and the slogan underneath in large letters:
HIGH FLIER.

Mma Makutsi looked at him. "Finishing
work early today?" she asked. "Ten o'clock
in the morning? You're a quick worker,
Charlie!"

The young man ignored this comment as he
sauntered over to Mma Ramotswe's desk.
"Mma Ramotswe," he said. "You've always
been kind to me." He paused, casting a glance
over his shoulder in the direction of Mma
Makutsi. "Now I've come to say goodbye. I'm
finishing work here soon. I'm going. I've come
to say goodbye."

Mma Ramotswe stared at Charlie in astonishment. "But you haven't finished your . . .
your . . ."

"Apprenticeship," supplied Mma Makutsi
from the other side of the room. "You silly boy!
You can't leave before you've finished that."

Charlie did not react to this. He continued
to look at Mma Ramotswe. "I haven't finished
my apprenticeship—I know that," he said.
"But you only need to finish your apprenticeship if you want to be a mechanic. Who said I
want to be a mechanic?"

"You did!" shouted Mma Makutsi. "When you signed your apprenticeship contract, you said that you wanted to be a mechanic. That's what those contracts say, you know."

Mma Ramotswe raised a hand in a calming gesture. "You needn't shout at him, Mma," she said quietly. "He is going to explain, aren't you, Charlie?"

"I'm not deaf, you know," said Charlie over his shoulder. "And I wasn't talking to you anyway. There are two ladies in this room—Mma Ramotswe and . . . and another one. I was talking to Mma Ramotswe." He turned back to face Mma Ramotswe. "I'm going to do another job, Mma. I am going into business."

"Business!" chuckled Mma Makutsi. "You'll be needing a secretary soon, I suppose."

"And don't bother to apply for that job, Mma," Charlie snapped. "Seventy-nine per cent or not, I would never give you a job. I'm not mad, you see."

"Ninety-seven per cent!" shouted Mma Makutsi. "See! You can't even get your figures right. Some profit you'll make!"

"Please do not shout at each other," said Mma Ramotswe. "Shouting achieves nothing. It just makes the person doing the shouting hoarse and the person being shouted at cross. That is all it does."

"I was not shouting," said Charlie. "Somebody else was doing the shouting. Somebody with big round glasses. Not me."

Mma Ramotswe sighed. It was Mma Makutsi's fault, this feeling between the two of them. She was older than Charlie and might have turned a blind eye to the young man's faults; she might have encouraged him to be a bit better than he was; she might have understood that young men are like this and that one has to be tolerant.

"Tell me about this business, Charlie," she said gently. "What is it?"

Charlie sat down on the chair in front of Mma Ramotswe. Then he leaned forward, his arms resting on the surface of her desk. "Mr J.L.B. Matekoni has sold me a car," he said, his voice barely above a whisper, so that Mma Makutsi might not hear. "It is an old Mercedes-Benz. An E220. The owner has a new one, a C-Class, and since this one has such a large mileage on it he sold it to the boss for very little. Twenty thousand pula. Now the boss has sold it to me."

"And?" coaxed Mma Ramotswe. She had

seen the Mercedes in the garage and had noticed that it had been parked at the side of the
building for over two weeks. She assumed that
they were waiting for some part that had been
ordered from South Africa. Now she knew that
there were other plans for the car.

"And I am going to start a taxi service," said
Charlie. "I am going to start a business called
the No. 1 Ladies' Taxi Service."

There was a gasp from the other side of the
room. "You can't do that! That name belongs to
Mma Ramotswe."

Mma Ramotswe, taken aback, simply stared
at Charlie. Then she gathered her thoughts.
The name that he had chosen was certainly de-
rivative, but was there anything wrong with
that? In one view, it was a compliment to have
a name one had invented being used by somebody else. The only difficulty would be if the
name were to be used by a similar business—by
a detective agency that wanted to take clients
away from them. A taxi company and a detective agency were two very different things, and
there would be no prospect of competition between them.

"I don't mind," she said to Charlie. "But
tell me: Why have you chosen that name?

You'll be driving the car—where do the ladies come into it?"

Charlie, who had been tense under Mma Makutsi's onslaught, now visibly relaxed. "The ladies will be in the back of the car."

Mma Ramotswe raised an eyebrow. "And?"

"And I will be in the front, driving," he said. "The selling point will be that this is a taxi that is safe for ladies. Ladies will be able to get in without any fear that they will find some bad man in the driver's seat—a man who might not be safe with ladies. There are such taxi drivers, Mma."

For a minute or so nobody spoke. Mma Ramotswe was aware of the sound of Charlie's breathing, which was shallow, from excitement. We must remember, she thought, what it is like to be young and enthusiastic, to have a plan, a dream. There was always a danger that as we went on in life we forgot about that; caution—even fear—replaced optimism and courage. When you were young, like Charlie, you believed that you could do anything, and, in some circumstances at least, you could.

Why should Charlie's taxi firm not succeed? She remembered a conversation with her friend Bernard Ditau, who had been a bank manager.

"There are so many people who could run their own businesses," he had said, "but they let people tell them it won't work. So they give up before they start."

Bernard had encouraged her to start the No. 1 Ladies' Detective Agency when others had merely laughed and said that it would be the quickest way of losing the money that Obed Ramotswe had left her. "He worked all those years, your Daddy, and now you're going to lose everything he got in two or three months," somebody had said. That remark had almost persuaded her to drop the idea, but Bernard had urged her on. "What if he hadn't bought all those good fat cattle?" he asked. "What if he had been too timid to do that and had left the money to sit gathering dust?"

Now she was sitting, in a sense, in Bernard's place. There was little doubt but that Mma Makutsi would be only too ready to throw cold water over Charlie's plan, but she decided that she would not do this.

"I will tell all my friends to use your taxi," she said. "I am sure you will be very busy."

Charlie beamed with pleasure. "I will give them a discount," he said. "Ten per cent off for anybody who knows Mma Ramotswe."

Mma Ramotswe smiled. "That is very kind of you," she said. "But that is not the way to run a business. You will need every pula you can make."

"If you make any, that is," muttered Mma Makutsi.

Mma Ramotswe threw a disapproving glance in Mma Makutsi's direction. "I am sure he will," she said. "I am sure of that."

After Charlie had left the office, Mma Ramotswe fiddled for a moment with a small pile of papers on her desk. She looked across the room at Mma Makutsi, who was studiously avoiding looking at her, and was paging through her shorthand notebook as if it contained some important hidden secret. "Mma Makutsi," she said, "I really need to talk to you."

Mma Makutsi continued to leaf through the notebook. "I am here," she said. "I am listening, Mma."

Mma Ramotswe felt her heart beating within her. I am not very good at this sort of thing, she told herself. "That young man," she said, "is just the same as any young man. He has his dreams, as we all did when we were his age. Even you, Mma Makutsi. Even you. You went to the Botswana Secretarial College—you sacrificed so much for that—your people up in Bobonong sacrificed too. You wanted to make something of yourself, and you did." She paused. Mma Makutsi was sitting quite still, no longer looking through the notebook, which she had laid down on the desk.

"Now everything has turned out well for you," Mma Ramotswe went on. "You have your house. You have that fiancé of yours. You will have money when you marry him. But don't forget that there are many others who still don't have what you now have. Don't forget that."

"I don't see what this has to do with anything," Mma Makutsi interjected. "I was merely pointing out what is very clear, Mma. That boy's business will fail because he is no good. Anybody can see that he is no good."

"No!" said Mma Ramotswe firmly. "You cannot say that he is no good! You cannot say that."

"Yes, I can," said Mma Makutsi. "I can say that because it's the truth, Mma. Your trouble . . ." She paused. "Your trouble, Mma, is that you're too kind. You let those boys get away with all sorts of things just because you're too kind. Well, I'm a realist. I see things as they really are."

"Oh," said Mma Ramotswe. And then she said again, "Oh."

"Yes," said Mma Makutsi. "And now, Mma, I shall resign. I do not have to work here and I have decided that it is time to resign. Thank you for everything you have done for me. I hope that you find the filing system is easy to use. You will find everything in the right place when I am gone."

And with that she rose to her feet and began to walk to the door. She stopped, though, and returned to her desk, where she opened a drawer and began to survey its contents. Mma Ramotswe noticed that she was wearing new shoes: burgundy suede shoes with bows on the toe caps. They were not the shoes of a modest person, she thought. They were . . . and then the description came to her. They were resignation shoes.

CHAPTER SIX

GO IN PEACE; STAY IN PEACE

MR J.L.B. MATEKONI had seen crises before. Usually these involved mechanical matters—distraught owners feeling desperate about cars which were needed for some important occasion; the non-arrival of spare parts; the eventual arrival of spare parts, but the wrong ones—there were many ways in which difficult situations could arise in a garage, but he had found that the best response to these was the same in every case. He would sit down and consider the situation carefully. Not only did this help to identify the solution to the problem, but it also gave him the opportunity to remind himself that things were not really as bad as they seemed; it was all a question of perspective. Sitting down and looking up at the sky for a few minutes—not at any particular part of the sky, but just at the sky in general— at the vast, dizzying, empty sky of Botswana, cut human problems down to size. It was not possible to tell what was in that sky, of course, at least during the day; but at night it revealed itself to be an ocean of stars, limitless, white in its infinity; so large, so large, that any of our problems, even the greatest of them, was a small thing. And yet we did not look at it like that, Mr J.L.B. Matekoni thought, and that made us imagine that a blocked fuel feed was a disaster.

He had not wanted Charlie to hand in his resignation, but when the apprentice had asked him about the possibility of using that car as a taxi, he had resisted the temptation to refuse him point-blank. That at least would have solved the problem in the short term. It would have put an end to his immediate plans to start a taxi service, but it would not have scotched the young man's hopes. So he had agreed to the proposition and had watched Charlie's face light up. Mr J.L.B. Matekoni had his reservations about the feasibility of the idea; there was scant profit to be made from taxis unless one over-charged—which some taxi drivers did—or drove too quickly—which all taxi drivers did. Charlie now had his driving licence, but Mr J.L.B. Matekoni had little confidence in his driving ability and had once stopped him and taken over when they were travelling together to pick up a consignment of parts and he had let Charlie take the wheel of the truck.

"We are not in a hurry," he said. "Those parts are not going anywhere. And there are no girls to impress."

The apprentice had sat in the passenger seat, shoulders hunched. He had been silent.

"I'm sorry to have to tell you off," said Mr J.L.B. Matekoni. "But that is my job. I have to advise you. That is what an apprentice-master has to do."

That conversation came back to him now. If he were really serious about his duties, he would have warned Charlie of the folly of not completing his training. He would have spelled out to him the risks of starting one's own business; he would have told him about cash-flow problems and the difficulty of getting credit. Then he would have gone on to warn him about bad debts, which presumably even taxi drivers encountered when people fled the car without paying or when, at the end of a journey, they confessed they did not have quite enough money to pay the fare and would five pula do?

He had done none of this, he reflected; he had said nothing. But his failure, and Charlie's departure, were not the end of the world. If the taxi service did not work, then Charlie could always come back, as he had done the last time he had given up his apprenticeship. That had been when he had gone off with that married woman and had come back, his tail between his legs, when that affair had come to its predictable end. That showed how these young men worked, he thought. They bounced back.

Mma Makutsi's departure, however, was a more serious matter altogether. Mma Makutsi resigned shortly before tea-time, when he and Mr Polopetsi came into the office, their mugs in their hands, expecting to find the tea already brewed. Instead they found Mma Ramotswe sitting at her desk, her head sunk in her hands, while Mma Makutsi was putting the contents of a drawer into a large plastic bag. Mma Makutsi looked up as the men entered the room.

"I have not made tea yet," she said. "You will need to put the kettle on yourselves."

Mr Polopetsi glanced at Mr J.L.B. Mate-koni; he stood in some awe of Mma Makutsi, and he was wary of her moods. "She is a changeable person," he had explained to his wife. "She is very clever, but she is changeable. One moment it's this; the next moment, it's that. You have to be very careful."

Mr J.L.B. Matekoni glanced at Mma Ramo-tswe, but she, looking up, merely nodded in the direction of the kettle.

Mma Makutsi continued to busy herself with her task of emptying the drawer. "The reason why I did not put on the kettle is that I have resigned."

Mr Polopetsi gave a start. "From making tea?"

"From everything," snapped Mma Ma-kutsi. "So I suspect that you will be doing more investigating, Rra, now that I am going. I hope that Mr J.L.B. Matekoni will be able to release you from your duties in the garage."

The effect on Mr Polopetsi of this remark was immediate. If he had wished to conceal his eagerness to occupy Mma Makutsi's position, then this wish was overcome by his sheer and evident pleasure at the thought of doing more investigative work. And Mma Makutsi, sensing this, decided to take the matter further. "In fact," she went on, slamming the drawer shut, "why don't you take over my desk right now? Here, try this chair. You can put it up a bit by turning this bit here. See. That is for short people like you, Rra."

Mr Polopetsi put his mug down on Mma Makutsi's desk and moved over to examine the chair. "That will be fine," he said. "I can adjust it. It looks as if it needs a bit of oil, but we have plenty of that in the garage, don't we, Mr J.L.B. Matekoni?"

It was meant to be a joke, and Mr J.L.B. Matekoni smiled weakly, and dutifully. He glanced again at Mma Ramotswe, who was now glaring at her assistant on the other side of the room. It seemed to Mr J.L.B. Matekoni that the most tactful thing to do would be to leave the office, and he turned to Mr Polopetsi. "I think that we should have tea a bit later, Rra," he said. "The ladies are busy."

"But Mma Makutsi . . . ," Mr Polopetsi began, but was silenced by a stare from Mr J.L.B. Matekoni, who had already started to move towards the door. Picking up his mug, Mr Polopetsi followed him out of the door and back into the garage.

Mma Ramotswe waited until the door had

been closed before she addressed Mma Makutsi. "I am very sorry," she said. "I am very sorry if I have offended you, Mma Makutsi. You know that I have a lot of respect for you. You know that, don't you? I would never deliberately be rude to you. I really would not."

Mma Makutsi, who had risen to her feet as the two men left, was reaching down for her bag. She straightened up and hesitated for a few moments before she spoke. It seemed as if she was looking for exactly the right words. "I am aware of that, Mma," she said slowly. "I know that. And I am the one who has been rude. But I have made up my mind. I have decided that I am fed up with being number two. I have always been number two, all through my life. I have always been the junior one. Now I am going to be my own boss." She paused. "It's not that you are a bad boss. You are a very good one. You are kind. You do not tell me what to do all the time. But I want to be able to speak as I wish. I have never been able to do that— ever. All my life, up in Bobonong, down here, I have been the one who has to watch my tongue and be careful. Now I do not want that any more. Can you understand that, Mma?"

Mma Ramotswe did. "I can see that. You are

a very intelligent woman. You have a piece of paper to prove it." She pointed to the framed diploma above Mma Makutsi's desk; the words **ninety-seven per cent** clearly legible even from afar. "Don't forget to take that, Mma," she said.

Mma Makutsi looked up at the diploma. "You could easily have got one of those yourself, Mma," she said.

"But I didn't," said Mma Ramotswe. "You did."

There was silence for a moment.

"Do you want me to stay?" asked Mma Makutsi. There was an edge of uncertainty in her voice now.

Mma Ramotswe opened her hands in a gesture of acceptance. "I don't think that you should, Mma," she said. "You need a change. I would love you to stay, but I think that you have decided, haven't you, that you need a change."

"Maybe," said Mma Makutsi.

"But you will come back and see me, won't you?"

"Of course," said Mma Makutsi. "And you will come to my wedding, won't you? You and Mr J.L.B. Matekoni? There will be a seat for you in the front row, Mma Ramotswe. With the aunties."

There was nothing more to do other than to retrieve the framed diploma from its place on the wall. When it was taken down, there was a white patch where it had been hanging, and they both saw this. Mma Makutsi had been there that long; right from the beginning, really, those humble days in the original office, when chickens came in, uninvited, and pecked at the floor around the desks.

Their words of farewell were polite—the correct ones, as laid down in the old Botswana customs. Tsamaya sentlê: go well. To which the reply was, Sala sentlê: stay well; mere words, of course, but when meant, as now, so powerful. Mma Ramotswe could tell that Mma Makutsi was regretting her decision and did not want to go. It would have been easy to stop this now, to suggest that while Mma Makutsi was replacing the diploma, she, Mma Ramotswe, would start to make the tea. But somehow it seemed too late for that. Sometimes one knew, as Mma Makutsi clearly did, when it was necessary to move on to the next stage of one's life. When this happened, it was not helpful for others to hold one back. So she allowed Mma Makutsi to leave, did nothing to stop her, and it was not until she had been gone for ten minutes or so that Mma Ramotswe began to weep. She wept for the loss of her friend and colleague, but also for everything else that she had lost in this life, and of which, unexpectedly, she was now by a flood of memories reminded: for her father, that great man, Obed Ramotswe, now late; for the child she had known for such a short time, such a precious time; for Seretse Khama, who had been a father to the entire country and who had made it one of the finest places on this earth; for her childhood. She wanted everything back, as we do sometimes in our irrationality and regret; we want it all back.

CHAPTER SEVEN

HOW DOES ONE BECOME MORE EXCITING?

IF I CAN FIX A CAR, Mr J.L.B. Matekoni told himself, then I can do a simple thing like find out whether a man is seeing a woman. And yet, now that he came to start the enquiry, he was not sure whether it would be quite as straightforward as he had imagined it would be. He could have asked Mma Ramotswe's advice, but she was preoccupied with the consequences of Mma Makutsi's departure and he did not want to add to her burdens. As far as the garage was concerned, Charlie still had to work a week's notice—he had spared him a longer period than that, although he would have been entitled to insist on a month. Fortunately, since it was a relatively quiet period—the school holidays, when people tended not to find fault with their cars and when thoughts of routine servicing were put aside—it would be easy for Mr J.L.B. Matekoni to take a few hours off every day, should the need arise. The younger apprentice was slightly more reliable than Charlie anyway, and could now cope with many routine garage tasks, and Mr Polopetsi was also showing himself to be a natural mechanic. Of course he had aspirations to Mma Makutsi's job, but Mr J.L.B. Matekoni doubted whether these ambitions would be satisfied. Mma Makutsi had done a lot of filing and typing, and he could not see Mr Polopetsi settling down to these mundane tasks. He wanted to be out and about, looking into things, and what Mma Ramotswe had said about his talents in this respect suggested that she might not be keen for him to do too much of that.

It was all very well being confident, but as you climbed the outside staircase of the President Hotel, on your way to meet the client for your first proper conversation with her, then you felt a certain anxiety. It was not dissimilar to the way you felt when, as an apprentice, you stripped an engine down by yourself for the very first time, decoked it and fitted new piston rings. Would everything fit together again?

Would it work? He looked over his shoulder at the scene in the square below. Traders had set up stalls, no more than upturned boxes in many cases, or rugs laid out on the concrete paving, and were selling their wares to passers-by: combs, hair preparations, trinkets, carvings for visitors. In one corner, a small knot of people clustered around a seller of traditional medicines, listening carefully as the gnarled herbalist explained to them the merits of the barks and roots that he had ranged in front of him. He at least knew what he was talking about, thought Mr J.L.B. Matekoni; he at least was doing what he had always done, and doing it well, unlike those who suddenly decide, in mid-life, that they want to become private detectives . . .

He reached the top of the stairway and entered under the cool canopies of the hotel's verandah. He looked about him; only a few of the tables were occupied, and he saw Mma Botumile immediately, sitting at the far end, a cup of coffee before her. He stood still for a moment and took a deep breath. She looked up and saw him and gestured to the empty chair at her table.

"I have been waiting, Rra," she said, looking at her watch. "You said . . ."

Mr J.L.B. Matekoni consulted his own watch. He had made a point of being on time and had not expected to be censured for lateness. She had said eleven o'clock, had she not? He felt a pang of doubt.

"Ten forty-five," she said. "You said ten forty-five."

He was flustered. "I thought I said eleven. I am sorry, Mma. I thought . . ."

She brushed aside his apology. "It does not matter," she said. "Where is Mma Ramotswe?"

"She is in the office," he said. "She has assigned me to this case."

Mma Botumile, who had been lifting her cup of coffee to her lips, put it down sharply. A small splash of coffee spilled over the rim of the cup and fell on the table. "Why is she not dealing with this?" she asked coldly. "Does she think that I am not important enough for her? Is that it? Well, there are other detectives, I'll have you know."

"There aren't," said Mr J.L.B. Matekoni politely. "The No. 1 Ladies' Detective Agency is the only agency. There are no other detectives that I know of."

Mma Botumile digested this information. She looked Mr J.L.B. Matekoni up and down before she spoke again. "I thought that you were the mechanic."

"I am," he said. "But I also do investigations." He thought for a few moments. "It is useful to have an ordinary occupation while at the same time you conduct enquiries." He had no idea why this should be so, but it seemed to him to be a reasonable thing to say.

Mma Botumile lifted up her coffee cup again. "Do you know my husband?" she asked.

Mr J.L.B. Matekoni shook his head. "You must tell me about him," he said. "That is why I wanted to meet you today. I need to know something more about him before I can find out what he is doing."

A waitress came to the table and looked expectantly at Mr J.L.B. Matekoni. He had not thought about what he would have, but now he felt that tea would be the right thing on a morning like this, which was getting hotter—you could feel it. He was about to order when Mma Botumile waved the waitress away. "We don't need anything," she said.

He watched in astonishment as the waitress walked off. "I thought that I . . . ," he began.

"No time," said Mma Botumile. "This is business, remember. I am paying for your time,

I take it. Two hundred pula an hour, or something like that?"

Mr J.L.B. Matekoni did not know what to say. There would be a fee, of course, but he had not thought about what it would be. He was accustomed to charging for mechanical work and he imagined that each case would have its mechanical equivalent. Finding out about an errant husband would be the equivalent perhaps of a full service, with oil change and attention to brakes. A more complex enquiry might be charged at the same rate as the replacement of a timing chain. He had not worked any of this out, but he would certainly not be charging two hundred pula an hour to sit and talk on the verandah of the President Hotel.

Mr J.L.B. Matekoni was a tolerant man, not given to animosity of any sort, but as he gazed at Mma Botumile he found himself developing a strong dislike for her. But he knew too that this was dangerous; he knew that as a professional person he should keep personal feelings strictly out of the picture. He had heard Mma Ramotswe talk about this before, and he had agreed with her. One simply could not allow one's feelings to get in the way of one's judgement. It was exactly the same with cars: emotion should not come into decisions about a car's future, no matter what the bonds between the car and the owner. But then there was Mma Ramotswe's tiny white van; if ever there were a case for not allowing emotion to cloud one's view of a vehicle, then that was it. He had nursed and cajoled that vehicle when good sense suggested that it should be replaced by something more modern, but Mma Ramotswe would have none of that. "I cannot see myself in a new car," she said. "I am a tiny white van person. That is what I want."

He lowered his gaze; Mma Botumile was staring back at him and he felt uncomfortable. "You must tell me about your husband," he said. "I must know the sort of things that he likes to do."

Mma Botumile settled back in her chair. "My husband is not a very strong man," she said. "He is one of those men who does not really know what he wants. I can tell, of course, what he wants, but he cannot." She looked at Mr J.L.B. Matekoni as if expecting a challenge to this, but when none came she continued. "We have been married for twenty years now, which is a long time. We met when we were both students at the University of Botswana. I

am a B.Com., you see. He is an accountant
with a mining company.

"We built a house out over near the Western
by-pass, near where the Grand Palm Hotel is. It
is a very fine house—you may have seen it from
the road, Rra. It has gates which go like this—
large gates. You know the place?"

Mr J.L.B. Matekoni did, and he had often
wondered who would build gates like those;
now he knew.

He nodded and waited for her to continue,
but she was silent, watching him over the rim
of her coffee cup.

"And was this marriage a happy one?" he
asked finally. He found that the question came
out in those words without his really having to
think very much about it. Where had it come
from? He suddenly remembered: years before,
he had been in the High Court in Lobatse,
waiting to give evidence in a case involving a
road accident, and he had slipped into one of
the courts to watch a case. He remembered the
lawyer standing at his table, facing a woman
who was sitting in the witness box, crying. And
the lawyer suddenly spoke and said to her:
"And was this marriage a happy one?" and the
woman had started to cry all the more. What a

ridiculous question, he had thought; what a ridiculous question to ask of a woman who was in floods of tears. Of course the marriage was not a happy one. But the question itself had sounded so impressive, that he had remembered it, little thinking that years later he would be able to use those precise words.

Unlike the witness, Mma Botumile did not burst into tears. "Of course it was happy," she said. "And still is. Or rather, could be, if he stopped seeing that other woman."

"Have you spoken to him about her?" Mr J.L.B. Matekoni asked.

Mma Botumile was dismissive. "Of course not! And, anyway, what could I say? I know nothing about this woman, whoever she is. That is for you to find out."

Mr J.L.B. Matekoni pondered this for a moment. "But you do know that he's seeing a woman, do you?" he asked.

"Oh, I know that all right," said Mma Botumile. "Women know these things."

Intuition, thought Mr J.L.B. Matekoni. That's what women claimed they had and men did not, or did not have enough of: intuition. He had often wondered, though, how one could know something without actually hearing it, or seeing it, or even smelling it. If one did not acquire knowledge from one's senses, then where would one acquire it? That's what he would have liked to ask Mma Botumile, but felt that he could not. She was not a woman, he felt, who would take well to being challenged.

"I see," he said mildly. "But, do you mind telling me how women know these things? I'm sure they do know them, but how come?"

For the first time in the course of their meeting, Mma Botumile smiled. "It's easier to talk to another woman about these matters," she said. "But since your Mma Ramotswe is so busy, I suppose that I shall have to talk to you, Rra."

Mr J.L.B. Matekoni waited.

Mma Botumile lowered her voice. "Men make certain demands of ladies," she said. "And if they stop, then it's a very good sign. Any woman knows that."

Mr J.L.B. Matekoni caught his breath.

There was a glint of amusement in Mma Botumile's eye. "Yes," she said. "That is always a sign that the man has another friend."

Mr J.L.B. Matekoni did not know what to say. He looked down at the table, and then at the floor. Somebody had spilled some sugar from the table, a small line of white grains, and

he noticed that a troop of ants, marshalled with
military precision, had arrived to carry them
off, minuscule porters staggering under the
weight of their trophies.

"So that is what you need to find out, Rra,"
said Mma Botumile, signalling to the waitress
to bring her bill. "You will have to follow him
and find out who this lady is. I can give you no
help about that—that is why I have asked you.
That is why you are being paid two hundred
pula an hour."

"I'm not," muttered Mr J.L.B. Matekoni.

HE LEFT THE PRESIDENT HOTEL uncertain what to do and unsure, he now realised,
whether he wanted to carry out this investigation at all. The meeting with Mma Botumile
had not been a satisfactory one. She had given
him no guidance as to where he might start
looking for her husband's girlfriend, and the
only suggestion that she had made was that Mr
J.L.B. Matekoni might follow him after work
one day and see where he went. "He certainly
doesn't come home straightaway," she said.
"He says that he's seeing clients, but I don't believe that, do you?" Mr J.L.B. Matekoni mut-

tered something which could have been yes or equally could have been no. He did not like being expected to take sides like this, and yet, he told himself, this is what must be expected of people like private detectives, or lawyers, for that matter. People paid them to take their side, and this meant that you had to believe in what the client wanted. The thought made him feel very uncomfortable. What if you were to be hired by somebody whom you could not bear, or if you found out that the person who had engaged you was lying? Would you have to pretend that you believed the lies—which would be impossible, thought Mr J.L.B. Matekoni— or could you tell them that you would have no truck with their falsehoods?

And then another thought struck Mr J.L.B. Matekoni as he made his way down the steps of the President Hotel. He had never met Mma Botumile's husband and he had no idea what he was like. But it occurred to him, nonetheless, that when he eventually met him—if he eventually met him—he would probably feel sorry for him and end up rather liking him. If he were to be married to Mma Botumile, whom he considered both rude and bossy, then would he not himself seek comfort elsewhere, in the arms of a good, sympathetic woman—somebody like Mma Ramotswe in fact? Of course Mma Ramotswe would never look at another man—Mr J.L.B. Matekoni knew that. He stopped. It had never once crossed his mind that Mma Ramotswe might take up with somebody else, but then many people who were let down in this way by their spouses never thought that this would happen to them, and yet it did. So there were many people who deluded themselves.

It was a very unwelcome thought, and Mr J.L.B. Matekoni felt himself becoming hot and uncomfortable as he stood there in front of the President Hotel, thinking the unthinkable. He saw himself coming home one evening and discovering a man's tie, perhaps, draped over a chair. He saw himself picking up the tie, examining it, and then dangling it in front of Mma Ramotswe and saying, **How could you, Mma Ramotswe? How could you?** And she would look anywhere but in his eyes and say, **Well, Mr J.L.B. Matekoni, it's not as if you have been a very exciting husband, you know.** It was ridiculous. Mma Ramotswe would never say a thing like that; he had done his best to be a good husband to her. He had never strayed, and he had helped around the house as modern husbands are meant to do. In fact, he had done everything in his power to be modern, even when that had not been particularly easy.

Suddenly Mr J.L.B. Matekoni felt unaccountably sad. A man might try to be modern—and succeed, to a degree—but it was very difficult to be exciting. Women these days had magazines which showed them exciting men—bright-eyed men, posed with smiling women, and everyone clearly enjoying themselves greatly. The men would perhaps be holding a car key, or even be leaning against an expensive German vehicle, and the women would be laughing at something that the exciting men had said, something exciting. Surely Mma Ramotswe would not be influenced by such artificiality, and yet she certainly did look at these magazines, which were passed on to her by Mma Makutsi. She affected to laugh at them, but then if she really found them so ridiculous, surely she would not bother to read them in the first place?

Mr J.L.B. Matekoni stood at the edge of the square, looking over the traders' stalls, deep in thought. Then he asked himself a question which, although easily posed, was rather more difficult to answer: How does a husband become more exciting?

CHAPTER EIGHT

AN ACCOUNT OF
A PUZZLING CONVERSATION

That evening, Mr J.L.B. Matekoni made his way to the address which Mma Botumile had given him as they had sat on the verandah of the President Hotel; sat tealess, in his case, because she had so selfishly dismissed the waitress. It was a modest office block, three storeys high, on Kudumatse Drive, flanked on either side by equally undistinguished buildings, a furniture warehouse and a workshop that repaired electric fans. He parked his truck on the opposite side of the road, in a position where he could see the front entrance to the offices, but sufficiently far away so as not to look suspicious to anybody who should emerge from the building. He was just a man in a truck; the sort of man, and the sort of truck, one saw all the time on the roads of Gaborone; quite unexceptional. Most of those men, and trucks, were busy going somewhere, but occasionally they stopped, as this man had done, and waited for something or other to happen. It was not an unusual sight.

Mr J.L.B. Matekoni looked at his watch. It was now almost five o'clock, the time when, according to Mma Botumile, her husband invariably left the office. He was a creature of habit, she said, even if some of these habits had become bad ones. If Mr J.L.B. Matekoni were to wait outside the office, he would see him coming out and getting into his large red car, which would be parked by the side of the building. There was no need to give a detailed description of him, she said, as he could be identified by his car.

"What make of car is it?" Mr J.L.B. Matekoni had asked politely. He would never describe a car simply by its colour, and it astonished him that people did this. He had noticed Mma Makutsi doing it, and even Mma Ramotswe, who should have known better, described cars in terms of their colour, without making any reference to make or engine capacity.

Mma Botumile had looked at him almost with pity. "How do you expect me to know that?" she said. "You're the mechanic."

He had bitten his lip at the rudeness of the response. It was unusual in Botswana, a polite country, to come across such behaviour, and when one did encounter it, it appeared all the more surprising, and unpleasant. He was at a loss as to why she should be so curt in her manner. In his experience bad behaviour came from those who were unsure of themselves, those who had some obscure point to make. Mma Botumile was a woman of position, a successful woman who had nothing to prove to anybody; certainly she had no reason to belittle Mr J.L.B. Matekoni, who could hardly have been any threat to her. So why should she be so rude? Did she dislike all men, or just him; and if it was just him, then what was there about him that so offended her?

Now, sitting in the cab of his truck, he looked over the road towards the side of the building where, he suddenly noticed, two large red cars were parked. For a moment he felt despair—this whole thing had been a mistake from the very outset—but then he thought: the odds were surely against there being two drivers of red cars who would leave the building at exactly five o'clock. Of course not: the first man to come out after five o'clock would be Mma Botumile's husband.

He consulted his watch again. It was one minute to five now, and at any moment Rra Botumile might walk out of the front door. He looked up from his watch, and at that moment two men emerged from the office building, deep in conversation with one another; two men in white shirtsleeves and ties, jackets slung over their shoulders, the very picture of the office-worker at the end of the day. Mr J.L.B. Matekoni watched them as they turned the corner of the building and approached the cars, lingered for a moment to conclude their conversation, and then each got into a red car.

For a few moments, Mr J.L.B. Matekoni sat quite still. He had no way of telling which of the two men was Mma Botumile's husband, which meant that either he would have to give up and go home, or he would have to make a very quick decision and follow one of them. It would be easy enough to drive off and abandon the enquiry, but that would involve going back to Mma Ramotswe and telling her that he had failed at his attempt at doing what he understood to be the simplest and most basic of the procedures of her profession. He had not read Clovis Andersen's **The Principles of Private Detection,** of course, and he wondered whether Mma Ramotswe's trusted **vade mecum** would give any instruction on what to do in circumstances like this. Presumably he would point out that you must at least have a description of the person you are interested in at the outset, which of course he had not obtained.

Mr J.L.B. Matekoni made a snap decision. He would follow the first car as it came out. There were no grounds for thinking that this was Mr Botumile, but he had to choose, and he might as well . . . Or should he go for the second? There was something about the second which **looked** suspicious. The driver of the first car was obviously acting confidently and decisively in leaving first. That showed a clear conscience, whereas the second driver, contemplating the dissemblance and the tryst that lay ahead, showed the hesitation of one with a guilty conscience. It was a slender straw of surmise, but one which Mr J.L.B. Matekoni grasped at in the absence of anything better. That would impress Clovis Andersen—and

Mma Ramotswe—he thought: a decision based on a sound understanding of human psychology—and from a garage mechanic too!

The snap decision, so confident and decisive, was reversed, and Mr J.L.B. Matekoni waited while the first of the two red cars swung out into the main road and drove off. At five o'clock on this road there was a fair bit of traffic to contend with, as people, anxious to return home, drove off to Gaborone West and onto the Lobatse Road, and to other places they lived; all of them going about their legitimate business, of course, unlike the second driver, who seemed to be hesitating. He had started his engine—a mechanic could tell that at a glance, even from that distance—but he was not moving for some reason. Mr J.L.B. Matekoni wondered why he should be waiting, and decided that this was a yet further indication of guilt: he was waiting until the driver of the other red car was well on his way, as he did not want that first driver to see him, the second driver, setting off in the wrong direction. That was clearly what was happening. Again, Mr J.L.B. Matekoni was astonished at the way in which these conclusions came to mind. It seemed to him that once one started to think about a problem like this, everything all fitted into place surprisingly neatly, like one of those puzzles one saw in the papers where all the numbers added up or the missing letters made sense. He had not tried his hand at those, but perhaps he should. He had read somewhere that if you used your mind like that, then you kept it in good order for a longer period of time, and you put off the day when you would be sitting in the sun, like some of the very old people, not exactly sure which day of the week it was and wondering why the world no longer made the sense that it once did. Yet such people were often happy, he reminded himself, possibly because it did not really matter what day of the week it was anyway. And if they remembered nothing of the recent past but still held on to memories of twenty years ago, then that too might not be as bad as people might think. For many of us, thought Mr J.L.B. Matekoni, twenty years ago was a rather nice time. The world slipped away from us as we got older—of course it did—but perhaps we should not hold on too tightly.

The red car ahead of Mr J.L.B. Matekoni went up Kudumatse Drive and continued on the road that led out to Kanye. The buildings became smaller—offices and small warehouses became houses; dirt roads went off on both sides to newly built dwellings, two-bedroomed embodiments of somebody's ambitions, dreams, hard work, carved out of what had not all that long ago been thorn bush, grazing for cattle. He saw a car he thought he recognised, parked outside one of these; a car that he had worked on only a few weeks ago. It belonged to a teacher at Gaborone Secondary School, a man who everybody said would one day be a headmaster. His wife went to the Anglican Cathedral on Sunday mornings, Mma Ramotswe reported, and sang all the hymns lustily, although quite out of tune. "But she is doing her best," added Mma Ramotswe.

Suddenly the red car slowed down. Mr J.L.B. Matekoni had been keeping his truck three vehicles behind it, as he did not want to be spotted by Mr Botumile, and now he was faced with a decision as to whether he should pull in—which surely would look suspicious—or overtake. Two cars ahead of him started to overtake, but Mr J.L.B. Matekoni did not follow them. Steering over to the side of the road, he watched what was happening ahead. The red car started to move more quickly, and then, with very little warning, swung round onto the other side of the road and headed back in the direction from which it had come. Mr J.L.B. Matekoni continued on his course. He had a glimpse of the driver of the red car—just a face, staring fixedly ahead, not enough to remember, or to judge—and then all he saw was the rear of the car heading back towards town. He looked in his driving mirror—the road was clear, and he turned, going some way off the edge of the tar, as his truck had a wide turning circle.

Fortunately the traffic returning to town was lighter, and Mr J.L.B. Matekoni soon found himself closing on Mr Botumile's car. He slowed down, but not too much, as this was an unpredictable quarry, like a wild animal in the bush that will suddenly turn and dart off in an unexpected direction to elude capture. Ahead of him the rays of the sinking sun had caught the windows of the Government buildings off Khama Crescent and were flashing signals. Red. Stop, Mr J.L.B. Matekoni. Stop. Go back to what you understand.

Mr Botumile drove through the centre of town, past the Princess Marina Hospital, and on towards the Gaborone Sun Hotel. Then he stopped, parking in front of the hotel just as Mr J.L.B. Matekoni turned his truck into a dif-

ferent section of the hotel parking lot and
turned off the engine. Then both men left their
vehicles and entered the hotel, Mr Botumile
going first, alone—he thought—and Mr J.L.B.
Matekoni following him a discreet distance behind, his heart beating hard within him at the
sheer excitement of what he was doing. This is
better, he thought, infinitely better than adjusting brake pads and replacing oil filters.

"MR GOTSO?" exclaimed Mma Ramotswe.
"Mr Charlie Gotso? Him?"

"Yes," said Mr J.L.B. Matekoni. "I recognised him immediately—who wouldn't? Charlie Gotso was sitting there, and when I saw him
I had to look away quickly. Not that he would
know who I am. He'd know who you are, Mma
Ramotswe. You've spoken to him, haven't you?
All those years ago when . . ."

"That was a long time ago," Mma Ramotswe said. "And I was just a small person to him. Men like that don't remember
small people."

"You are not small, Mma," Mr J.L.B.
Matekoni found himself protesting, but
stopped. Mma Ramotswe was not small.

She looked at him with amusement. "No, I am not small, Rra. You are right. But I was thinking of how I would mean nothing to a man like that."

Mr J.L.B. Matekoni was quick to assent. "Of course that's what you meant. I know men like that. They are very arrogant."

"He is a rich man," said Mma Ramotswe. "Rich men sometimes forget that they are people, just like the rest of us." She paused. "So there was Charlie Gotso, no less! And Mr Botumile went straight up to him and sat down?"

Mr J.L.B. Matekoni nodded. He and Mma Ramotswe were sitting at the kitchen table in their house on Zebra Drive. Behind them, on the stove, a pan of chopped pumpkin was on the boil, filling the air with that familiar chalky smell of the yellow pumpkin flesh. Inside the oven, a small leg of lamb was slowly roasting; it would be a good meal, when it was eventually served in half an hour or so. There was time enough, then, to talk, and for Mr J.L.B. Matekoni to give Mma Ramotswe an account of the enquiry from which he had just returned.

"This was outside," he said. "You know that bar at the back? That place. And since there were quite a few people there, and most of the tables were occupied, I was able to sit down at the table next to theirs without it appearing odd."

"You did the right thing," said Mma Ramotswe. Clovis Andersen, in **The Principles of Private Detection,** advised that it could look just as odd to distance oneself unnaturally from the object of one's attention as to come too close. **Neither too near nor too far,** he wrote. **That's what the Ancients called the golden mean, and they were right—as always!** She had wondered who these ancients were; whether they were the same people whom one called the elders in Botswana, or whether they were somebody else altogether. But the important thing was that Mr J.L.B. Matekoni, who had never read **The Principles of Private Detection,** should have done just the right thing without any specialist knowledge. This only went to show, she decided, that much of what was written in **The Principles of Private Detection** was simply common sense, leading to decisions at which one could have anyway arrived unaided.

Mr J.L.B. Matekoni accepted the compliment graciously. "Thank you, Mma. Well, there I was sitting at the table, so close to Charlie Gotso that I could see the place on his neck where he has a barber's rash—rough skin, Mma, like a little ploughed field. And there were flecks on his collar from the blood."

Mma Ramotswe made a face. "Poor man."

Mr J.L.B. Matekoni looked at her in surprise. "He is no good, that man."

"Of course not," Mma Ramotswe corrected herself. "But I would not wish anybody to be uncomfortable, would you, Mr J.L.B. Matekoni?"

He thought for a moment, and then agreed. He did not wish misfortune on anybody, he decided, even if they deserved it. Mma Ramotswe was undoubtedly right about that, even if she was inclined to be a little bit too generous in her judgements.

"They started to talk, and I pretended to be very interested in reading the menu which the waiter had brought me." He laughed. "I read about the price of a Castle lager and about the various sorts of sandwich fillings. Then I read it all again.

"In the meantime, I was listening as closely as I could to what they were saying. It was a bit hard, as there was somebody sitting nearby who was laughing like a donkey. But I did hear something."

Mma Ramotswe frowned. "Excuse me, Mr J.L.B. Matekoni," she said. "But why were you listening to them? Where was the woman?"

"What woman?" asked Mr J.L.B. Matekoni.

"The woman with whom Mr Botumile is having an affair," Mma Ramotswe replied. "That woman."

Mr J.L.B. Matekoni looked up at the ceiling. He had expected to see Mr Botumile meeting a woman, and when he had sat down next to Charlie Gotso he thought that perhaps the woman would arrive a bit later; that they both knew Mr Gotso. But then, even when it became apparent that no woman would be joining them, he found himself engrossed in the encounter that was taking place at the neighbouring table. This was more interesting than mere adultery; this was the edge of something much more important than that. He imagined now that he would be able to reveal to Mma Botumile that her husband was up to something far worse than that which she had imagined; he was consorting with no less a person than Charlie Gotso, the least salubrious of Gaborone's businessmen, a man who used intimidation and fear as instruments of persuasion; a bad man, in fact, to put it simply. And Mr J.L.B. Matekoni had no reluctance to use unadorned, direct language, whether about cars, or people. Just as there were some bad cars—cars that were consistently slow to start or that invariably had inexplicable, incorrigible rattles—so too there were bad people. Fortunately there were not too many of these in Botswana, but there were some, and Mr Charlie Gotso was certainly one of them.

"There was no sign of that woman," he conceded. "Maybe it was not his evening for seeing her. There will be time enough to find her."

"I see," said Mma Ramotswe. "All right. But what did they talk about anyway?"

"Mining," said Mr J.L.B. Matekoni. "Mr Botumile said something about bad results. He said that the cores had come in and that the results were not good."

Mma Ramotswe shrugged. "Prospecting," she said. "People do that all the time."

"Then he said: the share price will come down in two weeks, in Johannesburg. And Mr Gotso asked him if he was sure about that. And he replied yes he was."

"And then?" prompted Mma Ramotswe.

"Then Mr Gotso said that he was very pleased."

Mma Ramotswe was puzzled. "Pleased? Why would he be pleased about bad news?"

Mr J.L.B. Matekoni thought for a moment. "Perhaps it's because he is such an unpleasant man," he said. "Perhaps he likes to hear of the misfortune of others. There are people like that."

Yes, thought Mma Ramotswe. There were such people, but she did not think that Charlie Gotso was like that. He was the sort of person who would be unmoved by the misfortune of others; completely uninterested. All that he would be pleased about would be those things that were in his interests, that made him richer, and this raised a very difficult question: Why should the failure of prospectors to find minerals be good news for a bad man?

They finished their conversation on that note. Mr J.L.B. Matekoni had nothing further to report, and the pumpkin and the lamb, judging from the smell from the pot and from the oven, were both ready, or just about. It was time for dinner.

CHAPTER NINE

THE UNDERSTANDING OF SHOES

MMA MAKUTSI AWOKE the next morning slightly earlier than normal. It had been another cold night, and her room, which had no heating apart from a one-bar electric heater—which was turned off—was still chilly. When the sun came up properly, the light would flood in through her window and warm the place up, but that would not happen for twenty minutes or so. She looked at her watch. If she got up now, she would have fifteen minutes or so in hand before she went off to catch her minibus into work. She could use this time to do something constructive, some sewing, perhaps, on the new sewing machine which Phuti Radiphuti had bought her. She was making a dress for herself and had all the panels cut out, pinned together, and ready for the machine. Now all she needed was a bit of time. She could do fifteen minutes of work on it that morning and then, when she came home from work, she could devote at least two hours to the task, which might well be enough to finish it off.

But there would be no going to work that day, and now that she remembered this she opened her eyes wide, astonished by the realisation. I do not have to get up, she said to herself. I can stay in bed. She closed her eyes again, and nestled her head back into her pillow; but she could not keep her eyes closed, she could not drift back to sleep, for she was wide awake. On a cold morning an extra few minutes of sleep, snatched in denial of the imminent call of the alarm clock, would normally be irresistible. But not now; that which we have, we suddenly find we do not want. She sat up in bed, shivered, and tentatively lowered her feet onto the cement floor of her room. There might be running water in the house, and electric light, but in the villages and in the country they still had floors, here and there, which did not freeze your feet like this—floors made of the dung of cattle, sweet-smelling dung, packed down hard and mixed with mud to give a surface that was cool in the heat and warm to the touch in the cold weather. For all that modern buildings were more comfortable, there were some things, some traditional things, that could not be improved upon.

This thought of things traditional reminded her of Mma Ramotswe, and with a sudden jolt of regret she realised that she would not be seeing her former employer today. A day—a weekday too—with no Mma Ramotswe; it seemed strange, almost ominous, like a day on which something dark was due to happen. But she put that thought out of her mind. She had resigned and had moved on. That's what people said these days—they talked about moving on. Well, that's what she had done, and presumably people who moved on did not look back. So she would not cast an eye back to her old life as an assistant detective; she would look forward to her new life as Mrs Phuti Radiphuti, wife of the proprietor of the Double Comfort Furniture Store, **former** secretary.

It was strange having breakfast and not having to rush; strange eating toast without glancing at the clock; and strange, too, not having to leave the second cup of tea half-finished simply because time had run out. Breakfast that morning seemed not to finish—it merely petered out. The last crumbs of toast were cleared from the plate, the last sip of tea taken, and then . . . nothing. Mma Makutsi sat at her table and thought of the day ahead. There was the dress—she could easily finish that this morning, but somehow she did not want to. She was enjoying the making of that garment, and she had no material for another one. If she finished the dress, then there would be one less thing to do, and her new sewing machine would have to go back into the cupboard. She could clean the house, of course; there was always something to attend to in a house, no matter how regularly one swept and scrubbed. But although she kept the house spick-and-span, that was not a task that she actually enjoyed, and she had spent almost the entire last weekend giving it a thorough cleaning.

She looked about the room. Her living room, where she ate her breakfast, was sparsely furnished. There was the table at which she now sat—a table condemned by Phuti Radiphuti who had promised to replace it, but had not yet done so; there was a small second-hand settee that she had bought through a newspaper advertisement and which now sported the satin-covered cushions which Phuti Radiphuti had given her; there was a side table on which she had placed several small framed pictures of her family in Bobonong. And that, apart from a small red rug, was it.

She could do something more about decorating the room, she thought. But then if she was going to get married in January, when she would move to Phuti Radiphuti's house, there seemed little point in doing much to her own place. The landlord would be pleased, no doubt, if she went to the hardware store and bought some paint for the walls, but again there seemed to be no point in doing that. Indeed, there seemed to be little point in doing anything.

No sooner had she reached that conclusion, than she realised how absurd it was. Of course there was a point in doing something. Mma Makutsi was not one to waste her time, and she now told herself that her resignation should be a challenge to her to work out a new routine of activity. Yes, she would take advantage of this and do something fresh, something exciting with her life. She would . . . She thought. There must be something. She could get a new job, perhaps. She had read about a new employment agency which had opened which would specialise, it had been announced, in the placing of high-class secretaries. "This agency is not for everyone," the press announcement had read. "We are for the cream of the crop. We are for people who go the extra mile—every day."

Mma Makutsi had seen the advertisement in the **Botswana Daily News** and had been struck by the wording. She liked the expression **go the extra mile,** which had the ring of a journey to it; and that, she thought, was what life really was—it was a journey. In her case, the journey had started in Bobonong, and had been by bus, all the way down to Gaborone. And then it had become a metaphorical journey, not a real one, but a journey nonetheless. There had been the journey to her final grade at the Botswana Secretarial College, with the marks as milestones along the way: sixty-eight per cent in her first examination, seventy-four in the second; then on to eighty-five per cent; and finally, in a seemingly impossible leap, ninety-seven per cent, and the glory that had come with that. That had surely been a journey.

And then there had come the hunt for the first job—a journey of disappointing blind alleys and wrong turnings, as she discovered that at that level of secretarial employment a crude form of discrimination was at work. She had gone to interview after interview, dressed in the sole good dress that she possessed, and had discovered time and time again that the employer was not in the slightest bit interested in how she had done at the College. All that was required was that one should have passed and got the diploma; that was all. What was on the diploma did not matter, it seemed; all that counted was that one should be glamorous, which Mma Makutsi was realistic enough to know she was not. She had those large round glasses; she had that difficult skin; her clothes spoke of the hardship of her life. No, she was not glamorous.

Here was an agency, though, that implied that hard work and persistence would be rewarded. And the reward would come, no doubt, in the shape of a challenging and interesting job, with a large company, she imagined, in an office with air conditioning and a gleaming staff canteen. She would move amongst highly motivated people, who would be smartly dressed. She would live in a world of memos and targets and workshops. It would be a world away from the No. 1 Ladies' Detective

Agency, with its battered old filing cabinets and its two tea-pots.

She had made up her mind, and the decision made her feel more optimistic about the day ahead. She rose from the table and began to wash up the breakfast plates. Two hours later, having made satisfactory progress with her new dress, she put away the sewing machine, locked the house, and began to walk into town. It was a cool day, but the sun was still there; it was perfect, she thought; it was weather for walking, and for thinking as one walked. The doubts of the earlier part of the day had disappeared and now seemed so baseless, so unimportant. She would miss Mma Ramotswe, just as she would miss any friend, but to think, as she did, that her life would be empty without her was a piece of nonsense. There would be plenty of new colleagues once she started her new job and, without being disloyal to Mma Ramotswe, many of them would perhaps be a little bit more exciting than her former employer. It was all very well being of traditional shape, believing in the old Botswana values, and drinking bush tea, but there was another world to explore, a world filled with exciting, modern people, the people who formed opinions, who set the pace in fashion and in witty things to say. That was the world to which she could now graduate, although of course she would always have a soft spot for Mma Ramotswe and the No. 1 Ladies' Detective Agency. Even a thoroughly modern person would like Mma Ramotswe, in the way in which modern people can retain affection for their aunts back in the villages even though they really had nothing in common any more with those aunts.

She had kept the issue of the paper in which the advertisement appeared, and had noted down the address of the agency. It was not a long way away—a half hour walk at the most— and this walk went quickly, made all the quicker by the thoughts she was entertaining of the interview that no doubt lay ahead of her.

"Ninety-seven per cent?" the agency person might say. "Is that correct? Not a misprint?"

"No, Mma. Ninety-seven per cent."

"Well, that's very impressive, I must say! And there's a job which I think would be just right for you. It's a pretty high-level job, mind you. But then you've been . . ."

"An associate detective. Second from the top in the organisation."

"I see. Well, I think you're the lady for the job. The pay is good, by the way. And all the usual benefits."

"Air conditioning?"

"Naturally."

The thought of this exchange was deeply satisfying; absorbing too, with the result that she walked past her destination and had to turn back and retrace her footsteps. But there it was, the Superior Positions Office Employment Agency, on the second floor of a slightly run-down, but still promising-looking building not far from the Catholic church. Once she had climbed the stairs, she saw a sign pointing down a corridor inviting visitors to ring the bell on the door and enter. The corridor was dark, and had a slightly unpleasant smell to it, but the door of the agency office had been recently painted and, reflected Mma Makutsi, she was not going to work there, in that building, which was only a means to a much-better-appointed end.

It was a small room, dominated by a desk in the middle of the floor. At this desk there was a slight young woman with elaborately braided hair. She was applying varnish to her nails as Mma Makutsi entered, and she looked up with a vague air of annoyance that she should be disturbed in this task. But she greeted Mma Makutsi in the proper way before asking, "Do you have an appointment, Mma?"

Mma Makutsi shook her head. "Your advertisement in the **Daily News** said that none was necessary."

The receptionist pursed her lips. "You should not believe everything you read in the papers, Mma," she said. "I don't."

"Even when it's your own advertisement?" asked Mma Makutsi.

For a moment the receptionist said nothing. She dipped the varnish brush into the container and dabbed it thoughtfully on the nail of an index finger.

"You're an experienced secretary, Mma?" she asked at last.

"Yes," said Mma Makutsi. "And I'd like to see somebody more senior, please."

A further silence ensued. Then the receptionist picked up her telephone and spoke into the receiver.

"She'll see you in a few minutes, Mma," she said. "She's seeing somebody else at the moment. You can wait over there." She pointed to a chair in the corner of the room. Beside the chair was a small table laden with magazines.

Mma Makutsi sat down. She had encountered rude receptionists before and she wondered what it was about the job that seemed sometimes to attract unfriendly people. Perhaps it was that people did the opposite of what they really wanted to do. There were gentle prison guards and soldiers; there were unkind nurses; there were ignorant and unhelpful teachers. And then there were those unfriendly receptionists.

She did not have to wait long. After a few minutes the door to the inner office opened and a young woman walked out. She was carrying a folded piece of paper and was smiling. She walked over to the receptionist and whispered something into her ear. There was laughter.

When the young woman had left, the receptionist glanced at the door and gestured for Mma Makutsi to go in. Then she continued with her nail-painting. Mma Makutsi rose to her feet and made her way to the door, knocked, and without waiting for an invitation, went in.

THEY LOOKED at one another in astonishment. Mma Makutsi had not expected this, and the sight of this woman behind the desk deprived her of all the poise she had summoned for her entry. But in that respect she was equal with the woman behind the desk; equal in other respects too, as it was her old classmate from the Botswana Secretarial College, Violet Sephotho.

It was Violet who recovered first. "Well, well," she said. "Grace Makutsi. First the College. Then the Academy of Dance and Movement. Now here. All these crossings of our paths, Mma! Perhaps we shall even find out now that we are cousins!"

"That would be a surprise, Mma," said Mma Makutsi, without saying what sort of surprise it would be.

"I was only joking," said Violet. "I do not think we are cousins. But that is not the point. The point is that you have come here looking for a job? Is that correct?"

Mma Makutsi opened her mouth to reply, but Violet continued. "You must have heard of us. We are what are called head hunters these days. We find top people for top jobs."

"It must be interesting work," said Mma Makutsi. "I wondered whether . . ."

"It is," said Violet. "Very interesting." She

paused, looking quizzically at Mma Makutsi. "I thought, though, that you had a good job," she went on. "Don't you work for that fat woman who runs that detective business next to that smelly old garage? Don't you work for her?"

"That is Mma Ramotswe," said Mma Makutsi. "And the garage is Tlokweng Road Speedy Motors. It is run by . . ."

Violet interrupted. "Yes, yes," she said impatiently. "So you've lost that job, have you?"

Mma Makutsi gasped. It was outrageous that this Violet, this fifty-per-cent (at the most) person should imagine that she had been dismissed from the No. 1 Ladies' Detective Agency. "I did not!" she burst out. "I did not lose that job, Mma! I left of my own accord."

Violet looked at her unapologetically. "Of course, Mma. Of course. Although sometimes people leave just before they're pushed. Not you, of course, but that happens, you know."

Mma Makutsi took a deep breath. If she allowed herself to become angered, or at least to show her anger, then she would be playing directly into Violet's hands. So she smiled gently and nodded her agreement with Violet's comment. "Yes, Mma. There are many cases of people who are dismissed who say that they resigned. You must see a lot of that. But I really did resign because I wanted a change. That's why I'm here."

This submissive tone seemed to appeal to Violet. She looked at Mma Makutsi thoughtfully. "I'll see what I can do," she said slowly. "But I can't work miracles. The problem is that . . . Well, the problem, Mma, is one of **presentation.** These days it is very important that firms have a smart image. It's all about impact, you know. And that means that senior staff must be well presented, must be . . . of good appearance. That's the way it is in business these days. That's just the way it is." She shuffled a few papers on her desk. "There are a few high-level vacancies at the moment. A personal assistant post to a chief executive. A secretary to the general manager of a bank. That sort of thing. But I'm not sure if you're quite right for that sort of job, Mma. Maybe something in a Ministry somewhere. Or . . ." She paused. "Have you thought of leaving Gaborone? Of taking something down in Lobatse or Francistown or somewhere like that? Lots of people like those places, you know. There's not so much going on, of course, but it's a peaceful life out of town."

Mma Makutsi watched Violet as she spoke. The face revealed so much; that she had been taught by Mma Ramotswe, who had pointed out that the real meaning of what anybody said was written large in the muscles of the face. And Violet's face said it all; this was a calculated put-down, an intentional humiliation, possibly inspired by jealousy (Violet knew about Phuti Radiphuti and knew that he was well off), possibly inspired by anger over their vastly differing performances at the Botswana Secretarial College, but more probably inspired by pure malice, which was something which often just occurred in people for no apparent reason and with which there was no reasoning.

She rose to her feet. "I don't think you have anything suitable for me," she said.

Violet became flustered. "I didn't say that, Mma."

"I think you did, Mma," said Mma Makutsi. "I think you said it very clearly. Sometimes people don't have to open their mouths to say anything, but they say it nonetheless."

She moved towards the door. For a moment or two it seemed as if Violet was about to say something, but she did not. Mma Makutsi gave her one last glance, and then left, nodding to the receptionist on her way out, as politeness dictated. Mma Ramotswe would be proud of me, she thought; Mma Ramotswe had always said that the repaying of rudeness with rudeness was the wrong thing to do as it taught the other person no lesson. And she was right about that, as she was right about so many other things. Mma Ramotswe . . . Mma Makutsi saw the face of her friend and heard her voice, as if she was right there, beside her. She would have laughed at Violet. She would have said of her insults, **Little words, Mma, from an unhappy woman. Nothing to think twice about. Nothing.**

Mma Makutsi went out into the sunshine, composed herself, and began to walk home. The sun was high now, and there was much more warmth in it. She could get a minibus most of the way, if she waited, but she decided to walk, and had gone only a short distance when the heel of her right shoe broke. The shoe now flapped uselessly, and she had to take both shoes off. At home, in Bobonong, she had often gone barefoot, and it was no great hardship now. But it had not been a good morning, that morning, and she felt miserable.

She walked on. Near the stretch of open bush that the school used for playing sports, she picked up a thorn in her right foot. It was easy to extract, but it pricked hard for such a small thing. She sat down on a stone and nursed her foot, rubbing it to relieve the pain. She looked up at the sky. If there were people up there, she did not think that they cared for people down here. There were no thorns up there, no rudeness, no broken shoes.

She rose and picked up her shoes. As she did so, a rattly old blue taxi drove past, the driver with his right arm resting casually on the sill of the window. She thought for a moment, **That's a dangerous thing to do—another car might drive too close and that would be the end of your arm.**

She raised her own arm, suddenly, on impulse. The taxi stopped.

"Tlokweng Road, please," she said. "You know that old garage? That place. The No. 1 Ladies' Detective Agency."

"I will take you there, Mma," said the taxi driver. He was not rude. He was polite, and he made conversation with Mma Makutsi as they drove.

"Why are you going there, Mma?" he asked

as they negotiated the lights at the old four-way stop.

"Because that's where I work," said Mma Makutsi. "I took the morning off. Now it's time to go back."

She looked down at the broken shoe, now resting on her lap. It was such a sad thing, that shoe, like a body from which the life had gone. She stared at it. Almost challenging it to reproach her. But it did not, and all she heard, she thought, was a strangled voice which said, **Narrow escape, Boss. You were walking in the wrong direction, you know. We shoes understand these things.**

IF IT HAD BEEN a bleak morning for Mma Makutsi, it was equally bleak at the premises of the No. 1 Ladies' Detective Agency and Tlokweng Road Speedy Motors. In Mma Ramotswe's small office the desk previously occupied by Mma Makutsi stood forlorn, bare of paper, with only a couple of pencils and an abandoned typewriter upon it. Where three cups had stood on the cabinet behind it, along with the tea-making equipment of a kettle and two tea-pots, there now were only two—Mma

Ramotswe's personal cup and the cup that was kept for the client. The absence of Mma Makutsi's cup, a small thing in itself but a big thing in what it stood for, seemed only to confirm in Mma Ramotswe's view that the heart had been taken out of the office. Steps could be taken, of course: Mr Polopetsi could be invited to keep his mug there rather than on the hook which it occupied beside the spanners in the garage. But it would not be the same; indeed it was impossible to imagine Mr Polopetsi occupying Mma Makutsi's chair; much as Mma Ramotswe liked him, he was a man, and the whole ethos of the No. 1 Ladies' Detective Agency, its guiding principle really, was that it was a business in which women were in the driving seat. That was not because men could not do the job—they could, provided they were the right sort of men, observant men—it was simply because that particular business had always been run by women, and it was women who gave it its particular style. There was room in this world, Mma Ramotswe thought, for things done by men and things done by women; sometimes men could do the things done by women, sometimes not. And vice versa, of course.

She felt lonely. In spite of the sounds from the garage, in spite of the fact that immediately on the other side of the office wall was Mr J.L.B. Matekoni, her husband and helpmate, she felt alone, bereft. She had once been told by an aunt in Mochudi how, shortly after being widowed, she had seen her husband in empty rooms, in places where he liked to sit in the sun, coming back down the track that he always walked down; and these were not tricks of the light, but aches of the mind, its sad longings. And now, after her assistant had been absent for so short a time, she had looked up suddenly when she thought she heard Mma Makutsi say something, or had seen something move on the other side of the room. That movement was a real trick of the light of course, but it still brought home the fact that she was on her own now.

And that was difficult. Mma Ramotswe was normally quite content with her own company. She could sit on her verandah on Zebra Drive and drink tea in perfect solitude, with her only company that of the birds outside, or of the tiny, scrambling geckos that made their way up the pillars and across the roof; that was different. In an office one needed to be able to

talk to somebody, if only to make the surroundings more human. Homes, verandahs,
gardens were human in their feel; offices were
not. An office with only one person in it was a
place unfurnished.

On the other side of the wall, Mr J.L.B.
Matekoni felt a similar moroseness. It was perhaps not quite as acute in his case, but it was
still there, a feeling that somehow things were
not complete. It was as a family might feel, he
thought, if it sat down to dinner on some great
occasion and had one seat unoccupied. He
liked Mma Makutsi; he had always admired
her determination and her courage. He would
not like to cross her, of course, as she could be
prickly, and he was not sure whether she handled the apprentices very well. In fact she did
not; he was certain of it, but he had never quite
got round to suggesting to her that she should
change her tone when handling those admittedly frustrating young men. And of course
Charlie was going to go too, once he had finished tinkering with that old Mercedes and the
taxi licence application had been approved.
The garage would not be the same without
him, Mr J.L.B. Matekoni thought; there would
be something missing, in spite of everything.

Charlie, from the other side of the garage, where he was about to raise a car on the hydraulic ramp, glanced at Mr J.L.B. Matekoni and said to the younger apprentice standing beside him, "I hope that the Boss doesn't think that she's gone because of me. I hope he doesn't think that."

The younger apprentice wiped his nose on the sleeve of his blue overalls. "Why would he think that, Charlie? What's it got to do with you? You know what that woman's like. Nag, nag, nag. I bet that the Boss is relieved that she's gone."

Charlie thought about this possibility for a moment, and then dismissed it. "He likes her. Mma Ramotswe likes her too. Maybe even you like her." He looked at the younger man and frowned. "Do you? Do you like her?"

The younger apprentice shifted his feet. "I don't like her glasses," he said. "Where do you think she got those great big glasses?"

"An industrial catalogue," said Charlie.

The younger apprentice laughed. "And those stupid shoes of hers. She thinks she looks good in those shoes of hers, but most girls I know wouldn't be seen dead in them."

Charlie looked thoughtful. "They take your shoes off when you're dead, you know."

The younger apprentice was concerned. "Why?" he asked. "What do they do with them?"

Charlie reached forward and polished the dial of the panel that controlled the hydraulic lift. "The doctors take them," he explained. "Or the nurses in the hospital. Next time you see a doctor, look at his shoes. They all have very smart shoes. Lots of them. That's because they get the shoes when . . ."

He stopped. A blue taxi had drawn up in front of the garage and the passenger door was opening.

CHAPTER TEN

A SMALL BUSINESSWOMAN

WITH MMA MAKUTSI back in her usual place, the heavy atmosphere that had prevailed that morning lifted. The emotional reunion, as demonstrative and effusive as if Mma Makutsi had been away for months, or even years, had embarrassed the men, who had exchanged glances, and then looked away, as if in guilt at an intrusion into essentially female mysteries. But when the ululating from Mma Ramotswe had died down and the tea had been made, everything returned to normal.

"Why did she bother to leave if she was going to be away five minutes?" asked the younger apprentice.

"It's because she doesn't think like anybody else," said Charlie. "She thinks backwards."

Mr J.L.B. Matekoni, who overheard this, shook his head. "It's a sign of maturity to be able to change your mind when you realise that you're wrong," he explained. "It's the same with fixing a car. If you find out that you're going along the wrong lines, then don't hesitate to stop and correct yourself. If, for example, you're changing the oil seal at the back of a gearbox, you might try to save time by doing this without taking the gearbox out. But it's always quicker to take the gearbox out. If you don't, you end up taking the floor out and anyway you have to take the top of the gearbox off, and the prop shaft too. So it's best to stop and admit your mistake before you go any further and damage things."

Charlie listened to this—it was a long speech for Mr J.L.B. Matekoni—and then looked away. He wondered if this was a random example seized upon by Mr J.L.B. Matekoni, or if he knew about that seal he had tried to install in the old rear-wheel-drive Ford. Could he have found out somehow?

There was little work done in the agency that afternoon. Mma Makutsi restored her desk to the way she liked it to be: papers reappeared, pencils were resharpened and arranged in the right fashion, and files were extracted from the cabinet and placed back on the desk for further attention. Mma Ramotswe watched all this with utter satisfaction and, after she had offered to make the tea—an offer which Mma Makutsi politely declined, pointing out that she had not forgotten her role altogether—she asked her assistant if she would care to have the rest of the afternoon off.

"You may have shopping to do, Mma," said Mma Ramotswe. "You know that you can have the time off whenever you want for things like that."

Mma Makutsi had clearly been pleased by this, but again declined. There was filing to do, she insisted; it was extraordinary how quickly filing accumulated; one turned one's back for a few hours and there it was—piled up. Mma Ramotswe thought that this was also true of detection work. "No sooner do you deal with one case," she said, "than another turns up. There is somebody coming tomorrow morning. I should really be seeing people about that hospital matter, but I am going to have to be here to see this other person. Unless . . ."

She glanced across the room at Mma

Makutsi, who was polishing her spectacles with that threadbare lace handkerchief of hers. You would think, Mma Ramotswe said to herself, that she would buy herself a new handkerchief now that she had the money, but people held on to things they loved; they just did.

Mma Makutsi finished with her polishing and replaced her large round spectacles. She looked straight at Mma Ramotswe. "Unless?"

Mma Ramotswe had always insisted that she see the client first, even if the matter was subsequently to be delegated to Mma Makutsi. But things had to change, and perhaps this was the time to do it. Mma Makutsi could be made an associate detective and given the chance to deal with clients herself, right from the beginning of a case. All that would be required would be that the client's chair be turned round to face Mma Makutsi's desk rather than hers.

"Unless you, as . . . as associate detective were to interview the client yourself and look after the whole matter." Mma Ramotswe paused. The afternoon sun was slanting in through the window and had fallen on Mma Makutsi's head, glinting off her spectacles.

"Of course," said Mma Makutsi quietly. Associate detective. Whole matter. Herself. "Of course," she repeated. "That would be possible. Tomorrow morning? Of course, Mma. You leave it to me."

THE SMALL WOMAN sitting in the re-oriented client's chair looked at Mma Makutsi. "Mma?"

"Makutsi. I am Grace Makutsi."

"I had heard that there was a woman called Mma Ramotswe. People have spoken of her. I heard very good things."

"There is a woman of that name," said Mma Makutsi. "She is my colleague." She faltered briefly at the word **colleague.** Of course Mma Ramotswe was her colleague; she was also her employer, but there was nothing to say that an employer could not also be a colleague. She went on, "We work very closely together. As associates. So that is why you are seeing me. She is out on another case."

The small woman hesitated for a moment, but then appeared to accept that situation. She leaned forward in her chair, and Mma Makutsi noticed how her expression seemed to be a pleading one, the expression of one who wanted something very badly. "My name, Mma, is

Mma Magama, but nobody calls me that very much. They call me Teenie."

"That is because . . ." Mma Makutsi stopped herself.

"That is because I have always been called that," said Teenie. "Teenie is a good name for a small person, you see, Mma."

"You are not so small, Mma," said Mma Makutsi. But you are, she thought; you're terribly small.

"I have seen some smaller people," said Teenie appreciatively.

"Where did you see them?" asked Mma Makutsi. She had not intended to ask the question, but it slipped out.

Teenie pointed vaguely out of the window, but said nothing.

"Anyway, Mma," Mma Makutsi went on. "Perhaps you will tell me why you have come to see us."

Mma Makutsi watched Teenie's eyes as she spoke. The pleading look that accompanied each sentence was disconcerting.

"I have a business, you see, Mma," Teenie said. "It is a good business. It is a printing works. There are ten people who work there. Ten. People look at me and think that I am too small to have a business like that—they look surprised. But what difference does it make, Mma? What difference?"

Mma Makutsi shrugged. "No difference at all, Mma. Some people are very stupid."

Teenie agreed with this. "Very," she said. "What matters is what's up here." She tapped her head. Mma Makutsi could not help but notice that her head was very small too. Did the size of a brain have any bearing on its ability? she wondered. Chickens had very small brains but elephants had much bigger ones, and there was a difference.

"I started the business with my late husband," Teenie went on. "He was run over on the Lobatse Road eleven years ago."

Mma Makutsi lowered her eyes. He must have been small too; perhaps the driver just did not see him. "I am sorry, Mma. That was very sad."

"Yes," said Teenie. "But I had to get on with my life and so I carried on with the business. I built it up. I bought a new German printing machine which made us one of the cheapest places in the country to print anything. Full colour. Laminates. Everything, Mma."

"That is very good," said Mma Makutsi.

"We could do you a calendar for yourselves next year," said Teenie, looking at the almost bare walls, but noticing, appreciatively, the display of her own calendar. "I see that somebody has given you our calendar up there. You will see how well printed it is. Or we could do some business cards. Have you got a business card, Mma?"

The answer was no, but the idea was implanted. If one was an associate detective, then perhaps one was expected to have a business card. Mma Ramotswe herself did not have one, but that was more to do with her traditional views than with cost.

"I would like to have one," said Mma Makutsi. "And I would like you to print it for me."

"We shall do that," said Teenie. "We can take the cost off your fee."

That was not what Mma Makutsi had intended, but now she was committed. She indicated to Teenie that she should continue with her story.

Teenie moved forward in her seat. Mma Makutsi saw that her client's feet barely touched the floor in front of her. "I look after the people who work for me very well," said Teenie. "I never ask people to work longer hours than they want to. Everybody gets three weeks' holiday on full pay. After two years, everybody gets a bonus. Two years only, Mma! In some places you wait ten years for a bonus."

"Your people must be very happy," said Mma Makutsi. "It's not everybody who is as good to their staff as you are."

"That is true," said Teenie. She frowned before continuing. "But then if they are so happy, why do I have somebody who is stealing from me? That is what I cannot understand—I really can't. They are stealing supplies. Paper. Inks. The supply cupboards are always half-empty."

From the moment that Teenie mentioned staff, Mma Makutsi had anticipated this. It was one of the commonest complaints that clients brought to the No. 1 Ladies' Detective Agency, although not quite as common as the errant husband complaint. Botswana was not a dishonest country—quite the contrary, really—but it was inevitable that there would be some who would cheat and steal and do all the unhelpful and unpleasant things that humanity was heir to. That had started a long time back, at the point at which some Eden somewhere had gone wrong, and somebody had picked up a stone and hurled it at another. It was in us, thought Mma Makutsi; it was in all of us, somewhere deep down in our very nature. When we were children we had to be taught to hold it in check, to banish it; we had to be taught to be concerned with the feelings of others. And that, she thought, was where things went wrong. Some children were just not taught, or would not learn, or were governed by some impulse within them that stopped them from feeling and understanding. Later on, there was very little one could do about these people, other than to thwart them. Mma Ramotswe, of course, said that you could be kind to them, to show them the way, but Mma Makutsi had her doubts about that; one could be too kind, she thought.

"People steal," said Mma Makutsi. "No matter how kind you are to them, there are some people who will steal. Even from their own family, in their own house. That happens, you know."

Teenie fixed her pleading eyes on Mma Makutsi. It occurred to Mma Makutsi that the woman in front of her wanted her to say that people did not steal, that the world was not a place where this sort of thing happened. She could not give her that reassurance, because, well, because it would be absurd. One could not say the world was other than it was.

"I'm sorry about that," Mma Makutsi went on. "It obviously makes you unhappy, Mma."

Teenie was quick to agree. "It's like being hurt somewhere here," she said, moving her hand to her chest and placing it above the sternum. "It's a horrible feeling. This thief is not a person who comes at night and takes from you—it's somebody you see every day, who smiles at you, who asks how you have slept; all of that. It is one of your brothers or sisters."

Mma Makutsi could see that. She had been stolen from when she was at the Botswana Secretarial College. Somebody in the class had taken her purse, which contained all her money for that week, which was not very much anyway, but which was needed, every thebe of it. Once that was gone, there was no money for food, and she would have to depend on the help of others. Did the person who took the purse **know** that? Would that person **care** if he or she knew that the loss of the money would mean hunger?

"It always hurts," she said. There had been two days of hunger because she had been too proud to ask, and then a friend, who had heard what had happened, had shared her food with her.

Mma Makutsi folded her hands; they would have to progress from these observations on the human condition to the business in hand. "You would like me to find out who is doing this?" She paused and stared at Teenie with a serious look; it would be best for her to know that these things were far from easy. "When something is being stolen by somebody on the inside," she said, "it is not always easy. In fact, it can be very hard to discover who is doing it. We have to look at who's spending what, at who's living beyond their means. That's one way. But it can be hard . . ."

Teenie interrupted her. The pleading look now became something more confident. "No, Mma," she said. "It will not be hard. It will not be hard because I can tell you who is doing it. I know exactly who it is."

Mma Makutsi could not conceal her surprise. "Oh yes?"

"Yes. I can point to the person who's stealing. I know exactly who it is."

Well, thought Mma Makutsi, if she knows who is responsible, then what is there for me to do? "So, Mma," she said. "What do you want me to do? It seems that you have already been a detective."

Teenie took this in her stride. "I cannot prove anything," she said. "I know who it is, but I have no proof. That is what I want you to find for me. Proof. Then I can get rid of that person. The employment laws say: proof first, then dismissal."

Mma Makutsi smiled. Clovis Andersen in **The Principles of Private Detection** had something to say about this, she recalled—as had Mma Ramotswe. **You do not know anything until you know why you know it,** he had written. And Mma Ramotswe, who had read the passage out to Mma Makutsi with an admonitory wagging of her finger, had qualified this by saying that although this was generally true, sometimes she knew that she knew something because of a special feeling that she had. But what Clovis Andersen said was nonetheless correct, she felt.

"You will have to tell me why you think you know who it is," Mma Makutsi said to Teenie. "Have you seen this person taking something?"

Teenie thought for a moment. "Not exactly."

"Ah."

There was a short period of silence. "Has

anybody else seen this person taking something?" Mma Makutsi went on.

Teenie shook her head. "No. Not as far as I know."

"So, may I ask you, Mma: How do you know who this person is?"

Teenie closed her eyes. "Because of the way he looks, Mma. This man who is taking things, he just looks dishonest. He is not a nice man. I can tell that, Mma."

Mma Makutsi reached for a piece of paper and wrote down a few words. Teenie watched the pencil move across the paper, then she looked up expectantly at Mma Makutsi.

"I shall need to come and have a look round," said Mma Makutsi. "You must not tell the staff that I am a detective. We shall have to think of some reason for me to be visiting the works."

"You could be a tax inspector," ventured Teenie.

Mma Makutsi laughed. "That is a very bad idea," she said. "They will think that I am after them. No, you can say that I am a client who is interested in giving the firm a big job but who wants to have a good look at how things are run. That will be a good story."

Teenie agreed with this. And would Mma Makutsi be available that afternoon? Everybody, including the man under suspicion, would be there and she could meet them all.

"How will I know which is the one you suspect?" asked Mma Makutsi.

"You'll know," said Teenie. "The moment you see him. You'll know."

She looked at Mma Makutsi. Still pleading.

CHAPTER ELEVEN

DR CRONJE

WHILE MMA MAKUTSI dealt with her diminutive client, Mma Ramotswe made the brief drive out to Mochudi; forty minutes if one rushed, an hour if one meandered. And she did meander, slowing down to look at some cattle who had strayed onto the verge of the road. She was her father's daughter after all, and Obed Ramotswe had never been able to pass by cattle without casting his expert eye over them. She had inherited some of that ability, a gift really, even if her eye would never be as good as his had been. He had cattle lineages embedded in his memory, like a biblical narrative setting out who begat whom; he knew every beast and their qualities. And she had always dreamed that when he died, at the very moment at which that bit of the old Botswana went, the cattle had somehow known. She understood that this was impossible, that it was sentimental, but the thought had given her comfort. When we die there are many farewells, spoken and unspoken—and the imagined farewell of the cattle was one of these.

The cattle by the roadside were not in particularly good condition, Mma Ramotswe thought. There was little grazing for them at this time of the year, with the rains a few months away and such grass as there was dry and brittle. The cattle would find something, of course, leaves, bits and pieces of vegetation that would provide some sustenance; but these beasts looked defeated and listless. They would not have a good owner, Mma Ramotswe concluded as she continued on her journey. To start with, they should not be out on the verge like that. Not only was that a risk to the cattle themselves, but it was a terrible danger to anybody driving on the road at night. Some cattle were the colour of night and seemed to merge perfectly into the darkness; a driver coming round a corner or surmounting a hump in the road might suddenly find himself face-to-face with one of these cattle and be unable to stop in time. If that happened, then those in the car could be impaled on the horns of the cow as it was hurled through the windscreen—that had happened, and often. Mma Ramotswe shuddered, and concentrated on the winding strip of tar ahead. Cattle, goats, children, other drivers—there were so many perils on the road.

By the time she arrived in Mochudi, her dawdling on the road had made her late. She looked at her watch. It was twelve o'clock and she had arranged to meet the doctor at a restaurant on the edge of the town fifteen minutes earlier; he had to have an early lunch, he explained, as he would be on duty at the hospital at two. She wondered if he would wait; she had telephoned him out of the blue and asked to see him—there were many who would decline an invitation of that sort, but he had agreed without any probing into what her business with him might be. All she had said was that she was a friend of Tati Monyena; that, it seemed, was enough.

Mochudi had a number of restaurants, most of them very small affairs, one small room at the most, or a rickety bench outside a lean-to shack serving braised maize cobs and plates of pap; simple fare, but filling and delicious. Then there were the liquor restaurants, which were larger and noisier. Some of these stayed one step ahead of the police and the tribal authorities, and were regularly being closed down for the disturbance they created and their cavalier attitude to licencing hours. Mma Ramotswe did not like these, with their dark interiors and their groups of drinkers engaged in endless and heated debates over their bottles of beer; that was not for her.

There was one good restaurant, though, one that she liked, which had a garden and tables in that garden. The kitchens were clean, the food wholesome, and the waitresses adept at friendly conversation. She went there from time to time when she felt that she needed to catch up on Mochudi news, and she would spin out her lunch to two or three hours, talking or just sitting under one of the trees and looking up at the birds on the branches above. It was a good place for birds, a bird restaurant, and the more confident amongst their number would flutter down to the ground to peck at the crumbs of food under the tables, minute zebra finches, bulbuls, plain birds that had no name as far as she knew.

The tiny white van drew up in front of the restaurant and Mma Ramotswe alighted. A wide acacia tree stood at the entrance to the restaurant garden, an umbrella against the sun, and a dog sat just outside the lacy shadow of the tree, his eyes half closed, soaking up the winter sun. A couple of flies walked across the narrow part of his nose, but he did not flinch. Mma Ramotswe saw that only one of the outside tables was occupied, and she knew immediately that it was the doctor. Half Xhosa, half Afrikaner. It could only be him.

"Dr Cronje?"

The doctor looked up from the photocopied article he had been reading. Mma Ramotswe noticed the graphs across the page, the tables of results. Behind the things that happened to one, the coughs and pains, the human fevers, there were these cold figures.

He started to rise to his feet, but Mma Ramotswe urged him not to. "I am sorry to be late. It is my fault. I drove very slowly." She noticed that the doctor had green eyes; green eyes and a skin that was very light brown, the colour of chocolate milk, a mixture of Africa and Europe.

"Drive slowly," he mused. "If only everyone

would do that, we'd be less busy in the hospital, Mma Ramotswe."

A waitress appeared and took their order. He put his papers away in a small folder and then turned his gaze to Mma Ramotswe. "Mr Monyena told us that you might want to speak to people," he said. "So here I am. He's the boss."

He spoke politely enough, but there was a flatness in his tone. That explains it, thought Mma Ramotswe. That explains why he came.

"So he told you that I have been asked to look into those unexplained deaths," she said. "Did he tell you that?"

"Yes," he said. "Though why we need anybody else to do that beats me. We had an internal enquiry, you know. Mr Monyena was on that himself. Why have another one?"

Mma Ramotswe was interested. Tati Monyena had not told her about an internal enquiry, which must have been an oversight on his part.

"And what did it conclude?" she asked.

Dr Cronje rolled his eyes up in a gesture which indicated contempt for internal enquiries. "Nothing," he said. "Absolutely nothing. The trouble was that some people could not bring themselves to admit the obvious. So the enquiry petered out. Technically it hasn't been wound up."

The waitress now brought them their drinks: a pot of bush tea for Mma Ramotswe and a cup of coffee for the doctor. Mma Ramotswe poured her tea and took a first sip.

"What do you think it should have decided?" she asked. "What if you had been on it?"

The doctor smiled—for the first time, thought Mma Ramotswe—and it was not a smile that lasted long.

"I was," he said.

"You were?"

"I was a member of the enquiry. It was the hospital superintendant, Mr Monyena, one of the senior staff nurses, somebody nominated by Chief Linchwe, and me. That was it."

Mma Ramotswe took another sip of tea. Somebody had started to play music inside the restaurant, and for a few seconds she thought she recognised the tune as one that had been played by Note Mokoti, her former husband. She caught her breath; Note was over, gone, but when she heard his music, the tunes he liked to play, which she sometimes did, a tinge of pain could come. But it was a different tune, something like one that he played, but different.

"When you say that there was something very obvious that people could not admit, what was that, Rra?"

The doctor reached out and touched the rim of his coffee cup, idly drawing a finger round it. "Natural causes," he said. "Cardiac and pulmonary failure in two of the cases. Renal in the other. Case closed, Mma . . . Mma . . ."

He had already used her name, but she supplied it again. "Ramotswe."

"Ramotswe. Sorry."

They sat in silence for a moment. Then the doctor looked up into the tree, as if trying to find something. She saw the green eyes moving, searching. The green eyes were from the Afrikaner, but the softness of his face, a masculine softness but a softness nonetheless, came from the mother, came from Africa.

"So there's really nothing further to be done about it," Mma Ramotswe said gently.

The doctor did not reply for a moment; he was still looking up into the tree above them. "In my view, no," he said. "But that won't stop the talk, the pointing of fingers."

"At?" asked Mma Ramotswe.

"Me," he said. He looked down again and their eyes met. "Yes, me. There are people in the hospital who say that I'm bad luck. They look at me in that way . . . you know, that way which people use here. As if they're a bit frightened of you. They say nothing, but they look."

It was hard for Mma Ramotswe to respond to this. She had a sense that Dr Cronje was one of those people who did not fit in—wherever they were. They were outsiders, treated with a reserve which could easily become suspicion, and that suspicion could easily blossom into a whispering campaign of ugly rumours. But what puzzled her was why she herself should have this uneasy feeling about him, which she did. Why should she feel this discomfort in his presence when she knew next to nothing about him? It was intuition again; useful sometimes but on other occasions a doubtful benefit.

"People are like that," she said at last. "If you come from somewhere else, they can be like that. It is not easy to be a stranger, is it?"

He looked at her as she spoke; it seemed to her that he was surprised that she should speak like this, with such frankness. "No," he said, and then paused before he continued. "And that is what I have been all my life. All of it."

The waitress arrived with their plates. There was stew, and a plate of vegetables for each of them.

He looked at his plate. "I shouldn't talk like this, Mma. I have nothing to complain about, really. This is a good place."

Mma Ramotswe lifted up her fork, and then put it down again. She reached across and laid a hand upon his wrist. He looked down at where her hand rested.

"You mustn't be sad, Rra," she said.

He frowned, and laid down his knife.

"I wish I could go home," he said. "I love this country. I love it. But it's not home for me."

"Well you could go home," Mma Ramotswe said. She nodded in the direction of the border, not far across a few miles of scrub bush, behind the hills. "You could go home now, couldn't you? There's nothing stopping you."

"That place is not home any more," he said. "I left it so long ago, I don't feel at home there."

"And this place? Here?"

"It's where I live. But I can't ever belong here, can I? I will never be from this place. I will never be one of these people, no matter how long I stay. I'll always be an outsider."

She knew what he meant. It was all very well for her, she thought; she knew exactly where she came from and where she belonged, but there were many people who did not, who had been uprooted, forced out by need or victimisation, by being simply the wrong people in the wrong place. There were many such people in Africa, and they ate a very bitter fruit; they were extra, unwanted persons, like children who are not loved.

She wanted to say something to this man, this lonely doctor, but she realised there was little comfort she could give him. Yet she could try.

"Don't think, Rra," she said, "that what you are doing, your work in the hospital up there, is not appreciated. Nobody might ever have said thank you to you, but I do now, Rra. I say thank you for what you do."

He had lowered his gaze, but now he looked at her, and she found herself staring into those unnerving green eyes.

"Thank you, Mma," he said. And then he picked up his knife and fork and began to eat.

Mma Ramotswe watched discreetly as she started on her own plate of food. She saw the way his knife moved, delicately, with precision.

Mr j.l.b.matekoni talked to Charlie that afternoon.

"You can stop work today, Charlie," he said. "I have made up your final pay packet."

Charlie wiped his hands on a piece of paper towel. "This stuff isn't as good as lint, Boss," he said, frowning at the towel. "Lint gets grease off much better."

"Paper towel is the modern thing," said Mr J.L.B. Matekoni. "Paper towel and that scouring powder. That is very good for grease."

"Well, I won't need that any more," said Charlie. "Except maybe when I service the taxi."

"Don't forget to do that," warned Mr J.L.B. Matekoni. "It is an old car. Those old cars need regular oil changes. So change your oil every two months, Charlie. You will never regret that."

The apprentice beamed with pleasure. "I will, Boss."

Mr J.L.B. Matekoni looked at him from under his eyebrows. He doubted that the car would be well looked after, but he had steeled himself to let Charlie get on with his plans. And now it had come to the point where he would say goodbye and hand over the car. There was an agreement to be signed, of course, because Charlie did not have the money to pay for the vehicle and it would have to be paid off month by month for almost three years. Even then, he wondered whether he would ever see the money, or all of it, as of the two apprentices Charlie had always been the more financially irresponsible one and always tried to borrow towards the end of the month when money got tight.

Charlie glanced at the document which Mr J.L.B. Matekoni had drawn up and that had been typed out by Mma Makutsi that afternoon. He would pay six hundred pula a month until the cost of the car had been covered. He would make sure that it was insured. If he could not keep up the payments he would give the car back to Mr J.L.B. Matekoni, who would pay the book price for it. That was all.

"You should read that carefully," said Mr J.L.B. Matekoni. "It is a legal document, you know."

But Charlie reached out for a pen from his

employer's top pocket. He left a small grease stain on the edge of the fabric. "That's fine by me, Boss," he said. "You would never try to cheat me. I know that. You are my father."

Mr J.L.B. Matekoni watched Charlie as he signed with a flourish and handed over the piece of paper. There were greasy fingerprints on the document where the apprentice had held it. I have tried to teach him, Mr J.L.B. Matekoni said to himself. I have tried my best.

They went outside to where the old Mercedes-Benz was parked. Mr J.L.B. Matekoni handed over the keys to Charlie. "It's insured on my policy for the next two weeks," he said. "Then it's up to you."

Charlie looked at the keys. "I can hardly believe this, Boss. I can hardly believe it."

Mr J.L.B. Matekoni bit his lip. He had looked after this boy, every day, every day, for years now. "I know you'll do your best, Charlie," he said quietly. "I know that."

A door opened in the building behind them and Mma Makutsi appeared. Charlie put the keys in his pocket and looked nervously at Mr J.L.B. Matekoni.

"I have come to say goodbye," Mma Makutsi said. "And to wish you good luck with the business, Charlie. I hope that it goes well with you."

Charlie had been staring at the ground. Now he looked up and smiled. "Thank you, Mma. I will try."

"Yes," said Mma Makutsi. "I am sure that you will. And here's another thing. I'm sorry, Rra, if I have ever been unkind to you. I am sorry for that."

Nobody spoke. Mr J.L.B. Matekoni, who was holding the piece of paper which Charlie had signed, busied himself with folding it neatly and putting it into his pocket, a task which seemed to take a long time, and had to be re-done. Somewhere, on the road behind the garage, an engine revved up, coughed, and then died away into silence.

"That needs fixing," said Charlie, laughing nervously. Then, he looked at Mma Makutsi, and smiled at her. "If you need my taxi, Mma," he said, "I will be proud to drive you."

"And I will be proud to go in it," she said. "Thank you."

After that, there was little more to be said. Great feuds often need very few words to resolve them. Disputes, even between nations, between peoples, can be set to rest with simple acts of contrition and corresponding forgiveness, can so often be shown to be based on nothing much other than pride and misunderstanding, and the forgetting of the humanity of the other—and land, of course.

CHAPTER TWELVE

A GIFT FROM
MR PHUTI RADIPHUTI

AFTER THE DEPARTURE of Charlie, which happened shortly after four o'clock, Mr J.L.B. Matekoni found it difficult to settle back to work. Charlie had driven away in triumph, at the wheel of the Mercedes-Benz which Mr J.L.B. Matekoni had just made over to him. For the proprietor of Tlokweng Road Speedy Motors it was an emotional parting, and although Mr J.L.B. Matekoni was not one to show his feelings—mechanics do not do that—he had nearly been overcome by the moment. When he had first taken on the two apprentices, he had allowed himself to imagine that perhaps one of them would prove to be his helpmate and would in due course take over the garage. Charlie would have been the obvious choice, as the older of the two boys, but before very long it had become apparent to Mr J.L.B. Matekoni that such thoughts were no more than fond imaginings. But in spite of all Charlie's faults—his bad workmanship, his impetuosity, his endless attempts to impress girls—Mr J.L.B. Matekoni had conceived of a rough affection for him, as one will sometimes grow to love another for his human weaknesses. Now, with Charlie away, and the younger apprentice looking lost and disconsolate, Mr J.L.B. Matekoni felt curiously empty. It was not that he had no work to do—a station wagon belonging to an Air Botswana pilot, a much-loved car which Mr J.L.B. Matekoni had nursed through various mechanical illnesses, was waiting for him to replace some of its wiring. The old wires, pulled out and unravelled like a network of nerves, protruded from their hiding places; fuses lay beside them on the seats. But he could not bring himself to start this task, and so he put it off until the next day.

Now he would return to his other role—to the investigation of the errant Mr Botumile. His last observation of this man had revealed nothing more than that he kept surprisingly bad company. But that was not the same thing as adultery, and it was a suspected affair that had brought Mma Botumile to the door of the No. 1 Ladies' Detective Agency. She wanted to know the identity of the woman whom she suspected her husband was seeing—a reasonable thing for a wife to want to know, thought Mr J.L.B. Matekoni—and he was determined to find that out. What happened after that was another matter. Mma Botumile was a formidable person, and Mr J.L.B. Matekoni did not envy the other woman any encounter that she might have with her. That was not really his business, though. At the most, he imagined that he or Mma Ramotswe might be asked to warn the girlfriend off, which was something that could be done quite tactfully. All that would be necessary, he thought, would be to tell her that Mma Botumile knew, and that Mma Botumile was not the sort of woman who would countenance her husband's having an affair. A sensible girlfriend would then understand that a choice had to be made. She could fight for Mr Botumile and prise him away from his wife, or she could find another man. What she could not do was to continue to be a rival to Mma Botumile while her husband was still with her.

It was almost on impulse that Mr J.L.B. Matekoni went into the office to ask Mma Makutsi if he could borrow the agency camera. This camera had been bought at an early stage in the existence of the No. 1 Ladies' Detective Agency, in the belief that it would be necessary for the obtaining of evidence. Clovis Andersen had advised this, saying that **while one cannot say that a camera never lies, it is hard to beat photographic evidence. Many is the time that I have personally confronted a malefactor with a photograph of himself engaged in something discreditable and said, "There, who's that then? The Man in the Moon?"** It was Mma Makutsi who had read this passage, been impressed, and suggested the purchase of the camera. She had hardly ever used it, but the camera, ready and loaded with film, sat on a shelf behind Mma Ramotswe's desk, awaiting its moment.

Armed with the camera, Mr J.L.B. Matekoni had then left the garage, instructions having been given to the younger apprentice to lock up, and had driven in his truck to exactly that spot outside the office building where he had previously waited for Mr Botumile. He had been in position for ten minutes by the time that the front door opened and a man came out and headed for one of the two red cars parked to the side of the building. Although he was the first man out after five, this was not Mr Botumile but the other man, and Mr J.L.B. Matekoni ignored him as he got into the car and drove away. Then, a few minutes later, Mr Botumile appeared and climbed into his car.

Mr J.L.B. Matekoni followed the red car. The traffic was light, for some reason, and it was easy to keep a reasonable distance back without losing sight of his quarry. This time a new route was followed, and the red car drove back towards the Tlokweng Road. The main road was, of course, much busier, and he had to be careful not to lose sight of Mr Botumile's car, but he was close enough, and alert enough, not to miss it as it turned sharply off to the right a short distance after the shopping centre. Mr J.L.B. Matekoni was fairly familiar with the dirt road down which the red vehicle now travelled. This was not far from the garage, and he occasionally drove down here to test a car that he had repaired, especially if new suspension needed to be tried out. It was mostly a residential area, sparsely populated, although there were one or two business plots at the Tlokweng Road end. It was also a road for goats, he remembered, as a bit of land halfway down was given over to these destructive creatures. It had been stripped almost bare of vegetation, apart from a few thorn bushes which had defeated even the talents of the goats. Now, as he drove down it, following the small cloud of dust thrown up from the wheels of Mr Botumile's car, he saw a few goats standing by the side of the road, nibbling at a piece of sacking which had been blown against a fence. These were odd parts of the town; not quite the bush, which was just beyond the fences, but heading that way, prone to the incursions of animals.

Suddenly the rear lights of Mr Botumile's car glowed through the dust and he swung into the driveway of a house. Mr J.L.B. Matekoni, reacting quickly, slowed down and then drew in to the side of the road. He would wait a minute or so, he thought, before he drove past the house. This would give Mr Botumile time to get out of the car, if he was going to get out, or pick up his waiting girlfriend, if that was what he had in mind.

By the time he drove past, Mr Botumile was out of his car. Mr J.L.B. Matekoni saw him walking up a short path towards the door of the house. He saw the door open, and he saw a woman standing there, waiting. It was not much more than a brief glimpse, but it was etched indelibly in his mind—the man, his lover, the dispirited dust-covered vegetation in the yard of the house, the angle of the gate, which was off its hinge, the stand-pipe at the side of the house. Was this what a clandestine affair looked like?

He went further down the road until he came to a place where he could turn without being seen from the house. Then he drove back slowly, this time with the camera ready on his lap. As he drew level with the house, he slowed down slightly, and, manipulating the camera with one hand while the other hand was on the steering wheel, he took a photograph of the house. Then, his heart beating hard with the sheer excitement of it, he accelerated back in the direction of the Tlokweng Road. He felt confused. It had been an exhilarating experience in one sense, and he had felt the satisfaction of seeing what he had expected to see. But the act of taking the photograph seemed to him to have been an intrusion of a quite different degree from that of following Mr Botumile. He glanced down at the camera beside him on the seat of the truck; the sight of it, with its prying lens, made him feel dirty. This was not like being a mechanic; this was like being . . . well, it was like being a spy, an informant, a seeker-out of the tawdry secrets of others.

He thought that he would discuss it with Mma Ramotswe. It was impossible to imagine her ever doing anything that was wrong or shabby, and if she said that in this case the end justified the means, then he would be satisfied. But then he thought again: the whole point about this investigation was that he was doing it himself; he should not run off to Mma Ramotswe the moment anything difficult arose. No, he would have the film developed and he would show the photograph to Mma Botumile. But first he would find out who lived in that house so that he might reveal to her the chapter and verse of her husband's infidelity. He did not envy Mr Botumile after that, but then it was really not for him, Mr J.L.B. Matekoni, to pass judgement on a client's marriage, other than to come to the conclusion, privately, that if Mma Botumile were the last woman in Botswana and he were the last man, he would stay resolutely single.

WHILE MR J.L.B. MATEKONI wrestled with his conscience, Mma Makutsi was preparing a meal for Phuti Radiphuti in her house in Extension Two. The previous evening had been one of his days to eat at his aunt's house, and this meant that he would be looking forward to Mma Makutsi's cooking. Mma Makutsi cooked what Phuti Radiphuti wanted, whereas his aunt cooked what she thought he should eat. That evening, she had prepared fried chicken with rice into which sultanas had been sprinkled. There was also fried banana, which always seemed to go so well with chicken, and a small jar of Mozambiquan peri-peri sauce which gave a kick to everything. Phuti Radiphuti had revealed a taste for hot food, which Mma Makutsi was trying to acquire herself. She was making some progress in that, but it was slow, and frequent glasses of water were required.

Their conversation ranged over the events of the past few days. Mma Makutsi had debated with herself whether to reveal her abortive resignation, and had eventually decided that she would do so. She did not come out of the episode very well, she thought, but she had never concealed anything from him, and she did not want to start doing so now.

"I made a fool of myself yesterday," she said to him, as she stirred the fried chicken in the pan. "I thought I would go and get another job." That was all she said. She had thought that she would tell him everything, but now, in the end, she did not. There was no mention of the encounter with Violet and of the humiliation that had entailed; there was no mention of the broken shoe, nor of the ignominious barefoot walk, nor the thorn.

She was surprised by the strength of his reaction to the news. "But you can't do that!" he exploded. "What about Mma Ramotswe! You can't leave Mma Ramotswe!"

Taken aback, Mma Makutsi made an attempt to defend herself. "But there's my career to think about," she protested. "What about me?"

Phuti Radiphuti seemed unmoved. "What would Mma Ramotswe do without you?" he asked. "You are the one who knows where everything is. You have done all the filing.

You know all the clients. You cannot leave Mma Ramotswe."

Mma Makutsi listened to this with foreboding. It seemed to her that he cared more about Mma Ramotswe than he did about her. Surely as her fiancé he should side with her in all this, should have her interests at heart rather than those of Mma Ramotswe, worthy though she undoubtedly was?

"I came back very quickly," she said lamely. "I was only away for the morning."

Phuti Radiphuti looked at her with concern. "Mma Ramotswe relies on you, Mma," he said. "You know that?"

Mma Makutsi replied that she did. But there were times when one had to move on, did he not think . . .

She did not finish. "And I can understand why she cannot do without you," Phuti continued. "It is the same reason why I cannot do without you."

Mma Makutsi was silent.

Phuti reached for the bottle of peri-peri sauce and fiddled with the cap as he spoke. "It is because you are such a fine person," he said. "That is why."

Mma Makutsi gave the chicken a final stir

and then sat down. What had begun as a reproach had turned, it seemed, into a compliment. And she could not remember when she
had last been complimented for anything; she
had forgotten Mma Ramotswe's complimen-
tary remark about her red dress.

"That's very kind, Phuti," she said.

Phuti put down the bottle of sauce and
began to fish for something in the pocket of
his jacket. "I am not one to make a speech,"
he said.

"But you are getting better at it," said Mma
Makutsi. Which was true, she thought; that
dreadful stammer had been more or less ban-
ished since she had met him, even if it mani-
fested itself now and then when he became
flustered. But that was all part of his charm; the
charm of this man, her fiancé, the man who
would become her husband.

"I am not one to make a speech," Phuti repeated. "But there is something that I have
for you here which I want to give you. It is a
ring, Mma. It is a diamond. I have bought it
for you."

He slipped a box across the table to Mma
Makutsi. She took it with fumbling hands and

prised it open there on the table. The diamond caught the light.

"It is one of our diamonds," he said. "It is a Botswana diamond."

Mma Makutsi was silent as she took the ring from the box and fitted it onto her finger. She looked at Phuti and began to say something, but stopped. It was hard to find the words; that she who had been given so little, should now get this; that this gift, beyond her wildest yearnings, should come from him; how could she express what she felt?

"One of our diamonds?"

"Yes. It is from our land."

She pressed the ring, and the stone, to her cheek. It was cold to the touch; so precious; so pure.

CHAPTER THIRTEEN

THE GOOD IMPRESSION PRINTING WORKS

EVERYBODY, apart from Mr Polopetsi, and the younger apprentice of course, now had something to investigate. They approached this task with differing degrees of enthusiasm—Mr J.L.B. Matekoni, who believed that his investigation was almost over, felt buoyant. He now had photographic evidence—or at least one photograph of Mr Botumile's love nest—and all he had to do now was to find the name of the person who lived there. That was a simple enquiry which would not take long, and armed with the answer he could go to Mma Botumile and give her the information she needed. That would undoubtedly please her, but, more than that, it would impress Mma Ramotswe, who would be surprised at the speed with which he had managed to bring the enquiry to a satisfactory conclusion. The exposed film had been deposited at the chemist for developing and would be ready later that morning; there was no reason, then, why he should not see Mma Botumile the following day. To this end he telephoned her and asked if she would care to come to the office at any time convenient to her. He might have expected a snippy response even to that simple invitation. And that is what he got: no time, she said, was convenient. "I am an extremely busy woman," she snapped. "But you can call on me, maybe I will be in, maybe not."

Mr J.L.B. Matekoni sighed as he replaced the receiver. There were some people, it seemed, who were incapable of being pleasant about anything; that was what they were like when it came to the mending of their cars, and that was what they were like in relation to everything. Of course, the cars that such people drove tended to be difficult as well, now that he came to think about it. Nice cars have nice drivers; bad cars have bad drivers. A person's gearbox revealed everything that you could want to know about that person, thought Mr J.L.B. Matekoni.

He wondered whether Mr Botumile had been aware of his wife's irascible nature before he had asked her to marry him. **If** he had ever proposed marriage; it may well have been the other way round. Sometimes men cannot remember the circumstances in which they asked their wives to marry them, for the very good reason that no identifiable proposal was ever made. These are the men, thought Mr J.L.B. Matekoni, who are trapped into matrimony, who drift into it, who are eventually cornered by feminine wiles and find that a date has been set. In his own case he remembered very well the circumstances in which he had asked Mma Ramotswe to be his wife, but the memory of the way in which the day was actually selected was very much hazier. He had been at the orphan farm, he believed, and Mma Potokwane had said something about how important it was for a woman to know when a wedding would be—something like that—and then the next thing he knew was that he was standing under that big tree and Trevor Mwamba was conducting the wedding service.

Mr J.L.B. Matekoni, of course, was very content being the husband of Mma Ramotswe, and he would never conceive of a situation in which he would be unhappy with her. But how different it must be—and what a nightmare—to discover that the person whom one has married is somebody one just does not like. People did make such a discovery, sometimes only a week or two into the marriage, and it must be a bleak one. Mr J.L.B. Matekoni knew that you were supposed to make an effort with your marriage, that you should at least try to get on with your spouse, but what if you found that she was somebody like Mma Botumile? He shuddered at the thought. Poor Mr Botumile having to listen to that shrill, complaining voice every day, no doubt running him down, criticising his every move, his every remark, making a prison for him, a prison of put-downs and belittlements. There but for the grace of God, he thought, go I. This feeling for Mr Botumile, this sympathy, was the only drawback in the way he felt about the whole enquiry. And even then, in spite of his understanding of Mr Botumile's plight, he was proud of the fact that he had been able to be so professional about the whole matter. He had sympathised with the husband in this case, but he had not let it obscure the fact that he was working for the wife.

For Mma Makutsi, the investigation of Teenie's problem with her dishonest employee was less clear-cut. It might well be that one of the employees at the printing works looked shifty, but she very much doubted that his shifty looks alone meant that he was the thief. He might be, of course, and she would keep an open mind on that, but she could certainly not allow her investigation to be skewed by any presumption of guilt. Or that, at least, is what she told herself as she paid off the taxi that she had hired to take her from the agency office to the premises of Teenie's printing company. Thirty pula! She tucked the receipt carefully into the pocket of her cardigan; it would have cost two pula, at the most, to make the journey by minibus, but the exorbitant cost of the taxi could properly be passed on to the client, and anyway, she told herself, it would be quite in-appropriate for her to arrive at the printing works in a battered and over-loaded vehicle, complete with hands and feet sticking out of the windows. People noted how people trav-elled, and if she was going to pass herself off as a potential client of the company, then she should arrive in fitting style. Clovis Andersen probably said something about this in **The**

Principles of Private Detection, but even if he did not, common sense dictated it.

The Good Impression Printing Company occupied half of a largish building in the industrial site that lay beyond the diamond-sorting building. It was not a very impressive building—one of those structures that look like cheap warehouses and which have few windows. Above their door was a sign saying **Words mean business. Business means money. Make a good impression with the Good Impression Printing Company!** And below that was a picture of a glossy brochure out of which, as from a cornucopia, banknotes cascaded. It was a powerful message, thought Mma Makutsi, and it made her think that perhaps it was time to speak to Mma Ramotswe about a new sign for the agency. That might also have an illustration of some sort to brighten the signboard, but what might it be? A tea-pot was the image that most immediately sprang to mind, but that would hardly do: there was no particular association in the public mind between private detection and tea, even if tea-drinking was an important part of their day's activities. Mma Ramotswe drank six cups a day—at the office; she had no idea how much bush tea was consumed at home—and she herself drank four, or perhaps five, if one counted the occasional top-up. But this was no time to think about such things, she decided; this was a delicate enquiry, conducted **under cover,** and she would have to think herself into the part she was about to play—a client inspecting a potential supplier.

Mma Makutsi entered a reception area at the front of the building. It was not a large room and the receptionist's desk dominated the available space, leaving only a cramped corner for a few chairs. Beside these chairs was a small table on which paper samples and some trade magazines had been stacked.

There was a curious smell in the air, an almost acrid smell that took her a moment to recognise as the smell of ink. That took her back to the school in Bobonong, where they had a room with a duplicating machine and supplies of the ink that it used. It was an old machine of the sort that nobody used any more, and it had been forgotten by the authorities, but the school kept it going. The children had helped with the task of duplication, and she had watched in wonder as the newly printed pages emerged from beneath the circulating drum. And now, a world away from that place and those days, she remembered the smell of ink.

She gave her name to the receptionist, who telephoned and called through to Teenie Magama. Then she sat down on one of the chairs in the corner and waited until Teenie arrived.

She looked at the receptionist, a middle-aged woman wearing what looked like a housecoat but which she decided was actually a loose-fitting dress. Her outfit was far from smart, and Mma Makutsi found herself thinking, **It's not her. This woman has no spare cash. If she were stealing, then one would expect . . . Or would one? Desperation drove people to theft, did it not?** She looked at her more closely.

She decided on a general question. If you could think of nothing to say to somebody, you could always ask them how long they had been doing whatever it was that they were doing. People always seemed willing to talk about that. "Have you worked here very long, Mma?" Mma Makutsi asked.

The receptionist, who had been typing, looked up from her keyboard.

"I do not belong to this place," she said. "I am here because my daughter is sick. She is the one who has this job. I am standing in for her." She paused. "And I do not know what I am doing, Mma. I am just sitting here, but I do not know what I am doing."

Mma Makutsi laughed, but the woman shook her head. "No, I am serious, Mma. I really don't know what I'm doing. I try to answer the phone, but I end up cutting people off. And I do not know the names of any of the people in the works back there. Except for Mma Magama herself. That Teenie person. I know her name."

"There are many people who do not know what they are doing," said Mma Makutsi. "It is not unusual. In fact, maybe even most people do not know. They pretend to know, but they do not really know."

The receptionist smiled. "Then I am not alone, Mma."

Mma Makutsi tried another tack. "Is your daughter happy here?" she asked.

The woman's answer came quickly. "Very happy. She is very happy, Mma. She is always telling other people what a good boss she has. Not everybody can say that."

Mma Makutsi was about to say that she could, but stopped herself in time. She could not tell this woman about Mma Ramotswe because that would give away what she did and she was meant to be a prospective client, not a private detective. So she said nothing, and they drifted back into silence.

A few minutes later, Teenie appeared through a door behind the receptionist's desk. She was more plainly dressed than she had been when she had come to Mma Makutsi's office, and for a moment Mma Makutsi did not recognise her.

"Yes," said Teenie. "I am not looking smart now. These are my working clothes. And look, see what my hands look like. Ink!"

Mma Makutsi rose to her feet and examined Teenie's outstretched hands. "If I were a detective," she said as she saw the large ink stains, like continents, on Teenie's upturned palms, "I would say that you are a printer." Then she added hurriedly, glancing down at the receptionist as she spoke, "But I am not a detective, of course!"

"No, of course not," said Teenie. "You are not a detective, Mma."

The receptionist, who had been following the conversation between the two of them, looked up sharply. "You are a police-woman, Mma?"

Mma Makutsi noticed the concern in the woman's voice. "I am nothing to do with the police," she said. "Nothing at all. I am a businesswoman."

The receptionist relaxed visibly. Her sharp reaction, thought Mma Makutsi, was un-usual. She clearly had something to hide, but it was probably nothing to do with her daughter or the job at the printing works. Unless, of course, she knew that her daughter had been stealing from the works. Mothers and daugh-ters can be close; they tell each other things, and the knowledge that one's daughter was a thief would obviously make one dread the ar-rival of the police. But then she reminded her-self that there were plenty of people who were afraid of the police, even if they had clear con-sciences. These were people who had been the victims of bullying when young—bullying by severe teachers, by stronger children; there were so many ways in which people could be crushed. Such people might fear the police in the same way in which they feared all authority.

Mma Makutsi smiled at the receptionist and followed Teenie through the door into the works. The other woman was so small that even though Mma Makutsi was herself only of average height, she found herself looking down at the top of Teenie's head; at a small woollen bobble, in fact, which topped a curious tea-cosy style knitted cap which she was wearing. She looked more closely at it, wondering if she could make out an opening through which a tea-pot spout might project; she could not see an opening, but there was a very similar tea-cosy in the office, she remembered, and perhaps she or Mma Ramotswe might wear it on really cold days. She imagined how Mma Ramotswe would look in a tea-cosy and decided that she would probably look rather good; it might add to her authority, perhaps, in some indefinable way.

On the other side of the door was a short corridor. The smell she had picked up when she first came into the building was stronger now, and there was noise too, the obedient clatter of a machine performing some repetitive task. From the background somewhere, there came strains of radio music.

"Our new machine is on," said Teenie proudly. "That is it making that noise. Listen. That is our new German machine printing a brochure. They make very good machines, the Germans, you know, Mma."

Mma Makutsi agreed. "Yes," she said. "They do. They are . . ." She was not sure how to continue. She had been about to pass a further comment on the Germans, but realised that she actually knew very little about them. The Chinese one saw a lot of, and they seemed quiet and industrious too, but one did not see many Germans. In fact, she had seen none.

Teenie turned and looked up at her. The expectant, plaintive look was there; as if there was something important that Mma Makutsi might say about the Germans and which she desperately wanted to hear.

"I would like to go to Germany," said Mma Makutsi lamely.

"Yes," said Teenie. "I would like to visit other countries. I would like to go to London some day. But I do not think I shall ever get out of Botswana. This business keeps me tied up. It is like a chain around my ankle sometimes. You cannot go anywhere if you have a chain around your ankle."

"No," said Mma Makutsi, raising her voice now to compete with the sound of the German printing machine.

Mma Makutsi gazed about her. If she needed to act the part of the interested client, then it was not a difficult role for her to fill; she was very interested. They were in a large, high-ceilinged space, windowless but with an open door at the back. The sun streamed through the back door, but the main lighting was provided by a bank of fluorescent tube lights hanging from the ceiling. In the centre of the room stood the German printing machine, while four or five other complicated-looking machines were arranged around the rest of the area. Mma Makutsi noticed an electric guillotine, with shavings of paper below, and large bottles of what must have been ink on high racked shelves. There were several large supply cupboards, walk-in affairs, and stacks of supplies on trolleys and tables. It was a good place for a thief, she thought; there were plenty of **things.**

Next, she noticed the people. There were two young men standing at the side of the German printing machine: one engaged in some sort of adjusting task, the other watching a rapidly growing pile of printed brochures. At the far end of the room, two women were stacking piles of paper onto a trolley, while a third person, a man, was doing something to what looked like another, smaller printing machine. Just off the main space there were two blocked-off glass cubicles, small offices. One was empty, but lit; a man and a woman were in the other, the woman showing a piece of paper to the man. When Mma Makutsi looked in their direction, the woman nudged the man and pointed at her. The man looked across the room.

"You should introduce me to the staff," said Mma Makutsi. "Why don't we start with those two?" She indicated the two young men attending to the large printing machine.

"They are very nice young men," said Teenie. "They are my best people. They have a printer's eye, Mma. Do you know what a printer's eye is? It means that they can see how things are going to turn out even before the machine is turned on."

Mma Makutsi thought of the two apprentices. If there was such a thing as a mechanic's eye, then she doubted whether the apprentices had it.

"Printers used to be able to read backwards," said Teenie as they approached the machine and its two young attendants. "They could do that when type was set in metal. They put the letters in backwards."

"Mirrors," said Mma Makutsi. "They must have had mirrors in their heads."

"No," said Teenie. "They did not."

As they approached the printing machine, the two young men stopped what they were doing. One flicked a switch and the machine ground to a halt. Without the noise it had been making the works now seemed unnaturally quiet, apart from the radio in the background somewhere which could still be heard churning out the insistent beat of a rock tune, the sort of music that Mma Ramotswe described as the sound of an angry stomach.

The young men were dressed in work overalls and one of them now took a cloth out of his pocket and wiped his hands on it. The other, who had a large mouth, which he kept open, reached a finger up to fiddle with his nose, but thought better of it and dropped his hand to his side.

"This lady is a client," said Teenie. "She is very interested in printing. You could tell her about the new machine. She is called Mma Makutsi."

Mma Makutsi smiled encouragingly at the young men. She tried to keep her eyes off the face of the young man with the gaping mouth, but found that she could not; such a deep space, like the mouth of a cave, allowing one to see straight into his head. It was fascinating, in a curious, uncomfortable way.

The printer who had wiped his hands on the cloth leaned forward to shake hands with Mma Makutsi. He spoke politely to her, and told her his name. While this was happening, Mma Makutsi felt the eyes of the other young man on her. She glanced at him, but saw only the open mouth. Absurdly, temptingly, she wanted to put something into it: pieces of paper, perhaps, small erasers, anything that would block it up; it was ridiculous.

Then the young man spoke. "You are that lady from the detective agency," he said. "That place on the Tlokweng Road." The sound of his voice may have come from his mouth, but to Mma Makutsi it seemed that it really came from somewhere below, down in his chest or stomach.

Mma Makutsi looked at Teenie, who turned to stare up at her in blank surprise. "I am that lady," she stuttered. "Yes."

There was silence. Mma Makutsi was momentarily at a loss as to what to say. She felt an intense irritation that this young man, with his disconcerting mouth, should expose her so quickly. But then she began to wonder how he knew. It was flattering to think that she was well known, a public figure almost, even if it meant that she would be unable to carry out enquiries quite as discreetly as she hoped; certainly this enquiry was ruined now, as everybody here would know within minutes who she was.

Her surprise turned to anger. "So I am that lady," she snapped at the young man. "But that means nothing. Nothing at all."

"I've never met a detective," said the young man with the cloth. "Is it interesting work, Mma? Do you come to places like this to investigate . . ."

"Thefts," supplied the mouth.

Teenie gave a start. She had been watching the young men as they talked; now she spun round and looked at Mma Makutsi. Again there was that pleading look, as if she wanted Mma Makutsi to say that it was not true, that she was not a detective, and that she had certainly not come here to look into thefts.

Mma Makutsi decided that the best tactic would be to pretend to be amused by the very suggestion. "We do not spend all our time investigating," she said, smiling archly. "There are other things in our lives."

The young man with the large mouth cocked his head sideways as she spoke, as if he was trying to look at Mma Makutsi from a different angle. She glanced at him and found herself looking past his teeth and lips, into the very cave, the labyrinth. There were people who found such caves irresistible, she knew, who loved exploring. She imagined tiny people, equipped with minuscule ropes and picks, climbing into that mouth, leaning into the hot gusts of wind that came up from the lungs somewhere down below.

Teenie took Mma Makutsi's arm and led her off towards the offices. "They are not involved in it," she said. "They would never steal."

Mma Makutsi was not so sure. "One can't be too sure about that," she said. "Sometimes it is the most unlikely person who is to blame for something. We have had many cases where you would never have suspected the person who turns out to be guilty. Ministers of religion for example. Yes. Even them."

"I cannot imagine a minister of religion doing anything bad," said Teenie.

Mma Makutsi sighed. "Well, they do. There are some very wicked ministers of religion. They hardly ever get caught, of course, because nobody thinks of looking into their affairs. If I wanted to commit a crime and get away with it, you know what I would do? I would become a minister of religion first, and then I would commit the crime. I would know that I would get away with it, you see."

"Or a detective," said Teenie quietly.

"Or a . . ." Mma Makutsi had been about to agree with this, but was stopped by professional pride. "No," she continued. "I don't think that it would be a good idea to become a detective if you were planning to commit a crime. The people you worked with would know, you see, Mma. They would just know."

Teenie said nothing. They were now outside the office cubicle and Teenie was reaching for the handle of the door. The man and the woman inside were watching them.

"This is him," whispered Teenie. "This one inside."

Mma Makutsi looked in through the glass wall. Her eyes met the gaze of the man in the office. Of course, she thought. Now I see.

CHAPTER FOURTEEN

CHARLIE PICKS UP A PASSENGER

THE TAXI LICENCE for which Charlie had applied would be approved, he had been told, but the document itself, the important piece of paper, would not be ready for at least two weeks. For a young man of Charlie's age, and attitude, that was a long time—too long a time to wait for a mere bureaucratic formality. And so he had decided to start plying his trade rather than wait for the officials in the public transport department to get round to picking up their rubber stamps and validating his papers. Those idle civil servants! he thought. There are too many of them in this country. That is all that we make—civil servants. He smiled. He was a businessman now—he could think such thoughts.

The car which he had acquired from Mr J.L.B. Matekoni had been cleaned and polished until it shone. Charlie lived as a lodger with a maternal uncle, who had a small two-room house at the side of a busy street off the Francistown Road. The now gleaming Mercedes-Benz looked out of place among the shabby cars that stood outside these modest houses and Charlie was worried that it would be stolen. On the first night that the car spent in its new quarters, Charlie had decided to tie a piece of string to the front grille of the vehicle and then feed the other end of the string through the window of the room in which he slept. That would then be tied to his big toe before he got into bed.

"You will certainly wake up if the car is stolen," said his uncle, who had watched, bemused, as the string was unwound from its ball.

"That is why I am doing it, Uncle," Charlie had replied. "If I wake up when the car is moved, I can get out of bed and deal with the thieves."

The uncle had stared at his nephew. "There are two problems that I see," he said. "Two. The first is this: What if the string does not break? This new string is very strong, you know. I think it could probably take the weight of a man. It could pull your toe out of the window, with you still attached."

Charlie said nothing. He stared down at the ball of string. The label proclaimed: **Extra Strong.**

"Then there is another problem," said the uncle. "Even if the string woke you up and then broke before it pulled your toe off, what would happen then? How exactly are you going to deal with your car being driven away? Run after it?"

Charlie put the ball of string down on the table. "Maybe I will not do this," he said.

"No," said the uncle. "Maybe you shouldn't."

The car was not stolen that night. When Charlie awoke the next morning, he immediately rose from his mattress on the floor and pulled aside the thin cotton curtain that covered his window. The car was still there, exactly where he had left it, and he breathed a sigh of relief.

That morning he had arranged for a sign-painter to stencil the name of his taxi firm on the driver's door. This took barely an hour to do, but consumed almost half of the final week's pay that Mr J.L.B. Matekoni had given him. At least he would not have to pay for fuel just yet, as Mr J.L.B. Matekoni had given him a full tank of petrol as a parting gift. So now he was ready, apart from the licence.

Charlie stood outside the sign-painter's shop and admired the newly painted legend on the side of the car.

The sign-painter, a cigarette hanging out of the side of his mouth, contemplated his handiwork. "Why are you calling it the No. 1 Ladies' Taxi Service?" he asked. "Are you getting a lady driver?"

Charlie explained the nature of the service to the painter, an explanation which was followed by a brief silence. Then the painter said, "There are some very good business ideas, Rra. In my job, I see many businesses starting. But I hardly ever see one which is as good an idea as this."

"Do you mean that?" asked Charlie.

"Of course. This is going to be a big success, I can tell you, Rra. A big success. You are going to be very rich. Next month, maybe the month after that, you will be starting to get rich. You'll see. You come back and tell me if I'm wrong."

Charlie drove away with the sign-painter's prediction ringing in his ears. Of course the thought of being rich appealed to him; apart from that brief spell when he had been taken up by that wealthy, married, and older woman, he had known only poverty so far, had owned only a single pair of shoes, had made do with turned collars on his shirts. If he had the money, he could dress in a way which he knew would attract the girls; not that he had ever had any difficulty in doing that, but in a way which would attract a fancier sort of girl. That was what interested him.

He had intended to drive straight home in order to conserve fuel, but then, as he rounded a corner, a woman stepped out from a driveway and waved him down. For a moment he was puzzled, and then he remembered. **I am a taxi driver! I get waved down.**

He drew in at the side of the road, coming to rest immediately abreast of the woman. She stepped smartly to the back door and climbed in. He watched her in his rear-view mirror; a well-off woman, he thought; well-dressed, carrying a small leather briefcase.

"Where to?" he asked. He had not rehearsed the phrase, but it sounded right.

She told him that she wanted to go to the
bank at the top of the Mall. "I have an appointment," she said. "I am a bit late for it. I hope
that you can get me there quickly."

He shifted the car into gear and drove off. "I
will do my best, Mma."

In the mirror he saw the woman in the back
relax. "A friend was coming to collect me," she
said, looking out of the window as she spoke.
"She has obviously forgotten. It was a good
thing you came along."

"Yes, Mma. We are here to help."

The woman seemed impressed with this.
"Some of you taxi people are really rude," she
said. "You are not like that. That is a good
thing."

Charlie looked in the mirror again, his eyes
meeting his passenger's gaze. She was a good-
looking woman, he thought; a bit too old
for him, but one never knew. That last time,
when he had been involved with that older
woman, he had enjoyed a marvellous time,
until her husband . . . Well, one could never tell
how these things would work out. He glanced
into the mirror once more. She was wearing a
necklace with green stones and a pair of large
dangling ear-rings. Charlie liked ear-rings like

that. They were a sign that a woman liked a good time, he always thought. Perhaps he might ask this woman at the end of the journey whether he could come back and pick her up after her appointment. And she would say to him that this would be a very good idea because, as it happened, she had nothing to do and perhaps they could go out to a bar somewhere and have a beer because it was getting hot again, did he not think, and it would be a good thing to say goodbye to these winter nights when one really needed somebody nice and warm in one's bed to keep the chill away . . .

He did not see the traffic lights, which were red, against him; nor the truck that was approaching and that had no time to apply its brakes. Charlie, gazing in his rear-view mirror, saw nothing that lay ahead; not the frantic movements of the truck driver as he realised that impact was inevitable; not the crumpling of metal as the front of the car folded in; not the shattering of the windscreen as it fragmented into little pieces, like diamonds or droplets of water in the sun. But he heard the screaming of the woman in the seat behind him and a slow ticking sound from the engine of his car; he heard the slamming of the door of the truck as the driver, shaking, let himself out of his relatively unharmed cabin. He heard the protests of metal as his own door was prised open.

Another motorist had stopped and had put his arm around Charlie's passenger. She was standing beside the car, weeping with shock. There was no blood.

"Everybody is all right," said the other motorist. "I saw it happen. I saw it."

"I was coming that way," stuttered the truck driver. "The light was green."

"Yes," said the motorist. "I saw that. The light was green."

They looked at Charlie. "Are you all right, Rra? You are not injured?"

Charlie could not speak. He shook his head. He had escaped injury, thanks to the solidity of German engineering.

"God must be watching," said a passer-by, who had seen all three step unharmed from the wreckage. "But look at that car! I'm sorry, Rra. Your poor car."

Charlie had now sat down on the side of the road. He too was shaking. He was staring at his shoes; now he looked up and saw the ruins of his Mercedes-Benz, with its crumpled front, stained green by spurting coolant; at the metal rubbed bare where the truck had ground across it; at the buckled door with its newly painted sign. The ruptured metal had shortened the sign. **The No. 1 Ladies' Tax** it now read; a curious legend which caused the policeman who shortly afterwards arrived at the scene to scratch his head. Tax?

Charlie reached home four hours later. His aunt was there, and she could tell immediately that there was something wrong.

"I have had an accident," he said.

The aunt let out a wail. "Your beautiful new car?"

"It is finished, Aunty. That car is finished now."

The aunt looked fixedly at the ground; she had known, of course, that this, or something like this, would happen. Charlie, silent now that he had pronounced the requiem on his car, sat down. I am twenty, he thought. Twenty, and it is all finished for me.

CHAPTER FIFTEEN

MMA POTOKWANE ON THE SUBJECT OF TRUST, AMONGST OTHER THINGS

ON THE DAY following Charlie's accident—an accident of which nobody at the garage or the agency was yet aware—Mma Ramotswe decided not to work in her office but instead to go for a picnic. It was not a decision that was made on the spur of the moment; she had been invited almost two weeks previously by Mma Potokwane, had accepted, and then forgotten about it until a few hours before the gathering was due to take place. In some respects she would have preferred not to have remembered at all, as that would have given her a perfect excuse, even if a retrospective one, for not attending. But now it was too late: Mma Potokwane, the redoubtable matron of the orphan farm, would be expecting her and she had to go.

Mma Ramotswe and Mma Potokwane were old friends. Mma Makutsi, who had her difficulties with Mma Potokwane, the two having crossed swords on more than one occasion, had once asked Mma Ramotswe how they had first met. Mma Ramotswe had been unable to provide an answer. Some friends, she explained, seemed always to have been part of one's life. Obviously there was a first meeting, but in the case of old friends that was usually so long ago, and so mundane at the time, that all memory of it had faded. Such friends were like favoured possessions—a cherished book, a favourite picture—how one acquired them was long forgotten, they were just there.

It had not always been the smoothest of friendships and there were some aspects of Mma Potokwane's behaviour of which Mma Ramotswe frankly disapproved. Her bossiness was one such thing, particularly when it was directed at Mr J.L.B. Matekoni, who had long been incapable of refusing Mma Potokwane's requests to fix various antiquated pieces of equipment at the orphan farm. It was all very well for her to order the orphans about—that was what one expected of the matron of an orphanage, since it was undoubtedly good for the children to lead ordered lives—but it was another thing altogether for her to adopt a similar manner when it came to adults.

"I feel sorry for that woman's husband," Mma Makutsi had once remarked, following upon a call that Mma Potokwane had made to the office. "No wonder he doesn't ever say anything. Have you watched him? He just stands there. The poor man must be afraid to open his mouth."

Out of loyalty to her friend, Mma Ramotswe refrained from saying anything about this, but when she gave some thought to Mma Makutsi's less-than-charitable remark she had to acknowledge that it was probably true. Mma Potokwane's husband was a small man, neither as tall nor as well built as his wife, and he gave every appearance of being both physically and emotionally floundering in the wake created by his wife.

"I wonder why he married her," Mma Makutsi went on. "Do you think that he asked her, or did she ask him?" She paused as she mulled over the possibilities. "Maybe she even ordered him to marry her. Do you think that happened, Mma?"

Mma Ramotswe pursed her lips. It was difficult not to smile when Mma Makutsi got going on remarks like this, but she knew that she should not. It was none of Mma Makutsi's business how Rra Potokwane had proposed to Mma Potokwane; such things were the private business of man and wife and people had no right to pry into such areas. Mind you, Mma Makutsi might not be far wrong; she could just imagine Mma Potokwane instructing her mild, rather timid husband to marry her or face some unnamed unpleasant consequences.

"I wonder what their bed is like," went on Mma Makutsi. "I can just see their bedroom, can't you?—with her taking up most of the space on the bed and leaving only a few inches at the edge for him. Maybe he sleeps on the floor next to the bed. And then she wakes up and thinks: Where on earth did I put my husband? Do you think that is what happens, Mma Ramotswe?"

This was overstepping the mark. Mma Ramotswe did not like to speculate on the bedrooms, or beds, of others. That was private. "You mustn't talk like that," she said. "It is not funny."

"But you are smiling," Mma Makutsi said. "I can see that you are trying not to smile, but you are."

Mma Ramotswe had changed the subject at this point, but at home that evening she had narrated the conversation to Mr J.L.B. Matekoni and he had laughed. "Those two just can't get on," he said. "They are really the same, under the skin. In ten years' time, Mma Makutsi will be just like her. She has been ordering the apprentices around—for practice. Soon she will move on to Mr Phuti Radiphuti. Once they are married, then the ordering about will begin." He looked at Mma Ramotswe. "Not all men are fools, you know, Mma. We know the plans that you women have for us."

Oh, thought Mma Ramotswe, although she did not say **oh.** If Mr J.L.B. Matekoni thought that she had plans for him, then what exactly were they? There were undoubtedly women who had plans for their husbands; they were often ambitious for them in their jobs, and urged them to apply for promotion above the husbands of other women. Then there were

women who liked their men to have expensive
cars, to be wealthy, to dress in flashy clothes.
But she had no plans of that nature for Mr
J.L.B. Matekoni. She did not want Tlokweng
Road Speedy Motors to get any bigger or to
make more money. Nor did she want Mr J.L.B.
Matekoni to change in any way; she liked him
exactly as he was, with his old, stained veld-
schoen, his overalls, his kind face, his gentle
manner. No, if she had any plan for him it
was that they would continue to live together
in the house on Zebra Drive, that they would
grow old in one another's company, and maybe
one day go back to Mochudi and sit in the
sun there, watching other people do things,
but doing nothing themselves. Those were
plans of a sort, she supposed, but surely they
were plans that Mr J.L.B. Matekoni would
himself endorse.

Now, driving her tiny white van along the
road that led to the Gaborone dam, she let her
thoughts wander: Mma Potokwane, men and
their little ways, the Government, next year's
rains, Motholeli's homework problems: there
was so much to think about, even before she
started to dwell upon any of her cases. Once
she started to think about that side of her life,

Mochudi Hospital came to mind, with its cool corridors, and the ward where three people had died, all in the same bed. Three fingers raised, one after the other, and then lowered. Three stitches taken out of our shared blanket. She had talked to how many people now? Four, if one did not count Tati Monyena, who was really the client, even if it was the hospital administration that was paying. Those four people, the three nurses and Dr Cronje, had all endorsed the view that Tati Monyena had voiced right at the beginning—that the deaths were just an extraordinary coincidence. But if that was what everybody believed, then why had they sought to involve her in the whole business? Perhaps it was one of those cases where doubts simply refused to lie down until somebody independent, somebody from the outside, had come and put them to rest. So she was not a detective, then, but a judge brought in to make a ruling, as judges, chiefs, will do when with a few carefully chosen words they bury a cause of conflict or doubt. If that were so, then there was not much for her to do but to declare that she had looked into the situation and found nothing suspicious.

And yet she was not sure if she could honestly say that. It was true that she had looked into the situation, and while she had been unable to come up with any idea as to why the patients had died, she could not truthfully say that she had no suspicions. In fact, she had felt quite uncomfortable after her conversations with the nurses and with Dr Cronje; she had sensed an awkwardness, an unhappiness. Of course, that could have been nothing to do with the matter she was investigating—Dr Cronje was an unhappy man because he was in self-imposed exile; and as for the nurses, for all she knew they might have some cause for resentment, some work issue, some unresolved humiliation that gnawed away; such things were common and could consume every waking moment of those who allowed them to do so.

She reached the point at which the public road, untarred and dusty, a track really, entered the confines of the dam area. Now the road turned to the east and followed the base of the dam wall until it swung round in the direction of the Notwane River and Otse beyond. It was a rough road, scraped flat now and then by the Water Department grader but given to potholes and corrugated ridges. She did not push the tiny white van on such roads, and stuck to a steady fifteen miles per hour, which would give her time to stop should she see too deep a hole in the road or should some wild animal dash out of cover and run across her path. And there were many animals here; she spotted a large kudu bull standing under an acacia tree, its horns spiralling up a good four feet. She saw duiker too, and a family of warthogs scuttling off into the inadequate cover of the sparse thorn bush. There were dassies, rock hyrax, surprised in the open and running frantically for the shelter of their familiar rocks; as a girl, she had possessed a kaross made of the skins of these small creatures sewn together end to end, little patches of silky-smooth fur that had been draped across her sleeping mat and into which she had snuggled on cold nights. She wondered where that kaross was now; worn to the very leather, perhaps, abandoned, surviving as a few scraps of something, traces of a childhood which was so long ago.

Halfway along the dam, the road opened out onto a large clearing where somebody, a few years earlier, had tried to set up a public picnic ground. The attempt had been abandoned, but the signs of the effort were still there—

a small breeze-block structure with **Ladies** painted on one end and **Gentlemen** on the other, the lettering still just discernible; now, with the roof off and half the walls down, the two sexes were jumbled up together in democratic ruin. And beyond that, over a token wall, now toppling over in places and never more than a couple of feet high, was a children's playground. The ants had eaten the wooden support posts of the swings and these had fallen and been encased in crumbling termite casts; a piece of flat metal, which could have been the surface of a slide, lay rusted in a clump of blackjack weeds; there was an old braaivleis site, now just a pile of broken bricks, picked clean by human scavengers of anything that could be used to make a shack somewhere.

Mma Ramotswe arrived half an hour early, and after she had found a shady spot for the van, she decided to walk down to the edge of the water, some fifty yards away. It was very peaceful. Above her was an empty sky; endowed with so much room, so much light; on the other side of the dam, set back a bit, was Kgale Hill, rock upon rock. You could see the town on the other side of the wall, and you knew it was there, but if you turned your head the other way there was just Africa, or that bit of it, of acacia trees like small umbrellas, and dry grass, and red-brown earth, and termite mounds like miniature Babel towers. Paths led criss-cross to nowhere very much; paths created by the movement of game to the water, and she followed one of these down towards the edge of the dam. The water was light green, mirror flat, becoming blue in its further reaches. Reeds grew at its edge, not in clumps, but sparsely, individual needles projecting from the surface of the water.

Mma Ramotswe was cautious. There were crocodiles in the Notwane—everybody knew that—and they would be in the dam too, although some people denied it. But of course they would be here, because crocodiles could travel long distances over land, with that ungainly walk of theirs, seeking out fresh bodies of water. If they were in the Notwane, then they would be here too, waiting beneath the water, just at the edge, where an incautious warthog or duiker might venture. And then the crocodile would lunge out and seize its prey and drag it back into deeper water. And after that followed the roll, the twisting and churning, when the crocodile turned its prey round and round under water. That was how the end came, they said, if one was unfortunate enough to be taken by a crocodile.

There had been a bad crocodile attack at the end of the last rainy season, on the Limpopo, and Mma Ramotswe had discussed it with Mr J.L.B. Matekoni. He had known the victim, who was a friend of a cousin of his, a man who had a small farm up on the banks of the river and who had crossed the water in his boat to drive some cattle back. The cattle had somehow managed to cross the river to the wrong bank, onto somebody else's land, in spite of the fact that the water was high.

The Limpopo was not very wide at that point, but the central channel was deep, a place for a predator. The man was halfway across, seated in his boat with its small outboard motor, when a large crocodile had reared up out of the water and snatched him by the shoulder, dragging him into the river. The herd boy, who was with him in the boat, watched as it happened. At first he was not believed, as crocodiles very rarely attacked a boat, but he stuck to the story. They found what remained of the farmer eventually, and the herd boy was shown to be right.

She looked at the water. It was easy for a crocodile to conceal itself close to the edge, where there were rocks, clumps of half-submerged vegetation and lumps of mud breaking the surface. Any one of these could be the tip of a crocodile's snout, protruding from the water just enough to allow him to breathe; and, a short way away, two further tiny islands of mud were really his eyes, fixed on potential prey, watching. We are so used to being the predator, thought Mma Ramotswe. We are the ones to be feared, but here, at the edge of our natural element, were those who preyed on us.

Further out, a kingfisher hovered and then plummeted, stone-like, into the water; a splash of white spray, and then up again to a vantage point in the air. She watched this for a few moments, and smiled. Everything has its place, she thought; everything. And then she turned round and made her way slowly back up the track towards the van, to await the arrival of Mma Potokwane and the children. She thought she could hear an engine now, straining somewhere not too far away. That would be one of the orphan farm's minibuses, nursed and kept alive by Mr J.L.B. Matekoni, officially retired by Derek James, who ran the orphan farm office, and replaced with something newer, but brought back by Mma Potokwane, who could not bear to waste anything. The old minibuses were now used for work like this, since Mma Potokwane did not like the thought of the newer vehicles destroying their suspension on these bumpy roads.

There were two familiar old blue minibuses. The first one, driven somewhat erratically by Mma Potokwane, drew up close to where Mma Ramotswe was standing and the matron herself got out. She opened the rear door and a chattering group of children spilled forth.

Mma Ramotswe made a quick mental count. There had been nineteen children in a vehicle made for twelve.

Mma Potokwane guessed Mma Ramotswe's thoughts. "It was perfectly all right," she said. "Children are smaller. There's always room for one or two more children." She turned and clapped her hands. "Now, children, nobody is to go in the water. Play up here. Look, there used to be some swings over there. And a slide. So there's lots to do."

"Be careful of crocodiles," warned Mma Ramotswe. "You don't want to be eaten."

A small boy with wide eyes looked up at

Mma Ramotswe. "Would a crocodile eat me, Mma?" he asked politely. "Even me?"

Mma Ramotswe smiled. Even me. None of us thinks that we will be eaten; no child thinks that he will die. "Only if you weren't careful," she said. "Careful boys are never eaten by crocodiles. That is well known." As she spoke, she realised that this was not true: that farmer had been careful. But children could not be told the unvarnished truth.

"I'll be careful, Mma."

"Good."

Mma Potokwane had brought two of the housemothers with them, as well as a couple of volunteers from Maru-a-Pula School. The children flocked round the teenage volunteers while the housemothers set out the picnic on small trestle tables. Mma Potokwane and Mma Ramotswe found a small section of wall, shaded by a tree, and sat down on that.

Mma Potokwane drew a deep breath. "I am always happy when I am in the bush," she said. "I think everybody is."

"I certainly am," said Mma Ramotswe. "I live in a town, but I do not think my heart lives there."

"Our stomachs live in towns," said Mma

Potokwane, patting the front of her dress. "That is where the work is. Our stomachs know that. But our hearts are usually somewhere else."

They were silent for a while. Above them, in the branches of the acacia, a small bird hopped from twig to twig. Mma Ramotswe watched the children exploring the abandoned playground. Two boys were kicking at the fallen swing posts, causing the dried mud of the termites' activity to puff up in little clouds of dust.

She pointed to the boys. "Why do boys destroy things?"

Mma Potokwane sighed. "That is just what they do," she said. "When I first started to work with children, years ago, I used to ask myself questions like that. But then I realised that there was no point. Boys are the way they are and girls are the way we are. You might as well ask why those dassies sit on the top of rocks. That's just the way they are."

It was true, thought Mma Ramotswe. She liked doing the things that she liked doing, and Mr J.L.B. Matekoni was the same. She watched the children. "They seem very happy," she said.

"They are," she said. "Most of them have

had a bad start. Now things are going well for them. They know that we love them. That is all they need to know." She paused, and looked out over the water. "In fact, Mma Ramotswe, that's really all that a child needs to know—to know that it is loved. That is all."

Again, thought Mma Ramotswe, that was true.

"And if there's bad behaviour," Mma Poto-kwane went on. "If there's bad behaviour, the quickest way of stopping it is to give more love. That always works, you know. People say that we must punish when there is wrongdoing, but if you punish you're only punishing yourself. And what's the point of that?"

"Love," mused Mma Ramotswe; such a small, powerful word.

Mma Potokwane's stomach grumbled. "We must eat very soon. But, yes, love is the answer, Mma. Let me tell you about something that happened at the orphan farm. We had a child who was stealing from the food cupboard. Everybody knew that. The housemother in charge of that cupboard had seen the child do it. The other children knew.

"We talked to the child and told him that what he was doing was wrong. But still the stealing went on. And so we tried something different. We put a lock on the cupboard."

Mma Ramotswe laughed. "That seems reasonable enough, Mma."

"You may laugh," said Mma Potokwane. "But then let me tell you what we did next. We gave the key to that child. All the children have little tasks that they must do. We put that boy in charge of the cupboard."

"And?"

"And that stopped the stealing. Trust did it. We trusted him, and he knew it. So he stopped stealing. That was the end of the stealing."

Mma Ramotswe was thinking. At the back of her mind there was something that she thought she might say to Mma Makutsi about this. But her thoughts were interrupted by one of the housemothers bringing them a large tin plate on which several pieces of fruit cake had been laid, along with a number of syrup sandwiches. The housemother handed the plate to Mma Ramotswe and went back to the children.

Mma Potokwane glanced at her friend. "I think that is for both of us, Mma," she said anxiously.

"Of course," said Mma Ramotswe. "Of course."

They ate in silence, and contentment. The children, their mouths filled with syrup sandwiches, were quiet now, and again they could hear the birds.

"What we are trying to do with these children," said Mma Potokwane suddenly, "is to give them good things to remember. We want to make so many good memories for them that the bad ones are pushed into a corner and forgotten."

"That is very good," said Mma Ramotswe.

Mma Potokwane licked a small trace of syrup off a finger. "Yes," she said. "And what about you, Mma Ramotswe? What are your favourite memories? Do you have any that are very special?"

Mma Ramotswe did not have to think about that. "My Daddy," she said. "He was a good man, and I remember him. I remember walking with him along a road—I don't remember where it was—but I remember how we did not have to talk to one another, we just walked together, and were perfectly happy. And then . . . and then . . ."

"Yes?"

She was uncertain if she should tell Mma Potokwane about this, but she was her old friend, and she did. "Then there's another memory. I remember Mr J.L.B. Matekoni asking me to marry him. One evening at Zebra Drive. He had just finished fixing my van and he asked me to marry him. It was almost dark, but not quite. You know that time of the evening? That is when he asked me."

Mma Potokwane listened gravely to the confidence. She would reciprocate, she thought.

"Funny," she said. "I think it was the other way round with me. I asked my husband. In fact, it was definitely me. I was the one."

Mma Ramotswe, recalling her discussion with Mma Makutsi, suppressed a smile. **That's two things I need to tell her,** she said to herself.

CHAPTER SIXTEEN

A SHORT CHAPTER
ABOUT TEA

THE TEA REGIME at the No. 1 Ladies' Detective Agency was, by any standard, a liberal one. There was no official slot for the first cup of tea, but it was nonetheless almost always brewed at the same time, which suggested that it had a **de jure** slot in the day. This was at eight o'clock, when work had already been going on for half an hour or so—in theory at least—although Mma Ramotswe and Mma Makutsi often only arrived a few minutes before eight. The turning on of the kettle had become part of the ritual of opening the office for the day, alongside the moving of the client's chair away from the corner where it was placed at night and its positioning back into the middle of the floor, where it faced Mma Ramotswe's desk, ready for use. Then the window was opened the correct amount, and the doorstop put in such a position that it would allow for some circulation of air without admitting too much noise from the garage, a finely judged calculation which Mma Ramotswe herself undertook. After this there was a brief period for the exchange of information between Mma Ramotswe and Mma Makutsi—what Phuti Radiphuti had eaten for dinner the previous night, what Mr J.L.B. Matekoni had said about the bed he had dug for his beans, what Radio Botswana had announced on its early morning broadcasts, and so on. Once these snippets had been shared, the electric kettle would be boiling and the first, unofficial cup of tea would be served.

Official tea came two hours later, at ten o'clock. It was Mma Makutsi's responsibility to fill the kettle with water, which she did from the tap just outside the door that led to the garage. The sight of her holding the kettle under the tap was a signal to Mr Polopetsi that tea was about five minutes away, and he would then walk over to the sink on the other side of the workshop and begin to wash his hands free of grease. This, in turn, would be a signal to

Mr J.L.B. Matekoni to reach a decision on whether he would carry on with whatever he was doing, and have tea later, or whether he was at a point in the mechanical operation to set his tools to one side and take a break.

Mma Makutsi made the tea in two pots. One was her own pot, rescued from disaster some time ago when one of the apprentices had used it as a receptacle for drained diesel oil; astonishingly, it was none the worse for that experience. That had been one of the more serious points of conflict between her and the two young men, and had resulted in an exchange of insults and a storming-out by Charlie. Now, as she poured the hot water into the tea-pots, she remembered that difficult occasion and wondered how Charlie was faring with his new business. It was undoubtedly quieter without him; there were none of the sudden shouts that used to emanate from the garage when something was dropped or when an engine proved recalcitrant. He had a tendency to shout at engines, using colourful insults, and although Mma Ramotswe had instructed him never to do this when she had a client in the office, the exclamations still came. And now all was silence; the young apprentice, whom Mma Makutsi had seen when she came into work, had a hang-dog expression on his face and seemed to be listless and unhappy. It would be no fun for him, she thought, now that Charlie had gone, and she wondered whether he too might hand in his notice to go off and do something else. That would inevitably provoke a crisis for Mr J.L.B. Matekoni, who would never be able to cope with just himself and Mr Polopetsi to do all the work.

Mma Makutsi filled her own tea-pot and then reached for the small tin caddy in which Mma Ramotswe kept her supplies of red bush tea. She opened it, looked in, and then shut it again.

"Mma Ramotswe."

Mma Ramotswe looked up from her papers. She had received a letter from somebody who wanted her to look for a missing person, but the writer of the letter had signed it indecipherably, neglected to give a proper address, and had not mentioned the name of the missing person. She held the letter up to the light in the vain hope of some clue, and sighed. This was not going to be an easy case.

"Mma Ramotswe," said Mma Makutsi.

"Yes, Mma? Is the tea ready?"

Mma Makutsi held up the empty caddy and shook it demonstratively. "We have run out of bush tea," she announced. "Empty."

Mma Ramotswe put down the letter and glanced at her watch. It was shortly after ten o'clock. "But this is ten o'clock tea," she said. "When we had tea earlier this morning, there was bush tea."

"Yes, there was," said Mma Makutsi. "But that was the last bag. Now there is nothing left. The tin is quite empty. Look."

She opened the caddy and tipped it up. Only a few flecks of tea, the detritus of long-vanished bags, floated down towards the ground.

Mma Ramotswe knew that this was just a minor inconvenience; fresh supplies of tea could easily be obtained, but this could not be done in time for morning tea—unless she left the office and drove to the supermarket. If only Mma Makutsi had told her earlier on that they were down to the last bag, then she could have done this before ten o'clock. She wondered if she should say something about this to Mma Makutsi, but decided that she would not. She was still concerned that Mma Makutsi might suddenly revisit her decision to resign, and an argument over tea was exactly the sort of issue to precipitate that.

"It is my fault," said Mma Ramotswe. "I should have checked to see if we needed new tea. It is my fault, Mma."

Mma Makutsi peered into the tin again. "No," she said. "I think it is my fault, Mma. I should have pointed out to you earlier on that we were down to the last bag. That is where I failed."

Mma Ramotswe made a placatory gesture with her hand. "Oh no, Mma. Anybody can make that sort of mistake. One can be thinking of something else altogether and not notice that the tea is getting low. That has happened many times before."

"Here?" asked Mma Makutsi. "Are you saying that it has happened here? That I have forgotten many times before?"

"No," said Mma Ramotswe hurriedly. "Not you. I'm just saying that it has happened elsewhere. Everybody makes that sort of mistake. It is easily done. I cannot remember a single time when you have done this before. Not one single time."

This seemed to satisfy Mma Makutsi. "Good. But what are we going to do now? Will you have ordinary tea, Mma?"

Mma Ramotswe felt that she had no alternative. "If there is no bush tea, then I cannot very well sit here and not drink any tea. It would be better to drink a cup of ordinary tea rather than to have no tea to drink."

It was at this point that Mr Polopetsi came in. Greeting Mma Ramotswe and Mma Makutsi politely, he made his way to the teapot which Mma Makutsi had placed on top of the filing cabinet. He was about to reach for the pot to pour his tea but stopped. "Only one teapot," he said, looking at Mma Makutsi. "Is this bush tea or ordinary tea?"

"Ordinary," Mma Makutsi muttered.

He looked surprised. "Where is the bush tea, Mma?"

Mma Makutsi, who had been looking away, turned and faced him. "What is it to you, Rra? You drink ordinary tea, do you not? The pot is full of that. Go on, pour. There is plenty there."

Mr Polopetsi, a mild man—even milder than Mr J.L.B. Matekoni—was not one to argue with Mma Makutsi. He said nothing as he picked up the pot and began to pour. Mma Ramotswe, though, had been watching.

"It's all right, Rra," she said soothingly. "Mma Makutsi did not mean to be rude. Unfortunately we have run out of bush tea. It is my fault. I should have seen this coming. It is not a big thing."

Mr Polopetsi put down the tea-pot and picked up his mug, which he cupped with his hands, as if warming them. "Perhaps we should have a system," he said. "When the number of tea-bags in the tin drops down to five, then it is time for us to get more tea. When I worked in the pharmacy, we had a stock control system like that. When there was only a certain number of boxes of a drug on the shelves, we would automatically order more." He paused, and took a sip of his tea. "It always worked."

Mma Ramotswe listened in some discomfort. She glanced at Mma Makutsi, who had returned to her desk with her cup of tea and was tracing an imaginary pattern on her desk with a finger.

"Yes," Mr Polopetsi went on. "A system is a very good idea. Did they teach you about systems at the Botswana Secretarial College, Mma Makutsi?"

It was a moment of electric tension, thrilling in retrospect, but at the time it was dangerous to a degree. Mma Ramotswe hardly dared look at Mma Makutsi, but found her eyes drawn inexorably to the other side of the room, where the gaze of the two women met. Then Mma Ramotswe smiled, out of nervousness perhaps, but a smile nonetheless, and to her immense relief Mma Makutsi returned the smile. This was a moment of conspiracy between women, and it drew all the tension from the situation.

"We shall have to put you in charge of tea, then, Rra," said Mma Makutsi evenly. "Since you know all about systems."

Mr Polopetsi, flustered, mumbled a noncommittal reply and left the room.

"Well, that sorts that out," said Mma Ramotswe.

CHAPTER SEVENTEEN

PHOTOGRAPHIC EVIDENCE

ON THE MORNING that the No. 1 Ladies' Detective Agency ran out of bush tea, Mr J.L.B. Matekoni left Mr Polopetsi and the younger apprentice in charge of the garage. There was not a great deal of work—only two cars were in that morning, one, a straightforward family saloon, had been delivered for a regular service, which Mr Polopetsi was now quite capable of doing unaided, and the other required attention to a faulty fuel-injection system. That was trickier, but was probably just within the competence of the apprentice, provided his work could be checked later.

"I am going out to do some enquiries for Mma Ramotswe," Mr J.L.B. Matekoni announced to Mr Polopetsi. "You will be in charge now, Rra."

Mr Polopetsi nodded. There was a certain envy on his part of the fact that Mr J.L.B. Matekoni had been given this assignment which should, in his view, have been given to him. He had been led to understand that he was principally an employee of the agency, an assistant detective or whatever it was, and that his garage duties would be secondary. Now it seemed that he was expected to be more of a mechanic than a detective. But he would not complain; he was grateful for the fact that he had been given a job, whatever it was, after he had found such difficulty in getting anything.

Mr J.L.B. Matekoni drove his truck to the chemist's shop where he had left the photographs for developing. The assistant there, a young man in a red tee-shirt, greeted him jauntily. "Your photographs, Rra? They're ready. I did them myself. Money back if not satisfied!" He reached behind him into a small cardboard box and extracted a brightly coloured folder. "Here they are."

Mr J.L.B. Matekoni began to take a fifty-pula note from his wallet.

"I won't charge you the full cost," the

young man said. "You only had two exposures on the roll of film. Is there something wrong with your camera?"

Mr J.L.B. Matekoni wondered what the other photograph was. "Two photographs?"

"Yes. Here we are. Look. This one." The young man opened the folder and took out two large glossy prints. "That one is of a house. Down there, round the corner. And this one here . . . this one is of a lady with a man. He must be her boyfriend, I think. That is all. The rest—blank. Nothing."

Mr J.L.B. Matekoni glanced at the photograph of the house—it had come out very well and he could make out the figure of a woman standing on the verandah although the man on the steps, his head turned away from the camera and obscured by the low branch of a tree, could not be identified. But it was not Mr Botumile who was the object of interest here—it was the woman, and she was shown very clearly. He looked at the other photograph—it must have been on the roll of film already, taken some time ago and forgotten. He took it from the young man and stared at it.

Mma Ramotswe was standing in front of a

tree somewhere. There were a couple of chairs behind her, in the shade, and there, standing next to Mma Ramotswe, was a man. The man was wearing a white shirt and a thin red tie. He had highly polished brown shoes and a gleaming buckle on his belt. And his arm was around Mma Ramotswe's waist.

For a few moments Mr J.L.B. Matekoni simply stared at the photograph. His thoughts were muddled. Who is this man? I do not know. Why is his arm around Mma Ramotswe? There can be only one reason. How long has she been seeing him? When has she been seeing him? The questions were jumbled and painful.

The young man was watching; he had guessed that the photograph of Mma Ramotswe was a shock. Some of the photographs he handled were like that, he was sure; but he did not normally hand them to the husband. "This photograph of the house," he said, pushing it into Mr J.L.B. Matekoni's hand. "I know that place. It is off the Tlokweng Road, isn't it? It is the Baleseng house. I know those people. That's Mma Baleseng there. Mr Baleseng helped to teach soccer at the boys' club.

He is good at soccer, that man. Did you ever play soccer, Rra?"

Mr J.L.B. Matekoni did not respond.

"Rra?" The young man's voice was solicitous. I'm right, he thought: that photograph has ended something for him.

Mr J.L.B. Matekoni looked up from the photograph. He seemed dazed, thought the young man; on the point of tears.

"I won't charge you, Rra," said the young man, looking over his shoulder. "When there are only one or two photographs on a roll, we don't charge. It seems a pity to make people pay for failure."

Pay for failure. The words cut deep, each a little knife. I am paying for my failure as a husband, he thought. I have not been a good husband, and now this is my reward. I am losing Mma Ramotswe.

He turned away, only just remembering to thank the young man, and went back to his truck. It was so bright outside, with the winter sun beating down remorselessly, and the air thin and brittle, and everything in such clear relief. Under such light our human failures, our frailty, seemed so pitilessly illuminated.

Here he was, a mechanic, not a man who was good with words, not a man of great substance, just an ordinary man, who had loved an exceptional woman and thought that he might be good enough for her; such a thought, when there were men with smooth words and sophisticated ways, men who knew how to charm women, to lure them away from the dull men who sought, so unrealistically, to possess them.

He slipped the ignition key into the truck. No, he said to himself; you are jumping to conclusions. You have no evidence of the unfaithfulness of Mma Ramotswe; all you have is a photograph, a single photograph. And everything you know about Mma Ramotswe and her character, everything you know of her loyalty and her honesty, suggests that these conclusions are simply unfair. It was inconceivable that Mma Ramotswe would have an affair; quite inconceivable, and he should not entertain even the merest suspicion along those lines.

He laughed out loud. He sat alone in his truck and laughed at his stupidity. He remembered what Dr Moffat had told him about his illness—how a person suffering from depres-

sion could get strange ideas—delusions—
about what he had done, or what others were
doing. Although he was better now, and was
no longer required to take his pills, he had
been warned that there could be a recurrence
of such thinking, of irrational feelings, and he
should be on the look-out for them. Perhaps
that was what had happened—he had merely
had a passing idea of that nature and had allowed it to flower. I must be rational, he told
himself. I am married to a loyal, good woman,
who would never take a lover, who would
never let me down. I am safe; safe in the security of her affection.

And yet, and yet . . . who was in that
photograph?

WITH A SUPREME EFFORT, Mr J.L.B.
Matekoni put out of his mind all thoughts of
that troubling photograph and concentrated
on the photograph of Mma Baleseng and the
house. He had been to see Mma Botumile at
her own house, a large old bungalow just off
Nyerere Drive. It was an expensive part of
town, one in which the houses had been built
shortly after Gaborone had been identified as

the capital of the newly independent country of Botswana. The plots of land here were of a generous size, and the houses had the rambling comfort of the period, with their large rectangular rooms, and their wide eaves to keep the sun away from the windows. It was only later, when architects began to impose their ideas of clean-cut building lines, that windows had been left exposed to the sun, a bad mistake in a country like Botswana. In the Botumile house there was shade, and there were whirring fans, even now at the tail end of winter, and red-polished stone floors that were cool underfoot.

Mma Botumile received him on the verandah of the house, in a spot that looked out directly onto a spreading jacaranda tree and an area of crazy-paving. She did not rise to greet him as he was shown in by the maid, but continued with a telephone call that she was making. He looked up at the ceiling, and then studied the pot plants; averting his eyes from the rudeness of his hostess.

Eventually she finished with her call. "Yes, Rra," she said, tossing the cordless telephone down on a cushion beside her. "You have some information for me."

There was no greeting, no enquiry after his

health, but he was used to that now, and he did not let it upset him.

"I have carried out enquiries," he said solemnly. He looked at the chair next to hers. "May I sit down, Mma?"

She made a curt gesture. "If you wish. Yes. Sit down and tell me what you have found out about this husband of mine."

He lowered himself into the chair and took the photograph out of its envelope. "I have followed your husband, Mma," he began. "I followed him from his work in the evening and I was able to establish that he has been seeing another woman."

He watched her reaction to this disclosure. She was controlled, merely closing her eyes briefly for a few moments. Then she looked at him. "Yes?"

"The lady is called Mma Baleseng, I believe, and she lives over at . . ."

There was a sudden intake of breath by Mma Botumile. "Baleseng?"

"Yes," he said. "If you look at this photograph you will see her. That is her house. And that person there, whom you cannot see properly because of the tree, that is your husband going up the steps. Those are his legs."

Mma Botumile peered at the photograph. "That is her," she hissed. "That is her."

"Do you know her?" asked Mr J.L.B. Matekoni.

Mma Botumile looked up from the photograph and addressed him with fury. "Do I know her? You're asking me—do I know her?" She flung the photograph down on the table. "Of course I know her. Her husband works with my husband. They do not like one another very much, but they are colleagues. And now she is carrying on with my husband. Can you believe that, Rra?"

Mr J.L.B. Matekoni clasped his hands together. He wished that he had spoken to Mma Ramotswe about the proper way to convey information of this nature; was one expected to sympathise? Should one try to comfort the client? He thought that it would be difficult to comfort somebody like Mma Botumile, but wondered if he should perhaps try.

"I never thought that he would be carrying on with **her**," Mma Botumile spat out. "She's a very ugly woman, that one. Very ugly."

Mr J.L.B. Matekoni wanted to say, **But she can't help that surely,** but he did not.

"Maybe . . . ," he began, but did not finish. Mma Botumile had risen to her feet and was peering down the driveway.

"Oh yes," she said. "This is very well timed. This is my husband coming back now."

Mr J.L.B. Matekoni began to stand up, but was pushed back into his seat by Mma Botumile. "You stay," she said. "I might need you."

"Are you going to . . . ," he began to ask.

"Oh yes," she said. "I most certainly am going to. And he is going to have to too. I am going to ask him to explain himself, and I can just see his face! That will be a very amusing moment, Rra. I hope that you have a sense of humour so that you can enjoy it."

As Mma Botumile left to meet her husband, Mr J.L.B. Matekoni sat in miserable isolation on the verandah. It occurred to him that Mma Botumile could hardly detain him against his will, that he could leave if he so desired, but then if he did that Mma Ramotswe would be bound to hear of his abandonment of the case and she would hardly be impressed. No, he would have to stay and he would have to provide Mma Botumile with the support that she expected of him in the confrontation with her husband.

There were voices round the corner—Mma Botumile's voice and the voice of a man. Then she appeared, and behind her came the man whom he had heard. But it was not her husband; it was not Mr Botumile.

"This is my husband," said Mma Botumile, pointing, rather rudely, to the man behind her.

Mr J.L.B. Matekoni looked from face to face.

"Well?" said Mma Botumile. "Seen a ghost?"

Mr J.L.B. Matekoni was aware of the fact that Mr Botumile was looking at him in puzzlement and expectation. He decided, though, not to look at him, and concentrated on Mma Botumile instead.

"That is not the man," he said.

"What do you mean?" asked Mma Botumile. She turned to her husband, and almost as an aside said, "Your little affair. Finished. As of now."

No actor could have dissembled more convincingly than Mr Botumile, were he dissembling, which Mr J.L.B. Matekoni rapidly concluded he was not. "Me? Affair?"

"Yes," snapped Mma Botumile.

"Oh . . . oh . . ." Mr Botumile stared at Mr J.L.B. Matekoni for support. "It is not true, Rra. It is not true."

Mr J.L.B. Matekoni drew in his breath. Mma Botumile, Mma Potokwane—these powerful women were all the same, and one just had to stand up to them. It was not easy, but it had to be done. "He is not the man, Mma," he said loudly. "That is not the man I followed."

"But you said . . ."

"Yes, I said, but I am wrong. I saw another man leaving the office. He also drove a red car. I followed that man."

Mr Botumile clapped his hands together. "But that is Baleseng. He works with me. Baleseng is the financial controller. You followed Baleseng, Rra! Baleseng is having an affair!"

Mma Botumile directed a withering look at Mr J.L.B. Matekoni. "You stupid, stupid, useless man," she said. "And that stupid photograph of yours. That is a picture of Baleseng going back to his wife! You stupid man!"

Mr J.L.B. Matekoni took the insult in silence. He looked down at the table, at the photograph, now revealed to be so innocent. A faithful man returns to his wife: that could be the title of that picture. He had made a mistake, yes, but it was a genuine mistake, a mistake of the sort that anybody, including this impossibly arrogant woman, might make. "You're not to call me stupid," he said quietly. "I will not have that, Mma."

She glared at him. "Stupid," she said. "There. I have called you stupid, Rra."

But Mr J.L.B. Matekoni was thinking. It now dawned on him that he did have some information that might be of use to these people, even if it was something of a long shot.

"I followed this Baleseng twice, you know," he said. "And on the first occasion I saw something very interesting."

"Oh yes," sneered Mma Botumile. "You saw him go shopping perhaps? You saw him buy a pair of socks? Very interesting information, Rra!"

"You must not make fun of me," said Mr J.L.B. Matekoni, his voice rising, but still just under control. "You must not talk to me like that, Mma. You are very ill-mannered." He paused. "I saw him have a meeting with Charlie Gotso. And I overheard what they talked about."

The effect of this information was dramatic. Mr Botumile, who had been quietly smirking ever since he had been cleared of suspicion, now became animated. "Gotso?" he said. "He met Gotso?"

"Yes," said Mr J.L.B. Matekoni.

"What about?" asked Mma Botumile. "What did they talk about?"

"Mining," said Mr J.L.B. Matekoni.

Mr Botumile gave his wife a glance. "We must hear about this."

"Once you have apologised," said Mr J.L.B. Matekoni with dignity. "Then I shall tell you about it. But not before."

Mma Botumile's eyes widened. She was wrestling with conflicting emotions, it seemed, but eventually she turned to her husband. "I'm sorry," she said. "We can talk later."

Mr J.L.B. Matekoni cleared his throat. He had meant that she should apologise to him, and now she had apologised to **him.** She would have to apologise again, which would do her good, he thought, as this was a woman who had a lot of apologising to do.

As he waited for the apology, which eventually came, even if grudgingly given, Mr J.L.B. Matekoni thought: **I am a mechanic. I am not a detective. That has become well known.**

"Now, please tell us exactly what you heard them talk about," said Mr Botumile.

Mr J.L.B. Matekoni told them. There were holes in his account of what was said, but the Botumiles seemed ready to fill these in. At the end, smiling with satisfaction at what he had discovered, Mr Botumile explained to Mr J.L.B. Matekoni about share manipulation; about insider information; about having that precious advantage of advance knowledge. Charlie Gotso could have made a large profit on the company's shares, because he knew what was coming before anybody else did. And some of that profit, Mr Botumile explained, would go back to Baleseng.

"You've been an extremely good detective," said Mr Botumile at last. "You really have, Rra."

"Oh," said Mr J.L.B. Matekoni. He did not think that was true. Could one be good at something without knowing it? Could one accept the credit for an accidental result? Whatever the answers to these questions were, though, he had already made his decision. The things that we do best, he thought, are the things that we have always done best.

CHAPTER EIGHTEEN

WE DECEIVE OURSELVES,
OR ARE DECEIVED

Now mma makutsi," said Mma Ramotswe. "I want you to tell me about your case. That small woman . . ."

"Teenie."

Mma Ramotswe laughed. "I suppose she doesn't mind. But why do people put up with names like that? Sometimes we Batswana are not very kind in the names we give ourselves."

Mma Makutsi agreed. There had been a boy in Bobonong whose name meant **the one with ears that stick out.** He had lived with this and had seemed unconcerned. It was also true; his ears did stick out, almost at right angles to his head. But why land a child with that? And then there was that man who worked in the super-market whose name when translated from

Setswana meant **large nose.** His nose was large, but there were people with much larger noses than his and it was only because of his name that Mma Makutsi felt her eyes drawn inexorably to that dominating feature. It was tactless and unkind.

"I don't think she minds being called that, Mma," she said. "And she is very small. She's also . . ." She trailed off. There was something indefinably sad about Teenie, with her pleading look. She wanted something, she felt, but she was unsure what it was. Love? Friendship? There was a loneliness about her, as there was about some people who just did not seem to belong, who fitted in—to an extent—but who never seemed quite at home.

"She is an unhappy one," said Mma Ramotswe. "I have seen that woman. I do not know her, but I have seen her."

"Yes, she is unhappy," said Mma Makutsi. "But we cannot do anything about that, can we, Mma?"

Mma Ramotswe sighed. "We cannot make all our clients happy, Mma. Sometimes, maybe. It depends on whether they want to know what we tell them. The truth is not always a happy thing, is it?"

Mma Makutsi picked up a pencil on her desk and idly started a sketch on a piece of paper. She found herself drawing a sky, a cloud, an emptiness, the umbrella shape of an acacia tree, a few strokes of the pencil against the white of the paper. Happiness. Why should she see these things when she thought of happiness?

"Are you happy, Mma Ramotswe?" Her pencil moved against the paper. A pot now, a cooking pot, and these were the flames, these wavy lines below. Cooking. A meal for Phuti Radiphuti, for the man who had given her that diamond, to show that he loved her, and who did; she knew that. A girl from Bobonong, with a diamond ring, and a man who had a furniture shop and a house. All that has come to me.

"I am very happy," said Mma Ramotswe. "I have a good husband. I have my house on Zebra Drive. Motholeli, Puso. I have this business. And all my friends, including you, Mma Makutsi. I am a very happy woman."

"That is good."

"And you, Mma. You are happy too?"

Mma Makutsi put down her pencil. She looked down at her shoes, the green shoes with sky-blue linings, and the shoes looked back at her. **Come on, Boss. Don't beat about the bush. Tell her.** She felt a momentary irritation that her shoes should speak to her like this, but she knew that they were right.

"I am happy," she said. "I am engaged to be married to Mr Phuti Radiphuti."

"Who is a good man," interjected Mma Ramotswe.

"Yes, who is a good man. And I have a good job."

That was a relief to Mma Ramotswe, who nodded enthusiastically.

"As an associate detective," Mma Makutsi rapidly added.

Mma Ramotswe was quick to confirm this. "Yes. An associate detective."

"So I have everything I need in this life," concluded Mma Makutsi. "And I owe a lot of that to you, Mma. And I am thankful, really thankful."

There was not much more to be said about happiness, and so the conversation reverted to the subject of Teenie and her difficulties. Mma Makutsi told Mma Ramotswe of her visit to the printing works and of her meeting with the people who worked there. "I spoke to all of them," she said. "But they knew who I was—word got out very quickly after I had been identified. They all said that they did not know anything about things going missing. They all said that they could not imagine anybody stealing from the works. And that was it." She paused. "I'm not sure what to do now, Mma. There is one person whom Teenie suspects, and I must say that he seemed very shifty when I saw him."

Mma Ramotswe was intrigued. "Was that your instinct, Mma?"

"Oh yes," Mma Makutsi replied. "I know that you shouldn't judge by appearances. I know that. But . . ."

"Yes," said Mma Ramotswe. "But. And it's an important but. People tell you a lot from the way they look at you. They cannot help it."

Mma Makutsi remembered the man in the office and the way he had looked away when she had been introduced to him. And when he raised his eyes and met her gaze, they darted away again. She would never trust a man who looked that way, she thought.

"Maybe he is the one," said Mma Ramotswe. "But what can we do? Set some sort of trap? We have done that before in these cases, haven't we? We have put something tempting out and then found it in the possession of the thief. You could do that."

"Yes. Well . . ."

Then Mma Ramotswe remembered. Mma Potokwane had said something about this problem, had she not, on the picnic? There had been a child who was stealing from the food cupboard. And Mma Potokwane had solved the problem. Children, of course, were different, but not all that different when it came to fears and emotions.

"There is a story Mma Potokwane told me," said Mma Ramotswe thoughtfully. "She said that at the orphan farm they had a child who stole. And they solved the problem by giving the child the key to the cupboard. That stopped it."

Mma Ramotswe had half-expected Mma Makutsi to reject the idea out of hand. But her assistant seemed interested. "And that worked?" Mma Makutsi asked.

"No more thievery," said Mma Ramotswe. "The child had never known what it was like to be trusted. Once he was trusted, he rose to the challenge. Now, your shifty man at the printing works. What if he were put in charge of supplies? What if this Teenie person showed him that she trusted him?"

Mma Makutsi looked down at her shoes. **Give it a try, Boss!** She thought for a moment. "Maybe, Mma," she said. She sounded tentative at first, but then continued with growing conviction, "Yes. I'll suggest that he's put in charge of supplies. Then one of two things will happen: he'll stop thieving because he's trusted, or . . . or he'll take everything. One of those things will happen."

That was not the spirit of Mma Potokwane's story, thought Mma Ramotswe, but one had to acknowledge Mma Makutsi's realism. "Yes," said Mma Ramotswe. "It will decide matters one way or the other."

He'll steal the lot, Boss, whispered Mma Makutsi's shoes.

CHARLIE REAPPEARED that afternoon. Mr J.L.B. Matekoni was involved with a gearbox and the younger apprentice was engaged in a routine draining of oil. Mr J.L.B. Matekoni, who saw him first, stood up and wiped his hands on a paper towel. Charlie, standing at the entrance to the garage workshop, made a half-hearted gesture of greeting with his right hand.

"It's me, Boss. It's me."

Mr J.L.B. Matekoni chuckled. "I've not forgotten who you are, Rra! You have come back to see us." He looked behind Charlie, out onto the open ground in front of the garage. "Where's the Mercedes-B . . . ?" His voice died off at the end of the question. There was no Benz, no car.

Charlie's demeanour gave everything away—in the way his eyes dropped, in the misery of his expression, in his utterly defeated posture. The younger apprentice, who had come over to stand next to Mr J.L.B. Matekoni, looked nervously at his employer. "Charlie's back," he said, and tried to smile. "You see, Rra. He's come back now. You must give him his job back, Rra. You must. Please." He tugged at Mr J.L.B. Matekoni's sleeve, leaving a smudge of grease on the cloth.

Mr J.L.B. Matekoni glanced at the grease marks. It was maddening. He had told these boys time and time again not to touch him with their greasy fingers, and they always did it, always, tapping him on the shoulder, grabbing his arm to show him something, ruining his overalls, which he always tried to keep as clean as possible. And now this foolish young man had left his fingerprints on him again, and this other, even more foolish young man had probably succeeded in destroying an old but perfectly serviceable Mercedes-Benz. What could one do? Where could one start?

He addressed Charlie, his voice low. "What happened? Just tell me what happened. No this, no that. No, **It wasn't my fault, Rra.** Just what happened."

Charlie shifted awkwardly from foot to foot. "There was an accident. Two days ago."

Mr J.L.B. Matekoni took a deep breath. "And?"

Charlie shrugged. "I could not even get it brought here," he said. "The police mechanic looked at it. He said . . ." He moved his hand in a gesture of helplessness.

"A write-off?" asked the younger apprentice.

Charlie moved a hand up to cover his mouth. From behind his fingers, his voice was muffled. "Yes. He said that it would cost far more than it was worth to try to fix it. Yes, it's a write-off."

Mr J.L.B. Matekoni looked up at the sky.

He had brought these boys here, he had done his best, and everything they did, everything, went wrong. He asked himself if he had been like this as a young man, as prone to disaster, as incapable of getting anything right. He had made mistakes, of course; there had been several false starts, but nothing ever approaching the level of incompetence that these young men so effortlessly achieved.

He felt a sudden urge to shout at Charlie, to seize him by the lapels of his jacket and shake him; to shake him until some sense came into that head of his, full, as it was, with thoughts of girls and flashy clothes and the like. It was tempting, almost overpoweringly so, but he did not. Mr J.L.B. Matekoni had never laid an angry hand on another and would not start now. The dangerous moment passed.

"I was wondering, Boss," Charlie began. "I was wondering if I could come back here."

Mr J.L.B. Matekoni bit his lip. This was undoubtedly his chance to get rid of Charlie, if he wished to do so, but he realised, just as the possibility entered his head, that he was, in fact, relieved to have him back, even in these difficult circumstances. The car was still covered by his own insurance, but with the deductible element he would still be left out of pocket on its loss—almost to the tune of five thousand pula, he imagined. That was five thousand pula which Charlie's accident would cost him, and the young man would never have any means of paying that back. But these boys were part of the life of the garage. They were like demanding relatives, like drought, like bad debts—things that were always there, and to which one became accustomed.

He sighed. "Very well. You may start again tomorrow."

The younger apprentice, overjoyed, seized Mr J.L.B. Matekoni by the arm and squeezed hard. "Oh, Boss, you are such a kind man. You are so kind to Charlie."

Mr J.L.B. Matekoni said nothing. He carefully extricated himself from the young man's grip and walked back into the workshop. There were more grease stains where the younger apprentice had held him. He could have fumed about those, but did not. What was the point? he thought. Some things just are.

He went into the office, where he found Mma Ramotswe dictating a letter to Mma Makutsi, who was writing it down in shorthand. He stood in the doorway for a moment, until Mma Ramotswe signalled that he should come in.

"It's nothing private," she said. "Just a letter to somebody who has not paid his bills."

"Oh?" he said. "And what do you say?"

"If you do not pay the outstanding bill by the end of next month, we shall be obliged . . ." She paused. "That is as far as we got."

"We shall be obliged to . . . ," said Mma Ramotswe.

"Take action," offered Mr J.L.B. Matekoni.

"Yes," said Mma Ramotswe. "That is what we shall do." She laughed. "Not that we ever take action. But there we are. As long as people think that you're going to do something, that's enough."

"Bad debts are a very big problem," said Mr J.L.B. Matekoni. He was about to add "just like bad apprentices," but he did not. Instead, with the air of one conveying very mundane news, he said, "Charlie's back. Car crashed. Written off. He's coming back."

Mr J.L.B. Matekoni was watching Mma Makutsi as he gave this news, and when he looked over in the direction of Mma Ramotswe, he saw that she too was looking at her assistant. He knew of Mma Makutsi's difficulties with the apprentices, and particularly with Charlie, and he imagined the impending return would not be well received. But Mma Makutsi, aware of their scrutiny, did not react sharply. There was a moment, perhaps, when the lenses of her large round glasses seemed to flash, but this was only because a movement of her head caused them to catch the light; not a sign. And when she did speak, it was quietly.

"That is a great pity for him," she said. Then she added, "So that is the end of the No. 1 Ladies' Taxi Service." It was a simple epitaph, pronounced without any sense of triumph, without any suggestion of **I told you so.** As Mr J.L.B. Matekoni remarked to Mma Ramotswe over dinner that night, it was a kind thing for Mma Makutsi to have said, worthy, he suggested, of top marks.

"Yes," said Mma Ramotswe. "Ninety-seven per cent. At least."

They were seated alone at the table, Motholeli and Puso having eaten earlier and gone to their rooms to complete their homework.

"Poor boy," said Mma Ramotswe. "He was so looking forward to it all. But I'm afraid that I always thought it would end this way. Charlie is Charlie. He is the way he is, like the rest of us."

Yes, thought Mr J.L.B. Matekoni; like the rest of us. I am a mechanic; that is what I am; I am not something else. I suppose I have my ways which annoy other people—my keeping those engine parts in the spare room, for instance—that annoys Mma Ramotswe. And I do not always wash out the bath after I have used it; I try to remember, but sometimes I forget, or I am in a hurry. Things like that. But we all have some things we are ashamed of.

He looked at Mma Ramotswe. One of the things he was ashamed of was thinking that she could ever take up with another man, that she would leave him. He had tried to put those ideas out of his head because he knew that they were both unfounded and unfair. Mma Ramotswe would never deceive him—he knew that—and yet somewhere in the back of his mind those unsettling thoughts lurked, nagging, insistent. And then there had been that photograph. He had tried not to think about it, but he found that he just could not help it; try not to think of something and see how hard it is, he thought. There was Mma Ramotswe with another man, and the man had his arm about her. The camera had recorded it and he had found it. How could he **not** think about that?

Mma Ramotswe was buttering a piece of bread. She cut the bread into two pieces and popped one of them into her mouth. When she looked up from her task, she saw that Mr J.L.B. Matekoni was staring at her, with that look that he sometimes had, a slightly sad, confused look. She swallowed; a crumb tickled. "Is there something wrong?" she asked.

He shook his head, in false denial, and turned away, embarrassed. "No, nothing is wrong." But then he thought, But there is something wrong. There is.

He closed his eyes. He had decided to say something because he could not keep this within him any longer. But he was unable to look at her while he spoke. "Mma Ramotswe," he said. "Would you ever leave me?"

She had not anticipated anything like that. "Leave you?" she asked incredulously. "Leave you, Mr J.L.B. Matekoni?" And oddly, inconsequentially, she thought: Leave you to go where? To Francistown? To Mochudi? Into the Kalahari?

He kept his eyes closed. "Yes. For another man."

He opened his eyes slightly, just to catch a glimpse of the effect of his words. What he had said surprised even himself, and he wondered what effect it would have on Mma Ramotswe.

"But of course not," said Mma Ramotswe. "I am your wife, Mr J.L.B. Matekoni. A wife does not leave her husband." She paused. That was not true. Some wives had to leave their husbands, and she had done precisely that when she had broken up with her first husband, Note Mokoti. But that was different. "Of course I would never leave you," she went on. "I have no interest in other men. None at all."

Mr J.L.B. Matekoni opened his eyes. "None?"

"No. Only you. You are the one. There is no man like you, Mr J.L.B. Matekoni. There is no man who is as good, as kind." She stopped and reached out to take his hand. "That is well known, by the way."

He could not meet her gaze. He felt so ashamed of himself; but he was also touched by what she had said—for a man might easily imagine himself unloved—and he did not think it was untrue. But there was still that photograph.

He rose to his feet, gently pushing away her hand, and went across the room to pick up the small canvas bag which he sometimes took with him to the garage. He took out an envelope and felt within it for the photograph.

"There is this," he said. "There is this photograph. It was in the camera. That office camera."

He pushed the photograph over the table towards her. Frowning, she picked it up and examined it. She looked puzzled at first—he was watching her expression closely, with anxiety, with dread—but then she smiled. Her smile struck him as callous, hurtful; that she should smile at, make light of such a thing as this. He felt doubly betrayed.

"I had forgotten about that," she said. "But now I remember. Mma Makutsi took it shortly after we had bought the camera. It was taken outside the shop where we bought it. You know that place, just outside the Mall. Look, there is that bit of wall at the back."

He glanced at where she was pointing. "And that man?"

"I have no idea who he was," she said.

His voice was barely a whisper. "You do not even know his name?"

"No. And I don't know hers either."

"Whose?"

"Hers. The woman in the picture. The woman who looks like me. Or so Mma Makutsi told me. They ran that shop, you see, those two people. And Mma Makutsi whispered to me while we were buying the camera, **Look, Mma, that lady is your double.** And I suppose she did look a bit like me, and when we mentioned it, they thought so too. They laughed, and so we decided to try the camera out. We took that photograph, and forgot about it."

Mr J.L.B. Matekoni reached out and took the photograph. He peered at it. The woman looked like Mma Ramotswe, it was true; but on closer examination, of course it was not her. Of course not. The eyes were different; just different. He put down the photograph. He had been blind. Jealousy, or was it fear, had made him blind.

"You were worried," she said. "Oh, Mr J.L.B. Matekoni, I can understand now. You were worried!"

"Only a little bit," said Mr J.L.B. Matekoni. "But now I am not."

Mma Ramotswe looked at the photograph

again. "It's interesting, isn't it," she said. "It's interesting how we can look at things and think we see something, when it really isn't there at all."

"Our eyes deceive us," said Mr J.L.B. Matekoni. He was feeling waves of relief, like that relief which follows a flood in a dry land after rains, sudden, complete, overwhelming; he felt that, but could not find the words for his emotions, and so he said again, "Our eyes deceive us."

"But our hearts do not," said Mma Ramotswe. A silence followed this remark. Mr J.L.B. Matekoni thought, simply, **Yes.** But Mma Ramotswe thought: Is that really so, or does it merely **sound** right?

CHAPTER NINETEEN

THE PROPER PLACE OF MERCY

IT SEEMED TO MMA RAMOTSWE that a rather unusual, and unsettling, period had come to an end. If one believed those columns in magazines about the stars—and she had never understood how people could imagine that the stars had anything to do with our tiny, distant lives—then some heavenly bodies somewhere must have moved into a more favourable alignment. Perhaps the good planets had drifted from their normal position—which was directly above Botswana, and particularly above Zebra Drive, Gaborone, Botswana—and had now made their way back. For everything seemed to be in the process of satisfactory resolution. Mma Makutsi no longer spoke of resignation and seemed quite content with her new, vaguely defined post of associate detective; Charlie was back in the fold, the unfortunate No. 1 Ladies' Taxi Service no longer in existence, and, as a matter of tact, no longer mentioned, even by Mma Makutsi; Mr J.L.B. Matekoni seemed to have lost interest in conducting enquiries and had had his ridiculous anxieties laid to rest. Everything, in fact, seemed to have settled down; which was exactly the way Mma Ramotswe liked it to be. The world was full of uncertainty, and if the life of the No. 1 Ladies' Detective Agency and Tlokweng Road Speedy Motors, together with the lives of those associated with those two concerns, were all on an even keel, then at least some of that uncertainty was held at bay.

The world, Mma Ramotswe believed, was composed of big things and small things. The big things were written large, and one could not but be aware of them—wars, oppression, the familiar theft by the rich and the strong of those simple things that the poor needed, those scraps which would make their life more bearable; this happened, and could make even the reading of a newspaper an exercise in sorrow. There were all those unkindnesses, palpable, daily, so easily avoidable; but one could not think just of those, thought Mma Ramotswe, or one would spend one's time in tears—and the unkindnesses would continue. So the small things came into their own: small acts of helping others, if one could; small ways of making one's own life better: acts of love, acts of tea, acts of laughter. Clever people might laugh at such simplicity, but, she asked herself, what was their own solution?

Yet one had to be careful in thinking about such matters. It was easy to dream, but daily life, with its responsibilities and problems, was still there, and in Mma Ramotswe's case at least one pressing matter was still on her mind. This was her enquiry into the affairs of the hospital at Mochudi, and those three unexplained deaths. Or were they unexplained? It seemed to Mma Ramotswe that a perfectly credible explanation had been offered in each case. Ultimately we all died from heart failure, one way or another, even if there were all sorts of conditions which precipitated this. The hearts of these three had simply stopped because they could no longer breathe—or so claimed the medical reports they had shown her. And if everybody knew why these three patients were finding it difficult to breathe, then surely that was the end of the matter? Did they know that? It was hard for Mma Ramotswe to decide, because the doctors, it seemed, could not agree. But then there would always be disputes by experts as to why one thing happened and another did not. Even mechanics did this, as Mr J.L.B. Matekoni had often demonstrated. He would shake his head over the work of other mechanics who had attended to cars before they were brought to him. How could anybody have thought that a particular problem was a transmission problem when it was so clearly to do with something quite different, some matter of rods and rings and all the other complicated bits and pieces which made up the innards of a car?

Mma Ramotswe felt helpless in the face of medical uncertainty. It was not for her to make a pronouncement about why somebody died, and if that was the case, as it undoubtedly was, then she felt that all that she could do here was to exclude, if possible, some non-medical factor, something unusual that had resulted in three people all becoming late at the same time of the week and in the same bed. It was for this reason that she decided that the only thing to do—indeed the final thing that she intended to do in this particular investigation—would be to go to the hospital on a Friday at ten o'clock, which was one hour before the incidents had taken place, and to find out if there was anything to be noticed. One would have thought that the hospital authorities, and in particular Tati Monyena, would have thought of doing something like this, but then it had often struck Mma Ramotswe that people who were in the middle of things just did not pick up what might be glaringly obvious to those outside. She often saw things which other people missed—a fact which rather bemused her; that is why I have found my calling, she said to herself; I am called to help other people because I am lucky enough to be able to **notice** things. Of course, she knew where that particular ability came from—its roots were back in those early years under the tutelage of her cousin, who trained her to keep her eyes open, to notice all the little things that were happening when one did something as simple as go for a walk in the bush. Here, along the path, would be the tracks of the animals that had passed that way; there were the tiny prints of a duiker, the skittish miniature buck with its delicate miniature hooves; there were the signs of the labours of the dung beetle, pushing its trophy, so much bigger than itself, leaving those marks in the sand. And there, look, somebody had come this way while he was eating and had thrown the maize cob down on the ground, not all that long ago because the ants had not yet come to take possession of it. The cousin had an eye for these things, and the habit had been engrained in Mma Ramotswe's mind. At the age of ten, she had known by heart the number plate of virtually every car in Mochudi and had been able to say who had driven in the direction of Gaborone on any morning. "You have eyes like mine," said the cousin. "And that is a good thing."

Tati Monyena had responded enthusiastically to Mma Ramotswe's suggestion that she should visit the ward that Friday. "Of course," he said. "Of course. That is a very good idea, Mma. I shall give you a white coat if I can find one which is . . ." He had stopped himself, but Mma Ramotswe knew what he had been going to say, but had not, was **if I can find one big enough.** She did not mind. It was a good thing, in her view, to be of her particular construction, even if the manufacturers of white hospital coats failed to make adequate provision for the needs of those of traditional build.

"That will be fine," she responded quickly. "I will not get in the way. I will just watch."

"I shall tell the staff," he said. "You have my full authority. Full authority."

He was there to greet her when she arrived. He had been watching from his window, she thought, which suggested to her a certain anxiety on his part. That was interesting, but not really significant. This whole issue was not one which a hospital administrator would like; it had required an unsettling enquiry, it made people uneasy; there were far more important things to do. And of course there was probably a personal factor, as there so often was. Mma Ramotswe had asked about and had discovered that the next promotion for Tati Monyena would be to the post of Chief Administrator, a post which was already occupied by somebody else. But the woman who was in that post was also ambitious and there was a job in the Ministry of Health in Gaborone itself for which people thought she was the obvious candidate. That job was in the hands of a long-serving incumbent who was only eighteen months away from retirement and a return to a comfortable brick house he had built for himself in Otse. The last thing that Tati Monyena would want would be all these desirable changes to be disturbed by an administrative hiccup, a scandal of some sort. So of course the poor man would be looking out of his window and waiting for the arrival of the woman who was to put this whole awkward matter to bed, whose word would be final. Nothing untoward, she would say in her report. The end.

He greeted Mma Ramotswe outside and led her to his office. She saw a white coat on the chair. "For me?"

"Yes, Mma Ramotswe," he said. "It might be . . . it might be a slightly tight fit, I'm afraid. But it will mean that you will be unobtrusive. It's amazing how easy it is to wander about a hospital with a white coat on. Nobody will ask you what you're doing. You can do what you like."

He said this with a smile as he handed the coat to her. As she slipped it on, though, his words lingered. **Nobody will ask you what you're doing. You can do what you like.** If, for any reason, there was a mischief-maker in the hospital, then the way would be wide open for such a person to do what he liked. The thought had a strangely chilling effect. It would take a particular sort of evil, she imagined, to prey on patients in a hospital; but such things happened—the unimaginable did occur. Fortunately she had never encountered it, but perhaps that innocence of experience would inevitably be shattered if one was a detective, which, after all, she claimed to be. But I'm not that sort of detective, she told herself; not **that** sort . . .

In her white coat, tight at the arms, she remembered how on another occasion, at the very beginning of her career, she had impersonated a nurse to deal with the bogus father of Happy Bapetsi. That had worked, and the greedy imposter, who had claimed to be Happy's father, had been sent to Lobatse whence he had come, Mma Ramotswe's denunciations ringing in his ears. That had been a simple investigation, though, requiring no more than the wisdom of Solomon, and she had always had a clear idea of what she had to say, the lines she had to deliver. Her current circumstances were of course very different. She had no idea what she was going to say or do, or indeed of what she was looking for. She was searching for something unusual, something which had occurred at the same time on three Fridays, but she could not imagine what this might be. When she had asked the staff in the ward if anything special happened at that time of the morning, and on Fridays in particular, they had looked blank. "We have our tea round about then," one said. She had seized at this. Would nobody be looking after the patients while the nursing staff gossiped over a cup of tea? Her question had been anticipated. "We take turns to have tea," somebody else had quickly assured her. "Always. Always. This means that there is always somebody on duty. Always. That is the rule."

Tati Monyena walked with her to the ward, and introduced her again to the nurses she had already met. One smiled when she saw Mma Ramotswe in her white coat. Another looked at her in astonishment, and then frowned and turned away. They were busy, though, and had no time to speak to her. There was a man in a bed near the window who was breathing heavily, making a sound which was like that of gravel being walked upon. One of the nurses took his pulse and adjusted his pillow. There was a small framed photograph on the table beside him, left by a relative no doubt, a reminder, a little thing for a very ill person to have with him on his journey, along with all those other memories that make up the life of a man.

For the first little while, Mma Ramotswe felt like the intruder she was. It was an almost indecent feeling—that one was watching something that one should not be watching, like looking at another person in a moment of great privacy, but that feeling wore away as she stood by a window and watched the nurses at work. They were matter-of-fact in their manner: drugs were given, temperatures taken, entries made on charts. It was like an office, she thought, with its series of small tasks to be methodically carried out. That nurse over there, she thought, the one with the glasses, would be Mma Makutsi herself. And that young man who brought in the drugs trolley and who made some muttered comment to one of the nurses could be Charlie, and the drugs trolley, with its well-oiled, silent wheels, his Mercedes-Benz.

After three quarters of an hour, when she had begun to feel tired, Mma Ramotswe drew a chair over to the place where she had been standing. It was near a bed occupied by a silent, sleeping man. He had tubes inserted into his arms, and wires disappearing into the sleeve of his nightgown. He slept regardless, his face composed, peaceful, all pain, if he had been experiencing it, forgotten. She watched him and thought of her father, Obed Ramotswe, and of how he met his end, in just such a bed, and of how it had seemed to her at the time that a whole Botswana had died with him. But it had not. That fine country, with its good people, was still there; it was there in the face of this elderly man with his head upon that pillow and the sunlight, the warm, friendly sun of Africa, slanting through the window and falling upon him now in his last days.

She shifted in her chair and looked at her watch. It was almost eleven o'clock. The nurses, or some of them, would surely have their tea soon; but not today, perhaps, when they all seemed to be so busy. She closed her eyes for a moment, in comfortable drowsiness, feeling the sun from the window on her face. Eleven o'clock.

The double swing doors at the end of the ward were opened, and a woman in a light green working dress, the uniform of the hospital's support staff, bent down to put a doorstop in place. Behind her was a floor-polishing machine, a big, ungainly instrument like an oversized vacuum cleaner. The woman glanced at Mma Ramotswe as she pushed her floor polisher in, and then she bent down and switched it on. There was a loud whining sound as the machine's circular pad rubbed at the sealed concrete of the floor, and a smell of polish too, from some automatic dispenser attached to the handle. This was a well-run hospital, thought Mma Ramotswe; and a well-run hospital would also be battling against dirt on floors. That was where the invisible enemies were, was it not?—the armies of germs waiting for their chance.

She watched the woman fondly. She was a traditionally built cleaning lady doing an important, but badly paid job. There was no doubt that a number of children would be dependent on that job, on the money that it brought for their food, their school clothes, their hopes for a future. And here was this solid, reliable woman doing her job, as women throughout Botswana would be doing their various jobs at that very moment; her floor polisher whirring, its long electrical cable trailing behind it and out of the door into the corridor.

She was Mma Ramotswe, and she noticed things. She noticed the length of the cable, and all its coils, and she wondered whether there were not places in the ward where the polisher might be plugged in. Surely that would be easier, and would mean that this long cable could not threaten to trip people up in the ward or in the corridor. That would be far more sensible.

She looked about her. The ward was full of plugs, one at the head of each bed. And into each of these plugs there were fitted the lights, the injection pumps, the appliances that helped the patients to breathe . . .

She rose to her feet. The cleaning woman had now almost drawn level with her and they had exchanged a friendly glance, followed by a smile. She approached the woman, who looked up from her work and raised an eyebrow in enquiry before she bent down and switched off the polisher.

"Dumela, Mma."

The greeting was exchanged. Then Mma Ramotswe leaned forward and whispered to her urgently. "I must talk to you, Mma. Please can we go outside and talk? I won't keep you for long."

"What, now?" The woman had a soft, almost hoarse voice. "Now? I am working now, Mma."

"Mr Monyena," said Mma Ramotswe, pointing in the direction of Tati Monyena's office. "I am doing something for him. I am allowed to speak to anybody in working hours. You need not worry."

The woman nodded. The mention of Tati Monyena's name had reassured her, and she pushed her polisher to one side and followed Mma Ramotswe out of the ward. They went outside, to sit on a bench beneath a tree. A goat had strayed into the hospital grounds and was nibbling at a patch of grass. It watched them for a few moments and then returned to its task of grazing. It was becoming hot again. The cleaner said, "This is the end of winter."

They sat down. "Yes, winter is over now, Mma," said Mma Ramotswe. Then she said, "I noticed that you have a long cable on your polisher, Mma. It goes right out of the ward and into the corridor. Wouldn't it be easier to connect it to one of the plugs inside each ward?"

The cleaner picked up a twig from the ground at her feet and began to twist it. She was not nervous, though; that would have shown, and it did not.

"Oh yes," she said. "That's what I used to do. But then they told me not to. I was given very strict instructions. I should not use any of the plugs in the ward."

Mma Ramotswe felt herself swaying. It was as if she was about to faint. She drew a deep breath, and the swaying feeling went away. Yes. Yes. Yes.

"Who told you, Mma?" she asked. It was a simple question, but she had to struggle to get it out.

"Mr Monyena himself," said the cleaner. "He told me. He called me into his office and went on and on about it. He said . . ." She paused.

"Yes? He said?"

"He said that I was not to talk about it. I'm sorry I forgot. I did tell him that I would not talk about it. I shouldn't be talking to you, Mma. But . . ."

"But I have his full authority," said Mma Ramotswe.

"He is a kind man, Tati Monyena," said the

cleaner. And then, after thinking for a moment, she added, "He is my cousin, you know."

Which makes you mine, thought Mma Ramotswe.

SHE WALKED BACK to Tati Monyena's office, divested of her white coat, which she carried slung over her right arm. He was in, his door ajar, and he welcomed her warmly.

"It's lunch time," he said breezily, rubbing his hands together. "Well timed, Mma Ramotswe! We can have some lunch in the canteen. They do very good food, you know. Cheap, too."

"I need to talk to you, Rra," she said, putting the coat down on the chair before his desk.

He patted his stomach. "We can talk over lunch, Mma."

"Privately?"

He hesitated for a moment. "Yes, if that is what you want. There is a special table at one end that we can use. Nobody will disturb us."

They walked in silence to the canteen. Tati Monyena tried to make casual conversation, but Mma Ramotswe found herself too involved in her own thoughts to respond very much.

She was trying to make sense of something, and the sense was not apparent. He knew, she thought; he knew. But if he knew, then why ask her? An outside whitewash—that was what he wanted.

They helped themselves at the hot-food counter and made their way over to a small, red-topped table at the far end of the canteen. Tati Monyena, sensing that something important was coming, had now become edgy. As he lowered his tray onto the table, Mma Ramotswe could not help but notice that there was a tremor in his hands. He is shaking because he senses that I know something, she thought. Now he is feeling dread. There will be no senior job for him now. This was not the part of her job that she liked: the painful spelling out of the truth, the exposure.

She looked down at her plate. There was a piece of beef on it, some mashed potatoes, and green peas. It was a good lunch.

Suddenly, without having thought about it beforehand, she felt impelled to say grace. "Do you mind if I say grace for us?" she said quietly.

He gave his assent. "That would be good," he said. His voice sounded strained.

Mma Ramotswe lowered her head. The

smell of the beef was in her nostrils; and that of the mashed potatoes too, a slightly chalky, earthy smell. "We are grateful for this good food," she said. "And we are grateful for the work of this hospital, which is good work. And if there are things that go wrong in this place, then we remember that there is always mercy. As mercy is shown to all of us, so we can show it to our brothers and sisters."

She did not really know why she said this, but she said it, and when she stopped, and was silent, Tati Monyena was silent too, so that she heard his breathing from across the table. "That is all," she said, and looked up.

When she saw his eyes, she did not need to tell him that she had found out what had happened.

"I saw you talking to the cleaner," he said. "From my office. I saw you talking to her."

Mma Ramotswe kept her gaze upon him. "If you knew, Rra, all along, then why . . ."

He raised his fork, and then put it down again. It was as if he had been somehow defeated, and there was no point now in eating. "I found out by chance, only by chance. I asked who had been present in the ward just before the third patient went and one of the nurses happened to mention that the cleaner had left the ward just before it happened. She always polished the floor there at the same time on a Friday morning. So I spoke to her and asked her to tell me exactly what she did in the ward."

Mma Ramotswe encouraged him. She was keen to hear his description of events, and relieved to find out that it tallied with what the cleaner had told her. This meant that he was no longer lying.

"She told me," Tati Monyena went on. "She told me that she plugged her polisher in near the door. Near the bed by the window. I asked her how she did this and she said that she simply unplugged the plugs that were already in. Just for a few minutes, she said. Just for a few minutes."

Mma Ramotswe looked down at her mashed potatoes. They were getting cold, and would become hard, but this was no time for such thoughts. "And so she unplugged the ventilator," she said. "Just long enough for the patient to become late. And then she plugged it back in. But the damage had been done."

"Yes," said Tati Monyena, shaking his head with regret. "That machine is not the most modern machine. It has an alarm, which probably sounded, but with the whirring sound of that old floor polisher nobody would hear it. Then, when the nurses checked, they found that the machine was still operating properly, but the patient was gone. It was too late."

Mma Ramotswe reflected on this. "So did the cleaner know what had happened?"

"She knew that there had been an incident in the ward," Tati Monyena replied. "But of course she did not know that it had anything to do with her. She . . ." He stopped. He was looking at Mma Ramotswe with an expression that said only one thing, **Please understand.**

She picked up her fork and dug it into the potatoes. A little skin had formed on the top, a powdery white skin. "You didn't want her to know that she had killed somebody, Rra? Is that it?"

His voice was urgent as he replied; urgent, and full of relief that she should understand. "Yes," he said. "Yes, Mma. Yes. She is a very good woman. She has small children and no husband. The husband is late. You'll know why. He was ill with that for a long time, Mma, a long time. She herself is on . . . on treatment. She is one of the best workers we have in the hospital, and you can ask anybody, anybody. They will all say the same."

"It is not just because she is your cousin?"

This took him by surprise, and he looked aghast. "That is true," he said. "But what I said about her is also true. I did not want her to suffer. I know how she would feel if she found out that she was responsible for somebody's death. How would you feel, Mma, if you knew that about yourself? And she would lose her job. It wouldn't be my decision, it would be the decision of somebody back there . . ." He gestured through the window, in the direction of Gaborone. "Somebody in a big office would say that she had been responsible for the deaths of three people and should be fired. They would say, carelessness. They wouldn't blame me, though, or the head of the medical staff, or anybody else; they would blame the person at the bottom, that lady. Fire the cleaner, and end the matter there."

Mma Ramotswe took a mouthful of potato. It was slightly bitter in the mouth, but that was what truth was sometimes like too. She could think about this problem, and then think about it again, looking at it from every direction. Whichever way one thought of it, though, it would still have the same feel to it, would still raise the same questions. Three people had died. They were all elderly people, she had found out, and none of them had dependants. Nothing could be done to help them now, wherever they were. And, if they were anything like the elderly people of Mochudi whom she had known, people of Obed Ramotswe's generation, they would not be ones to want to make difficulties for the living. They would not want to see that woman put out of her job. They would not wish to add to her difficulties; that poor woman who was working so hard, with that other thing hanging over her head, that uncertain sentence.

"You made the right decision, Rra," she said to Tati Monyena. "Now let us eat our lunch and talk about other matters. Relatives, for example. They are always doing something new, aren't they?"

Now he knew what her grace had meant, and he wanted to say something about that, to thank her for her mercy, but he could not talk. He expressed his relief in tears, which he mopped at, embarrassed, with a handkerchief that she supplied, wordlessly. There was no point in telling somebody not to cry, she had always thought; indeed there were times when you should do exactly the opposite, when you should urge people to cry, to start the healing that sometimes only tears can bring. But if there was a place for tears of relief, there might even be a place for tears of pride—for the people who worked in that hospital, who looked after others, who took risks themselves of infection, of disease—from an accidental cut, a needle injury incurred at work; there were many tears of pride to be shed for them, for their bravery. And one of them, she thought, was Dr Cronje.

THE NEXT DAY, Mma Ramotswe dictated a report for Tati Monyena's superiors, which Mma Makutsi took down in shorthand, ending each sentence with a flourish of her pencil, as if to express satisfaction at the outcome. She had told her assistant what had happened at the hospital, and Mma Makutsi had listened, open-mouthed. "Such a simple explanation," she said. "And nobody thought of it until you did, Mma Ramotswe."

"It was just something I saw," said Mma Ramotswe. "I did not do anything very special."

"You are always very modest," said Mma Makutsi. "You never take any credit for these things. Never."

Mma Ramotswe was embarrassed by praise, and so she suggested that they continue with the report, which ended with the conclusion that no further action was required in respect of incidents in which nobody was to blame.

"But is that true?" asked Mma Makutsi.

"Yes, it is true," said Mma Ramotswe, adding, "No blame can be laid at that woman's door. In fact, she deserves praise, not blame, for her work. She is a good worker."

She looked at Mma Makutsi with a look that she rarely used, but which was unambiguously one which closed a matter entirely.

"Well," said Mma Makutsi, "I suppose you're right."

"I am," said Mma Ramotswe.

The report was finished, typed by Mma Makutsi—in an error-free performance, as one might expect of such a graduate of the Botswana Secretarial College. Then it was time for tea, as it so often was.

"You told that woman, Teenie, about the key to the supplies?" said Mma Ramotswe. "I wonder how that went. It's a test of Mma Potokwane's advice, I suppose."

Mma Makutsi laughed. "Oh, Mma, I forgot to tell you. She telephoned me. She did as I suggested and put that man in charge of all the supplies. The next day, everything was gone. The whole lot. And he had gone too."

Mma Ramotswe looked into her cup. She wanted to laugh, but prevented herself from doing so. This result was both a success and a failure. It was a success in that it demonstrated to the client beyond all doubt who the thief was; it was a failure in that it showed that trust does not always work. Perhaps trust had to be accompanied by a measure of common sense, and a hefty dose of realism about human nature. But that would need a lot of thinking about, and the tea break did not go on forever. "Oh well," she said. "That settles that. Mma Potokwane's advice **sounded** good, though."

Mma Makutsi agreed that it did, and they talked for a few minutes about the various affairs of the office until Mr J.L.B. Matekoni came in for his tea. He was wiping his hands on a cloth and smiling. He had been struggling with a particularly difficult gearbox and at long last he had solved the problem. Mma Ramotswe looked out of the window, at that square of land, at the acacia tree that fingered into the empty sky; a little slice of her country that she loved so much, Botswana, her place.

Mma Ramotswe smiled at Mr J.L.B. Matekoni. He was such a good man, such a kind man, and he was her husband.

"That engine I've been working on will run so sweetly," he remarked as he poured his tea.

"Like life," she said.

africa
africa africa
africa africa africa
africa africa
africa

ABOUT THE AUTHOR

Alexander McCall Smith is the author of the huge international phenomenon The No. 1 Ladies' Detective Agency series, and of The Sunday Philosophy Club and 44 Scotland Street series. He was born in what is now known as Zimbabwe and was a law professor at the University of Botswana and at Edinburgh University. He lives in Scotland.